CALIFORNIA
FIRE AND LIFE

California
FIRE AND LIFE

by Don Winslow

ALFRED A. KNOPF   *New York*   1999

THIS IS A BORZOI BOOK
PUBLISHED BY ALFRED A. KNOPF, INC.

Copyright © 1999 by Don Winslow

www.randomhouse.com

Knopf, Borzoi Books, and the colophon are registered trademarks of Random House, Inc.

Library of Congress Cataloging-in-Publication Data
Winslow, Don, [date]
California fire and life / by Don Winslow. — 1st ed.
        p.   cm.
    ISBN 0-679-45431-4 (hc)
            I. Title.
    PS3573.I5326C35   1999
  813'.54—dc21   98-50910
                            CIP

Manufactured in the United States of America

First Edition

To the claims guys and their defenders. It was an honor.

ACKNOWLEDGMENTS

Many people—most of whom it would be imprudent to thank by name—helped me in the research of this book, and I thank them all. Among those I can name, my undying gratitude to the ever patient Dr. Edward Ledford, president of the Zoex Corporation in Lincoln, Nebraska, for his guidance and counsel in regard to gas chromatographs, mass spectrometers and countless other issues involving the testing of debris samples. My thanks as usual to David Schniepp for sharing his knowledge of arcane surfing matters and south coast lore and legend. My gratitude to my wife, Jean Winslow, for her patient and expert drafting of the floor plans of the Vale house and for countless kindnesses.

CALIFORNIA
FIRE AND LIFE

1

Woman's lying in bed and the bed's on fire.

She doesn't wake up.

Flame licks at her thighs like a lover and she doesn't wake up.

Just down the hill the Pacific pounds on the rocks.

California fire and life.

2

George Scollins doesn't wake up, either.

Reason for this is that he's lying at the bottom of the stairs with a broken neck.

It's easy to see how this might have happened—Scollins's little Laguna Canyon house is a freaking mess. Tools, wood, furniture lying all over the place, you can hardly walk across the floor without tripping on something.

In addition to the tools, wood and furniture, you have paint cans, containers of stain, plastic bottles full of turpentine, cleaning rags . . .

This is also the reason the house is a bonfire.

Not surprising, really.

Not surprising at all.

California fire and life.

3

Two Vietnamese kids sit in the front of a delivery truck.

The driver, Tommy Do, pulls it off into a parking lot.

"Middle of freaking nowhere," says Tommy's buddy, Vince Tranh.

Tommy doesn't give a shit, he's happy to be getting rid of the load, a truck full of hot stuff.

Tommy pulls over by a Caddy.

"They love their Caddies," Tranh says to him in Vietnamese.

"Let 'em," Tommy says. Tommy's saving for a Miata. A Miata is cool. Tommy can see himself cruising in a black Miata, wraparound shades on his face, a babe with long black hair beside him.

Yeah, he can see that.

Two guys get out of the Caddy.

One of them's tall. Looks like one of those Afghan hounds, Tommy thinks, except the guy's wearing a dark blue suit that has got to be *hot* standing out there in the desert. The other guy is shorter, but broad. Guy wears a black Hawaiian print shirt with big flowers all over it, and Tommy thinks he looks like a jerk. Tommy has him tabbed as the leg breaker, and Tommy is going to be glad to get his money, unload and get the fuck back to Garden Grove.

As a general rule, Tommy doesn't like doing business with non-Vietnamese, especially these people.

Except the money this time is too good.

Two grand for a delivery job.

The big guy in the flowered shirt opens a gate and Tommy drives through it. Guy closes the gate behind them.

Tommy and Tranh hop out of the truck.

Blue Suit says, "Unload the truck."

Tommy shakes his head.

"Money first," he says.

Blue Suit says, "Sure."

"Business is business," Tommy says, like he's apologizing for the money-first request. He's trying to be polite.

"Business is business," Blue Suit agrees.

Tommy watches Blue Suit reach into the jacket pocket for his wallet, except Blue Suit takes out a silenced 9mm and puts three bullets in a tight pattern into Tommy's face.

Tranh stands there with this *oh-fucking-no* look on his face but he doesn't run or anything. Just stands there like *frozen,* which makes it easy for Blue Suit to put the next three into him.

The guy in the flowered shirt hefts first Tommy, then Tranh, and tosses their bodies into the Dumpster. Pours gasoline all over them then tosses a match in.

"Vietnamese are Buddhists?" he asks Blue Suit.

"I think so."

They're speaking in Russian.

"Don't they cremate their dead?"

Blue Suit shrugs.

An hour later they have the truck unloaded and the contents stored in the cinder block building. Twelve minutes after that, Flower Shirt drives the truck out into the desert and makes it go boom.

California fire and life.

4

Jack Wade sits on an old Hobie longboard.

Riding swells that refuse to become waves, he's watching a wisp of black smoke rise over the other side of the big rock at Dana Head. Smoke's reaching up into the pale August sky like a Buddhist prayer.

Jack's so into the smoke that he doesn't feel the wave come up behind him like a fat Dick Dale guitar riff. It's a big humping reef break that slams him to the bottom then rolls him. Keeps rolling him and won't let him up—it's like, *That's what you get when you don't pay attention, Jack. You get to eat sand and breathe water*—and Jack's about out of breath when the wave finally spits him out onto the shore.

He's on all fours, sucking for air, when he hears his beeper go off up on the beach where he left his towel. He scampers up the sand, grabs the beeper and checks the number, although he's already pretty sure who it's going to be.

California Fire and Life.

5

The woman's dead.

Jack knows this even before he gets to the house because when he calls in it's Goddamn Billy. Six-thirty in the morning and Goddamn Billy's already in the office.

Goddamn Billy tells him there's a fire and a fatality.

Jack hustles up the hundred and twenty steps from Dana Strand Beach to the parking lot, takes a quick shower at the bathhouse then changes into the work clothes he keeps in the backseat of his '66 Mustang. His work clothes consist of a Lands' End white button-down oxford, Lands' End khaki trousers, Lands' End moccasins and an Eddie Bauer tie that Jack keeps preknotted so he can just slip it on like a noose.

Jack hasn't been inside a clothing store in about twelve years.

He owns three ties, five Lands' End white button-down shirts, two pairs of Lands' End khaki trousers, two Lands' End guaranteed-not-to-wrinkle-even-if-you-run-it-through-your-car-engine blue blazers (a rotation deal: one in the dry cleaners, one on his back) and the one pair of Lands' End moccasins.

Sunday night he does laundry.

Washes the five shirts and two pairs of trousers and hangs them out to unwrinkle. Preknots the three ties and he's ready for the workweek, which means that he's in the water a little before dawn, surfs until 6:30, showers at the beach, changes into his work clothes, loops the tie around his neck, gets into his car, pops in an old Challengers tape and races to the offices of California Fire and Life.

He's been doing this for coming up to twelve years.

Not this morning, though.

This morning, propelled by Billy's call, he races to the loss site—37 Bluffside Drive, just down the road above Dana Strand Beach.

It takes him maybe ten minutes. He's pulling around on the circular driveway—his wheels on the gravel sound like the undertow in the trench at high tide—and hasn't even fully stopped before Brian Bentley walks over and taps on the passenger-side window.

Brian "Accidentally" Bentley is the Sheriff's Department fire investigator. Which is another reason Jack knows there's been a fatal fire, because the Sheriff's Department is there. Otherwise it would be an inspector from the Fire Department, and Jack wouldn't be looking at Bentley's fat face.

Or his wavy red hair turning freaking *orange* with age.

Jack leans over and winds down the window.

Bentley sticks his red face in and says, "You got here quick, Jack. What, you carrying the fire *and* the life?"

"Yup."

"Good," Bentley says. "The double whammy."

Jack and Bentley hate each other.

That old thing about if, say, Jack was on fire, Bentley wouldn't piss on him to put it out? If Jack was on fire, Bentley would drink gasoline so he could piss on Jack.

"Croaker in the bedroom," Bentley says. "They had to scrape her off the springs."

"The wife?" asks Jack.

"We don't have a positive yet," Bentley says. "But it's an adult female."

"Pamela Vale, age thirty-four," Jack says. Goddamn Billy gave him the specs over the phone.

"Name rings a bell," Bentley says.

"Save the Strands," Jack says.

"What the what?"

"Save the Strands," Jack says. "She's been in the papers. She and her husband are big fund-raisers for Save the Strands."

A community group fighting the Great Sunsets Ltd. corporation to prevent them from putting a condo complex on Dana Strands, the last undeveloped stretch of the south coast.

Dana Strands, Jack's beloved Dana Strands, a swatch of grass and trees that sits high on a bluff above Dana Strand Beach. Years ago, it was a trailer park, and then that failed, and then nature reclaimed it and grew over and around it, and is still holding on to it against all the forces of progress.

Just holding on, Jack thinks.

"Whatever," Bentley says.

Jack says, "There's a husband and two kids."

"We're looking for them."

"Shit."

"They ain't in the house," Bentley says. "I mean we're looking for *notification* purposes. How'd you get here so soon?"

"Billy picked it off the scanner, ran the address, had it waiting for me when I got in."

"You insurance bastards," Bentley says. "You just can't wait to get in there and start chiseling, can you?"

Jack hears a little dog barking from somewhere behind the house. It bothers him.

"You name a cause?" Jack asks.

Bentley shakes his head and laughs this laugh he has, which sounds more like steam coming out of a radiator. He says, "Just get out your checkbook, Jack."

"You mind if I go in and have a look?" Jack asks.

"Yeah, I do mind," Bentley says. "Except I can't stop you, right?"

"Right."

It's in the insurance contract. If you have a loss and you make a claim, the insurance company gets to inspect the loss.

"So knock yourself out," Bentley says. He leans way in, trying to get into Jack's face. "Only—Jack? Don't bust chops here. I pull the pin in two weeks. I plan to spend my retirement annoying bass on Lake Havasu, not giving depositions. What you got here is you got a woman drinking vodka and smoking, and she passes out, spills the booze, drops the cigarette and barbecues herself, and that's what you got here."

"You're retiring, Bentley?" Jack asks.

"Thirty years."

"It's about time you made it official."

One reason—out of a veritable smorgasbord of reasons—that Jack hates Accidentally Bentley is that Bentley's a lazy son of a bitch who doesn't like to do his job. Bentley could find an accidental cause for virtually *any* fire. If Bentley had been at Dresden he'd have looked around the ashes and found a faulty electric-blanket control. Cuts down on paperwork and court appearances.

As a fire investigator, Bentley makes a great fisherman.

"Hey, Jack," Bentley says. He's smiling but he's definitely pissed. "At least *I* didn't get *thrown* out."

Like me, Jack thinks. He says, "That's probably because they don't realize you're even there."

"Fuck you," Bentley says.

"Hop in the back."

The smile disappears from Bentley's face. He's like *serious* now.

"Accidental fire, accidental death," Bentley says. "Don't dick around in there."

Jack waits until Bentley leaves before he gets out of the car.

To go dick around in there.

6

Before the scene gets cold.

Literally.

The colder the scene, the less chance there is of finding out what happened.

In jargon, the "C&O"—the cause and origin—of the fire.

The C&O is important for an insurance company because there are accidents and there are *accidents.* If the insured negligently caused the accident then the insurance company is on the hook for the whole bill. But if it's a faulty electric blanket, or a bad switch, or if some appliance malfunctions and sets off a spark, then the company has a shot at something called subrogation, which basically means that the insurance company pays the policyholder and then sues the manufacturer of the faulty item.

So Jack has to dick around in there, but he thinks of it as dicking around with a purpose.

He pops open the trunk of his car.

What he's got in there is a folding ladder, a couple of different flashlights, a shovel, a heavy-duty Stanley tape measure, two 35-mm Minoltas, a Sony Hi8 camcorder, a small clip-on Dictaphone, a notebook, three floodlights, three folding metal stands for the lights and a fire kit..

The fire kit consists of yellow rubber gloves, a yellow hardhat and a pair of white paper overalls that slip over your feet like kids' pajamas.

The trunk is like *full.*

Jack keeps all this stuff in his trunk because Jack is basically a Dalmatian—when a fire happens he's there.

Jack slips into the overalls and feels like some sort of geek from a cheap sci-fi movie, but it's worth it. The first fire you inspect you don't do it, and the soot ruins your clothes or at least totally messes up your laundry schedule.

So he puts on the overalls.

Likewise the hardhat, which he doesn't really need, but Goddamn

Billy will fine you a hundred bucks if he comes to a loss site and catches you without the hat. ("I don't want any goddamn workmen's comp claims," he says.) Jack clips the Dictaphone inside his shirt—if you clip it outside and get it full of soot, you buy a new Dictaphone—slings the cameras over his shoulder and heads for the house.

Which in insurance parlance is called "the risk."

Actually, that's *before* something happens.

After something happens it's called "the loss."

When a risk becomes a loss—when what could happen *does* happen—is where Jack comes in.

This is what he does for California Fire and Life Mutual Insurance Company—he adjusts claims. He's been adjusting claims for twelve years now, and as gigs go Jack figures it's a decent one. He works mostly alone; no one gives him a lot of shit as long as he gets the job done, and he always gets the job done. *Ergo,* it's a relatively shit-free environment.

Some of his fellow adjusters seem to think that they take a lot of shit from the policyholders but Jack doesn't get it. "It's a simple job," he'll tell them when he's heard enough whining. "The insurance policy is a contract. It spells out exactly what you pay for and what you don't. What you owe, you pay. What you don't, you don't."

So there's no reason to take any shit or dish any out.

You don't get personal, you don't get emotional. *Whatever* you do, you don't get *involved.* You do the job and the rest of the time you surf.

This is Jack's philosophy and it works for him. Works for Goddamn Billy, too, because whenever he gets a big fire, he assigns it to Jack. Which only makes sense because that's what Jack did for the Sheriff's Department before they kicked him out—he investigated fires.

So Jack knows that the first thing you do when you investigate a house fire is you walk around the house.

SOP—standard operating procedure—in a fire inspection: you work from the outside in. What you observe on the outside can tell you a lot about what happened on the inside.

He lets himself in through the wrought-iron gate, being careful to shut it behind him because there's that barking dog.

Two little kids lose their mother, Jack thinks, least I can do is not lose their dog for them.

The gate opens into an interior courtyard surrounded by an adobe wall. A winding, crushed gravel path snakes around a Zen garden on the right and a little koi pond on the left.

Or *former* koi pond, Jack thinks.

The pond is sodden with ashes.

Dead koi—once gold and orange, now black with soot—float on the top.

"Note," Jack says into the Dictaphone. "Inquire about value of koi."

He walks through the garden to the house itself.

Takes one look and thinks, *Oh shit.*

7

He's seen the house maybe a million times from the water but he hadn't recognized the address.

Built back in the '30s, it's one of the older homes on the bluff above Dana Point—a heavy-timbered wood frame job with cedar shake walls and a shake roof.

A damn shame, Jack thinks, because this house is one of the survivors of the old days when most of the Dana headlands was just open grass hillside. A product of the days when they really *built* houses.

This house, Jack thinks, has survived hurricanes and monsoons and the Santa Ana winds that sweep these hills with firestorms. Even more remarkably, it's survived real estate developers, hotel planners and tax boards. This sweet old lady of a house has presided over the ocean through all that, and all it takes is one woman with a bottle of vodka and a cigarette to do her in.

Which *is* a shame, Jack thinks, because he's sat on his board looking at this house from the ocean all his damn life and always thought that it was one of the coolest houses ever built.

For one thing, it's made of wood, not stucco or some phony adobe composite. And they didn't use green lumber to frame it up either. In the days when they *built* houses, they used kiln-dried lumber. And they used real log shakes on the exterior and were content to let the ocean weather it to a color somewhere between brown and gray so that the house became a part of the seascape, like driftwood that had been washed up on the shore. And a lot of driftwood, too, because it's a big old place for a single-story building. A big central structure flanked by two large wings set at about a thirty-degree angle toward the ocean.

Standing there looking at it, Jack can see that the central and left sections of the house are still intact. Smoke damaged, water damaged, but otherwise they look structurally sound.

The wing to the right—the west wing—is a different story.

You don't have to be a rocket scientist to figure out that the fire started in the west wing. Generally speaking, the part of a house that suffers the most damage is where the fire started. You know this because that's where the fire burned the longest.

Jack steps back and photographs the house first with one camera and then the other. He has one loaded with color film and the other with black-and-white. Color is better for showing the damage, but some judges will only allow black-and-white shots into evidence, their theory being that color shots—especially in a fatal fire—are "prejudicially dramatic."

Might *inflame* the jury, Jack thinks.

Jack thinks that most judges are dicks.

A lot of adjusters just take Polaroids. Jack uses 35 mm because the images enlarge so much better, which is important if you need them as exhibits in court.

So some bottom-feeding plaintiff's attorney doesn't take your shitty Polaroids and stick them up your ass.

"Polaroids are hemorrhoids." Another of Goddamn Billy's pithy sayings.

So just on the odd chance the file might end up in court, Jack's covering all his bases. Which is why he keeps two 35s handy in the car, because it would be a waste of time to have to reload and then go take each shot again.

He grabs shots of the whole house with each camera and then jots down a note describing each shot and giving the time and date that he took the picture. He notes that he used Minolta cameras, notes the serial numbers of both cameras, the type of film and its ASA. He speaks the same information into the tape recorder, along with any observations he may want to have for his file.

Jack takes these notes because he knows that you *think* you're going to remember what you took and why, but you won't. You got maybe a hundred losses you're working at any given point and you get them mixed up.

Or as Billy Hayes poetically puts it, "It's writ, or it's shit."

Billy's from Arizona.

So Jack says, "Frame One, shot of house taken from south angle. August 28, 1997. West wing of house shows severe damage. Exterior walls standing but will probably have to be torn down and rebuilt. Windows blasted out. Hole in roof."

The easiest way to the other side of the house is through the central section, so Jack lets himself in the front door.

Jack opens it and he's looking straight out at the ocean like he's going to fall into it, because there are big glass sliders with a view that stretches from Newport Beach to the right down to the Mexican islands to the left. Catalina Island straight ahead of you, Dana Strands just down to your left, and below that Dana Strand Beach.

And miles and miles of blue ocean and sky.

You're talking two million bucks just for the view.

The big glass door opens onto a deck about the size of Rhode Island. Below the deck is a sloping lawn, a rectangle of green in all this blue, and in the green there's another rectangle of blue, which is the swimming pool.

A brick wall borders the lawn. Trees and shrubs line the side walls, and the trees and shrubs are edged by a border of flowers. Down to the left there's a pad with a clay tennis court.

The view is totally killer but the house—even this main section that didn't burn—is a fucked-up mess. Drenched with water and the all-pervading acrid stench of smoke.

Jack takes some shots, notes the smoke and water damage on his tape and then goes out into the yard. Takes some shots from this angle and doesn't see anything to change his mind that the fire started in the west wing, which must be the bedroom. He walks to the outside of the west wing, over to one of the windows, and carefully removes a shard of glass from the window frame.

First thing he notices is that it's greasy.

There's a thick, oily soot on the glass.

Jack makes this observation into the tape but what he doesn't speak into the record is what he's *thinking*. What he's thinking is that a residue on the inside of the glass can mean the presence of some kind of hydrocarbon fuel inside the house. Also, the glass is cracked into small, irregular patterns, which means it was fairly near the origin of the fire and that the fire built up fast and hot. He doesn't say any of this, either; all he says into the tape is strictly the physical details: "Glass shows greasy, sooty residue and small-pattern crazing. Radial fracture of glass indicates that it was broken by force of fire from inside the house."

That's all he says because that can't be argued with—the evidence is the evidence. Jack won't put his analysis or speculation on tape because if a lawsuit happens and it goes to trial, the tape will be subpoenaed, and if his voice is on there speculating on potential hydrocarbon fuel in the house, the plaintiff's lawyer will make it sound like he was prejudiced, that he was looking for evidence of arson and therefore skipped over evidence of an accidental fire.

He can just hear the lawyer: "You were focused on the possibility of arson from Moment One, weren't you, Mr. Wade?"

"No, sir."

"Well, you say right here on your taped notes that you thought . . ."

So it's better to leave your thoughts out of it.

It's sloppy work to start thinking ahead of yourself, and anyway, there could be other explanations for the oily soot. If the wood inside the room didn't burn completely, it might leave that kind of residue, or there could be any number of petroleum-based products in the house quite innocently.

Still, there's that barking dog, which is really going at it now. And the bark is not an angry bark, either, not like a dog defending its turf. It's a scared bark, more like a whine, and Jack figures the dog must be terrified. And thirsty. And hungry.

Shit, Jack thinks.

He photographs the piece of glass, labels it and puts it into a plastic evidence bag he keeps in a pocket of the overalls. Then, instead of going into the house—which is what he really wants to do—he goes to look for the dog.

8

The dog probably got out when the firemen broke in, and it's probably traumatized. The Vale kids will be worried about the dog, and anyway, maybe it'll help them feel a little better to get their dog back.

Jack kind of likes dogs.

It's people he's not so crazy about.

Nineteen years (seven with the Sheriff's, twelve with the insurance company) of cleaning up after people's accidents have taught him that people will do about anything. They'll lie, steal, cheat, kill and litter. Dogs, however, have a certain sense of ethics.

He finds the Vales' dog hiding under the lower limbs of a jacaranda tree. It's one of those little fru-fru dogs, a house dog, all big eyes and bark.

"Hey, pup," Jack says softly. "It's all right."

It isn't, but people will lie.

The dog doesn't care. The dog is just happy to see a human being and hear a friendly voice. It comes out from under the tree and sniffs Jack's hand for some kind of clue as to his identity and/or intentions.

"What's your name?" Jack ask.

Like the dog's going to answer, right? Jack thinks.

"Leo," a voice says, and Jack about jumps out of his geeky paper overalls.

He looks up to see an older gentleman standing across the fence. A parrot sits on his shoulder.

"Leo," the parrot repeats.

Leo starts wagging his tail.

Which is what Yorkies do for a living.

"C'mere, Leo," Jack says. "That's a good dog."

He picks Leo up and tucks him under one arm, scratching the top of his head, and walks over to the fence.

He can feel Leo trembling.

There's that thing about people resembling their pets, or vice versa? Jack always thought that applied to just dogs, but the parrot and the older gentleman kind of look like each other. They both have beaks: the parrot's being pretty self-explanatory and the older gentleman's nose being shaped just like the parrot's beak. The man and the bird are like some interspecies kind of Siamese twins, except that the parrot is green with patches of bright red and yellow, and the older gentleman is mostly white.

He has white hair and wears a white shirt and white slacks. Jack can't see his shoes through the hedge, but he's betting that they're white, too.

"I'm Howard Meissner," the old guy says. "You must be the man from Mars."

"Close," Jack says. He offers his left hand because he has Leo tucked under his right. "Jack Wade, California Fire and Life."

"This is Eliot."

Meaning the parrot.

Which says, *"Eliot, Eliot."*

"Pretty bird," Jack says.

"Pretty bird, pretty bird."

Jack guesses the parrot's heard the "pretty bird" bit before.

"A shame about Pamela," Meissner says. "I saw the stretcher go out."

"Yeah."

Meissner's eyes get watery.

He reaches over the fence to pet Leo and says, "It's all right, Leo. You did your best."

Jack gives him a funny look and Meissner explains, "Leo's barking woke me up. I looked out the window and saw the flames and dialed 911."

"What time was that?"

"Four forty-four."

"That's pretty exact, Mr. Meissner."

"Digital clock," Meissner says. "You remember things like that. I called right away. But too late."

"You did what you could."

"I'm thinking Pamela is out of the house because Leo is."

"Leo, Leo."

"Leo was outside?" Jack asks.

"Yes."

"When you heard him barking?"

"Yes."

"You're sure about that, Mr. Meissner?"

"Pretty bird, pretty bird."

Meissner nods. "I saw Leo standing out there. Barking at the house. I thought Pamela . . ."

"Did Leo usually sleep outside?" Jack asks.

"No, no," Meissner says, like dismissively.

Jack knows it's a stupid question. No one's going to leave a little dog like this outside at night. He's always seeing signs for lost Yorkies and cats, and with all the coyotes around here you know it's like "B Company ain't comin' back."

"Coyotes," Jack says.

"Of course."

Jack asks, "Mr. Meissner, did you see the flames?"

Meissner nods.

"What color were they?" Jack asks.

"Red."

"Brick red, light red, bright red, cherry red?"

Meissner thinks about this for a second, then says, "Blood red. Blood red would describe it."

"How about the smoke?"

No question about it, no hesitation.

"Black."

"Mr. Meissner," Jack asks, "do you know where the rest of the family was?"

"It was Nicky's night with the kids," he says. "A blessing."

"They're divorced?"

"Separated," he says. "Nicky's been staying with his mother."

"Where does she—"

"Monarch Bay," he says. "I told this to the police when they were here, so that they could notify."

Except, Jack thinks, Bentley tells me they're still looking.

"I feel for the kids," says Meissner. He sighs one of those sighs that come only from advanced age. The man has seen too much.

"In and out. In and out," Meissner says. "Chess pieces."

"I know what you mean," Jack says. "Well, thanks, Mr. Meissner."

"Howard."

"Howard," Jack says. Then he asks, "Do you know why they were separated? What the issues were?"

"It was Pamela," he says sadly. "She drank."

So there it is, Jack thinks as he watches Meissner walk away. Pamela Vale has a night without the responsibility of the kids so she gets hammered. At some point she lets Leo out to go pee, forgets he's out there and ends up in bed with a bottle and some cigs.

So Pamela Vale is drinking and smoking in bed. The vodka bottle tips over and most of the contents spills onto the floor. Pamela Vale either doesn't notice or doesn't care. Then, with a burning cigarette still in her hand, she passes out. The sleeping hand drops the cigarette onto the vodka. The alcohol ignites into a hot flame, which catches the sheets, and the blankets, and the room fills with smoke.

Normally it would take ten to fifteen minutes for the cigarette to ignite the sheets. Ten to fifteen minutes in which Pamela Vale might have smelled smoke, felt the heat, woke up and stamped her foot on the cigarette and that would have been that. But the vodka would ignite instantly, at a much greater heat than a smoldering cigarette—enough to ignite the sheets—and because she's passed out she never has a chance.

It's the smoke, not the flames, that kills Pamela Vale.

Jack can picture her lying in bed, passed out drunk, her respiratory system working even though her mind has shut down, and that respiratory system just sucks in that smoke, and fills her lungs with it, until it's too late.

She suffocates on smoke while she's asleep.

Like a drunk choking on his own vomit.

So there's that small blessing for Pamela Vale. She literally never knew what hit her.

They had to scrape her off the springs, but she was dead before the intense heat merged her flesh into the metal. She never woke up, that's all. The fire broke out, her system inhaled a lethal dose of smoke, and then the fire—fueled by all her belongings and her home—became fast and hot and strong enough to melt the bed around her.

An accidental fire, an accidental death.

It's one of those cruel but kind ironies of a fatal house fire. Cruel in the sense that it chokes you with your own life. Takes those crucial physical things—your furniture, your sheets, your blankets, the paint on your walls, your clothes, your books, your papers, your photographs, all the intimate accumulations of a life, a marriage, a physical existence—and forces them down your throat and chokes you on them.

Most people who die in fires die from smoke inhalation. It's like lethal injection—no, more like the gas chamber, because it's really a gas, carbon monoxide, the old CO, that kills you—but in any case you'd prefer it to the electric chair.

The technical phrase in the fire biz is "CO asphyxiation."

It sounds cruel, but the kind part is that you'd sure as hell prefer it to burning at the stake.

So there it is, Jack thinks.

An accidental fire and an accidental death.

It all fits.

Except you have the sooty glass.

And flames from burning wood aren't blood red—they're yellow or orange.

And the smoke should be gray or brown—not black.

But then again, Jack thinks, these are the observations of an old man in bad light.

He carries Leo back to the car. Opens up the trunk and digs around until he finds an old Frisbee he left in there. Gets a bottle of water from out of the front seat and pours some into the Frisbee. Sets Leo down and the little dog goes right for the water.

Jack finds an old Killer Dana sweatshirt in the trunk and lays it on the passenger seat. Rolls the windows halfway down, figuring that it's early enough in the morning that the car won't get too hot, and then sits Leo down on the sweatshirt.

"Stay," Jack says, feeling kind of stupid. "Uhh, lie down."

Dog looks at Jack like he's relieved to be getting some kind of order and settles down into the sweatshirt.

"And don't, you know, *do* anything, okay?" Jack asks. Classic '66 Mustang, and Jack's spent hours refurbishing the interior.

Leo's tail whacks against the seat.

"What happened in there, Leo?" Jack says to the dog. "You know, don't you? So why don't you tell me?"

Leo looks up at him and wags his tail some more.

But doesn't say a word.

"That's okay," Jack says.

Jack deals with a lot of snitches. Seven years in the Sheriff's Department and twelve in insurance claims and you deal with a lot of snitches. One of the ironies of the game: you rely on snitches and at the same time you despise them.

Another plus for the dog column.

Dogs are stand-up guys.

They never snitch.

So Leo says nothing except for the fact that he's alive. Which sets off this sick little alarm in Jack's brain.

What Jack knows is that people will never burn the pooch.

They'll burn their houses, their clothing, their business, their papers—they'll even burn each other—but they'll never torch Fido. Every house fire Jack's ever worked that turned out to be arson, the dog was somewhere else.

But then again, Jack thinks, so were the people.

And Pamela Vale was good people.

Raising all that money to save the Strands.

So let it go.

He peels off the overalls and the rest of it.

The house inspection will have to wait for a little while.

You got two kids going through a divorce, then their mother dies and their house burns down. Better get them their dog.

Small consolation for a shitty deal.

9

Goddamn Billy Hayes strikes a match, cups his hands against the breeze and lights his cigarette.

He's sitting on a metal folding chair in the cactus garden outside his office at California Fire and Life, claim files in his lap, reading glasses on his nose and a Camel in his lips.

The cactus garden was Billy's idea. Since the People's Republic of California banned smoking in the workplace, Billy has been the company chairperson of COSA, the California Outdoor Smokers Association. He figured since he spent most of his time out in the courtyard anyway, it might as well be someplace he liked, so he had it rebuilt as a cactus garden.

If you need to talk to Billy and he isn't in his office, he's outside sitting on his folding chair, working on his files and sucking on a stick. One time Jack came in on a Sunday night and moved Billy's desk out there. Billy thought that was just about as amusing as filtered cigarettes.

Billy came from Tucson twenty years ago to head up Cal Fire and Life's Fire Claims Division. He didn't want to come, but the company said it was "up or out," and up meant coming out to California. So here he is, sitting out among the ocotillo and barrel cactus and the sand and the rocks amidst the aroma of sage, tobacco and carbon monoxide coming off the traffic streaming by on the 405.

Goddamn Billy Hayes is a small man—five-six—and so thin he looks like one of those dolls where there's just wire under the little clothes. Got a sun-shriveled tan face, a silver crew cut and eyes as blue as Arctic ice. He wears good blue suits over cowboy boots. Used to keep a .44 Colt holstered on his belt—back when he had a few arson losses on some mob-owned buildings in Phoenix, and the Trescia family intimated that if he didn't pay up maybe *he'd* have an "accident."

Here's how Billy handles that.

Goddamn Billy walks into young Joe Trescia's real estate office with the .44 in his hand, pulls the hammer back, sticks the barrel up under young Joe's nose and says, "I'm about to have me one hell of a goddamn *accident* here."

Five wise guys standing there—scared too shitless to reach for their own hardware because it's clear this little nut ball would splatter Joe Jr.'s brains all over the wall. Which would make Joe Sr. very unhappy, so they just stand there sweating and saying silent prayers to St. Anthony.

Young Joe looks up the blue steel barrel at those blue steel eyes and says, "I've decided to look elsewhere for our insurance needs."

But that was the old days, and they don't let you do that kind of thing anymore, especially not in California, where it would be deemed *inappropriate.* ("I mean, goddamn it," Billy said, relaying the story to Jack one night over Jack Daniel's with beer chasers, "in a state where they won't let you *smoke,* you know they ain't gonna let you splatter some greaseball's brains all over the wall.") So the pistol now sits on the top shelf of Billy's bedroom closet.

What we got now instead of guns, Billy thinks, is we got lawyers.

Not as fast, but every bit as lethal and a hell of a lot more expensive.

Only thing more expensive than having lawyers is *not* having lawyers, because what insurance companies do these days—in addition to selling insurance and paying claims—is they get sued.

We get sued, Billy thinks, for not paying enough, paying too slow, paying too *fast,* but especially for not paying at all.

Which is what you got to do when you got an arson, or a phony theft, or a car accident that didn't really happen, or even a dead insured who isn't really dead but who's slurping piña coladas in Botswana or some such goddamn place.

You gotta deny those claims. Say, Sorry, Charlie, no money; and then of course they sue you for "bad faith."

Insurance companies are scared shitless of bad faith lawsuits.

You end up spending more on lawyers and court costs than you would have just to pay the goddamn claim, but *goddamn it,* you just can't go around paying money you don't owe.

Another Goddamn Billy dictum: "We don't pay people to burn their own houses down."

Unless, of course a judge and/or jury disagrees with you.

Finds that you "unreasonably" denied the claim or paid less than you should. Then you're in *bad faith* and you're also neck deep in a downwardly swirling shitter, because they hit you with not only the "contractual damages," but also "compensatory damages," and—if they really hate you—punitive damages.

Then you *do* pay your insureds to burn their own house down, and you *also* pay them compensatories for the pain and anguish you caused them, and you pay a few million in punitive damages if the scumsucking, bottom-feeding goddamn plaintiff's attorney has managed to whip the jury into a froth about how mean and nasty you were to the poor insureds who burned their own goddamn house down in the first place.

So it's entirely possible—possible, *shit*, it's happened—to deny a $10,000 theft claim and get popped for a cool mil in a bad faith judgment.

You get the right lawyer, the right judge and the right jury, the very best thing that can happen to you in your whole life is that your insurance company denies your claim.

Which is why Billy sends Jack Wade out on the Vale loss, because Jack is the best adjuster he's got.

Goddamn Billy's thinking these thoughts while he's looking through the Vales' homeowner's policy and what he sees is that this loss is a beaut: a million-five on the house itself; $750,000 on personal property, propped up with another $500,000 in special endorsements.

Not to mention a dead wife.

With a $250,000 life policy on her.

All of which is why he handed this one to Jack Wade.

He knows Jack, so he knows that whatever else happens, Jack is going to do the job.

10

Here's the story on Jack Wade.

Jack grows up in Dana Point, which in those days is a small beach town with a couple of motels, a few diners and surf to die for. In fact, so many surfers actually die for the surf that the beach gets the nickname Killer Dana.

Jack's old man is a contractor so Jack grows up working. Jack's mom is a contractor's wife so she *gets it*: as soon as her little boy is big enough to hold a hammer he's on jobs with his dad after school, weekends and summers. Jack's seven years old and he's holding the hammer for his dad until his dad reaches back and then *smack*, that hammer's in Dad's palm because little Jack is *on the job*. He gets bigger he gets to do bigger stuff. Jack's thirteen, he's in there tacking framing, hanging Sheetrock, toeing in footings. He's sixteen he's on roofs nailing down the shingles.

Jack *works*.

When he isn't working he does what every other kid in Dana Point does—he surfs.

Learns this from his old man, too, because John Sr. was one of the early guys out there on a longboard. John Sr. was out there riding a Dale Velzy ten-foot wooden longboard in the days when surfers were considered bums, but John Sr. doesn't give a shit because he knows he works for a living and bums don't.

This is what John Sr. tells Jack like maybe only a million times on the beach or on the job. What he tells him is, "There's work and there's play. Play is better, but you *work* to earn the play. I don't care what you do in this world, but you do *some*thing. You earn your own living."

"Yeah, Dad."

"Yeah, yeah, yeah," John Sr. says. "But I'm telling you, you do the job, you do it right, you earn your paycheck. Then the rest of your time is yours, you don't owe anybody shit, you don't owe any explanations, you have paid your way."

So Jack's father teaches him to work and to surf. Turns him on to all the good stuff: In-N-Out Burgers, Dick Dale & His Del-Tones, *tacos carne asada* at El Maguey, longboards, the beach break at Lower Trestles, the old trailer park at Dana Strands.

Young Jack thinks it might be the most beautiful place in the world, this long ridge overlooking Dana Strand Beach. The trailer park has been closed for years; all there is now is a few decrepit old buildings and some trailer pads, but when he's up there among the eucalyptus and the palms which overlook the gorgeous stretch of beach that curves into the big rock at Dana Head, well, it's the most beautiful place in the world.

Young Jack spends hours there—hell, *days* there—on the last undeveloped hillside on the south coast. He'll surf for a while, then hike up the ravine that leads up the bluff and slip under the old fence and wander around. Go sit in the old rec hall building where they used to have Ping-Pong tables and a jukebox and a kitchen that put out burgers and dogs and chili for the trailer park patrons. Sometimes he sits there and watches the lightning storms that crash over Dana Head, or sometimes he sits up there during the whale migration and spots the big grays moving north up the coast. Or sometimes he justs sits there and stares at the ocean and does nothing.

His dad doesn't let him do a lot of nothing. John Sr. keeps him pretty busy, especially as young Jack gets older and can handle more work.

But sometimes when they've finished a big job they take the truck down to Baja and find some little Mexican fishing village. Sleep in the back of the truck, surf the miles of empty beach, take siestas under palm trees in the ferocious midday heat. In the late afternoon they order fish for dinner and the locals go out and catch it and have it ready by the time the sun goes down. Jack and his dad sit at an outdoor table and eat the fresh fish, with warm tortillas right off the grill, and drink ice-cold Mexican beer and talk about the waves they caught or the waves that caught them or just about *stuff*. Then maybe one of the villagers gets out his guitar, and if Jack and his dad have had *enough* beers they join in singing the *canciones*. Or maybe they just lie in the back of the truck listening to a Dodgers game through the crackle of the radio, or just talk to the background of a mariachi station, or maybe just fall asleep staring at the stars.

Do a few days of this and then drive back to *el norte* to go back to work.

Jack graduates from high school, does a couple of semesters at San Diego State, figures *that* ain't it and takes the test for the Sheriff's Department. Tells his dad he wants to try something different from Sheetrock and 2 by 6s for a while.

"I can't blame you," says his dad.

Jack aces the written exam, and he's bulked up from the construction work and the surfing, so he gets on with the Orange County Sheriff's Department. Does the usual gigs for a few years—serves papers, picks up fugitive warrants, does car patrols—but Jack is a *smart* kid and wants to move up and there's no spot in Major Crimes so he applies for fire school.

Figuring that if you know *con*struction you got a jump on *destruc*tion.

He's right about this.

He *rips* fire school.

11

"Prometheus," the little man in the tweed suit says.

Jack's like, *Pro-who?* And what the hell does it have to do with fire?

The lecturer acknowledges the blank stares of the class.

"Read your Aeschylus," he says, adding to the general puzzlement. "When Prometheus gave *fire* to mankind, the other gods chained him to a boulder and sent eagles to pick at his liver for all eternity. If you consider what man has done with fire, Prometheus got off easy."

Jack had expected fire school to be taught by a fireman—instead he has this tweed-jacket professor named Fuller from the chemistry department of Chapman mumbling about gods and eternity and telling the students in a thick Irish accent that if they don't understand the *chemistry* of fire, they can never understand the *behavior* of fire.

First thing Jack learns in fire school is, What is fire?

Nothing like starting with the basics.

So . . .

"Fire is the active stage of combustion," the professor tells Jack's class. "Combustion is the oxidation of fuel that creates flame, heat and light."

"So combustion is flame, heat and light?" Jack says.

The professor agrees, then asks, "But what is flame?"

The class's reaction is basically, *Duhh*.

It's easy to *describe* flame—it's red, yellow, orange, occasionally blue—but defining it is something else. Fuller lets the class sit with this for a minute, then he asks a very unprofessorlike question: "Are you telling me that no silly bastard in this room has ever lighted a fart?"

Ahhh, says the class.

Ahhh, thinks Jack. Flame is burning gas.

"Burning *gases*," Fuller says. "So combustion is the oxidation of fuel that creates burning gases, heat and light. Which begs what question?"

"What is oxidation?" Jack asks.

"Full marks for the surfer dude," Fuller says. "What's your name?"

"Jack Wade."

"Well, Master Jack," Fuller says, "oxidation is a series of chemical reactions that occur when an atom—that is, *matter*—forms a chemical bond with a molecule of oxygen. Now don't you all wish you'd paid more attention in Chemistry 101?"

Yes, thinks Jack. Definitely. Because Fuller starts drawing chemical equations on the board. While the chalk is screeching, Fuller's saying, "In order for oxidation to occur, a combustible fuel—we'll talk about fuel in a few minutes—and oxygen must come together. This is called an exothermic—that is, heat-producing—reaction."

He draws an equation : $2H_2 + O_2 = 2H_2O$ + heat.

"A basic oxidation reaction," Fuller says. "When you combine hydrogen and oxygen, you get two molecules of water, and heat. Heat is measured in BTUs—British thermal units. One BTU is the amount of heat that it takes to raise the temperature of one pound of water by 1 degree Fahrenheit. So the more heat you have, the greater the temperature you're going to get. Put simply, the more BTUs, the hotter the fire."

Fuller continues, "Look, gentlemen, to sustain a fire you need to have three things working together: oxygen, fuel and heat. If you have no oxygen, oxidation obviously can't take place—no fire. If you have no fuel, there is nothing to oxidize—no fire. If the fuel doesn't contain enough mass of heat, then the fire dies out."

He strikes a match.

"Observe," he says. "We have oxygen, we have fuel, we have heat."

The match burns for a few seconds, then goes out.

"What happened?" Fuller asks. "We had plenty of oxygen, but not a lot of fuel and not a lot of heat."

He strikes another match.

"I will now attempt to burn down the classroom."

He holds the match to the metal desk.

The flame makes a slight scorch on the metal, then burns out.

"What happened?" Fuller asks. "We have oxygen, we have heat, it's a big desk—plenty of fuel—where is our sustained fire?"

"Most metals don't burn easily," Jack says.

"Most metals don't burn easily," Fuller repeats. "Which is the lay person's way of talking about flammability. Some substances burn more easily than others. Witness . . ."

He rips a page from a legal pad, strikes another match and holds the match to the paper.

"It *ignites* immediately," he says. He drops the burning paper into a metal trash can and puts a lid on it.

"Thereby depriving it of oxygen," he notes. "Look, paper has a lower *flash point* than the metal of the desk. Flash point is the temperature at which a fuel ignites. A simple match will ignite paper but doesn't have nearly the BTUs to create enough temperature to reach the flash point of the metal in this desk. It simply can't sustain the oxidation reaction needed to set the desk on fire and keep it on fire.

"Now, were we to add more fuel to the fire, and developed enough BTUs to raise the temperature, there is a point at which we could indeed melt the desk.

"It's a chain reaction, gentlemen—a chemical chain reaction. Difficult to break down into a description because it is a never-ending cycle of chain reactions which are really quite fascinating in detail. But for practical purposes it's all about fuel. The amount of fuel, the flash points of that fuel and the conductivity of that fuel.

"So, the amount of fuel—in proper terminology the fuel *load,* or the fuel *mass.* Why is it important to establish a fuel load for a structure that has suffered a fire? If, for instance, you find a melted metal desk in a burned structure where the pre-fire fuel load could not have produced sufficient BTUs to melt that metal, you have an anomaly which you need to resolve.

"You'll want to be taking notes on this because you'll need this terminology to pass the bloody test."

Jack takes notes.

He doesn't want to pass the bloody test.

He wants to ace it.

12

So he has to learn certain definitions.

Like fuel load.

Fuel load is the total potential BTUs per square foot of the structure in question. You calculate it by determining the total pounds of matter in the structure and multiplying the total weight by the total BTUs of the various materials in the structure—8,000 BTUs per pound of wood, 16,000 BTUs per pound of plastic, et cetera et cetera et cetera.

Certain materials give off more heat than others. Wood, about 8,000 BTUs. Coal, about 12,000. Flammable liquids, somewhere between 16,000 to 21,000 BTUs.

Another term: heat release rate. This is the speed at which a fire grows, depending on the fuel upon which it is feeding. Some materials burn fast and hot, others are slow. HRR is measured in BTUs per second, otherwise known as kilowatts. A plastic trash bag, filled with the usual garbage, is going to have somewhere between 140 and 350 kilowatts. A television set about 250. A two-square-foot pool of kerosene, 400. Kerosene gives you a hot, fast fire.

Jack learns that fuel load isn't just fuel load, but is divided into two parts: dead load and live load. Dead load is the total weight of the materials in the structure plus the total weight of any permanent built-ins. Live load is the total weight of the materials of items added to the structure—furniture, appliances, artwork, toys, people and pets. The irony of the phrase "live load" is that if they are found in the fire, they are most likely dead.

Conductivity—that is to say, the amount of heat a substance on fire transfers. Some materials retain most of their heat; some transfer it to other materials in the structure. Jack learns for a fire to spread it has to encounter material that is conductive, that transfers and adds to the BTUs. Paper, for example, is highly conductive. Water isn't—it absorbs more heat than it transfers. Air is highly conductive, being made up of about 21 percent oxygen. So most structural fires spread by convection, meaning the transfer of heat by a circulating medium, usually air. Fire burns up, because that's where the air is.

"It's all about fuel," Fuller lectures. "You are what you eat, and fire is no different. You can determine its severity, its origin, its direction and rate of spread, and how long it burned, by the fuel in the structure."

Jack aces the chemistry test.

Fuller passes out the results, which apparently launch him to new rhetorical heights.

"So," he asks, "what happens in a fire?

"It has all the dramatic structure of your classic three-act play, gentlemen. It has the rhythm of a love affair.

"Oxidation occurs. Act One: The Smoldering Phase. The seduction, if you will, the chemical reaction between oxygen and solid molecules in which the oxygen tries to induce heat in the solid matter. The seduction might take a fraction of a second—in the case of a hot number like gasoline or kerosene or some other liquid accelerant, the roundheels of the flammable street corner, I might tell you. Switching metaphors, liquid accelerants are the aphrodisiacs of the fire seduction. They are the storied Spanish fly, the fine wine, the manly cologne, the American Express Platinum Card left casually by the side of the couch. They can get the passion ignited in a big hurry.

"Or the smoldering phase might last hours or even days. The material, the fuel, wants to be wined and dined, courted, taken to dinner and the movies. Come to Sunday dinner and meet my parents. But fire is a patient seducer, comrades. If it can just hang in there long enough to generate a little heat, if the affair is given a little air to breathe, it lingers. A kiss on the neck, a hand under the blouse, the steamy heat of the backseat at a drive-in movie, fellows. Working, working, trying to melt the fuel to liquid and then into burning gas. A questing hand under the skirt, trying to generate enough heat to reach the ignition point, smoldering, smoldering and then . . .

"Ignition. Act Two: The Free-Burning Phase. The flash point is reached. Open flames, my boys. Passion. Heated gas is lighter than air so it rises—witness your Goodyear blimp. It starts eating up the air and then it hits the ceiling. If the fire is hot enough to ignite the ceiling materials you have more ignition. The fire might even blast a hole in the roof to get to that easy, tasty air. The heated gases themselves become a source of radiation, now spreading the heat downward to ignite material below. This is why the ceiling might burn, by the way, before the furniture does.

"It all depends on your fuel, gentlemen. Is she an ice maiden with a high flash point and a tepid HRR? The affair will die from lack of passion. She's a frigid bitch, my jolly boys—do your worst, she won't respond. Or is she a hot number? A low flash point, a steaming HRR? Then hold on, buckoes, you are in for a ride. If she's hot enough and big enough, your fire will reach a critical temperature. The heat will radiate down from the ceiling hot enough to overwhelm the ignition point of all the materials underneath it, and then the fairies start flying.

"What do I mean by that esoteric and somewhat effeminate reference regarding flying fairies? Just before flashover, boys, you might see little pockets of gas in the air ignite—little licks of flame dancing in the air. That is the 'fairies flying,' and that is the time to put it in Reverse, gentlemen, because if you see the fairies flying, it is a prelude to—

"WHOOSH! Act Three: The Flashover Phase. All the exposed surfaces reach ignition point, and now you have an out-of-control fire. An undeniable passion that sweeps everything before it. Nothing can resist it, every substance opens its legs and joins the orgy. The heat is transferred upward by the air, downward by radiation and sideways by conduction. It thrashes in passion in all directions. The intensity *doubles* with each 18-degree rise in temp. It gets hotter and faster, faster and hotter. This is fire's orgasm, gentlemen, the fiery consummation of the affair. It roars and screams and groans and moans. It howls like a banshee into the air. It burns until it runs out of fuel or someone comes along and puts it out.

"And now," Fuller says, "we shall have a cigarette."

He lights his cig and leans back against the desk in a parody of sexual satisfaction and exhaustion. After a minute he says, "Three phases of fire, ye thirsters after knowledge: smoldering, free burning and flashover. The first act often dies from its own lack of energy, it suffocates from lack of air; the second phase can be put out by prompt and appropriate action; the third phase, flashover—well, Katie, bar the door.

"So what is fire? A dry chemical interaction between molecules. A three-act drama that often ends in tragedy. A metaphor for sex, which reveals itself in our language of love, i.e., the 'heat of passion': 'You get me so hot, baby.' The stereotypical seduction setting of the bearskin rug in front of a roaring fire. The heat that can only be extinguished by the emission of cooling exothermic fluids.

"This is the chemistry that old Prometheus instinctively understood," Fuller says. "He gave it to man and man has used it to warm his caves, to cook his food and—being human—to incinerate his fellow man in all manner of nasty combustion.

"Well, let the sparks fly. Let the eagles feast."

He finishes his cigarette, tosses it into the trash can, then says, "Let's go dance with the bitch."

Dance with the bitch?

13

The crazy bastard puts them into a burning building.

Jack loves it.

Fire school—*outrageous,* man.

The little Irish dude walks them out onto this big concrete square where there's this two-story concrete building that looks like an air control tower designed by some sort of Soviet architectural committee. Thing's got doors and windows and fire escapes all over it and there's firemen standing around looking at the students like they are meat.

Firemen have these little smirks on their faces, like *good morning, welcome to our world. Welcome to your hosing.*

Firemen standing in front of a stack of oxygen masks.

Which makes the students a little, you know, *apprehensive,* then one of the older firemen comes up and starts giving them a briefing about how to put on the masks and how to use them.

Five minutes later Jack is standing in a crowded mass of his fellow students on the second floor of the concrete building, and it's hot and sweaty and then it's pitch black because the door slams. Some of the boys start scrambling to put their masks on, but a voice comes over the PA screaming, *Not yet!!!!*

There's something we want you to experience first, gentlemen.

Suffocation.

More properly, asphyxiation.

First thing Jack feels is like this intense heat, then the room starts filling with smoke. Jack's like, *This is wild,* and wild it is because what you got here is a bunch of men crowded into a dark locked room, part of which is on fire.

Jack gets the game.

The game is, you put your mask on before the order comes, you are *out of there*—out of the building, out of the school—so Jack squats down as close as he can manage to the floor, where there's still some air. But it's only a minute or so before his eyes start burning and tearing, and then he starts choking and gagging, and everyone is choking and gagging, and Jack feels this moment of absolute primal terror—which is like *panic,* man. He feels it and appreciates it—this is what they *want* me to feel, this is the moment they want me to confront. Want me to give in, freak out, lose it.

Which is what a couple of guys do—they're history, they're past tense—but Jack is like, *Fuck that.* Jack's been held under by a wave more than once in his young life. He's already experienced not breathing, so he's like, *Bring it, dudes.*

I will fucking die in here before I reach for the mask.

But is nevertheless very pleased to hear Fuller scream, *Put your masks on, you silly bastards,* except it's no gimme putt in the dark, with your elbows banging against other elbows, and you can't see a damn thing, and your brain is telling your hands to like *Hurry the fuck up* and your fingers are telling your brain *Fuck you* and then you get the mask on and it's like *Aaaaaahhhhh.*

A completely new appreciation for oxygen.

Then the door comes open and a big beautiful rectangle of light penetrates this contrived little mock hell and some guys are standing and some are keeled over and Jack sees this one guy crouched on the floor. In bad shape, man—dude is still fiddling with his mask. Dude is going to be out in a second, so Jack pushes his down to the guy and holds the mask to the guy's face and gets him strapped in and then Fuller's voice comes across the PA screeching, *Get out of there, you total idiots!*

Jack rips his mask off long enough to yell, "Guys! Be cool!"

The guy nearest the door stands at the side and plays traffic cop, pushing guys through one at a time. Jack's boy is in bad shape, though, can't straighten up, so Jack gets a shoulder under his arm and lifts. Waits his turn by the door and carries the guy out onto the fire escape.

Which is on fire, of course.

Just fucking outrageous, Jack thinks as he looks up and sees that the roof of the tower is a mass of flames, and the railing of the fire escape is a line of flame, and flames are bursting out the windows they have to get past.

Jack spots Fuller and the head fireman watching them from a nearby tower, so he sets his boy down and gives him a little shove down the stairs, which is too crowded for the guy to fall anyway, and even if he does, it's better for him to be seen taking a header than getting carried out of there.

Just to make things more fun, the firemen are spraying them with a hose, so by the time Jack makes it down the stairs he's half-choked, semiblinded, singed, bruised and soaked.

The whole class is sprawled out on the concrete, not caring that they're lying in puddles, just happy to be breathing and *not on fire* when Fuller comes over and looks down at them.

Fuller lights himself another cig, has himself a long smirk and asks, "Any questions?"

Jack raises his hand.

"Mr. Wade?"

"Yeah," Jack says. "Can I go again?"

Fire school.

What a ride.

Better than Knott's Berry Farm.

14

Fire school.

Jack's having more fun than a boy should have.

Going to class, studying his ass off, hitting a few beers with the boys in the dorm after shutting the books.

Fire school is very cool.

33

Next thing they get into after fire chemistry is construction. This time it's no Irish professor but a local good-old-boy contractor with a civil engineering degree who takes them through how a house is built.

This contractor is classic. Got that greased-back pompadour So-Cal left-over-from-the-Oklahoma-days look. White short-sleeved shirt with a pocket protector. Mechanical pencil and a protractor peeking out of the pocket.

And the boy knows his shit.

This is the easy part of fire school for Jack, because he's been there. Every piece of terminology that the guy writes on the board, Jack has, like *done*. They're not talking chemistry, drama, sex and Greek mythology now; they're talking dormers, downspout straps, cripples, floor joists and headers. Talking newels and king posts and trusses and wall sheathing, and these are all things that Jack's dad taught him the hard way. Which is like, carrying the shit around, putting it in, putting it in wrong and having to rip it out and do it all over again, so Jack knows whereof the contractor speaks.

Next thing they do is they go over to the shell of a building they got set up in a big old Quonset-hut hangar.

Damn thing looks like a dinosaur in a museum.

A two-room house with dormer windows—half of it just the structural shell, the other half finished out with walls, shingles, doors and windows and the rest of the enchilada.

First each student has to walk around naming every piece of wood in the skeleton half. Name it—"door buck, stud, collar beam"—then identify the size and type of the lumber—pine 3 by 6, 2 by 4, so on and so forth. Once the whole class can do that, they go over to the finished-off side and now they have to get into window sashes, types of glass, chair rails, balusters—all the stuff that Jack has come to know as "dead load," fuel for the fire.

Jack aces construction.

Next thing they look at is appliances. Go into a big empty warehouse with fire extinguishers all over the place and light fires under television sets, blenders, radios, alarm clocks, you name it. They learn how these behave when introduced to varying degrees of heat. Which is like, badly, because these puppies don't want to burn. I mean maybe if you've spent forty-seven minutes giving yourself carpal tunnel syndrome on the remote control box and still can't find anything worth watching you might want to set fire to the old Panasonic twenty-inch with picture-in-picture, but what Jack learns is that this is no easy task. You want to toast the TV, you have to bring some serious heat.

So all day they're setting fire to stuff and at night Jack humps the books. No suds sessions now; the work's getting harder and all you have to do to get your locker cleaned out is screw up one exam. Guys are dropping like fat men in a marathon. Like, *Timmmberrrrrrr!!!!*

So Jack's up half the night cramming Ohm's law ("The current flowing through resistance is equal to the applied voltage divided by the resistance") into his brain, or trying to memorize the ignition temperature of magnesium (1,200°F) or the length of time it will take an inch of number-two lumber to burn at a temperature of 4,500°F (forty-five minutes).

Like all day they're running electrical engineers at them, fire investigators at them, heating contractors at them. They're even running freaking lawyers at them, so at night Jack's not only boning up on the explosive properties of methane, the ignition temperature of magnesium and the decomposition of cellulose under an open flame ($C_6H_{10}O_5 + 6O_2 = 5H_2O + 6CO_2$ + heat), now he also has to learn the significance of *Michigan v. Tyler* and *The People v. Calhoun* and he also has to master the Federal Rules of Evidence regarding the collection and preservation of evidence at a fire scene for the purposes of an arson prosecution.

Dig it, this is the same Jack Wade who couldn't force-feed himself two chapters of *Moby-Dick* and now he's writing papers covering constitutional law. This is the dude who punked out of Algebra 101 and now he can tell you how much carbon monoxide will be produced by a specific mass of polyurethane burning at a given temperature.

Jack is hanging in there very strong.

Learns how to document a fire scene: how to draw a floor plan, how to overlay the progress of the fire on that plan, how to take photographs, what photographs to take and how to light them, how to take notes, how to take samples, how to collect and preserve evidence, how to interview suspects, how to interview witnesses, when to make an arrest, how to testify in court.

Guys are washing out—there are more empty desks in the classrooms, more available stools in their rare sessions at the bar—but Jack is hanging tough.

Surprising himself.

Taking all they can give.

Then they bring in Captain Sparky.

15

His real name isn't Sparky.

It's Sparks.

You got a guy named Sparks who becomes a fireman anyway, you got a tough guy. You got a guy who doesn't give Shit One about what anyone else thinks.

It's Jack who hangs the nickname Captain Sparky on him, because it's kind of inevitable. Sparky has no apparent sense of humor. Captain Sparky is as serious as a CAT scan, and he tells the students right off the bat that he's out to get them.

Captain Sparky stands in front of the class in his dress blues and says, "Gentlemen, the whole reason you are here, the entire purpose for providing you with this multi-thousand-dollar education, is for you to be able to go to the scene of a fire and determine its cause and origin. If you should pass this class, that will become the sole purpose of your professional life."

Looks at the class like he's Jesus Christ telling Peter he's supposed to build the church. Looking at them like he's thinking, Fat chance you dim bulbs could find your asses with both hands, let's not talk about building no church.

Anyway, hopeless as they are, they're all he's got, so he carries on with, "People's lives, futures and financial well-being will depend on the accuracy of your determinations as to cause and origin. Your conclusions will be the basis for decisions to prosecute or not to prosecute, to convict or acquit, to hold individuals or corporations liable or not liable in civil suits. So your competence, or lack thereof, will be very critical to individuals and societies. I will do my level best to ensure that we unleash no incompetents upon the public. You will not get the benefit of the doubt. This is a pass/fail course—you pass with a grade of A. Anything below that, you fail."

Which intimidates Jack not at all because this is basically the way he was raised. You do the job right or you do it again *until* you do it right or you just get out.

So Jack's like, *Bring it on, Captain Sparky.*

"The first rule of cause and origin," the captain says, "and I quote—

and you will commit this to memory—is, '*Unless all relevant accidental causes can be eliminated, the fire must be declared accidental, the presence of direct evidence to the contrary notwithstanding.*'

"That is to say, that unless you can rule out all possible accidental causes, you may not conclude that the fire was intentionally set. You must classify the cause of the fire as 'Unknown.'

"Now let's look at the other classifications of accidental causes . . ."

Natural, Electrical and Chemical.

Natural—your basic Act of God. Lightning, wildfire, the apocalypse. A gimme putt, because when a house gets hit by lightning . . .

Electrical—a major source of accidental fires, Jack learns. So major a source that for a few days Jack thinks he's studying to be an electrician. They're running electrical engineers and electrical contractors through the classroom and Jack's up late at night studying standard electrical plans for your basic two-bedroom two-bath model home.

They've got the class examining burned-out cords—"Was the cord burned *by* the fire or was it the *source* of the fire? You need to know"— and electrical outlets and electric blankets and fuse boxes. The class learns how to determine if someone tampered with a circuit breaker in order to give the appearance of an accidental electric fire. They learn how people can accidentally set fire to their houses by overloading extension cords, or leaving them where the dog can chew on them, or by splicing wires or by generally trying to get more electric power than their system was designed to handle.

Electricity is heat, Jack learns, subject to all the physical laws and consequences thereof. It is, in effect, an incipient smoldering phase awaiting the kiss that will send it to ignition.

Chemical—propane, natural gas, methane explosions. Then you're looking for code violations, sloppy installation, mechanical breakdowns. Once again Jack feels as if he's learning a new trade, because they're bringing heating contractors in and they break down oil heaters and pumps, propane tanks and insertion systems, nozzles, ignition systems. They learn what they're supposed to look like and what they look like when things go wrong.

And another chemical cause—smoking in bed. One of the most common causes of household fires and a beaut. A king-size polyurethane mattress has an HRR of 2,630 (over three times that of a big dry Christmas tree), so if you light one of those up it's going to transfer the heat to about everything else in the room, including the inhabitants.

So those are the three basic causes of accidental fires.

"To determine the precise cause of origin," Captain Sparky tells them, "you have to identify the *point* of origin."

Point of origin is the whole game. You find the origin you're almost always going to determine the cause. You're going to find the frayed wire, the flawed heater, the mattress that looks like somebody napalmed it.

Cause and origin is the thing.

Which is why they make it the final exam.

What they do is they burn a house.

The faculty goes out to a condemned two-bedroom ranch house on the edge of town and sets it on fire. Captain Sparky takes the class out there and says, "Gentlemen, here's the final exam. Do an inspection, do an investigation, and determine the cause and origin."

Get it right, you pass.

Get it wrong, sayonara.

Jack's cool with this. This is the way it should be. Get it right or get your feet in gear. Jack's ready.

Then Sparky says, "Gentlemen, you are all in the same boat. Work together. Turn in a collective report as to cause and origin. The correct C&O, the entire class passes the course. Incorrect C&O, you all fail."

But no, you know, pressure.

"You have until 0700 tomorrow, gentlemen. Good luck."

Sparky tosses down a notebook giving the names and addresses of the neighbors, who get paid fifty bucks each for memorizing a set of facts, in case they're asked by the students. Same with a pair of owners. Sparky tosses this down and walks off.

Leaving the students standing there looking at this burned-out shell and thinking, *Oh fuck,* when Jack says, "Let's get to work."

He organizes the class. Decides someone better do that in a hurry before fifteen men go through like a herd of elephants and trample the evidence. So Jack's like, "First thing we do is a walk around the exterior and everyone take notes. Ferri, start taking pictures. Garcia, how about doing a diagram? Krantz and Stewart, canvass the neighbors. Myers, interview the owners and get it on tape . . ."

Some of the guys stand there looking at Jack like, *Who made you God?*

Jack says, "Hey, guys, I ain't flunking this course."

So let's get after it.

Four in the morning, they're back in the dorm talking it over.

Fuse box fire is what they come up with.

Overloaded circuit breaker.

They have heavy char around the fuse box and the worst heat damage in the area directly above the box. A big V-pattern with its base as wide as the fuse box.

A no-brainer as far as that goes.

The guys that did the dig-out report no pour patterns on the concrete slab. No spalling, no signs of accelerant.

Owners were home at the time of the fire.

Neighbors report nothing unusual.

Burn patterns consistent with source.

Materials burned and not burned consistent with HRRs.

They're ready to go in: a Class C Fire—Accidental Fire of Electrical Origin.

"I don't think so," Jack says.

To groans from fourteen exhausted men.

"The fuck you mean you don't think so?" Ferri asks. He's like, annoyed.

"I mean I don't think so," Jack says. "I think this is an incendiary fire."

"Fuckin' Wade," seems to be the general opinion. "Don't be an asshole . . . Wade, don't be such a pain . . ." A firestorm, as it were, of protest. Which Ferri leads: "Look, we've been working this for fifteen-plus hours. We're beat. Don't come in here with your cop bullshit and try to make an overloaded fuse box into a federal case."

"Someone tampered with the circuit breaker," Jack says. "The plastic sheathing on the calibration screw is missing."

"Far as I'm concerned, Wade," Ferri says, "the only sheathing that was missing was what your father forgot when he knocked up your mother."

Jack says, "Calibration screws *always* have plastic sheathing on them. Where is it?"

"It melted off."

"It wouldn't melt off," Jack says. "It would melt *on*. There's no sign of that. Someone recalibrated the circuit breaker. To do that they had to break the sheath off the calibration screw. I'd look at the owners."

"We looked at the owners," Krantz said. "They looked all right to us."

"Did you call the mortgage company?" Jack asks.

"No," Krantz says.

"Why not?"

"We were looking at a fuse box fire . . ."

"Are the owners employed?"

"Yeah."

"Did you check with the employers?"

"No . . ."

"Shit," Jack says. Like he's going to bust Krantz one.

"I'm *sorry*," Krantz says.

"Don't be *sorry*," Jack says. "Do your fucking job."

"Chill out," Ferri says.

"You chill out," Jack says. "These assholes had a job to do and—"

"Look, hotshot," Ferri says. "Just because you want to show off—"

"Explain the missing sheathing, Ferri," Jack says. "Anybody?"

No takers.

"Let's vote," Ferri says.

Knowing it's 14 to 1.

"Vote my ass," Jack says.

"What are you, the dictator here?"

"I'm right."

Your basic awkward silence. Finally, one of the guys—the guy Jack had pulled from the concrete tower—says, "Shit, Jack, you'd *better* be right."

They write up the report. Electrical fire, deliberately caused by tampering with the circuit breaker.

Jack walks into the classroom with the weight of the whole class on his shoulders. Six weeks of eighteen-hour days times fourteen men—that's a lot of heat.

Captain Sparky walks in and picks up the report from the desk. Stands reading it as fifteen guys grip. Sparky looks up from the report and asks, "Are you *sure* this is what you want to go with?"

Jack says, "We're sure, sir."

"I'll give you another chance," Sparky offers. "Go out for an hour, reconsider and redo."

Jack's like, *Shit*. I walked the whole freaking class off a cliff. And now Sparky, of all people, is throwing us a rope. All we have to do is reach up and grab it.

Ferri raises his hand.

"Yes?" Sparky says.

Ferri's got balls, Ferri's a man. He points to the report and says, "That's our conclusion, sir. We'll stand with it."

Sparky shrugs.

Like, suit yourselves, losers.

Says, "Well, I gave you a chance."

Takes a red pen and starts slashing the report.

Jack feels like shit. Feels thirteen pairs of eyes burning into his back. Ferri looks over and shrugs. Like, win some, lose some.

Ferri's a man.

Sparky finishes the massacre, looks up and says, "I never thought you'd get the sheath."

Just like Captain Sparky, Jack thinks—you have the right answer and he tries to sell you the wrong one. Just so he can flunk your collective ass.

"Class dismissed," Sparky says. "Good job, gentlemen."

Graduation ceremony tomorrow. Try to dress like grown-ups.

Fire school.

What a ride.

All of which is to say that when it comes to fire, Jack knows what he's doing. Which is why Goddamn Billy's not concerned when Jack comes into his office with a dog under his arm.

16

Actually, *out* into his office, because Billy's sitting out beside the giant saguaro he had imported from south Arizona.

It's a Billy kind of a day, Jack thinks—hot, dry and windy. Kind of day that reminds you that Southern California is basically a desert with a few tenacious grasses, overirrigation and a freaking army of gifted and dedicated Mexican and Japanese gardeners.

"So?" Billy asks.

"Smoking in bed," Jack says. "I was just starting to set up the file."

"Save you the trouble," Billy says. He hands Jack a folder.

Jack instantly turns to the Declarations Page. The "Dec Page" is a one-sheet detailing the types and amounts of the insurance coverage.

A million-five on the house.

No surprise there. It's a large, elegantly crafted house overlooking the ocean. The mil and a half is just for the structure. The lot is probably another mil, at least.

$750,000 on the personal property.

The max, Jack thinks. You can insure your personal property at a value up to half of the insurance on the structure. If you have personal property worth more than that, you need to get special endorsements, which Vale sure as hell did.

"Holy shit," Jack says.

$500,000 in special endorsements.

What the hell did he have in the house? Jack asks himself. To come up with $1,250,000 in personal property? And how much of it was in the west wing?

"When did the underwriters start smoking crack?" Jack asks.

"Be nice."

"These endorsements are *very* whacked," Jack says.

"It's California." Billy shrugs. Which is to say, of course it's whacked— *everything* is whacked. "How much of this stuff is destroyed?"

"Don't know," Jack says. "I haven't been in the house yet."

"Why not?"

"I found their dog outside," Jack says. "I thought I'd better get it back to them first."

Billy hears that the dog was outside and raises a significant eyebrow.

Sucks on his cig for a second then says, "It got out when the firemen came in?"

Jack shakes his head. "No soot, no smoke. Fur wasn't singed."

Because dogs are usually heroes. Fire breaks out, they don't run, they *stick*.

"The dog was outside before the fire," Jack says.

"Don't go off half-cocked," Billy warns.

"I'm fully cocked," Jack says. "I figure Mrs. Vale let the dog out to do its thing and forgot about it. She was hammered. Anyway, I want to get it to the kids."

"Well, you'll have your chance," Billy says. "Vale called a half-hour ago."

Say what?

"You're kidding," Jack says.

"He wants you to come over."

"*Now?*" Jack asks. "His wife has been dead for what, six hours, and he wants to start adjusting his claim?"

Billy snuffs out the cigarette on the rocks. The butt joins its dead brothers in an arc around Billy's feet.

"They're separated," Billy says. "Maybe he's not all that torn up."

He gives Jack the address in Monarch Bay and strikes another match.

Then says, "And—Jack? Get a statement."

Like he has to tell him.

Billy knows that most other adjusters would just take the Sheriff's statement, attach it to their reports and start adjusting the claim.

Not Jack.

You give a big file to Jack Wade, he'll work it to death.

Billy figures this is because Jack doesn't have a wife, or kids, or even a girlfriend. He doesn't have to be home for dinner, or to the school for a ballet recital, or even out on a date. Jack doesn't even have an ex-wife, so he doesn't have his every other weekend or three weeks in the summer with the kids, or I-have-to-get-to-Johnny's-soccer-game-or-he'll-end-up-back-in-therapy time demands.

What Jack does have is his job, a couple of old surfboards and his car.

Jack has no life.

He fits the Vale file like a custom-made boot.

Jack's walking back through the lobby when Carol, the receptionist, calls and tells him that Olivia Hathaway is here to see him.

"Tell her I'm not in," Jack says.

Olivia Hathaway is all he needs right now.

"She saw your car in employee parking," the receptionist says.

Jack sighs, "Do you have a meeting room?"

"One-seventeen," the receptionist says. "She requested it. It's her favorite."

"She likes the painting of the sailboat," Jack says. "Can you look after this dog for a few minutes?"

"What's its name?"

"Leo."

Five minutes later Jack's sitting in a small room across the table from Olivia Hathaway.

17

Olivia Hathaway.

She's a tiny woman, eighty-four years of age, with beautiful white hair, a handsomely chiseled face and sparkling blue eyes.

Today she's wearing an elegant white dress.

"It's about my spoons," she says.

Jack already knows this. He's been dealing with Olivia Hathaway's spoons for over three years now.

Here's the story on Olivia Hathaway's spoons.

Three years ago Jack gets a theft file. An eighty-one-year-old widow by the name of Olivia Hathaway has had a burglary at her little house in Anaheim. Jack goes out there and she's waiting for him in the kitchen with tea and freshly baked sugar cookies.

She won't discuss the loss until Jack has had two cups of tea, three cookies, told her his entire genealogy and received a report on what each of Olivia's nine grandchildren and three great-grandchildren is doing. Now, Jack has five other loss reports to do that day, but he figures she's a charming, lonely old lady so he's okay with spending the extra time.

When she finally gets down to it, it turns out that the only thing that has been stolen is her collection of spoons.

Which is weird, Jack thinks, but he's looking out the window at a gigantic model of the Matterhorn replete with fake snow, the Crystal Cathedral and a gigantic pair of mouse ears on a billboard, so, like, what's weird?

Olivia's just had an appraisal done ("I'm not going to live forever, you know, Jack, and there's a matter of a will") and the spoons are worth about $6,000. At this point, Olivia gets a little weepy because four of the spoons are sterling silver, handed down from her great-grandmother in Dingwall, Scotland. She excuses herself to get a tissue and then comes back in and asks Jack if there's anything that he can do to help recover her spoons.

Jack explains that he isn't the police, but that he will contact them to get a report, and that all he can really do, sadly, is reimburse her for the loss.

Olivia understands.

Jack just feels like shit for her, goes back to the office and calls Anaheim PD for the loss report, and the desk sergeant just laughs like hell and hangs up.

So Jack punches Olivia Hathaway in on the PLR (Prior Loss Report, pronounced "pillar") system and finds that Olivia Hathaway's spoons have been "stolen" fourteen times while insured with thirteen different insurance companies. They have, in fact, been stolen once a year since Mr. Hathaway's death.

Olivia's spoons are what's known in the insurance business as 3S, Social Security Supplement.

The amazing thing is that thirteen out of thirteen prior insurance companies have paid the claim.

Jack gets on the phone and calls number eleven, Fidelity Mutual, and it turns out that an old buddy named Mel Bornstein handled the claim.

"Did you do a PLR?" Jack asks.

"Yup."

"And you saw the priors?"

"Yup."

"Why did you pay?"

Mel laughs like hell and hangs up.

Jack tracks down adjusters number nine, ten and thirteen, and they're each pretty much in helpless hysterics when they hang up the phone.

Three long years later Jack understands why they paid an obviously phony claim.

But he doesn't back then. Back then he's in a quandary. He knows what he should do: by law, in fact, he's obligated to report the fraud to the NICB (National Insurance Crime Bureau), cancel her policy and deny the claim. But he just can't bring himself to turn her in and leave her without insurance (What if there was a fire? What if someone slipped and fell on her sidewalk? What if there was a real burglary?), so he just decides to deny the claim and forget about it.

Right.

Two days after he sends her the denial letter she shows up at the office. They have the same conversation roughly twice a month for the next three years. She doesn't write letters, she doesn't go over his head, she doesn't complain to the Department of Insurance, she doesn't sue. She just keeps coming back, and back, and back, and they always have the same conversation.

"Jack, you've neglected to pay me for my spoons."

"I didn't neglect to pay you for your spoons, Mrs. Hathaway," Jack says. "Your spoons were not stolen."

"Of course they were, Jack."

"Right, they were stolen fourteen times."

She sighs, "The neighborhood is not what it used to be, Jack."

"You live outside of Disneyland."

Like, *Be on the lookout for a large rodent carrying spoons. Suspect is approximately five feet tall with large circular ears and white gloves.*

"I need you to pay me for my spoons," Olivia says.

"Your spoons have been paid for thirteen times."

She thinks she has him. "But they have been stolen *fourteen* times."

"Mrs. Hathaway," Jack says. "Are you asking me to accept that on thirteen prior occasions the spoon thieves have returned your spoons to you? And that they've been stolen again . . . and again and again and again . . . No, please don't haul out the cookies."

But she does.

She always does.

She always sits there looking lovely, smiling, speaking softly, never raising her voice, and she always brings a Ziploc bag of sugar cookies.

"I know how you like these, Jack."

"I can't take any cookies, Mrs. Hathaway."

"Now," she says, reaching into her handbag and coming out with a stack of photographs, "little Billy has gone to junior college to study computer programming . . ."

Jack lowers his head and thumps it repeatedly on the table as Olivia continues her recitation of the daily lives and personal development of each and every child, grandchild, great-grandchild and their spouses.

". . . Kimmy is living—*in sin*—with a motorcycle repairman from Downey . . ."

Thump . . . thump . . .

"Jack, are you listening?"

"No."

"Now, Jack, you've neglected to pay me for my spoons."

"I didn't *neglect* to pay you for your spoons; your spoons were not stolen."

"Of course they were, dear."

"Right, they were stolen fourteen—I thought Kimmy was living with an electrician."

"That was *last* month."

"Oh."

"Cookie?"

"No thank you."

"Now, about my spoons . . ."

It's forty-five more agonizing minutes of the Olivia Hathaway Water Torture (drip . . . about my spoons . . . drip . . . about my spoons . . . drip . . .) before he can get rid of her and head out to Vale's mother's house in Monarch Bay.

18

Monarch Bay.

Aptly named.

Absolutely primo real estate location on the south coast.

Monarch Bay sits on the border between the towns of Laguna Niguel and Dana Point and went through Bosnia-esque civil strife as to which town it would belong to. To most people's surprise, the residents chose Dana Point over the more tony Laguna Niguel, even though Dana Point in those days was just the harbor and a bunch of fast food joints, surf shops and cheap motels on a strip of the PCH.

The Dana Point that Jack loved.

The choice pissed a lot of people off, especially the owners of the Ritz-Carlton/Laguna Niguel just down the beach, who never changed the resort's name, even though it's technically in Dana Point and not Laguna Niguel.

This is fine with Jack, who doesn't particularly want to be associated with the beautiful resort people. As far as Jack's concerned, the resort is basically a place for the young surf bums to work as waiters and supplement their meager incomes by screwing the rich wives that they've otherwise serviced at lunch. More than a few of whom live in the exclusive gated community of Monarch Bay.

You roll up to the gates of Monarch Bay in a Ford Taurus, you'd better be there to clean something. You'd better have some ammonia and rags in the backseat.

Otherwise, this is a gate for Mercedes and Jags and Rollses.

Jack does feel a little uncool in the Taurus, but he switched to a company car because somehow it just didn't feel right to go to a house where people have lost a loved one and show up in a '66 Mustang with a Hobie on top.

Feels disrespectful.

Getting the company car was a hassle.

To get a company car, you have to go to Edna.

Edna has those glasses with the little metal-bead chain hanging around her neck.

Jack says, "Edna, I need a car."

"Are you asking or telling?"

"Asking."

"We don't have any with surfboard racks on them."

Jack smiles. "It was my last call of the day. Three Arch Bay, so, you know . . ."

"I do know," Edna says. "I saw the crew vacuuming the sand out."

What Jack doesn't tell Edna is that he left two six-packs with the pool car crew for the inconvenience. Something he always does. The guys in the crew love Jack. They'd do anything for Jack.

"Sorry," he says.

"Company cars are *not* for pleasure," Edna says, pushing the keys at him.

"I promise I won't have any pleasure in it."

All of a sudden Edna has these images of twisted carnal goings-on in the backseat of one of her cars and her hand pauses on the keys.

"*Tell* me you boys don't—"

"No, no, no, no," Jack says, taking the keys. "Not in the *back*seat, anyway."

"Slip 17."

"Thank you."

So Jack takes a Taurus to Monarch Bay.

Where the guard gives the car a long look, just to make a point, and then asks, "Is Mr. Vale expecting you?"

Jack says, "He's expecting me."

The guard looks past Jack on the front seat and asks, "You're what? The dog groomer?"

"That's right. I groom the dog."

The house is a mock-Tudor mansion. The lawn is as manicured as a dowager's hand and a croquet set has been meticulously measured out on the grass. A rose garden edges the north wall.

Hasn't rained in three months, Jack thinks, and the roses are dripping with moisture, fresh as a blush.

Vale meets him in the driveway.

He's one good-looking man. He's about six-three, Jack guesses, thin, with black hair cut unfashionably long except somehow it looks *perfectly* stylish on him. He's wearing a beige pullover over faded jeans and Loafers. No socks. Wire-rim John Lennon glasses.

Very cool.

He looks younger than forty-three.

The face is movie-star handsome and mostly it's the eyes. They have a slight upward slant and they're the gray-blue color of a winter sea.

And intense.

Like when Vale looks at you he's trying to make you do something. Jack has the feeling that most people do.

"Would you be Jack Wade?" Vale asks.

There's the slightest trace of an accent, but Jack can't work out what it is.

"Russian," Vale explains. "The actual name is Daziatnik Valeshin, but who wants to sign all those checks that way?"

"Sorry to meet you under these circumstances, Mr. Vale."

"Nicky," Vale says. "Call me Nicky."

"Nicky," Jack says. "Here's Leo."

"Leonid!" Nicky yells.

The little dog goes nuts, starts twirling around and stuff. Jack opens the door and Leo jumps out and leaps into Nicky's outstretched arms.

"Again," Jack says, "I'm sorry about Mrs. Vale."

"Pamela was young and very beautiful," Nicky says.

Which is definitely what you want to be, Jack thinks, if you're going to be married to a rich guy and live in a house overlooking the ocean. "Young and beautiful" is the baseline qualification. You aren't young and beautiful, you don't even get to fill out the application.

Still, it's a weird thing to say at a time like this.

Jack says, "I know she did a lot of work for Save the Strands. I know you both did."

Nicky nods. "We believed in it. Pamela spent a lot of time in the Strands—painting, walking with the children. We'd hate to see it ruined."

"How are the children doing?" Jack asks.

"I believe the expression is 'As well as can be expected.'"

One odd fucking dude, Jack thinks.

He must see it on my face, Jack thinks, because Nicky says, "Let's cut through the pretense, Jack. Obviously you know that Pamela and I were separated. I loved her, the children loved her, but Pamela couldn't decide which she loved more—her family or the bottle. Still, I had every hope of a reconciliation. We were working toward one. And she *was* young, and very beautiful, and under these circumstances that is what I seem to bring to mind. A protective reflex of the mind, I suppose."

"Mr. Vale . . . Nicky—"

"In all honesty, I don't know exactly what I am supposed to be feeling right now, or even what I *do* feel. All I know is that I need to to put my children's lives in order, because they have been in chaos for quite some time, all the more so this morning."

"I wasn't—"

Nicky smiles and says, "You weren't saying anything, Jack, you are too polite. But inside you are offended by my apparent lack of grief. I grew up as a Jew in what your news readers like to call 'the former Soviet Union.' I learned to watch men's eyes more than their mouths. I'll bet that in your world, Jack, people lie to you all the time, don't they?"

"I hear some lies."

"More than *some*," Nicky says. "People can get money from you and so they lie to get it. Even otherwise honest people will exaggerate their loss just to cover the deductible, am I right?"

Jack nods.

"And I will probably try to do the same," Nicky laughs. "Big deal— I'll come up with a number, then you'll come up with a number, and we'll negotiate. We'll make a deal."

"I don't make deals," Jack says. "I just carry out the policy."

"Everyone makes deals, Jack."

"Not everyone."

Nicky puts his arm around Jack's shoulders.

"I think we can work together, Jack Wade," he says. "I think we can do business."

Nicky invites him in.

"I don't want to intrude," Jack says.

"I'm afraid you'll have to," Nicky says. He gives Jack a smile that makes him a co-conspirator. "Mother made tea."

Well, Jack thinks, if Mother made tea . . .

19

Mother is beautiful.

A small, perfect gem.

Sable hair pulled back tight against the whitest skin Jack's ever seen. She has Nicky's blue eyes, only darker. The color of deeper water.

Head up, spine sergeant major straight.

No, not sergeant major, Jack corrects himself, ballet instructor.

She's wearing August-appropriate white. A midlength summer dress edged in gold. She doesn't shop in Laguna, Jack thinks—too funky and too many gays—but in Newport Beach. Come Labor Day, no matter how hot, she'll lose the whites and go to beige and khaki. The first of November she'll switch to black.

Jack starts, "Mrs. Vale—"

"Valeshin."

"Mrs. *Valeshin*," Jack says. "I'm sorry for your loss."

"I understand that she was smoking in bed," Mother says. She has more of an accent and there's this slight edge, like Pamela *deserved* to choke to death in the dark, Jack thinks. Like she had it coming.

"That's the preliminary finding," Jack says.

"*And* drinking?" Mother adds.

"There's some indication that she might have been drinking," Jack says.

"Won't you come in?" she asks.

Now that I've paid admission, Jack thinks.

The inside of the house is a museum.

No DO NOT TOUCH signs, Jack thinks, but they're not needed. You just *know*, like, DO NOT TOUCH. The place is immaculate. The floors and furniture shine. No dust would dare settle.

Dark, too, like a museum.

Dark-stained hardwood floors with Persian carpets. Oak doors, moldings and window frames.

Big old dark fireplace.

In contrast, the living room furniture is white.

White sofa, white wingback chairs.

White like a *challenge* white. White like nobody spills here, or dribbles, or drops. White, like a statement that life can be clean if everyone just maintains discipline and pays attention and tries.

Furniture, Jack thinks, as ethic.

Nicky motions for Jack to sit down on the sofa.

Jack tries to sit without leaving an indentation.

"You have a beautiful home," Jack says.

"My son bought it for me," she says.

"You've been to the house?" Nicky says.

"Just for a preliminary look."

"Is it a total loss?" Nicky asks.

"Most of the structure is still there," Jack says, "although there's a lot of smoke and water damage. I'm afraid the west wing is going to have to be torn down."

"Since the coroner called," Nicky says, "I've been trying to steel my nerves to go over there and see . . . And of course the children are terribly upset."

"Sure."

Nicky waits for what he feels is a decent interval, then asks, "How do we proceed with the claim?"

Like, we've done our sensitive moment, let's get down to business.

Jack runs it down for him.

The life insurance claim is simple. Jack requests a death certificate from the county and once he gets it, bang, he writes a draft for $250,000. The fire claim is a little more complicated because you're looking at three different "coverages" under the policy.

Coverage A is for the structure itself. Jack needs to examine the house in detail and come up with an estimate of what it's going to cost to rebuild. Coverage B is for personal property—furniture, appliances, clothing—and Nicky will need to fill out a Personal Property Inventory Form, to tell the company what he lost in the fire.

"I see you also have a bunch of special endorsements added to your Coverage B," Jack says.

Which is a *humongo* understatement, Jack thinks. Special endorsements to the tune of three-quarters of a million bucks.

And nice fat premiums for California Fire and Life.

The perpetual circle jerk, Jack thinks.

"My furniture," Nicky says. "I collect eighteenth-century English. Mostly George II and III. I collect, I sell, I buy. I'm afraid the bulk of my collection was in the west wing. Is there . . . ?"

Jack shakes his head.

Nicky winces.

Jack says, "I'll need to have you complete a PPIF—Personal Property Inventory Form—so we can sort out what's destroyed and what isn't. There's no hurry on that, of course."

"I have a videotape," Nicky says.

"You do?"

"Just a couple of months before the fire," Nicky says, "Pamela and I decided we should finally follow our agent's advice and videotape the house and our belongings. Would that be helpful?"

Yeah, that would be helpful, Jack thinks.

"Sure," Jack says. "Where *is* the tape?"

"Here at Mother's," Nicky answers.

Then Nicky says, "You mentioned a third coverage."

"Coverage D," Jack says. "Additional Living Expenses. That's for any expenses you incur while you're out of your home. Rent, restaurant bills, that sort of thing, until you get settled. I can also write drafts from that coverage to give you an advance on your personal property so you can buy clothes . . . toys for the kids . . ."

"How thoughtful," Nicky says.

"You have plenty of insurance," Jack says.

Mother says, "Nicky and the children will be staying here until the house is rebuilt."

"That's great," Jack says.

"I'm charging them $2,000 a month in room and board."

Those deep blues look at him like it's a challenge, like she's daring him to say something. Something along the order, Jack thinks, of what kind of mother charges rent to her widowed son and her homeless grandchildren?

Jack says, "Actually, $2,000 is a little low. For instance, if Nicky were to rent an equivalent home, we would pay for that."

"Daziatnik is staying *here*," she says.

"Of course he can stay where he wants," Jack says. "I'm just saying that wherever he decides to stay, we'll pay the rent."

She says, "After all, why should I subsidize the insurance company?"

"No reason," Jack says. "In fact, I can issue an advance of $25,000 on your Coverage D," Jack says.

"When?" Nicky asks.

"Now."

(Another Billyism: Get an advance in their hands. *Pronto.* People been burned out of their home, get some clothes on their backs. Kids lose their home, at least they can get some goddamn toys to play with. They feel better.)

And if they lose their mom, Billy?

Well, I can bring them their dog.

Silence. Mother has just figured out that she's lost face by winning a battle she didn't need to fight, and she doesn't like it.

So while she's pissed off anyway, Jack says, "I'm going to need to get a recorded statement. It doesn't have to be today."

"A recorded statement?" Nicky asks. "Why?"

"Routine with any fire," Jack says.

One of Goddamn Billy's rules in this cynical world: Take a statement as soon as you can. Get their story on the record so they can't walk away from it. If they're not involved with the fire, it doesn't matter; if they are . . . well, Billy's right again. Get a statement. Get it in detail. Get it early.

(Another Billyism: If you're planning on getting in a fight with someone, it's a good idea to first get their feet stuck in concrete.)

Nicky's looking at him with his charming smile.

"Did you bring a tape recorder?" he asks.

You bet.

20

"This is Jack Wade from California Fire and Life," Jack says into the tape recorder. "The date is August 28, 1997. The time is 1:15 p.m. I am taking a recorded statement from Mr. Nicky Vale and his mother, Mrs. Valeshin. I am making this record with the full knowledge and permission of both Mr. Vale and Mrs. Valeshin. Is that correct?"

"That is correct," Nicky says.

"Correct."

"And will you validate the date and time for me?"

"It is correct as stated," Nicky says.

"Then we can proceed," Jack says. "If at any time I turn off the tape, I will make a note for the record of the time we go off record and the time we resume. Now, could you each state and spell your full legal names for me?"

It's a delicate thing, taking a recorded statement. On the one hand, you have to observe the formalities so you get a useful record that will stand up in court. On the other hand, it's not a sworn statement or a legal proceeding, so you have to walk a fine line between the formal and the casual. So after they state and spell their names, Jack flips back into talk show mode and says, "Mr. Vale—"

"Nicky."

"Nicky, why don't you start by giving me a little background on yourself?"

Because Jack knows that the first thing you do is get the subject talking. About anything, it doesn't matter. The idea is to get them into the habit of responding to your questions and just plain talking. Also you learn something right off the bat: if your guy balks at talking about himself, he's going to balk at everything else and then you have to wonder what he's protecting.

There's a more cynical reason. Jack knows it like every other investigator knows it—the more a subject talks the more chance he has to lie. To fuck up, give inconsistencies, *lie* on the record. Get his feet stuck in the concrete.

Most people hang themselves.

It's a basic truth that Jack knows: if you're dragged out of your bed by the cops at four in the morning and they want to talk to you about the Kennedy assassination, the Lindbergh kidnapping or aiding and abetting freaking Pontius Pilate, what you do is you keep your fucking mouth shut. Doesn't matter if they ask you your height, your favorite color or what you had for breakfast that morning, you keep your fucking mouth shut. If they ask you if night is darker than day, or whether up is higher than down, you keep your fucking mouth shut.

There are four words, and only four words, you can say.

I want my lawyer.

When your lawyer gets there he'll give you some sage advice.

He'll tell you to keep your fucking mouth shut.

And if you do that, if you follow that sage advice, you will in all probability leave the police station a free man.

There are usually three reasons people talk.

One, they're scared.

Nicky Vale isn't scared.

Two, they're stupid.

Nicky Vale isn't stupid.

Three, they're arrogant.

Bingo.

Nicky Vale starts talking about himself.

He was born in St. Petersburg, which was Leningrad when he was born but now is St. Petersburg again. This name thing matters like shit to Nicky Vale, because it wasn't any more giggles being a Jew in Leningrad than it was being a Jew in St. Petersburg.

You can change your name as often as you want ("I should know, right?" Nicky adds), but you can't change your spots, and those Bolshevik bastards are the same and will always be the same. Czarist, Bolshevik, Stalinist or glasnostnik, it's all the same because they're still and always anti-Semites.

"We have served," Nicky observes, "as an indispensable factor knitting the Russian social fabric. We have done them an enormous favor: over the centuries of conflict we have provided a unifying focus of hatred."

So Nicky grows up as an outsider. Excluded from sports clubs, social clubs and the Young Communist League, young Nicky lives in a physical and social ghetto.

"What we had," Nicky says, "is what those Bolshevik bastards will never have: a legitimate culture. We had God, we had literature, we had music, we had *art*. We had an immutable *past*, Jack, that could not change and did not change with the tides of political purges and the shifting sands of doctrine. What makes a Jew is the Jewish past. So they excluded us. Excluded us from *what*?"

Well, not the army.

Nicky gets drafted. Greetings, Jewboy, here's hoping you get smacked.

So if you think it's fun being Jewish in Leningrad, try being a Russian Jew in Afghanistan. They hate you twice. They can't figure out if they hate you more for being a Russian or for being a Jew. It's like hatred squared or cubed or something.

Nicky doesn't help matters.

"I was stupid," Nicky says. "I wore a Star of David on a chain around my neck. For what? So in case I'm captured they can torture me twice as long? But when you're young . . ."

Nicky survives his tour in mullah-land.

Comes home to what?

The same old crap.

So what he wants is out.

"Glasnost comes," Nicky says, "and the bastards try to curry favor by opening the gates to release people they don't want in the first place."

The hypocrisy is stunning to Nicky but all right with him. While the gate is open he's determined to walk through it. Mother wants to go to Israel but Nicky . . .

"Well, I have seen my war," Nicky says. "I've seen enough of people being blown up. And Israel, well, to be frank . . ."

Young Nicky has other ideas. Young Nicky has heard of the land of dreams, the land of golden sands and golden hair. The land where a young man with no money and no background and little formal education—but energy, smarts and determination—can still make a splash. Young Nicky wants to go to California.

They have some family here. Some cousins who made the escape and live in L.A. and are doing all right. They give Nicky a gig driving town cars on the airport run. A couple of years of this, Nicky buys his own car. Then two, then three. Then a used-car lot, then a parts whole-sale business. Then he goes in with several partners and buys an old apartment building. Fixes it up and sells it. Buys another. Then another. Now he has a fleet of cars, two used-car lots and his parts business.

Leverages them to buy an apartment complex in Newport Beach. Converts them to condos and makes a killing. Leaves his money on the table, so to speak, and buys another. Pretty soon he's in the crazy '80s real estate market. Sometimes buying commercial property and selling it on the same day. Gets into development, buying raw land and developing town houses, condos, country clubs.

Orange County is booming and Nicky with it.

"The only problem with Americans?" Nicky says. "You don't appreciate what you have here. Every time I hear an American running this country down I laugh."

He's booming and blooming, enough to get into a sideline which is his true love.

Art.

Paintings, sculpture, fine furniture.

Especially fine furniture.

"It is, to use a hackneyed phrase, the craftsmanship," Nicky says. "In those days they cared about quality. About the quality of the wood, the quality of the workmanship. Attention to the smallest detail. Devotion to the aesthetic of the whole. They built furniture to be useful, to be beautiful and to last. They didn't just throw it together, destined for the trash heap or the yard sale.

"And there is something about *wood*, isn't there? Do you know what I mean? For the sacrifice of a beautiful tree something beautiful should be created. To see those fine grains of mahogany and walnut shaped into something exquisite and lasting. And something that you use every day—a chair, a cabinet, a bed—you have a *relationship* with the wood, with the woodworker, with the designer. You become part of the continuum of history. Can you understand that, Jack?"

"Yes."

He really can. It's why he spends half his free time sanding old wooden longboards in his garage.

"So when I made my fortune," Nicky says, "I indulged my passion. I bought Georgian furniture. Some I sold, some I traded, most I kept to fill my home. To create a space around me that fed my soul. That's my story, Jack: Russian Jew turned California cabbie turned English gentleman. Only, as they say, in America. Only in California."

"Why only in California?"

"Come on, you know." Nicky laughs. "It is truly the land of dreams. That's why people come here. They say it's the weather, but it's really the atmosphere, if you will. In California you are unhooked from time and place. You can untie yourself from the bonds of history, nationality, culture. You can free yourself from what you *are* to become what you *want* to be. *Whatever* you want to be. No one will stop you, scorn you, criticize you—because everyone else is doing the same thing. Everyone breathing the same ether but from our own individual clouds. Endlessly floating, shifting and changing shape. Sometimes two clouds drift together, then apart and then together again. Your own life is what you want it to be. Like a cloud, it *is* what you imagine."

Nicky stops and then laughs at himself.

"So," he says, "if a Russian Jew wants the sunshine and the freedom and the ocean and the beaches *and* to be an English country gentleman all at the same time, in California he simply loads his house full of expensive furniture and creates his own reality. . . . So much of it gone now. Gone in the fire."

Not to mention your wife, Jack thinks.

Which, in fact, you don't mention.

But the fire, Jack says. Not to be offensive, but please tell me where you were the night of the fire.

Now that we're, you know, chatting.

21

Here, Nicky tells him like it's simplicity itself.

I was here.

And he shrugs, like fate is an inexplicable thing.

"And thank God," Mother says, "the *children* were here."

"When did you pick the children up?" Jack asks.

"About 3 o'clock," Nicky says.

"Was that the usual arrangement?"

"There was no usual arrangement, strictly speaking," Nicky says. "Sometime middle to late afternoon."

"And were you here from 3 o'clock on?"

"No," Nicky says. "I believe we went out to dinner around 6 or 6:30."

"Where?"

"How is that relevant?"

Jack shrugs. "I don't know at this point what's relevant and what isn't."

"We went to the Harbor House. The kids like that you can have breakfast all day. They had pancakes." He adds, "I'm sorry, I don't recall what I had."

With just a whiff of sarcasm.

"What time did you get home?"

"Eight-thirty."

"It was closer to 8:45," Mother says.

"Eight forty-five, then," Nicky says.

"Big pancakes," says Jack.

"They are, in fact," Nicky says. "You should try them."

"I eat breakfast there almost every Saturday."

"Then you know."

"I'm a Denver omelet guy myself."

Nicky says, "We went for a walk after dinner. Down around the harbor."

"What did you do after you got home?"

Nicky says, "I'm afraid we watched television. The children are, after all, Americans."

"Do you recall—"

"No," Nicky says. "The shows are all the same to me. I suppose you could ask the children."

Not me, Jack thinks. Even I couldn't ask two little kids, *Do you recall what you were watching the night your mommy died?* I'm hardcore, but I'm not *that* hardcore.

"What time did you put the kids to bed?"

Nicky looks to his mother.

"It was 10:15," she says, with a hint of disapproval.

It's a hint, but Nicky picks up on it like it fell on his head.

"Summertime," he says. "They have no school to get up for, so I'm afraid I'm a bit lenient . . ."

She says, "Children need a routine."

Jack asks, "What did you after the children went to bed?"

"I am an American now, too." Nicky laughs. "I watched television. A movie on HBO."

"Cinemax," Mother corrects.

"Cinemax," Nicky says with a look at Jack that says, *Mothers*.

"Do you recall what the movie was?"

"Something with John Travolta," Nicky says. "About stealing an atomic weapon. Very post–cold war."

"Did you watch the whole thing?"

"It was quite suspenseful."

"That's a yes?"

"Yes."

Jack turns to Mother.

"Did you watch it with him?"

"Am I under suspicion of something?" she asks.

"No one's under suspicion of anything," Jack says. "It's just the rules."

You have a $2 million claim, I have to ask the questions.

Mother says, "I was reading a book while Daziatnik watched the film, but I was, yes, in the room with him."

"Did you go to bed after the movie?" Jack asks Nicky.

"Yes."

"What time was that?"

"About 12:30, I suppose."

"No," Mother says. "You went out for a swim and then sat in the spa."

Nicky smiles. "She's right. I took a brandy out with me."

"So you went to bed around . . . ?"

"One-thirty, it must have been."

"How about you, Mrs. Valeshin?" Jack asks. "Did you go to bed after the movie was over?"

She answers, "Yes. I turned the light out at 1 o'clock."

So much for the prelims, Jack thinks. He asks Nicky, "When did you get up?"

"When the telephone rang."

"That was the—"

"The authorities calling to inform me of the . . . of my wife's death."

"I'm sorry to have to—"

"No, you are performing your job," Nicky says. "I asked you to come do just that, didn't I? Your next question is, Do I recall the time? Yes, I do. When I heard the phone ringing I looked at the clock. You know, what fool is calling at this hour? It was 6:35. I am quite certain. This is not the sort of thing you forget."

"I understand," Jack says.

"Then I went and woke up Mother," Nicky says. "I told her and we discussed how to tell the children. We decided to let them sleep for a while longer. I believe it was around 7:30 when we woke them up to tell them."

"So you were in bed from roughly 1:30 to 6:30," Jack says.

"That's correct."

"No," Mother says. "You got up to check on the children. Michael was crying and I was about to get up when I heard you. That was at—"

Let me guess, Jack thinks. That was at 5 o'clock.

"—four forty-five."

Okay, close.

"Mother is, as usual, right," Nicky says. "Now that she mentions it, I recall that I got up to check on Michael. He was back asleep, of course, by the time I got to their room. I probably stopped to use the toilet on my way back to bed, Jack."

Jack asks some more questions then tells Nicky that he'll need tax returns and bank statements.

"Why?" Nicky asks.

Because I want to see if you have a financial motive for burning your house down.

"Just part of the process," Jack says.

"Do you think I had the house burned down?" Nicky asks. "A case of 'Jewish lightning,' as I've heard said?"

"I don't think anything," Jack says.

Under the gaze of Nicky's blue eyes.

Mother says, "Daziatnik, why don't you go get the children?"

Daziatnik goes to get the children.

Mother gives Jack her iciest smile and says, "Perhaps I should reconsider the room and board."

"That's between you and your son, Mrs. Valeshin."

He watches while she thinks for a few seconds.

Then she says, "Perhaps *three* thousand . . ."

Jack can't wait to go surfing. Let a violent ocean pound his body and clean his soul.

"Do you have children, Mr. Wade?" she asks.

"No," Jack says. "No wife, no kids."

"Why not?"

Jack shrugs. "Too selfish."

I work, I surf, I work on my longboards in my garage.

Sunday nights I do laundry.

"When you have children," she says, "you will understand life. When you have grandchildren, you will understand eternity."

Mrs. Valeshin, Jack thinks, I don't know if I could stand it if I understood life, never mind eternity.

Nicky comes in with the kids.

22

Heartbreakers.

Jack takes one look at them and hears this cracking sound in his chest.

Seven-year-old Natalie and four-year-old Michael.

They stand, one under each paternal hand, picture perfect. The little girl has her father's blue eyes, red and puffy now from crying. Black hair done in a single braid. A little skirt outfit of yellow and plaid. The boy's eyes are brown. And enormous. He's also dressed for company, a little sky-blue polo shirt and white tennis shorts.

Museum pieces, Jack thinks.

"Say hello to Mr. Wade," Mother tells them.

They mumble a hello and Jack feels embarrassed that they even *have* to say hello to a stranger on the same day their mother dies. All he can think of to say is, "I brought Leo. He's fine."

The kids start to smile and then stop.

Jack adds, "He's outside."

They don't move.

Not a muscle, not an inch.

And it isn't Daddy's hands on their shoulders, Jack sees. It's Grandma's eyes.

They are Doing What's Expected, Jack thinks.

Except it isn't what *I'd* expect. I'd expect them to go tearing out that door to go hug and kiss and make a big deal over that little dog.

But they're as still as statues.

"We're having tea," Mrs. Valeshin says. "Tea for the adults, lemonade for the children."

She gets up and comes back a minute later with a tray. A pitcher of iced tea, another of lemonade, and five glasses. She sets the tray on the coffee table, pours the glasses and sits back down.

Natalie and Michael sit next to Jack on the sofa. He notices that they're doing the same thing he's doing, sitting on the very edge of the cushion, their butts barely touching the fabric.

Looking straight ahead.

The tea is sweet, Jack notices. Strong and sugary.

And they all sit in silence. Like it's some sort of weird summer sacrament, Jack thinks. The First Sip, or something.

Until Mrs. Valeshin says, "I'm raising your rent, Daz."

Like it's some wonderful joke.

"Oh, Mother."

"Well," she says, "why should the insurance company get off lightly? Right, Mr. Wade?"

"We pay what we owe, Mrs. Valeshin."

"And what company are you with?"

"California Fire and Life."

"Perhaps I should consider switching to you," she says. "I'm with Chubb now."

"They're a fine company," Jack says.

He imagines trying to adjust a claim in this house and decides he'd rather spoon a can of Drāno down his throat.

Then Michael spills his lemonade.

Lifts the glass and just misses his mouth, and the lemonade goes down his shirt, his shorts and onto the sofa. Nicky yells, "Michael!" and the boy drops his glass on the carpet.

Pandemonium.

Cool Nicky loses it.

Totally.

He screams at Michael, *You stupid boy!* Michael sits there, paralyzed, in a pool of lemonade, while Natalie laughs hysterically. *Shut up!* Nicky screeches at her. Raises his hand and the girl stops laughing.

Mother yells, *Resolve!* and it takes Jack a second to realize she's talking about carpet cleaner, not some moral exhortation, then she and Nicky hustle into the kitchen. Yelling at each other like the house is on fire, Jack thinks, then feels bad because it's a poor choice of words.

Michael gets up, walks to one of the wingback chairs, bends straight over at the waist and starts to *sob*.

Jack doesn't know what the hell to do, then he sets down his papers and goes to the boy.

Jack picks him and holds him.

Michael sobs against his chest and holds him tight.

"Next time?" Jack says to him. "Ask for grape juice."

Natalie looks up at Jack and says, "Daddy says Mommy is *all . . . burned . . . up*."

In a singsong voice.

All burned up.

23

Hector Ruiz has done this a couple of dozen times, so it's no big deal.

Another day at the office.

He's driving an Aerostar van with six people in the back, following Martin up the Grand Avenue entrance ramp onto the 110. He checks his rearview mirror. Octavio's right behind him—smack where he's supposed to be—in a shit-brown '89 Skylark, which is good because Octavio is the crucial dude in this gig.

Octavio fucks up, it could get ugly.

But Octavio, he don't fuck up.

Octavio is a *player*.

So is Jimmy Dansky, who for an Anglo anyway is pretty trustworthy. Dansky's cruising—or better be, anyway, in the right-hand lane on the 110 South—in a black '95 Camaro, and Dansky is one terrific driver, which is a happy thing because the timing on this is tricky.

Hector checks his speedometer and eases it down to thirty.

Sees Martin kick up his Toyota Corolla to hit the highway.

Just as Dansky's Camaro swerves right, into the entrance lane.

Dansky hits the horn.

Martin slams on the brakes.

Hector stands on his own brakes, cranks the wheel to the right and just *nicks* Martin's right rear bumper.

Looks into his rearview and here comes Octavio.

Brakes squealing.

And BAM.

Octavio's *so* good, man.

Octavio is the only dude Hector ever wants to make his play with, man, because Octavio makes this sound like the big bang but only hits them at about ten miles per hour. Octavio leaves skid marks like an F-16 landing on a flight deck but the impact is like, minimal.

Like, I've been kissed harder.

The two cars look like shit, though. This is because Hector and Octavio smacked the bumpers up pretty good in the garage before putting them back on the cars. Matched the paint jobs and everything, but then again, they're pros.

Hector hollers into the back, "It's showtime!"

Hector slides out of the car, starts screaming in Spanish at Octavio, who's screaming back. Six dudes from Sinaloa in the back of the Aerostar moaning, *Oh my neck, Oh my back, Oh my neck.*

Doctor will diagnose soft tissue injuries and treat them for *months.* Refer them to physical therapy, man, and bill for ultrasound and massage and chiropractic sessions and all that shit that never happens except on paper.

Hector yells at Octavio, "You better be insured, man!"

"I'm insured!" Octavio yells back.

"Who's your insurance company?!"

Octavio whips out his insurance card.

Like American Express, only better, because you don't have to pay the bill.

"California Fire and Life!" Octavio yells.

Just like they've done it a couple of dozen times before.

Just another day at the office.

24

Mommy is all burned up.

Jack's so bummed he doesn't know whether to drive the car or suck on it.

The totally downer picture of Pamela Vale's death smacks him in the face: marriage fucked up, kids off at nightmare grandma's house, a lonely woman hits the vodka and the cigs and gets a longer oblivion than she was looking for.

Tough shit, he thinks. So what? She's not the only person who died today.

So, why do I care?

It's just the whole damn thing, he decides. It's drunk Pam Vale burning herself up in her bedroom, it's Bentley taking about ten minutes to call her death an accident, it's the grieving husband hustling to the phone to ask about his money, it's the All-Star Anal Retentive Mother from Hell charging her widowed son and motherless grandchildren bust-out retail for room and board.

And it's the kids, with their alkie mother and their shifting-cloud father and a grandmother who's about as warm as a steel ruler, and it's *Daddy says Mommy is all burned up.*

And there's this *thing*—this feeling, this suspicion, this paranoia, this sick *thing*—smoldering in the back of his cynical brain. The sooty glass, the dog outside, the blood-red flame, the black smoke . . .

Daddy says Mommy is all burned up.

Call Me Nicky, Jack thinks.

Call you a sick twist.

Telling your kids that.

Be honest, Jack tells himself. The main reason you don't like Nicky is because he's a real estate developer. One of those classic '80s schlock artists who made the big quick dollar throwing up shit all over the south coast. Shaving off the hillsides, pounding out building pads on bad soil, tossing up condos and apartment buildings with cheap materials and shoddy construction.

That's *your* fucking California, Call Me Nicky. You invent your own California and ruin mine. Reinvent yourself and invent me out.

And now he gets Nicky's involvement with Save the Strands. A fucking developer fighting development. Of course, the Vale house looks out over the Strands. It's just a NIMBY thing—Not in My Back Yard. I got my million-dollar view—don't fuck it up. I got *my* California.

Shit.

Like you're any different.

You're the same guy without the money.

It's not Nicky Vale.

It's *me,* Jack thinks.

My pathetic fucking excuse for a life, which mostly consists of sifting around in the ashes of other people's lives, trying to put things back together again. Like that can happen, like that can ever happen.

Putting ashes together again.

"Christ, listen to yourself," he says.

Fucking pathetic, self-pitying, burned-out.

Cold ashes.

Jack, the ace fire guy, a burnout case.

Now, *that's* funny.

The cell phone rings.

"I shouldn't be telling you this," the voice says.

But . . .

25

The voice takes him back a long way.

Back to the days when he graduates from fire school and goes back to the Sheriff's Department and they put him in the Fire Inspector's Unit.

Jack is a comer, a real potential star.

He works his ass off, takes every seminar offered, goes to fires that aren't even his. The joke is that every firefighter in south Orange County is afraid to barbecue a burger because they're afraid Jack will show up.

Jack, he figures he has life just about dicked.

He has a trailer across the PCH from Capo Beach, so he's ten minutes from Trestles, ten minutes from Dana Strand, and twenty from Three Arch Bay, and he can always just go across the highway to surf Capo if he's pressed for time. He's got a primo '66 Mustang that needed only a little Bondo, and he gets a yellow paint job on that hummer, wires the sound system himself and puts on a rack and he is rolling.

Rolls out to a firebombing scene one day and everything else he could want in life is standing out in front of the Jewish Community Center waiting for him.

Letitia del Rio.

It's *hard* to look good in an Orange County Sheriff's Department deputy's uniform, but Letty gets it done. Black hair an inch longer than regulation, golden brown skin, black eyes in a face that is stunningly beautiful, and a body that is pure sex.

"This shouldn't be a tough one for you," Letty says to Jack as he walks up. She juts her chin at a teenage skinhead being loaded into an ambulance. "Adolf Jr. over there threw a Molotov cocktail and set himself on fire."

"They think it's the liquid," Jack says, "not the fumes."

"That's because they sleep through their classes," she says.

Jack shakes his head. "It's because they're morons."

"Well, that too."

Two minutes later he hears himself asking her out.

"What did you say?" she asks.

"I guess I asked you to dinner," Jack says.

"You guess?" she asks. "I'm not going out on a *guess*."

"Would you go out to dinner with me?"

"Yes."

Jack blows out the savings account on a meal at the Ritz-Carlton.

"You're trying to impress me, huh?" she asks.

"Yeah."

"That's good," Letty says. "I'm glad you're trying to impress me."

Next date, she insists on Mickey D's and a movie.

Date after that she cooks him a Mexican dinner that is only the best meal he's ever had. He tells her so.

"It's genetic," Letty says.

"Did your parents come from Mexico?"

She laughs. "My family was living in San Juan Capistrano when it was still part of *Spain*. Do you speak Spanish, white boy?"

"A little."

"Well, I'll teach you some more."

She does.

She takes him into her bedroom and Jack thinks he learns not only a little Spanish but the entire meaning of life when she steps out of her jeans and unbuttons her white blouse. She's wearing a black bra and black panties and her smile says that she knows it's sexy and she looks down at the bulge in his pants and says, "I make you *hard*, huh?"

"Yeah."

"Good," she says. Then smiles and says, "What I've got for *you*, baby . . ."

She's not kidding.

You can take all those classroom definitions of fire, Jack thinks, but you don't know about heat until you have Letty del Rio swirling on you. He reaches up to touch her breasts but she grabs his hands and pushes them down on the bed and holds them down while she keeps moving on him. She's focusing his attention to just where she wants it; it's like, *Once you've been in* here, *you're never going to want to be anywhere else. You are* home, *baby.* And when he's about to come, she reaches underneath him and lightly *strums*—later she'll call this her "Mexican guitar"—and while he's coming she's talking dirty in Spanish.

She's not only gorgeous and smart, she's tough and hardworking and ambitious and she *gets* it. Like, they're necking on his couch in the trailer when the scanner squawks about a fire on a houseboat, and after a minute Letty sighs *Go ahead* because she knows Jack has never done a boat fire before. Letty's so cool she's even there when he gets back and she lets him tell her all about it.

Some of their dates, they go to the shooting range together where Letty invariably beats him and then busts his balls about it all through dinner, telling him that because he lost and she won he has to do any-thing she says when they get home.

"*Any*thing," she says, touching his dick with her toe. Then she starts murmuring *en español* what she wants him to do to her, and when he asks her what it all means she says, "You just start doing. I'll let you know when you get it."

She's so cool she goes down to Mexico with him and sleeps in the back of the truck he borrows from his dad, and when they get back she says, *Sweetie, that was wonderful. Next time, a hotel.*

Pretty soon they're spending all of their off time together. They go to the beach, to movies, they go out to clubs and dance. They make love and talk about cases. They talk about marriage and kids.

"I want two kids," she says.

"Just two?"

"What? I'm Mexican, I'm supposed to want ten?" she says. "I'm one of those *modern* Mexican women. I read *Cosmo,* I read *Ms.,* I give head. Two kids, you can help me make them."

"No, I'm one of those old-fashioned Anglo men," Jack says. "You have to marry me first."

"Maybe," she says. "But if you want to propose to me, I want the din-ner, the flowers . . ."

Jack starts saving for a ring.

So he has a place, a car, a woman.

And a job he loves.

Wakes up and goes to sleep to the sound of the ocean, sometimes sweetened by the sound of Letty's breathing.

Then Kazzy Azmekian's carpet warehouse burns down.

It's a big freaking fire, so they put two guys on it.

Jack and a more experienced guy.

Brian Bentley.

26

The Atlas Warehouse fire is an arson.

Jack's in there doing his inspection and what he sees are a bunch of cleaning rags left by a baseboard heater, but he's also smelling enough gas fumes to get you through New Jersey on Empty.

The night watchman, some poor old semiretired guy from a second-rate rent-a-cop company, doesn't get out. Probably asleep in there or something, and of course the smoke detectors have been disabled, so the guy dies from smoke inhalation.

So you got an arson and a murder, maybe second-degree but still a murder, and so Jack wants the arsonist *bad*.

Jack and Bentley are in the burned-out building doing their inspection when an old Mexican gentleman walks up to them and says that he heard that a man had died, and he wants to do the right thing.

Jack's bowled over.

Like, here they are standing in the black hole of this used-to-be-a-building and this man walks up like a ghost. White suit, white shirt and carefully knotted tie—Jack figures the man must have dressed up to come talk to the police because he thinks it's an important thing to do. The man just walks up and introduces himself.

"I'm Porfirio Guzman," he says. "I saw what happened."

Mr. Guzman lives in the apartment building across the street, hears a noise about three in the morning, looks out his window and sees a man come out of the warehouse, throw gasoline cans into his trunk and drive off.

"Can you describe the man?" Jack asks him.

Guzman got a good look at him. And the car. And the license plate.

"I see him toss the cans into his trunk," he says. "A few moments later I see the flames."

Jack learns that Mr. Guzman is sixty-six years old. Takes tickets at a local movie theater, pays his rent. Quiet voice, distinguished-looking, a real gentleman.

"Are you willing to testify to this?" Jack asks.

Guzman looks at him like he's crazy.

"Sí," he says. "Of course."

He'll make a hell of a witness.

Except the guy he fingers is Teddy Kuhl.

Jack and Bentley bring Mr. Guzman in to look at pictures and he picks out Teddy Kuhl. Teddy's the leader of a crew of white biker trash that does odd jobs for the so-called businessmen who own shit like the Atlas Warehouse. Teddy and his crew do the odd collections, extortions, vandalism, protection, arson and murder.

The second Jack sees Mr. Guzman point at Teddy's picture and nod his head, Jack *knows* that Kazzy Azmekian had his own place burned down. He also knows he has a problem, because if Guzman makes a statement or takes the stand he's going to get killed.

A dead-solid lock.

"We can't let him testify," Jack says to Bentley.

"He don't, we have no case."

They have an arson but no arsonist.

"He does testify," Jack says, "he's dead."

Bentley shrugs.

Jack's brooding on this all the time they're going out to pick up Teddy. This is not a difficult thing to do. If Teddy's not out actually committing some hideous form of nastiness, he's on the third stool from the door at Cook's Corner in Modjeska Canyon, either planning some hideous form of nastiness he's about to commit or celebrating some hideous form of nastiness he just did. Anyway, Jack's working on the situation as they go over there, jerk Teddy off his stool, cuff him and take him back to the station. By the time they have Teddy in the interview room Jack knows what he needs to do.

Get a confession.

Jack grabs a cup of coffee and then goes into the room to work him.

Teddy's a real asshole. He even *looks* like a real asshole. Long blond hair thinning in front. A purple sleeveless T-shirt to show off his arm muscles. Couple of tattoos, one of which appears to be an anatomically correct teddy bear in a state of arousal. He's even got jailhouse tattoos on his fingers, which when interlocked together spell out L-E-T-S-L-O-V-E.

Jack turns on the tape recorder and asks, "Is it Kuhl like in 'cool' or like in 'mule'?"

"Teddy Cool."

Jack says, "A warehouse burned down last night, Teddy Cool."

Teddy shrugs. Says, "That's a real *bish,* man."

Jack asks, "What did you say?"

"That's a real *bish.*"

"Bish?" Bentley asks. "You mean *bitch*? You got a speech impediment there, Teddy?"

"Yeah," Teddy says. "Maybe I do, you fat son of a bish."

Jack asks, "Where were *you* last night?"

"What time?"

"About 3 a.m."

"Fucking your mother."

"You were at the Atlas Warehouse."

Jack watches Teddy thinking. Mulling over that if they have him at the scene, it's either a snitch or a witness. If it's a snitch, he's one of the crew. If it's a witness . . .

"Your mom's a drag in the sack, man," Teddy says. "Gives lousy head. But I guess you'd know that."

"You were at the warehouse."

"Your sister, on the other hand . . ."

"You left a gas can behind," Jack says. "Got your prints on it."

He'd told this lie once to a young amateur who had blurted out, "Bullshit, I was wearing gloves!"

Teddy doesn't go for it, though.

"Wasn't me," he says.

"Don't be a dumb shit," Jack says. "We got you. Why take a hit for Kazzy Azmekian? He wouldn't take one for you. Give us Azmekian, we'll get you some credit with the DA."

Bentley chimes in, "Theodore, you have priors. Unless you do something to help yourself, you could be looking at double-digit time here. You could be dating Rosie for ten, twelve years."

"Or you could write us a statement," Jack says. "Like, now."

Teddy lifts his middle finger, sticks it in his mouth and sucks it, then points it at Jack.

Out in the hallway, Jack says to Bentley, "We gotta get a statement. We can't let Guzman testify."

"Man knew what he was getting into," Bentley says.

"Teddy'll have him banged out."

"I'm not losing an arson-murder," Bentley says.

Jack shakes his head. "Either we get Teddy's statement or we just say fuck it."

Bentley looks at the floor for a long time. Finally says, "You do what you think you have to do."

The selective use of the second person doesn't elude Jack.

He asks, "We're together on this?"

They look at each other while Bentley thinks it over. Then he says, "Yeah."

They go into the room. Bentley leans against the wall in the corner as Jack sits down across the table from Teddy. Jack turns on the tape recorder, says, "You don't know how to write, you can give it to us on tape."

Teddy leans over the desk, gets into Jack's face.

"You don't got no fuckin' gas can, you don't got no fuckin' prints," he says. "What you got is a fuckin' witness, and by the time this thing gets to trial . . . well, don't you just hate it when bad things happen to good people? Ain't it a real *bish*?"

Jack turns off the tape recorder. Takes off his jacket and lays it on the back of the chair.

Jack's a big guy. Six-four and muscled. He comes around behind Teddy, says, "Teddy *Coooool.*" Then cups his palms and slams them against Teddy's ears.

Teddy screams and slumps down in the chair, holding his hands over his ears and shaking his head. Jack picks him up and tosses him against the wall. Catches him on the rebound and bounces him off the other wall. Does this three or four times before he lets Teddy fall to the floor.

"You set the fire, Teddy."

"No."

Jack picks Teddy halfway up, then drives his knee into Teddy's chest. The air comes out of Teddy's lungs with a grunt that makes Jack sick. But it's like, *Do the job and do it right,* so he knees Teddy two more times then shoves him down so that his head bounces off the concrete floor.

He backs off and Teddy goes fetal.

"Don't you just hate it," Jack says, "when bad things happen to good people?"

"You're crazy, man," Teddy moans.

"That would be a good thing for you to keep in mind, Teddy," Jack says. "Now, are you going to give it up or do we start again?"

"I want a lawyer."

Jack knows he has to move him, and quick. Teddy gets a lawyer, he'll find out there's a murder rap hanging out, and then it's over.

"Did you say something?" Jack asks. "Because you're really tripping, man. Bouncing off the walls. PCP, Teddy? Or did you get hold of some skanky meth?"

Jack stomps on him, four times, hard.

Teddy balls up.

"C'mon," Jack says. "It's an arson. You'll get eight, serve what, three? You can do three."

Teddy's lying on the floor sucking for breath.

Bentley's turned away, his face into the corner.

"Or do you want to start again, Teddy?" Jack asks. "Because this time I'm really going to *hurt* you. I go about two twenty, so if I jump and land on your back . . ."

"Maybe I did the fire."

"Maybe?"

"I did the fire," Teddy says. "But Azmekian hired me to do it and I'll say that in court."

Jack feels the weight of the world go off his shoulders. He's been carrying Guzman's life and he didn't want to drop it.

About ten seconds later Teddy's in the chair, writing like mad. Gives it up totally. When he's done, Bentley says to him, "Asshole, a guy *died* in the fire. You just wrote yourself a murder beef."

Which just cracks Bentley up.

Jack's down the hall, he can hear Bentley laughing and Teddy screaming, *You motherfuckers! You lying asshole motherfuckers!*

Gets over that, though, and *really* starts laying it on Azmekian, giving up other fires, all kinds of shit. Teddy's digging like a fucking gopher, man, trying to tunnel away from that body in the warehouse.

Jack, he's in the can puking.

He never lit a guy up before.

End of the workday, he goes and finds his dad and they surf until it's black out. Tells Letty he doesn't want company that night.

27

The story on Jack Wade, Part Three.

Jack's on the stand in Azmekian's criminal trial.

Jack listens to the DA's question, turns to the jury and says, "The modus operandi of the fire matched that of several known arsonists, including Mr. Kuhl. We brought Mr. Kuhl in for questioning, confronted him with the evidence against him, and he wrote a statement confessing to setting the fire and implicating Mr. Azmekian."

"What sort of evidence?"

Jack nods. "Mr. Kuhl left behind one of the gasoline cans at the scene, and we found fingerprints that matched Mr. Kuhl's."

Jury's eating him up.

"Was Mr. Kuhl under any duress to sign the statement?"

Jack smiles. "None."

The DA calls Kuhl, who looks properly criminal-like in jailhouse Day-Glo orange. Kuhl's in County awaiting his own trial, so he has a lot riding on his testimony. He doesn't get the job done on Azmekian, he gets to carry the dead night watchman. They get through the preliminaries and then the DA throws the big fat pitch across the plate.

"Did you set the fire at the Atlas Warehouse?"

"No."

Goddamn Billy's in the gallery and he about swallows his teeth because Cal Fire has denied Azmekian's fire claim based on Teddy Kuhl's statement. Azmekian filed a lawsuit, of course, and they're three months from the civil trial. Which will be a slam dunk if Azmekian has to shuffle to the stand in ankle bracelets.

The DA isn't all that thrilled, either. He gulps and asks a question that provides commuter entertainment in the Greater Orange County legal community for weeks to come.

He asks, "You *didn't*?"

"Nope."

The DA goes back to his table and starts scrambling through his papers. Comes up with Kuhl's statement, and starts reading it out loud. Then asks, "Didn't you write this statement and testify to its truth under oath?"

"Yeah," Kuhl says, and pauses with a jailhouse joker's perfect timing. "But I lied."

Jack gets this sinking feeling.

His career, going right through the floor and into the shitter.

As the DA croaks, "No further questions."

Azmekian's lawyer has a few, though.

"You said you lied in that statement, Mr. Kuhl."

"Yeah."

"Why did you lie?"

Kuhl grins at Jack, then says, "Because Deputy Wade there was beating the crap out of me."

He goes on with great glee to say that Wade threatened to really hurt him if he didn't give up Azmekian. How he would have said anything to stop the beating. How he doesn't even know Azmekian. No, sir, never set eyes on him before today.

Jack's sitting there watching this performance and wondering who got to Kuhl. Who was so scary that Teddy would trash his deal and risk a murder conviction?

Then he hears the lawyer ask, "Do you recognize Deputy Wade in this courtroom?"

"Sure," Kuhl says. "The cocksucker's sitting right there."

The predictable hell breaks loose.

The judge bangs his gavel, the defense attorney moves for dismissal, the DA demands that Kuhl be arrested for perjury on the spot, the defense attorney demands that Jack be arrested for perjury on the spot, the bailiff whispers to Teddy he better not fucking say cocksucker on the stand ever again or he'll whale the living shit out of him in the van, the defense attorney moves for a mistrial, the DA moves for a mistrial, the judge says there's not going to *be* any mistrial, not on his damn calendar, anyway, and the next thing Jack knows the judge has sent the jury off and is holding an evidentiary hearing where Jack is the star witness.

Superior Court Justice Dennis Mallon is one pissed-off judge.

He has the dark suspicion that someone is jerking his leash here and he thinks that person might be Deputy Wade. So he gets Jack in front of him, reminds him that he's still under oath and asks in no friendly tone of voice, "Deputy, did you *coerce* this statement from this witness?"

Jack's problem—well, one of Jack's many problems—is that he doesn't have time to think this through. If Jack were more experienced he would have taken the Fifth, which would have tubed the prosecution but probably saved his own ass. Jack's not thinking that way, though. What he's thinking is that he has to protect his witness. He's also thinking that it's Career Felon and All-World Scumbucket Teddy Kuhl's word against his and Bentley's—like, they're up against a guy who's got a teddy bear with a *hard-on* on his arm—so Jack decides to gut it out.

"No, Your Honor."

"Is there *any* truth to what this man Kuhl is saying?"

"None, Your Honor."

Me and him, we're lying motherfuckers, Your Honor.

Judge Mallon scowls and then the defense attorney asks permission to approach the bench. He and the DA and the judge all whisper and hiss stuff that Jack can't hear and when the huddle breaks, it's the defense attorney asking Jack the questions.

"Deputy Wade, how did you come to suspect my client of this arson?"

"His *modus operandi* matched that of the fire."

"That's not true, is it?"

"Yes, it is."

"You said you had a gas can with my client's prints on it, is that your testimony?"

"Yes."

"And did you?"

"Yes."

Which strictly speaking is true, because he and Bentley went out and got a gas can, jammed Teddy's hand onto it, placed it on the site and "found" it.

"You *planted* that evidence, didn't you?"

"No, sir."

"Did you beat up my client?"

"No."

"You *beat* this so-called confession out of him, didn't you?"

"No."

Jack hangs tough.

Billy Hayes is watching this and thinking that Deputy Wade is a genuine tough guy.

Judge Mallon lets Jack off the stand but instructs him not to leave the courtroom. Jack sits in the gallery sweating bricks while there's another endless huddle at the bench, the clerk makes a phone call, and twenty minutes later Brian Bentley walks in.

Walks right past Jack without looking at him, and the back of his jacket is *soaked.*

He takes the oath, and the stand, and the judge asks him how the statement was obtained and Bentley tells him that Jack Wade beat the confession out of Theodore Kuhl.

Bentley is sweating like a sauna as he turns into a Chatty Cathy doll on the stand. Tells about how Jack told him to leave the room and when he came back in Wade was stomping on Theodore Kuhl and threatening to really hurt him. How he had pulled Wade off the suspect, explained to the suspect that they had an eyewitness—

No, no, no, Jack's mind is screeching.

—who could place him at the scene, so he might as well try to help himself, and how based on that, Kuhl had written his statement. How Jack had forced Kuhl to put his prints on the gasoline can and then planted that evidence, and it was all so unnecessary because they did have an eyewitness—

"I want that witness produced," Judge Mallon tells the DA.

No, no, no, no.

"Yes, Your Honor."

"What's the witness's name, Deputy Bentley?"

"Mr. Porfirio—"

Jack stands up and yells, *"No!"*

"—Guzman."

Jack, he wants to race out of the courtroom and get to Guzman first, except he's in handcuffs because the judge orders him arrested for perjury. Teddy's sitting there grinning at him. Azmekian is smiling at Billy Hayes, who's calculating how many millions it will take to settle his lawsuit. Bentley's on the stand wiping his brow with a handkerchief as he reaches for his spiral notepad to give up Guzman's address.

Which he does, in front of God, the judge and the defense attorney, and when the sheriffs go to pick up Mr. Guzman—sur*prise,* he's disappeared.

Dropped off the face of the earth.

Jack always hopes that he's in Mexico somewhere, in some village by the sea, drinking cold beer to some sweet *canciones.* He knows it's far more likely that Teddy's crew took him out.

And it's my fault, Jack thinks.

I didn't do the job.

I didn't do it well.

And I got that good gentleman killed.

As Teddy Kuhl *walks*, as Kazzy Azmekian gets two million bucks from California Fire and Life, as Jack pleads out to perjury in exchange for unsupervised probation and his uncontested dismissal from the department.

All through this Jack doesn't say shit. Doesn't rat out Brian Bentley, doesn't say a word in his own defense, doesn't offer any explanations. Just takes the ass kicking and goes.

Worst thing is, he can't get a job.

28

Any job.

He's a lying felon. A corrupt, brutal cop. And with that kind of reference he can't get a gig asking, *Would you like fries with that, sir?* And his dad's retired, so that's out, and then a few months later his dad dies while on a sport boat fishing off Catalina, and Jack disappears inside himself into his trailer across the PCH from Capo Beach and drinks beer for breakfast and surfs but after a couple of months he stops surfing.

Letty wants to stick it out with him. Letty is *there*, man, she ain't going anywhere. She is one hundred percent solid gold, she walks the talk. She'll even walk down the aisle with him, have kids, do a life. She tells him that and he looks at her like she's some freaked-out skell and says, "Married? What are you, drunk?"

She starts to answer, *No, asshole, you are*, but she swallows her temper and says, "I thought you wanted to get married."

He laughs. "I don't even have a job!"

She says, "I have a job."

"What, you'll support us?"

"Sure," Letty says. "Until you find something."

"There's nothing to find."

"It's not like you're busting your ass looking."

Unless they got jobs at the bottom of Budweiser cans.

"What do you want from me?" Jack asks.

"I want us to get married," Letty says. "I want us to have a life. I want kids."

Jack says, "I won't bring kids into this shitty world."

"Jack, you got beat," Letty says. "You lost a case—"

"I lost *everything.*"

"Not everything."

"I got a man killed!"

"Not *everything*, Jack!" Letty yells.

"Yeah," Jack says. "What are you doing here, anyway?"

"What am I *doing* here?"

"Go away, Letty."

"I don't want to."

"I want you to."

"No, you don't," Letty says. "Don't throw me away, Jack. I'm too good to throw away."

"You're too good to hold on to, Letty."

"Don't give me that self-pitying shit. If I didn't want to be here, I'd—"

"What are you, fucking deaf? I'm telling you to get out! Leave! Go! Split! *¡Pintale!*"

"I'm gone."

First word in Spanish he ever says to her and it's *Go away.*

"I'm gone," she repeats.

"Good."

"Yeah, good."

She slams the door shut behind her.

Two months later Jack's unemployment has about run out when Billy Hayes trots his cowboy boots up Jack's steps and into the trailer where Jack's slumped on the sofa, drinking a beer and watching the Dodgers on TV. Jack recognizes him as the insurance guy he jammed up, so Jack asks, "What, are you here to give me shit?"

Billy says, "No, I'm here to give you a goddamn job."

Jack stares at him for a long time, then says, "Mr. Hayes, I did everything they said I did."

"You have some construction background," Goddamn Billy says. "And you already been to fire school, so you save me some money right there. I figure you can make a pretty decent adjuster. Basically, it's putting people's houses back together. You want the job or not?"

"I want the job."

"Seven o'clock tomorrow morning," Goddamn Billy says. "And leave the beer at home—"

"I will."

"—unless you bring one for me."

So Jack goes to work for Cal Fire and Life.

Twelve years later he's sitting in Nicky Vale's mommy's driveway getting a phone call from the past.

29

There's no smoke in Pamela Vale's lungs.

Is what the woman whispers over the phone.

I shouldn't be telling you this but I thought someone *should know, the autopsy showed no smoke in her lungs.*

30

Dr. Winston Ng is thrilled to see Jack.

"Go away" is what Ng says when Jack appears in his office. Ng has just taken a minute to sit down and have a cup of old rancid coffee and he doesn't want to be hassled. And Jack Wade is a hassle.

"You had a fire fatality in here this morning," Jack says. "Mrs. Pamela Vale?"

"No kidding?"

Jack says, "She didn't have any smoke in her lungs."

"Who have *you* been talking to?"

I don't know, Jack thinks. But he asks, "Did you test for carbon monoxide?"

Ng nods. "I tested her blood for a level of carboxyhemoglobin."

Carbon monoxide loves red blood cells. CO enters the body, seeks out those red blood cells and goes there. In the body of a person who dies from CO asphyxiation, you'd expect to find, for instance, two hundred times more CO than oxygen in the red blood cells. You'd find a high level of carbon monoxide in the blood.

"What was the saturation level?" Jack asks.

"Under 9 percent," Ng answers.

Which is negligible, Jack knows. A charred body will absorb small amounts of CO through the skin.

"Postmortem lividity?" Jack asks.

"Blue-black."

"Should have been bright red," Jack says. Carbon monoxide turns the blood bright red. "Blisters?"

"A few," Ng answers. "Small, filled with air."

Jack nods. It's what he'd expect on a body that was dead before the fire. Otherwise the blisters would be larger and filled with fluid. He asks, "Rings?"

"No rings."

Same thing. A live body in a fire develops inflamed rings around the blisters. Not so with a dead body.

"She was dead before the fire," Jack says.

Ng pours a second cup of coffee, for Jack. Hands him the styrofoam cup and says, "You know she was or you wouldn't be here busting my balls."

"I'm not busting your balls."

"Yeah you are." Ng plops down on his old wooden desk chair. Slides open a drawer in the gray metal desk and takes out a file. Tosses it on the desk and says, "You didn't see this."

Jack opens the manila file and about pukes.

Photos of Pamela Vale.

Half of her anyway.

Her legs are pretty much burned off. Shinbones exposed. Her arms are bent and pulled up, her fingers clawed as if she's trying to protect herself. Her face is intact, violet eyes open and staring.

Jack gags.

"Hey," Ng says, "you come here busting my balls, you get what you ask for."

"Shit," Jack says.

"Indeed," Ng says. "Any thoughts for me on why we have half of her intact?"

"The leg bones are exposed," Jack says. It would take twenty-five to thirty minutes at 1,200°F for an average structural fire to burn through to the shinbones. Except this fire didn't burn that long. But he says, "Fall-down effect, probably. Shielded her torso and face from the flames."

"Lucky girl," Ng says.

Jack makes himself look at the photos again and says, "She went pugilistic."

He's not talking about boxing exactly, except for the fact that when a human body is exposed to high heat its arm and leg muscles contract, the arms pulling up into a classic boxer's pose. One reason that it wouldn't do this would be if rigor mortis had set in.

"Rigor?"

"No."

"No smoke in her lungs, no carbon smudges around her mouth, low carboxy, and she went pugilistic," Jack says.

Ng says, "She died before the fire but not long before the fire."

"Faceup or facedown?"

"Faceup."

Most people who die *in* a fire are found facedown. It's not a situation where you lie down on your back and wait for it.

"And this is an accidental death?" Jack asks.

"That's what the cops say," Ng says. "And the cops would never ever lie."

"She had alcohol in her blood."

"Yup."

"A lot?"

"She would have been considered legally drunk."

"Enough to pass out?"

"Hard to tell," Ng says. "I also found traces of barbiturates."

"So it could've happened," Jack says. "She's drinking and taking pills and smoking, she passes out, the cigarette ignites the alcohol . . ."

"Say she is unconscious," Ng says. "She's still breathing. She's inhaling smoke. No, this woman was dead before the fire."

"So how did she die?"

They sit there for a second, then Ng says, "There's no bruising around the throat, no ligature marks, no apparent trauma to the trachea. There are no signs of a struggle, as they say on TV. I wanted to talk to the husband about it but his lawyer shut me down. The cops won't pick it up. They say it's an accidental fire, accidental death. Now you know what I know."

"It doesn't strike you as funny that a guy gets a call that his wife died in a fire and ten minutes later he has a lawyer?" Jack asks.

"I'm an ME. I don't analyze live behavior," Ng says. "Yes, of course it strikes me as funny."

Jack asks, "Sexual activity?"

"Those parts were consumed by the fire," Ng says. "Why?"

"Some sicko rapes her, sets a fire."

Ng shrugs. Says, "I saved blood and tissue samples. If there's interest I can send them off to a specialist, get an opinion on violent suffocation."

"Can I see the body?" Jack asks.

"The body's gone," Ng says.

"Already?"

"I released it," Ng says. Sees the look on Jack's face and says, "Jack, what do you want me to do? I have a fire inspector's report that says accidental, smoking in bed. I have a bloodstream juiced with alcohol and barbiturates—"

"She died *before* the fire."

Ng nods. "She drops the cigarette, loses consciousness and ODs before the fire ignites. It's all consistent. If you're fishing for reasons to not pay the claim—"

"Fuck you, Winston."

"I'm sorry," Ng says. "It's been a long shift. That was unworthy."

"Yeah, it's been a day. So . . ."

"So I'm calling it an overdose."

An accidental fire and an accidental death.

"That's cool, Winston. I just wanted an explanation."

"No need to apologize."

"How are the kids?"

"Fine," Ng says. "I think they'll be glad when school starts again. I know *I'll* be glad when school starts again."

"Elaine?"

"Busy," Ng says. "I hardly see her. She's in that EBD phase—'everything but dissertation.'"

"Tell her I said hello."

"You got it," Ng says. "Hey, you want the End of a Long Day Dark-Humor Special?"

"Sure."

"Mrs. Vale?" Ng says. "They're going to cremate her."

Jesus, Jack thinks.

Again?

31

Jack watches Pamela Vale walk around the house.

It's pretty eerie. He's sitting in an A-V room back at California Fire and Life, watching the video that Nicky had given him.

They had to scrape her off the springs.

Now here she is, Pamela Vale walking around the same room that's now full of cold, black ash. Where Jack saw her blood baked onto the melted bedsprings. Now she's looking into the camera and talking to him.

Very weird, almost voyeuristic. He's seen pictures of her charred, naked body—right down to the leg bones—and now she's walking around talking to him.

Young and very beautiful, is that how Nicky had put it? And no kidding, because Pam Vale is—

—*was,* Jack reminds himself, a very beautiful young woman.

It's sick, Jack thinks, because if you didn't keep yourself aware that this woman is dead, you'd be falling in love with her. She's wearing a print sundress that shows her body. She has black satin hair framing a heart-shaped face, but her eyes are what really get to you.

Purple.

Violet.

Some shade in there that he's never seen before.

They grab the camera, they grab *your* eyes and hold them.

And her voice.

Is pure sex.

Even narrating this inventory that Nicky's walking her through. He's holding the camera and whispering instructions. But it's not Nicky's voice softly telling her what to do, it's *her* voice describing, the television, the VCR, the paintings, the sculptures, the furniture, that gets to Jack. He expected it to be that high-pitched beach-girl trophy-wife kind of voice but it isn't. It's a woman's voice—a woman who was a wife and a mother of two kids and a manager of an expensive, complicated household—it's a voice with some real life experience behind it and it's deeper than he expected, and fuller. It's a mature woman's voice and it's pure sex.

Even in this video of Nicky's, basically saying *Dig my possessions and this sexy woman is one of them.*

She knows it. You can see in her eyes that she knows what he's about.

But she's above it.

How? Jack wonders.

Maybe it's the kids—she has the status as their mother and maybe that's enough. Or maybe she's just loaded, anesthetized into a pleasant zonk which gets her through the day. He decides the question is unanswerable and irrelevant and tries to concentrate on what she's saying.

And on the room.

The video is invaluable to Jack because it shows the room before the fire.

It's huge, of course, with high, peaked ceilings. There's the center beam and the rafters coming down off it. Highly polished pine flooring. The wallpaper is white and rich with gold pattern striping. It shouldn't work. Thick red draw curtains come over the sliders that lead onto the deck outside the bedroom. Oval, gilded mirrors and old English hunting prints in walnut frames complete the effect.

Jack rewinds the tape, takes out a notebook and stops and starts the tape as he jots down Pamela's narration. He has Nicky's inventory on his lap and he's trying to match the descriptions up with the listed items and prices.

Of Nicky's precious furniture.

She poses by a desk, gesturing with both hands. ("Show them what they'll win, Vanna.") At Nicky's prompting she says, "This is a George III mahogany pedestal desk, made in about 1775. It has fluted columns at the corners, and note the unusual carved scroll feet."

The camera pans down to the unusual carved scroll feet.

Jack scans the inventory and finds the desk.

Evaluated at $34,000.

Pam continues, "The mirror above it is a *Kent* mirror of carved gilded wood with a shell-backed neoclassical head. This piece was made in about 1830."

Jack thinks she sounds like Jackie Kennedy giving a tour of the White House.

The mirror's estimated at $28,000.

It goes on and on.

"This side table is circa 1730 and is clearly inspired by the Italian Renaissance with its carved gilded wood and gesso motifs. But also note that the carved acanthus leaves on the curved legs point toward the neoclassical."

$30,500.

"These are a pair of George I gilt chairs."

$25,000.

"This is a George I card table."

$28,000.

"This is one of our real treasures," Pamela says. "A rare bombé-based red-lacquered and japanned bureau-cabinet from about 1730. It has clawed and hairy paw feet. Also, serpentine-shaped corners with attenuated acanthus leaves. A very rare piece."

True enough, Jack thinks. Fifty-three grand worth of rare.

The camera lingers over the cabinet, and Jack has to admit that he admires the workmanship. It's all fine furniture, lovingly and carefully built.

To last.

The tour goes on.

A pair of mahogany George II armless chairs.

$10,000.

A 1785 Hepplewhite with Prince of Wales feathers.

$14,000.

A 1745 gilded Matthias Lock rococo console table.

$18,000.

Jack's scribbling notes and prices and he's also noting what he should find when he does the sift.

He *should* find, he thinks, handles from the cabinets. Maybe some remnants from the thickest part of the wood furniture—from the balled and clawed feet and bases. Some fragments should have survived and should be found in the deep char.

Back to the tape.

Georgian furniture, even in the bathroom.

A George II dressing table. A bargain at $20,000.

A George III silent valet. A gimmick for $1,500.

The cabinetry in and around the twin sinks done in walnut to match the period. Expensive tiled cabinet tops in mock marble. The freakin' towel racks done in scrolled acanthus walnut.

Then back to the bedroom for the *pièce de résistance.*

The bed.

Outrageous.

Calling it a four-poster, Jack thinks, is like calling the Great Wall of

China a fence. This bed has four posts all right, but each post has a gilded walnut base with royal-blue inlays. The bases support cylindrical posts of gilded mahogany leading up to rectangular walnut pedestals with carved angels on top. The top pedestals themselves are sheathed in heavy white silk with the coat of arms of what Jack figures had to be some duke or lord or something. The four posts support a frame from which hang two layers of heavy, draped gold fabric, very old and delicate. Judging from the video, there must have been supports across the top of the frame, because a cupola of sorts sits on top of the bed. The cupola is ringed with carved gilded eagles and topped off with a carved castle tower which grazes the ceiling. The bed canopy is tied off to each of the posts.

All of which, Jack thinks, would explain why the top part of Pam Vale's body wasn't burned in the fire. Doubtless the canopy burned early and dropped down on top of her, smothering the flames and protecting the top part of her body.

At the head of the bed is a panel painted with the coat of arms.

This is a very serious bed.

Pamela Vale describes it: "This is the pride of our collection, a neoclassical bed designed by Robert Adam in 1776. It is all the original piece—except for the mattress and box spring, because we need *some* creature comforts, you know—and some of the fabric, which has been replaced. This piece . . ."

Jack flips through the inventory to find the price.

$325,500.

For a bed which is now mostly char.

All that old wood, all that gilding, all that fabric . . .

. . . would go up like a torch.

Maybe it would blow a hole in the roof.

But it would also fill Pamela Vale's lungs full of smoke.

As would the rest of Nicky Vale's fine furniture. Even the stuff that's in the other two wings is going to be smoke- and maybe water-damaged, but right now Jack's interested in what's totally lost.

He punches the values of the destroyed items into the calculator.

$587,500.

And change.

Jack checks the date handwritten on the label: June 21, 1997.

On June 21, Jack thinks, Nicky Vale videotapes an inventory of all his precious belongings. Less than two months later they're all burned up.

Including his wife.

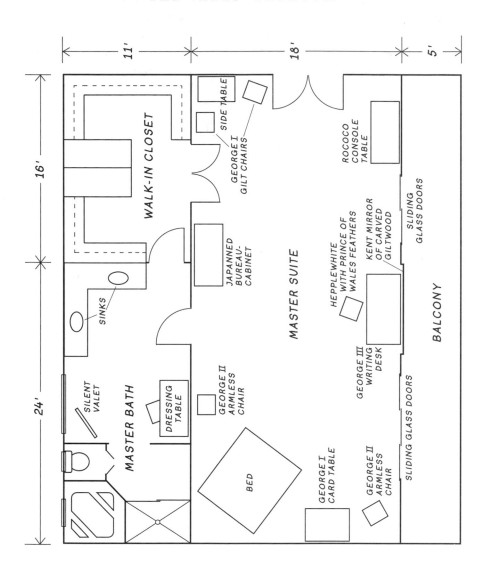

11' 18' 5'

16'

24'

WALK-IN CLOSET

SIDE TABLE

GEORGE I GILT CHAIRS

ROCOCO CONSOLE TABLE

MASTER SUITE

HEPPLEWHITE WITH PRINCE OF WALES FEATHERS

KENT MIRROR OF CARVED GILTWOOD

SLIDING GLASS DOORS

JAPANNED BUREAU-CABINET

SINKS

BALCONY

GEORGE III WRITING DESK

GEORGE II ARMLESS CHAIR

SILENT VALET

MASTER BATH

DRESSING TABLE

BED

GEORGE I CARD TABLE

GEORGE II ARMLESS CHAIR

SLIDING GLASS DOORS

Who in terms of cold cash is worth another $250,000.

So before we even talk about the structure and the rest of the personal property, we're looking at $837,500.

No wonder Nicky's in a hurry to settle his claim.

We're talking major bucks here.

32

Hector Ruiz is pulling a rare doubleheader.

Or a double rear-ender, to be more precise, because he has a new old van in position on the Katella on-ramp onto the 57 in Anaheim. New fake license, new cargo of wetbacks, Octavio behind him, Martin in front of him, Dansky on the freeway.

A doubleheader is rare because two of these things are hard—not to mention tiring, *ese*—to pull off in one day, but Hector and his wife are moving into a new apartment and she has her eye on this bedroom set, so . . .

And Hector has never been afraid of work.

He checks his speedometer and eases it down to thirty.

Sees Martin kick up his Dodge Colt to hit the highway.

Just as Dansky's Camaro swerves into the merge lane.

Dansky hits the horn.

Martin slams on the brakes.

Hector hits his own brakes, cranks the wheel to the right and just *nicks* Martin's right rear bumper.

I am *sooo* good, Hector thinks.

Looks into his rearview and here comes Octavio.

Hector blinks and looks again because it isn't Octavio, it's a gas tanker and he's got to be doing sixty-five and the driver is standing on the brakes and you can hear those big truck brakes compressing down but they ain't gonna make it, man.

"It's show time," Hector says to himself about a half-second before the fuel tanker crashes into the van and both vehicles explode in a fireball that reaches high into the soft California night.

Channel 5 Eyewitness News gets lucky and has a helicopter out there doing traffic so they get a SkyCam picture of the multiple-fatality crash and lead with it on the 11 o'clock news.

It makes a hell of a teaser.

Blue Suit leans over in his chair and asks, "Is that one of ours?"

"Could be one of ours."

When they see Jimmy Dansky out there explaining to some blond reporter that there was "this flash in the sky and I'm just lucky to be alive," they know it's one of theirs.

Standing near the wreckage, the reporter says something about at least eight people dead, all appear to be Mexican Americans.

Flower Shirt looks at the burning van and says, "Hey. Refried beaners."

"You're disgusting," Nicky Vale says to him.

33

The funeral's a riot.

It starts off well enough.

Jack's sitting in the back of the Surf Jesus Episcopal Church, which is not the real name, of course, but it's what the locals call it because the steeple is a curved sweep of white stone that resembles a topping wave—like, Jesus is hip, Jesus is cool, Jesus can tube a twelve-foot point break in his sleep.

Pray for surf.

And surf Jesus.

Jack's a little surprised they're holding the service at a Christian church, but then he finally figures out that while Nicky's Jewish, Pamela was a shiksa, which is probably another reason the mother-in-law was not exactly transported with joy when her son married Pam.

The turnout's decent. The church isn't packed—it's a big church—but there's enough people that the place doesn't look empty. The mourners are mostly South County money. They look healthy and prosperous in that way that shows that they *work* at looking healthy and prosperous. They have health club bodies and tennis tans, and they all know each other, Jack thinks as he watches them greet each other and catches bits of subdued conversations.

. . . a shame about Pamela . . .

. . . into spinning now . . .

. . . graphite handle . . .

. . . and I've lost twelve pounds . . .

. . . Nicky is devastated *. . .*

. . . reclining bicycle, which doesn't put so much stress on the knees, so . . .

. . . at least there won't be a custody fight now . . .

. . . save the kids that *agony, anyway . . .*

. . . cardio-kickboxing . . .

There's fair turnout from Save the Strands. Jack knows this because a number of the mourners sport "Save the Strands" buttons, which Jack thinks is very freaking weird at a funeral.

There are times when you just, you know, give it up.

The family comes in from a side door at the front of the sanctuary. Nicky, Mother Valeshin and the kids. All dressed in black, the color, Jack thinks, of fire.

Nicky looks particularly—and there's no other word for it, Jack thinks—elegant. Wide-shouldered, narrow-lapeled silk jacket over silk trousers. White collarless shirt, black suede shoes. It's like Nicky has been flipping around in the special *GQ* Mourning Edition, "A New Look for Hip Young Widowers," and taken the pages into the Armani store at Fashion Island.

He has a benign, grief-stricken, but-I-have-to-be-brave-for-the-children expression on his face and he looks, Jack has to admit, just god-damn great.

The dozen or so divorcees in the crowd are doing everything but actually moaning, Jack thinks, and if Nicky doesn't get laid right after the coffee cake, Jack's missed his bet.

The kids look like something out of *Masterpiece Theatre*—perfectly costumed, exquisitely mannered, ineffably sad.

The minister lays a kindly hand on the kids and then takes the pulpit. Waits for the organ music to fade and then smiles at the congregation.

Jack thinks he recognizes him from television. He has the official television minister combed-back pompadour of silver hair, except this isn't one of your cracker-southern greased-back jobs, this is a seventy-five-dollar styling from Jose Ebert. He has the official minister sky-pilot eyeglasses, the black robe edged in purple and the white collar that looks weirdly like Nicky's.

Anyway, he finishes smiling then says, "We're here to celebrate a life . . ."

Then gives the usual God is a great guy but your loved one died any-way and I have no explanation for the seeming contradiction so let's not talk about death, let's talk about life and didn't Pamela have a wonderful life and a loving husband and two beautiful children and wasn't she a wonderful wife and mother and life is beautiful and now Pamela is with my buddy God in a better place than even south Orange County and we're going to scatter her ashes over the ocean that she loved so much, by the Strands that she loved so much, and every time we look at the ocean and the Strands we'll think of Pamela, and Jesus loves her and God loves her and Jesus loves you and God loves you and we must all love each other every day because you never know when God is going to toss the banana peel under your foot and bang you out *like that,* and of course the minister doesn't actually say that last bit; it's what Jack is thinking.

No, the good doctor what's-his-name—I *know* I've seen him on the tube begging for bucks—goes on about how we must all form a community to help Nicky and the kids, it takes a village, and thank God they have a loving grandmother to help care for them and Jack's looking in the rack in the pew in front of him for a barf bag and he hears the woman across the aisle from him sort of *snort,* and then the minister looks up at the tongue-and-groove red cedar ceiling and says, *"Lord Jesus, we pray . . ."*

Followed by a long prayer for the soul of Pamela Vale, and that the *healing process* begin for Nicky and Natalie—and for the first time Jack realizes that's Mother Valeshin's first name—and the children, and then the organ plays some horror movie background piece and when Jack looks up Nicky is at the pulpit asking people to share memories of Pamela.

And they do. One by one, about ten or so mourners stand up and tell about a day they spent with Pam at the beach, how Pam loved the sunset, how Pam loved her kids . . . One woman gets up to tell about a shopping spree she and Pam went on, and another about a whale-watching trip they went on . . .

But nobody wants to tell about Pam drinking, about Pam throwing up at a party, about Pam driving the Lexus into the big pine tree by the driveway, about Pam so zonked on Valium they find her passed out in her car outside a garden party. Nobody wants to talk about the screaming fights she and Nicky had, about the flying goblets, about the time she threw her drink in his face at that party on the boat, about Nicky tapping every willing divorcee, bored wife and ambitious cocktail waitress on the south coast . . .

All of that has faded into the sunset that Pam loved so much.

So everything is going just skippy, Jack thinks, when there's a lull and Nicky—misty-eyed but gently, bravely smiling—asks if there is anyone else who would like to say anything.

Which is when a woman's voice from behind Jack yells, "YOU KILLED MY SISTER, YOU SON OF A BITCH!"

This is pretty much when the riot starts.

34

"YOU KILLED MY SISTER!"

Nicky's jaw drops to where the collar would be on his collarless shirt and Jack thinks, *Well, you asked.*

The minister looks frantically around to see if there are any reporters there, especially with cameras, as the woman yells again, "YOU KILLED MY SISTER, YOU SON OF A BITCH!"

Stands there in front of Surf Jesus and everybody and literally points the finger at Nicky.

The other mourners freeze in their seats. They don't try to stop her or calm her down or anything because this woman is clearly intent on mayhem and no one's going to risk a ten-thousand-dollar nose job getting in her way.

Two security guys do.

Jack didn't notice them before, these two guys in black suits who come down from the back of the church to like *quell* the situation. They reach the woman just before Jack does.

"Get your damn hands off me!" the woman yells as one of the security guys lays a thick hand on her shoulder. She knocks his hand off her, and then both of them grab her and start to pull her into the aisle.

The woman looks at the crowd in the church, points at Nicky again, and says, "HE KILLED MY SISTER! HE KILLED PAM!"

The heavyset security guy clamps his hand over her mouth and locks his forearm across her neck.

"Let her go," Jack says to him.

"The lady needs to leave."

Guy has a Russian accent.

"She's leaving," Jack says.

The other guy—tall, thin but *wired*—turns to Jack. "You want to get involved here?"

Same accent.

"Whatever," Jack says.

The guy wants to stroke him one, it's in his eyes, but there's something else that's saying *best behavior,* so he backs down. Jack can see him memorizing his face, though, for future reference.

Jack looks at the heavyset guy and repeats, "Let her go."

First guy nods and the other muscle releases his grip. Jack says to the woman, "Come on."

"He killed Pam."

"Everybody heard you."

He reaches out his hand and takes her arm.

"Come on."

She comes with him.

Jack can still hear the children in the background yelling for their aunt. Looks down there and sees Michael in tears. Mother Valeshin's face set in stone. Nicky looking like he could kill.

So does the boss muscle guy. He gives Jack a badass look.

"Yeah, it's okay with me," Jack says.

"We'll see."

"Yeah."

Jack walks the woman out of the church.

Into the front seat of his car.

"Jesus, Letty," Jack says. "You could have told me she was your sister."

I shouldn't be telling you this but I thought someone should know, the autopsy showed no smoke in her lungs.

35

She's still a looker, Jack thinks.

Shiny black shoulder-length hair, dark Mexican eyes, a body that won't quit. Makeup perfect, just enough jewelry, clothes perfect. It's hotter than hell out but she's wearing a white blazer over her jeans. Jack knows she wears the blazer to disguise the .38 clipped on her belt.

He's half-surprised she didn't just shoot Nicky.

"My half sister," Letty says. "Same mother, different father."

"I didn't even know you had a sister," Jack says.

"She wasn't around much," Letty says. "In those days she didn't want to remember that she was half-Latina. Christ, I just *lost* it in there."

"It's okay."

"It's not okay. I'm supposed to be a professional."

"Letty, you're not *working* this, are you?"

She shakes her head. "Ng finds no smoke in her lungs, he calls over to us and I'm catching. Lucky me. I get to the morgue and I'm like, Oh my God. It's Pam. But I keep my mouth shut that she's my sister because I want to stay on top of what happens."

"Jesus, Letty."

"You know Ng. Ng wants to go out and interview Vale right away. But we better contact the fire inspectors first so they don't get their panties in a wad. He gets Bentley on the horn and—"

"'Don't fuck up my fishing.'"

"You got it," Letty says. "Accidental fire, accidental death. I ask him how come there's no smoke in her lungs and he says 'superheated air.'"

"Superheated air?" Jack asks. "What, he thinks she dropped her cigarette onto a hydrogen bomb?"

"I guess," Letty says. "Anyway, Ng is like, *Fuck Bentley.* He gets on the phone to Vale to tell him he's coming over and Vale's *lawyer* conferences in, says he's representing."

Pretty simple, Jack thinks.

Letty calls Bentley, Bentley calls Vale, Vale calls his lawyer.

"So anyway," Letty says, "that ends any chance of interviewing Vale. I mean, I'm about ready to bring him in anyway, then my boss calls me in. He's been getting his ass chewed on by Bentley's boss, and my boss tells me, *Sorry, I don't have the stroke right now to take on the Sheriff's.* I'm like, *The fire inspector blew it,* and he's, *I know the fire inspector blew it, but Bentley already filed his report that says accidental, and the Sheriff's isn't going to put its guy on the stand and make him eat his own report.*"

"And?"

"And nothing, Jack," Letty says. "That's it. Major Crimes won't take over the file, and I get assigned to a Missing Persons on two Vietnamese punks with about thirty-seven priors each. *Get thee out and find Tranh and Do.* Teach *me* a lesson."

Jack knows the lesson. The lesson is you don't make another deputy look bad.

"So you called me," Jack says.

"Bentley said you'd been fucking around over there."

"And you knew I'd pursue it."

Letty shrugs. "He killed her, Jack. I know he did."

Jack takes her by the hand. Says, "Your sister died from an overdose of pills and alcohol. I saw the ME's report."

Letty shakes her head.

"She didn't drink."

Say what? Jack thinks.

Say *what*?

36

"I mean she quit," Letty says. "Had quit. Like, over a *year* ago."

They're sitting outside at a table at Harpoon Henry's, down at Dana Point Harbor. Their table overlooks the channel, so they can sit in the sun and watch the sailboats and sportfishing boats come in and out. Jack had heard that the yellowtail were running like crazy and so they're fresh and that's why he takes her here.

Letty says, "She, you know, went to rehab. That famous place where they make you take your own garbage out. Like *that's* a big deal. Anyway, she came out, she was clean. Doing the meetings and all that."

"Maybe she had a slip that night," Jack says.

"She didn't have a *slip*," Letty says. "She was doing great."

They stop talking because the waitress comes with food: grilled yellowtail tuna with roast potatoes and yellow and red peppers. A minute later Bob, the owner, is at the table to say hello to Jack.

"How's the surf?" he asks.

"Pretty good," Jack says. "The water's warm."

"I think that's why we're hitting the yellowtail."

"Trunk water," Jack says.

"Trunk water," Bob agrees.

"Bob, this is Letty . . ."

"It's still del Rio," Letty says.

"I'm Bob. How's your meal?"

"It's great," she says.

"Well, let me know if you need anything," Bob says. He smiles at Jack and takes off.

"Bob's your buddy?" Letty asks.

"He's a good guy."

"He always come around to get a look at who you're fucking?"

"Hey, Letty . . ."

"Sorry," she says. "What's trunk water?"

"It's water that's so warm you don't need a wet suit," Jack answers. "You can go in wearing just your trunks."

"So you're still surfing?" she asks.

Jack answers, "Work to live and live to surf."

He says, "There's a purity to the ocean. A cleanliness. It's an absolute."

"Wow," she says, only half making fun of him. "An *absolute*."

Jack says, "The ocean's going to do what it's going to do—what it *has* been doing for millions of years—with you or without you. So if you go into the ocean you just *deal* with its . . . absolute power. Which I find soul cleansing."

She says, "Good for you it's a big ocean."

Which makes them both laugh, and they eat in silence for a while and look out at the boats and then he gets the guts to say, "Letty, isn't it possible that she was having a real rough night and hit the bottle and the pills again?"

"No."

"Letty . . ."

She shakes her head. "You'd have to *know* her."

"Tell me," Jack says.

Tell me about Pam.

37

She wanted to be a princess.

Is what Letty tells him.

My little sister Pam always wanted to be a princess. She would make crowns from construction paper, and gowns from whatever old stuff was laying around the attic, and she would talk me into pulling her around in the wagon like she was Cinderella and we had to get back before mid-night or the wagon would turn into a pumpkin. Which would have been about the only thing to grow on the place.

We're growing up on a shit-poor farm outside Perris; what my step-father is mostly growing is withered lettuce, withered corn and a few withered tomatoes because he doesn't have the money to irrigate. We have a few cows, some sheep, and "Dad" even tried raising goats for the milk products but the dairy equipment is too expensive so that goes bust, too.

I'm the tomboy and Pam's the princess. I want the Chuck Taylor high-tops and she wants the glass slippers. I want to dunk, she wants to dance.

Stepfather drinks and *mi madre* works: a workaholic and an alco-holic and it's sort of a dysfunctional trickle-down theory: I catch the work thing but the taste for the booze trickles down to Pam.

But I loved her, Letty tells him, and this you must understand, Jack: Pam was a wonderful person.

A loving, giving, dear and wonderful person.

When Dad and Mom would fight, like eight nights a week, I'd be upstairs in our bedroom trying to block out the noise and Pam would come up and tell me stories to *get me out of there*, you know? It's like I took care of her physically, she took care of me emotionally. She'd tell the greatest stories about princes and princesses and fairyland and monsters and dragons and wizards and handsome knights. As we got older the details changed but the basic plots stayed the same. She'd say how we were going to go off to college and join the same sorority and meet these totally wonderful guys and get married.

We'd get out of Perris and come here—Letty waves a hand around the harbor and the ocean—to the gold coast, where the money and the good times are, and we'd have money and good times.

And looking at her, you'd believe her. For one thing, she was drop-dead gorgeous—have you seen any pictures of her? She was *so* beauti-ful, Letty says. The kind of striking looks that made you think she could come out here and get guys. Guys with looks and money.

And she did, Jack says.

She did, Letty agrees.

She's seventeen when she splits. A junior in high school. I'm already with the Sheriff's when she takes off. For a long time I blamed myself, because I got my own apartment and left her alone out on that farm.

Anyway, she can't take it anymore so without a word to anyone she splits for L.A.

Gets herself a shitty little place in Santa Monica she shares with four other girls and gets a job serving drinks at some yahoo bar. Gets hit on a thousand times a night but she's not about to go out with—never mind go to bed with—the young guys who take turns buying pitchers.

She saves every cent she can and buys one good bathing suit, one good day dress, one good evening dress and then she hits the beach. She has that jet-black hair and Liz Taylor eyes and the big boobs and little butt and she goes out trolling for the A-list guys. She's on the beach in this little black number and she gets attention, she gets invited to parties and if she likes the address, she goes.

Pretty soon she's hitting so many parties she cuts her work nights down to three a week, and no weekends, thank you very much. All she needs is rent money, really, because she's eating at the parties, she's going out to lunch, she's going out to breakfast.

She's hitting parties in Hollywood, in Brentwood, in Beverly Hills. She's sailing to Catalina, she's doing day trips on fishing boats, she's cruising down for dinners in Newport Beach and Laguna.

And the girl's not putting out.

You gotta *get* this, Jack. Pam's not giving it up, for anyone. And the guys put up with it, they're so smitten. She has the face and the body and the personality. And she's funny and warm, she has the whole package, so they keep chasing.

And she's not getting caught.

Pam's waiting for the real thing.

She wants the whole Cinderella deal. She wants the prince, and the money, and she wants love.

She's not a gold digger, Jack. She has plenty of opportunities, but she tells me, I have to love him, Letty. I have to love him.

She's at a party at Las Brisas in Laguna Beach when she meets Nick. The restaurant sits on the edge of a cliff overlooking the ocean. The jacarandas are in full scented bloom, lanterns glow from trees, a Mexican guitar plays love songs, and the moonlight sparkles on the water.

Nick sees her and walks her outside.

First words out of his mouth?

You look like a princess.

38

His mother didn't approve, Letty says.

No kidding? says Jack.

They've finished lunch and they're walking along the marina. Hundreds of sailboats and motorboats bob with the outgoing tide.

A twenty-two-year-old high school dropout? Letty says. From some farm? Mother Russia *hated* her. If you have to marry a shiksa, you can't find a rich shiksa? From an established family?

"Good thing she didn't know Pam was half Mexican," Letty says. "She would have had a stroke. Maybe it wasn't such a good thing . . ."

Anyway, Mother Russia hated her.

But Nick knows he's holding the trump card.

"Grandchildren," Jack says.

"You got it."

Nick is getting up there and Mother Russia is getting nervous that the family name will die with her bachelor son. And also, the usual rumors are going around: He's thirty-five and unmarried?

Anyway, Mother Russia summons Pam and Nick into the living room of the living dead and says, "My son is infatuated with you, but that's just because he can't get into your pants."

Pam says, "Mrs. Valeshin, *if* he ever *does* get into my pants, he'll be more infatuated than ever."

This makes Mother choke on her tea and gives old Nick a woody that lasts at least until the honeymoon.

Huge wedding, held outside at the House. They have a rabbi and a minister, who talk a lot about how they share a common cultural heritage and after all, Jesus *was* a Jew. It's plain that Nick's paid them not to step too hard on the religious thing, so they're a little vague on the details but very heavy on the humanism. Anyway, Nick and Pam exchange rings and step on glasses and they're pronounced man and wife.

"Wait a second," Jack says. "You were invited?"

"As her *friend*," Letty says. "I'm ashamed to tell you that I went. *Mi madre* had already worked herself to death, stepfather too drunk to give a damn. And I didn't want to ruin it for her. She was happy. Christ, Mother Russia was freaked she wasn't Jewish—if they'd found out she was half Mexican they would have annulled the marriage and made her do the dishes. Or half of them, anyway."

Splashy reception, of course, right there at Monarch Bay, and I was hoping for balalaikas and guys doing that dance where they squat and kick but there is none of that. This party is so Orange County money you could fall asleep standing.

But Pam, she is a princess.

To the manor born, like she's taken lessons or something.

What I kept hearing as I wend my numbed body around the party: *Where* did he *ever* find *her*?

And it's said in *admiration*.

Envy.

Pam's a star.

If the movie ends there, Letty says, you have fucking *Sabrina*.

But the movie doesn't end there, Jack thinks.

It ends the way everything ends.

In ashes.

39

Which the wind blows into their eyes.

They're standing in the driveway looking at the house. It's against Jack's better judgment, but Letty wants to see it and he figures it's better if he's along.

"What they're doing now?" Letty says. "They're taking the boat out in the ocean to scatter her ashes. He doesn't want any *part* of her around."

Which has been true for years, Letty tells him.

After Michael was born.

The son.

A Valeshin.

I thought I was a princess, Pam had told her. *What I am is a brood-mare.*

She's still in the hospital with Michael when Nick nails a waitress at the Salt Creek Inn. She hears about it from a friend who comes with flowers and spite.

Not to like stress *you, darling, but . . .*

It doesn't end there.

Nick has God knows how much tied up in leveraged real estate. Balloon payments looming, then the bottom drops out. Orange County goes bankrupt and you can't get a construction loan at any price. Even money can't buy money.

First real estate, then the furniture. People can't make their mortgages, they're not going to buy George II side tables, so what was an investment becomes a collection. Nick gets his ego wrapped up in it. The damn furniture become his *possessions.* Even on the rare occasions when he gets an offer, he won't part with them.

And they need the money, they're so stretched out.

He mortgages the house, at God knows what psychic cost.

Prime interest and his balls.

He takes it out in coke and fucking, Letty says. The money goes up his nose and out his dick.

Pam becomes the quintessential lonely South County wife and starts to drink. First it's liquid lunches; after a while she's already primed by the time lunch rolls around. Sobers up in the afternoons for the kids, gets them dinner, bathes them, puts them to bed, then drinks herself to sleep.

"Letty . . . ," Jack says.

"I know," Letty says. "But I'm telling you she was *sober.*"

"Maybe not that night," Jack says. "You know, Nick has the kids, he's going to divorce her . . ."

Letty shakes her head. "*She* was divorcing *him.*"

"Oh."

Pam finally gets tired of it, Letty tells him. Tired of his fucking around, his coke, his lying, his smacking her when the real estate deal falls through or when she objects to him buying a five-thousand-dollar sculpture with money they don't have.

Tired of herself, too. Tired of the way she feels and looks. And horrified that she's starting to see her kids through the long-distance smoked lens of pills and alcohol.

So she checks herself into rehab.

I don't know what went on in there, Letty says, but Pam went in a *faux* princess and came out a real woman. She must have *dealt* with stuff there, because she comes out, she's different. More real, somehow. Warmer.

She starts calling, inviting me over. Even introduces me as her half sister. We speak Spanish together, which makes Nick crazy. I spend time with the kids—take them to the beach, take them to the country—

"What do you know about the country?" Jack asks.

"I live there now," Letty says. "I bought a little place up along the Ortega Highway, Cleveland National Forest. Are we talking about me or Pam?"

"Pam."

Pam comes out of rehab warmer.

And *strong.*

Gives Nick an ultimatum: Straighten up or the marriage is over.

She hauls him into counseling. *That* works. Three weeks later she comes home to find him in their bed with some coke whore from Newport Beach. She tells Nick to pack his bags and get out.

Nick storms out and comes back an hour later with a head full of blow and beats the crap out of her. Princess Pam would have taken it, but this Pam goes into court the next day and gets a restraining order, *throws* his ass out.

He runs to Mommy. She calls Pam and tells her that she'll never, ever get the kids. She's an unfit mother. The Vale lawyers will take her apart.

You'll take my kids, Pam says—get this, Jack—*over my dead body.*

Set on fire, Jack thinks, melted *into* their bed, cremated again and scattered over the ocean.

"He was terrified of a divorce," Letty says. "He's already up to his ears in debt and she's going to take half. And the house, and the kids . . ."

Daddy says Mommy is all burned up.

"You have motive," Jack says, "but—"

"He *told* her he was going to kill her," Letty says. "He'd break into the house when she was gone and take things. Leave her threatening notes. Call her on the phone late at night and *tell* her he was going to kill her."

"Jesus Christ."

"She called me the morning before she died," Letty says. She starts to cry as she's telling this.

He came over to pick up the kids, Pam had said. *And he whispered in my ear, I'm coming back tonight. I'm coming back and I'm going to kill you.*

"I begged her to come out and stay with me that night, but she wouldn't," Letty says. The tears pour down her face now. "I should have *made* her. I should have come and stayed with *her.* I should have—"

"Letty—"

"He has the kids, Jack," she says. "That rotten bastard and that bitch are going to raise her kids."

"Looks like it."

"Over my dead body," Letty says.

Then she starts to cry. Breaks down right there and would maybe collapse except he holds her. Asks her, "Do you want to come home with me?"

She nods.

As they're pulling out of the driveway, Jack notices a car parked on the street.

Two guys stand by the car.

Same guys who were in the church.

Nicky's hired security.

40

Jack lives in your basic Southern California neofascist "gated community." A walled-in cluster of tile-roofed condos and town houses sitting like a castle on a shaved-off hill on the corner of Golden Lantern and Camino Del Avion.

"When did you move from the trailer?" Letty says as she gets out of her car in the Guest Parking slip.

Jack says, "When they tore the park down to build condos I couldn't afford. So I bought this place."

This place is a one-bedroom condo on the top floor of a three-condo unit. There are two units below him, sort of out and away as they slope down the hill. As a matter of fact, the two units get a little more out and a little more away every day because they're literally moving downhill.

Jack explains, "They built this back in the boom days in the '80s when they couldn't throw this shit up fast enough. Everybody and his uncle was a contractor all of a sudden and there was big money to be made, so they cut corners with a chain saw. They were in too big a hurry to compact the soil properly, so every building pad is on shifting ground. The whole damn complex is slowly sliding downhill. The homeowners association is trying to sue the contractors, but they're long gone in the recession. So now the association is suing the contractors' insurance company. And so on and so on . . . Anyway, the complex is heading back toward the ocean."

"I thought that was only supposed to happen when the Big One hits," Letty says. The Big One being the Earthquake, the apocalyptic event that everyone in So-Cal jokes about and dreads.

"It won't take the Big One," Jack says. "See those hills behind us? Those are about the last undeveloped hillsides on the south coast. There's another stretch above Laguna, and another one above San Clemente.

"It's fire season—hot, dry, windy—and those hills are covered with brush. One spark on a windy day and we'll be fighting the fire from the beach again. It'll blow down these canyons, surround all these complexes, some will burn down, others will make it.

"After fire season comes the rainy season. We haven't had a serious one in a few years, but we're due. So say we get a big fire and the brush is burned off those slopes. Then the rains come . . .

"The mother of all mudslides. All these hillsides that they shaved off and built this crap on, they're all coming down. All these condos and town houses built on shifting soil? They'll collapse from the bottom up because the ground will literally give out beneath them. We'll slide down the hill in a flow of cheap materials, bad construction and mud.

"First Mother Nature burns it, then she flushes it."

"You'd like that, Jack, wouldn't you?"

They're standing in the street by his garage. Beneath a row of condo buildings that are all exactly identical.

Jack says, "Maybe I would."

Maybe then they wouldn't get a chance to ruin the Strands.

There's a note on his garage door.

Owners of one-car garages are expected to park their vehicle in that garage, not in parking slots on the street. The garages are intended for vehicles, not surfboard workshops.

—The Homeowners Association

"Surfboard workshop?"

"I have a couple of old boards in there," Jack says. Because of the cantilevered design of the building, Jack's garage sits directly below his kitchen. He pushes a remote button on a handheld clicker and the garage door opens with a metallic groan.

A surfboard workshop isn't a bad description, Letty thinks.

Jack has two old longboards on sawhorses and a couple more hung up on racks. The garage smells of surf wax and wood finish. There are posters from old surf movies on the walls.

"You never change, Jack," Letty says.

"This is the best one," Jack says. He rubs a hand along an old wooden longboard stretched across two sawhorses. It has three grains of wood, dark wood blended into light—beautifully jointed, seamless. A flawless piece of work. "Made by Dale Velzy back in 1957."

"It was your dad's."

"Yeah."

"I remember these things."

"I can see that."

"You're stuck in the past," she says.

"It was better then," Jack says.

"Okay."

They go up the sixteen concrete steps to his door.

Jack's condo is Plan C—"The Admiralty." To the right as you come in is a small but functional kitchen with a window that looks out at the cul-de-sac end of the condo complex, and on a clear day has a view of Saddleback Butte to the east. To the left is a dining alcove and then a living room with a fireplace. The bedroom is off the living room to the left.

A sliding glass door off the living room leads to a small balcony.

"*Mira*," Letty says. "You have some view."

She steps out onto his balcony.

"Yeah," Jack says, nodding to a strip mall that sits across Golden Lantern down to the right. "I can see Hughes Market, Burger King and the dry cleaners. In a west wind, I can smell the grease from Burger King. An east wind, I get garlic from the Italian place."

"Come on," Letty says, because the view from the balcony is spectacular. Disregard the strip mall, and the condos down the slope, and look straight ahead and you have miles of ocean horizon. You can see Catalina Island to the right and San Clemente Island straight ahead. Dana Point Harbor is behind a knoll just to the left and then it's open coast all the way down to Mexico.

"You must have some great sunsets," Letty says.

"It's pretty," Jack says. "In the winter the ocean rises up like this big blue bar of color. It's two miles away, but at least I can see it."

"Are you kidding? This is a million-dollar view."

The place cost him $260,000—cheap by local standards.

Letty says, "I think I'm going to start crying again."

"Do you want someone with you or do you want to be alone?"

"Alone."

He's about to say *Mi casa es su casa*, but thinks better of it.

"The place is yours," Jack says.

"I don't mean to kick you out."

"I have things I can do downstairs," he says. "If you need me, stamp on the floor or something. I'll hear you."

"Okay."

He gets out quick because even saying okay her voice quivers and her eyes are full. So he goes down in the garage and works on the board. Takes a sheet of 000 sandpaper, folds it over a block of wood and runs it up and down the length of the board. Slowly, lightly, he gets into a rhythm, sanding the old balsa down to a high, smooth finish.

Upstairs he can hear her sobbing. Sobbing and yelling and throwing pillows and stuff and he half expects to get a call from the association telling him that his condo is a residence, not a funeral home or a shrink's office, and that open displays of grief are in violation of the CC&Rs.

It's an hour and a half before it gets quiet up there.

Jack waits another twenty minutes and then goes up.

She's asleep on his couch.

Her face is puffy and her eyes are slits, but they're closed anyway. Her black hair is splayed out on the pillow.

Watching her sleep is something wonderful and painful. Letty asleep is like an underground fire—placid and beautiful on the surface, but something always smoldering underneath, waiting to ignite. He remembers that from when they were together and he'd wake up earlier and look at her lying there and he'd ask himself what he ever did that someone that beautiful and that good could be with him.

And twelve years later, he thinks, I'm still in love with you.

So what? he thinks. I threw you away.

Like something tossed into the ocean, and now a wave washes up on my little stretch of the beach. Life giving you back something you don't deserve.

Don't get carried away, he thinks. Take a step away from yourself. She's not back because she loves you; she's back because she needs you.

Because there was a fire and her sister died.

He gets a spare blanket from the hall closet and puts it over her.

Her story doesn't change a thing. Pam had a history of alcoholism, a history of pills. Her blood tested positive for both.

Nothing Letty says can change *that* story.

The only thing that can really tell the story, Jack knows, is the fire.

41

Fire has a language.

It's small wonder, Jack thinks, that they refer to "tongues of flame," because fire will talk to you. It will talk to you while it's burning—color of flame, color of smoke, rate of spread, the sounds it makes while it burns different substances—and it will leave a written account of itself after it's burned out.

Fire is its own historian.

It's so damned proud of itself, Jack thinks, that it just can't help telling you about what it did and how it did it.

Which is why first thing the next morning Jack is in the Vales' bedroom.

He stands there in that dark fatal room and he can hear the fire whispering to him. Challenging him, taunting him. Like, *Read me, you're so smart. I've left it all here for you but you have to know the language. You have to speak my tongue.*

It's okay with me, Jack thinks.

I speak fluent fire.

Start with the bed.

Because Bentley called it the point of origin and because that's just what it looks like.

They had to scrape her off the springs.

In fact, Jack can see the traces of dried blood on the metal. Can smell the unmistakable smell of a burned body.

And the bedsprings themselves—twisted, congealed. It takes a hot fire to do that, Jack knows. This kind of metal only starts to melt at 2,000°F.

That's the fire telling you, *I'm* bad, *baby. I'm a badass fire and I did her in the bed.*

Then there's the hole in the roof. What's known in the trade as a BLEVE, a boiling liquid evaporation explosion. Also known as a chimney effect. The fire ignites at the point of origin, and the superheated gases rise and form a fireball. The fireball hits the ceiling and *boom.* Which certainly means that something hot and heavy happened around the bed. Fire saying, *I'm so bad you can't even keep me in the room, Jack. I'm so big and bad I have to fly. Break out, baby. Show my stuff to the sky.*

Jack looks down and sees where Bentley dug through the ashes on the floor by the left side of the bed, and he can see the vodka stain—the spalling—literally burned into the wood floor. He can see some shards of smoked, oily glass, including the neck of the bottle.

He can see where Bentley got his theory.

But the lazy bastard just stopped there. Saw an Insta-Answer and grabbed at it so he could start packing for the big fishing trip.

So Jack keeps looking.

Not only because he thinks Bentley is a cretin, not only because of Letty's story, but also because it's just laziness to repeat someone else's work. That's where mistakes—if indeed there is a mistake here—get perpetuated. One lazy bastard after another copying each other's work.

A circle jerk of error.

So start again.

Start from scratch with no preconceptions and listen to the fire.

The first thing that the fire is telling him is that it burned a whole lot of stuff in this room, because Jack's standing in char up to his ankles. He clips his Dictaphone inside his shirt and starts talking notes.

"Note ankle-deep char," Jack says. "Indicates the probability of heavy fuel load. Whether primarily live load or dead load I can't tell at this point."

The heavy char tells Jack something else he isn't going to speak into the tape. Usually heavy char means a hot, fast fire, simply because it shows that fire had the chance to burn a lot of stuff—*fast*—before the Fire Department could get there and put it out.

So the next thing he looks at is the char *pattern.*

If fire has a language, then the char pattern is its grammar, its sentence structure, its subject-verb-object. And the sentences this pattern is banging out are like Kerouac on speed, because it's like verb-verb-verb, it's talking about a fire that was *moving,* man, not stopping for periods or commas or nothing.

Jack's thinking that this fire was *rolling.* Because Jack's looking at what's known in the business as "alligator" char. It looks like what it sounds like, the skin of an alligator. What happens is that a hot fire moves fast. It burns quickly and moves on, so it leaves sharp lines of demarcation between what it burns and what it doesn't. Turns out looking like alligator skin.

The hotter the fire, the faster it burns, the bigger the alligator you got.

Jack's looking at one big alligator here.

He scans the charred remains of what had been the expensive white-and-gold wallpaper, which is going to cost a bundle to replace, and he questions whether this wallpaper, pricey as it was, was sufficient fuel to feed this hungry an alligator.

He doesn't say that into the tape recorder, though. He keeps those thoughts to himself. What he says into the recorder is, "Moving along the west wall of the bedroom, I observe large, alligator-type char."

Observing it's one thing, recording it's another, because the room is black, and black photographs like nothing. So Jack hauls out his portable flash unit and starts "painting" the room with the light.

He stands in one corner and looks through the camera viewfinder as he moves the light out from one wall toward the center of the room. He observes where the light fades so he knows where he'll need to start for the next shot. He snaps his shots—color and black-and-white—and then moves the flash in toward the center of the room. Then he moves to another corner and repeats the process and so on and so forth until he has the room covered. He jots down a note for every shot he takes and speaks what he's doing into the tape recorder.

Then he draws a rough sketch of the room and notes where he was standing for each shot and what part of the room the shot covered. So when the smart-ass lawyer asks him, "You don't really *know* that you were standing in the southwest corner when you took this photograph, do you?" Jack can whip out the notebook and say, "Actually I do, counselor, because it's my practice to make notes of my location when . . ."

Because the point is, Jack thinks, that you have to do it every time. Take your time, do it right, go on to the next task.

So the next thing he does is measures.

Gets out a steel tape and measures the dimensions of the room and notes certain "landmarks" from which he can triangulate. He has a number of marks to do it from, because the big furniture in the room left heat shadows.

Pale marks on the wall—reverse silhouettes, if you will—where the heavy furniture shielded the wall from the initial flashover. So he uses two of the heat shadows as triangulation points and moves on, goes back to listening to the fire.

What else does the fire have to say?

The char on the rafters.

Same thing, alligator char on the wood, sharp lines of demarcation between the bottom edge of the rafters, which is heavily charred, and the top edge, which isn't.

Nothing unusual there, Jack thinks. Fire burns up, so you'd expect to see the bottom edges of the rafters more heavily charred than the top. And you'd expect to see the heaviest char directly above the bed, where the fire burned the longest. What you wouldn't necessarily expect is what Jack's seeing, and that is that there are *several* areas of the rafters that are showing heavier char than others. One over by the opposite wall, one by the closet, another by the door that leads into the bathroom.

"Note heavy char on rafters above bed," Jack says. "Sharp lines of demarcation. Note also, heavier char on rafters near closet and near entrance to bathroom."

Jack takes out a steel ruler and jams it into the middle of a char blister on the rafter above the bed.

"Char is one and three-eighths inches deep on rafter above bed," he says, and then does the same for the other two areas. "One and three-eighths on area near closet. One and three-eighths on area by entrance to bathroom."

Then he measures two points in the rafters that look less heavily charred. The char is an inch deep.

Which is interesting, Jack thinks, because there can't be *three* places where the fire burned the longest. Not accidentally. Of course, there could be other explanations. Depends on what was sitting *under* those charred rafters. Maybe there was something really tasty for the alligator, something that burned hot and deep and long. That could explain the apparent anomaly.

Then again, the dog was out in the yard when it wasn't supposed to be. And the flames were the wrong color, and the smoke was the wrong color.

That, combined with three hot spots on the rafters, is starting to get Jack pissed off.

Jack knows what Bentley did. Bentley looked at the hole in the roof above the bed, looked at the heavy char on the rafters above the bed, dug the ashes from around the bed and saw that the fire had burned into the floor. Saw the broken vodka bottle and the burned mattress and the twisted bedsprings and figured he had his point of origin.

Because there should be only one point of origin and smoking in bed is the number-one cause of fatal bedroom fires.

Which is good as far as it goes, Jack thinks, but it doesn't go far enough.

So Jack goes looking for V-patterns.

42

Fire burns up and out.

Like a V.

It ignites at the base of the V and flames up—because fire burns up, where the oxygen is—and out, as the atmosphere in the room tries to equalize the heat and pressure.

It burns up and out from its point of origin and often it leaves a V-pattern mark. In which case the fire *points* to where it started.

Now, when a fire starts in the middle of the room, you're not going to see a V-pattern, because there's no surface for the fire to mark. When a fire starts away from a wall, what you'd expect to see instead of a V-pattern is a circular pattern on the ceiling above the point of origin.

Which there certainly is. Above the bed there's not only a circular burn pattern, there's a freaking *hole* blown through the roof. But there's also ankle-deep ash and deeper char on several places on the rafters and there's a hole in the roof and there's a dog barking outside.

Jack starts in what used to be the closet.

The closet is a walk-in.

Or a hike-in, because this closet is maybe a little smaller than Delaware.

And calf-deep in ash, which Jack would expect because there's a lot of stuff in closets. That's the purpose of a closet, right? To put stuff in it, and because this is a humongous walk-in closet belonging to rich people you're going to expect that the alligator had a banquet in here.

Especially if you have clothes hanging from a pole, because fabrics are tasty to eat and you also have a lot of nice oxygen underneath them.

And you're going to have a lot of ash because you're going to have a lot of "fall down." Fall down is just what it sounds like; it's stuff that burns and then falls down onto the floor.

Again, the basic principle of fire is that it burns up. It burns up, seeking oxygen and fuel. Insufficient oxygen, the fire smothers. Insufficient fuel, the fire burns out. The situation a fire *really* likes is when it can burn upward and find fuel there. Fuel like clothing. Fuel like boxes stored on shelves, and then the shelves themselves.

So the fire zooms up and consumes those things, and the carbonized material—char—falls down on the floor. A lot of times there's enough fall down to smother the fire on the floor. That's why you can go into a fire site and the ceiling is burned but the floor—where the fire started—isn't.

See, sometimes fire will go up and then *across*. The fire isn't even burning across the floor, it's up along the ceiling, where the fuel is. It burns the nice fuel up there and gets hotter and hungrier and then you have what's known as the convection effect. The fire up top generates so much heat that the *heat*—not the flame—ignites the material on the floor and then the floor goes up.

But it all has to start somewhere.

Which is at the base of a V, and the reason Jack's looking in the closet is because Jack is a cynical bastard.

A cynical bastard thinks that if someone is going to start a fire, the closet is a good place to do it because it's not immediately visible and the fall-down effect often obscures the evidence.

So Jack's down on his knees digging away the ash at the back wall of the closet and it doesn't take long before he finds what he's looking for—a tall narrow V marking on the wall. Important that it's narrow instead of wide. A wide V is the fire telling you that it spread normally, just the usual grazing on the usual feed. A narrow V is the fire telling you something else.

The fire saying, *I was hot.*

I was *fast.*

Something else with this V. The apex doesn't come to a point. It looks like a V with the point cut off, more like ⋁.

Which is the fire hinting to Jack, *Yo, dude, maybe I had a little help.* A little *boost.* Maybe I had me a little something to get me, you know, *started.*

In an accidental fire, the V will be pointed. But if the fire had a little help—say, if someone poured an accelerant on the floor—then the apex of the V is going to be as wide as the pool of the accelerant. Because you don't so much have a point of origin as you have a *pool* of origin, all of which ignites at the same moment.

So now, Jack thinks, we have not just one point of origin, we have at least two.

Which is one too many.

If there's one thing Jack knows about an accidental fire, it's that it has one—count them, *one*—point of origin.

An accidental fire doesn't start accidentally in two places.

It's not possible.

Jack pushes aside the charred remains of what appears to have been some coats on the floor by the wall at the bottom of the V.

Could swear he hears the fire laughing.

Because there's a hole in the flooring. As wide as the base of the V.

Which makes Jack think that maybe Letty is right.

Maybe Pam was murdered.

43

Letty del Rio is standing in a chop shop in Garden Grove, hip deep in cut-up cars, and she's got five Vietnamese kids against the wall with plastic ties around their wrists and not one of the jokers will tell her anything about what she wants to know.

That is, what were Tranh and Do up to when they did their duet Houdini act.

And she doesn't really want to run these boys in for the cars, because it is a major pain in the ass for little results, but that's what she's going to do unless they start showing a marked improvement in their attitude.

Letty says to the interpreter, "Tell them they'll get five to eight on the cars."

She unwraps a stick of gum and pops the Juicy Fruit into her mouth as the interpreter translates her threat and gets a response.

"They say they'll get probation," he tells her.

"No," she says. "Tell them I'll personally fuck them with the judge. Tell them that."

He tells them that.

He gets their answer and says, "They say your sex life is your business."

"Cute boys," Letty says. "Very cute boys. Tell the cute boys they better not have sheets because I'll rattle their probation officer's cage until he violates them. Tell them I'll make sure they get into one of those tough-love juvenile boot camps where they do push-ups till they puke. No, don't tell them that. I *know* they speak English."

Shit, Letty thinks, these kids were born right here in Little Saigon, which is technically in California but in real-life terms is still in the Republic of (South) Vietnam. They all speak English until they get popped, then they dummy up and go for the interpreter bit because they know it's hard for a prosecuting attorney to work up any mojo when he has to wait for the translation.

It pisses Letty off.

"You speak English, don't you?" she says to the kid who looks the oldest. The kid who's been giving the other kids the shut-your-mouths looks. Checks his ID and the kid's name is Tony Ky. "I'm looking for Tranh and Do and I *know* they were involved with your little parts dealership here. So I'm going to bring the heat on you, and I'm not ever going to stop bringing the heat until you help me out. No, don't say a *word* to the interpreter—I don't need your smart mouth. You just think about what I'm telling you."

Like it's going to do any good, Letty thinks.

This is a closed world, Little Saigon, and it ain't going to open up for her. So she's pissed off at these kids, and she's pissed off at her boss for sending a Latina into a closed, Asian, male world.

Like they're going to talk to me, she thinks.

And she's also pissed off that she's going to have to go talk to Uncle Nguyen, who is the one person who could open up mouths for her, and Uncle Nguyen just gives her a headache. Uncle Nguyen used to be a cop back in Big Saigon, the old Saigon, so he has this annoying we're-all-cops camaraderie bullshit and he also isn't going to tell her a thing. Or tell anyone else to tell her a thing.

Shit, if Tranh and Do have been whacked, Uncle Nguyen would have had to *okay* them getting whacked, so that's probably a dead end. But it's a street she has to walk down to make the boss happy.

But I'll get a headache, she thinks.

She tells the uniforms to take the kids in and then she starts searching the shop.

The thing you have to love about the Vietnamese, Letty thinks, is that they keep records. Here they have this beautiful scam going, stealing each other's cars and stripping them, selling the parts and collecting the insurance, and they just have to keep lists of whose cars they "stole" and how much they paid.

Thinking, like the old-time bookies, that they can flash the paper before the cops come through the door.

Sorry, you lose. Deputy del Rio is faster than your average cop.

Smarter, too.

And much faster and smarter than your average fucked-up kid who doesn't have the *cojones* to at least *try* to get himself into a junior college or something and chops cars instead.

Letty has *no* sympathy.

So Letty's poking around the shop, looking for the record books, and she collects every slip of paper in the joint. Logs them in as potential evidence and has them translated.

Tells the translator, "I want to see—right away—anything with the names Tranh or Do on it."

Which, Letty thinks, is kind of like standing down in Chula Vista and saying you want to see anything with the name Gonzalez on it. But what are you going to do?

44

Fire burns *up*.

Because that's where the oxygen is.

Fire burns up . . .

unless . . .

. . . it has a *reason* to burn *down*.

Jack knows that there's a limited universe of possibilities as to what that reason could be. Anything poured on the floor to get a fire going—in the lingo, an *accelerant*—seeps *down*, as any liquid will. *Down*—into the flooring—and the fire follows. Follows *down* because now it has a reason, the accelerant, which is better fuel than oxygen. The fire eats up that nice tasty accelerant—gasoline, kerosene, styrene, benzene—and *then* burns *up*. Fast, hot and mean.

So Jack's looking at this hole in the flooring—about two feet long and a foot wide—where the fire burned through and he's wondering why. He shines his light into the hole and onto the floor joist. The top of the joist directly beneath the hole is charred. The bottom looks unaffected. Jack leans over and shines the light onto the joist just beyond the hole.

Sees what he expects to see: finger-shaped stains on the top part of the joist.

"Note splatter pattern on joist beneath hole in closet flooring," he says into the tape.

That's all. He doesn't say that this is what you'd expect to see in an accelerated fire—the splatter pattern where the poured accelerant has seeped through the flooring and along and into the joist.

Fucking Bentley, Jack thinks. Lazy fucking Bentley. Sees his point of origin, brushes some ash aside and pronounces cause and origin. Gets the poles out and goes fishing.

Doesn't bother to look, doesn't bother to do a dig-out.

You *have* to dig out the char before you can determine the cause of the fire. At least this is what Jack was always taught. You *have* to do a dig-out. And not just where you think the point of origin is, but over the whole structure.

See, it's hard to burn a house.

Most people think that it's easy, but most people are wrong. A fire needs a lot of oxygen and a lot of fuel to get big and grow strong, and in a lot of house fires, there just isn't the oxygen or the fuel load to sustain a real hummer of a fire. Arson fires that Jack has worked, he goes in and finds holes punched in the walls to vent the fire, or windows left open. He once investigated a fire in a house that was under construction, and they'd taken the frigging *drywall* out so that the fire would have enough oxygen to spread through the house.

And it isn't just a matter of oxygen and fuel load—it's a matter of time.

Time before the fire trucks roll in.

In the old days it was different—the country was more rural, houses were farther away from the fire stations, nobody had automatic alarms and sprinkler systems and all that happy crap.

But now—especially in the Southern California megalopolis—everything is wired. Everybody's hooked in. A fire goes off, it trips the sprinkler system, it trips the security alarm, the Fire Department is at most ten minutes away and firefighters arrive in force.

You want to burn a structure down—or burn out a wing of your house—you're in a game of Beat the Clock. You start the fire in just one spot, you're bound to lose that game. The unrelenting math of physics is just against you.

You have to reset the math.

You do it two ways.

First, you accelerate the fire. You generally take some fossil fuel and ignite a fire that's more hare than tortoise. The other thing you do is you set more than one fire. An arson fire is usually not a single fire but several fires, because it has more than one point of origin. You need more than one because even a highly accelerated single fire is not going to do the damage you need before it runs out of clock.

You need several accelerated fires to (a) get to the areas you want destroyed and (b) to increase the total amount of BTUs to get your convection effect working for you. Get enough heat going in the structure so that the flames don't necessarily have to spread the fire—the heat will reach the ignition point of the materials in the structure and then WHOOSH.

Flashover phase.

The fire out of control.

The alligator in a feeding frenzy.

Orgasm, as Fuller would have put it.

Of course, Jack knows that the convection effect doesn't always happen that way. A guy sets two or three fires and one or two of them die out before they get the necessary heat going. So what a lot of arsonists will do is connect the fires so the flames move through the structure. So they pour accelerant from one place to the other, or sometimes they make what's known in the business as "trailers," often bedsheets twisted up and run through the house from pool of accelerant to pool of accelerant.

A little highway for the fire to get up some speed.

And the evidence burns itself up.

Unless you speak fire, in which case the evidence is there—like a hole in the flooring and a splatter pattern on the joists.

Showing that the fire burned down instead of up.

Physics, Jack thinks, never lies.

The laws of nature are laws that even plaintiff attorneys and judges can't overrule. You throw a ball up in the air, it comes down. You get under a wave, it rolls you on the bottom. Fire ignites and burns *up* unless it has a physical reason to burn down.

Jack kneels there, sweating inside his white paper overalls, the smell of ash penetrating his sinuses, and part of him wishes he were out in the cold blue water under a cool blue sky instead of knee-deep in ash in a closed black room that smells like fire and death.

He goes through the whole photography process again, lighting and shooting the V-pattern, the hole, the joist and the closet as a whole. In color and black-and-white. Records the information on his notes and into the microphone.

When he's done with all that, he takes out a plastic evidence bag from the overalls. Some guys like to use paint cans, but Jack worries that the metal in the cans could contaminate the samples. Likewise, your basic grocery store Ziploc bags. So Jack buys special evidence bags which have been treated and sterilized. They're more expensive, but he figures that in the long run they're a lot cheaper than having your samples kicked out of court. He scoops some char out of the hole and places it in the bag. Seals the bag and then labels it, giving the date, time, description and exact location where the sample was taken. Then he signs the label.

He records the same information into his notebook and speaks it into the tape recorder.

Jack being a belt-and-suspenders kind of guy.

He repeats this process several more times, taking a small chunk of the joist, the flooring itself and then a char sample from a different part of the closet, away from the V-pattern and the hole. He takes material from an area he thinks will be clean in order to get a comparison sample, hopefully one that doesn't contain an accelerant. Otherwise, if the samples *do* test positive for accelerants, the argument can be made that they're inherent in the wood itself. Pine flooring, for example, can have a lot of turpentine in it. So you try to get a "clean" sample to show the difference.

He takes samples from several locations around the room.

I'm going to have to do a dig-out, Jack thinks.

The whole room.

Literally dig out all the char in the room to expose the flooring to see holes, potential pour patterns, spalling on the concrete slab below the floor—all "indicia," as they say in the trade, of an accelerated fire.

He picks up his shovel and starts to dig.

Beginning in the closet. Figures he'll start in that corner, where he knows that there's a problem, and then work his way out across the whole bedroom. He scoops up char and tosses it into one of the large plastic garbage cans he brought with him. He'll need the char later when he goes to do the sift.

As he digs he sometimes scoops up larger pieces of material—partially burned clothing, pieces of appliances, remnants of furniture. He sets aside the larger pieces—some brass cabinet handles, copper hasps, a claw handle foot—but records all of them in his notes. He sketches the location of the larger pieces on his floor plan, photographs them and puts them into plastic evidence bags.

All of this takes time.

When he's done digging out the open floor space, he's exposed what's left of the flooring.

Stands back and takes a look and the fire is really talking.

The pour pattern that starts in the closet leads to the bed.

"Go figure," Jack says.

If Bentley had done his fucking job, he might have traced it back the other way, from the vodka pour back to the closet. But he didn't—Jack did—and to Jack, what he's looking at now is like reading a book.

Someone poured a great deal of accelerant in the closet. Jack knows this because the flooring is burned clear through, exposing the concrete pad beneath. Then someone poured a trail of accelerant from the closet over to the bed. Jack can see the pour pattern, a pale spalling on the wood. Here and there a hole where the fire burned the hottest.

But there's no hole beside the bed where the remnants of the vodka bottle were. Whoever poured the juice was careful not to pour it there.

Jack lifts up the charred mattress and spring and moves them over. What he'd expect to see underneath would be a relatively undamaged floor. Again, you're talking about the fall-down effect. If the fire started on the floor beside the bed, it would have ignited the wood frame of the bed. When the frame collapsed, the mattress and box spring would have dropped down, shielding the floor beneath.

But that's not what he sees.

Not what he hears, either, because the fire is talking to him again.

Yapping at him, *chirping* at him, *I did her right here, baby. I did her right in her bed. Blew through the freaking roof, baby.*

Because there's heavy ash where there shouldn't be.

Jack digs through the ash.

Underneath it there's a big hole. Irregularly shaped, but roughly the size of the bed. Wider, in fact, on the side opposite the bottle remnants.

Jack keeps digging.

Digs right down through the flooring to the concrete pad beneath.

Scoops the char off the pad, and what he sees is a white stain where the concrete was scorched.

Spalling.

It's another sign of a set fire, because, once again, fire burns up unless it has a reason to burn down. You have spalling like this, you have juice dripping down onto the concrete, luring the alligator down for a snack.

So Jack's standing there and he has the hole beneath him, and above him, there's the hole in the roof.

"Jesus Christ," Jack says.

The fire is screaming at him.

Feels like it's coming from inside his soul.

Whoever set the fire poured accelerant under the bed. Then doused Pamela Vale with it. Doused it from her hips down her legs. Then lit a match.

No professional arsonist does that, Jack thinks.

Not on a strictly business fire, anyway. You douse a woman in a bed like that, it's personal. It's sexual. It comes out of rage.

Jack goes through his whole routine again. Photographs the floor in black-and-white and color, logs the photos, videos the room, then sketches the pour pattern onto a floor plan of the room. Belt and suspenders, because he wants a lot of evidence to go in front of a jury.

The best thing would be if the jury could visit the site, but he knows that's not likely to happen. For one thing, the chances of getting an injunction against demolition and reconstruction of this room are practically nil, and two, judges rarely allow a site visit, especially when there's been a fatality. It could prove to be too emotional and prejudice the jury.

What it could prove, Jack thinks, is that Nicky Vale burned his wife up in their marital bed. If I could walk a jury through this place and explain to them what they're seeing . . .

But fat chance of that, so he documents the scene the best he can—photos, video, sketches—then grabs samples from around the pour pattern and under the bed. For each potential "dirty" sample, a potential "clean" one for comparison. He puts them into plastic evidence bags and logs them in.

The samples are *everything* now.

If the samples test positive for accelerants, it makes total bullshit out of the smoking-in-bed theory.

Then it's not an accidental fire *or* an accidental death.

It's arson.

And murder.

Jack heads off to see Accidentally Bentley.

Tell him he needs to reopen the Vale file.

POUR PATTERN*

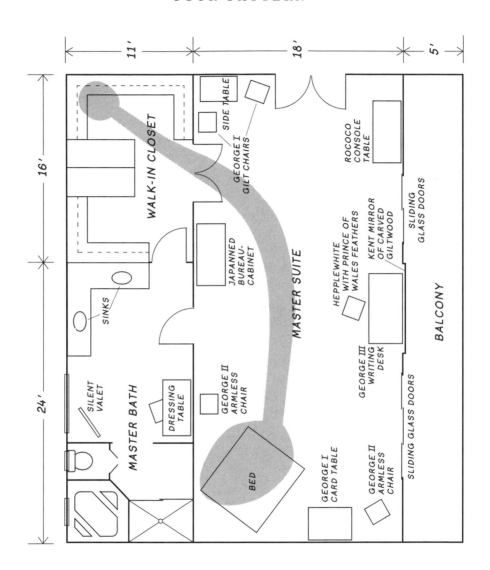

11'   18'   5'

16'   24'

WALK-IN CLOSET

SIDE TABLE

GEORGE I GILT CHAIRS

ROCOCO CONSOLE TABLE

SLIDING GLASS DOORS

JAPANNED BUREAU-CABINET

MASTER SUITE

HEPPLEWHITE WITH PRINCE OF WALES FEATHERS

KENT MIRROR OF CARVED GILTWOOD

SINKS

GEORGE III WRITING DESK

BALCONY

SILENT VALET

MASTER BATH

DRESSING TABLE

GEORGE II ARMLESS CHAIR

BED

SLIDING GLASS DOORS

GEORGE I CARD TABLE

GEORGE II ARMLESS CHAIR

*Shaded area indicates pour pattern

45

You got it wrong again, you dumb lazy fuck!

Is what Jack wants to say to Accidentally Bentley. But Jack doesn't figure that's exactly diplomatic, so he settles for, "I think you might want to reconsider your call on the Vale fire."

"Get out of here," Bentley says. He's sitting at his desk at the Sheriff's office. Actually, he's cleaning out his desk, and what he means by *Get out of here* is not *You're kidding;* what he means is *Get out of here.*

Bentley jerks his thumb toward the door.

Which looks good to Jack, too, but he reminds himself that he's here to try to get Bentley to reopen the investigation, so he takes a breath and says, "Brian, the house has all the indicators."

"Such as?"

"Deep char."

"There was a lot of stuff in the house."

"Alligator char on the beams."

"Old wives' tale," Bentley says. He doesn't even look at Jack. He's busy putting stuff into a cardboard box. "Could mean something, could mean nothing."

"Spalling on the concrete pad."

"Same."

"The damn bed frame was annealed."

Bentley puts a coffee mug in the box. "Jack, if you're saying this was a hot fire—okay, it was a hot fire. I'm telling you, there was a fuel load in that place could have burned Chicago. Now get out of here."

A couple of deputies standing at another desk look over.

"I found a pour pattern," Jack says.

"There was no pour pattern."

"You didn't do a dig-out."

"Didn't *need* to do a dig-out."

"The hell you *mean* you didn't *need* to do a dig-out?!"

The deputies are watching now. Ready to step in if this guy needs moving.

Bentley yells back, "The deceased was smoking in bed! The most common cause of fire fatality there is!"

"There was no smoke in her lungs!" Jack yells. "Less than 10 percent CO in her blood."

"She was *drinking*!" Bentley hollers. "She was bombed on booze and pills! She OD'd!"

"But first she went around the room pouring accelerants?" Jack asks. "Gives herself her own Viking funeral? Come on, Brian."

"The fuck you talking about, accelerants."

"I took debris samples, and they're going to come up positive—"

"Bullshit."

"—and I just want to give you a chance to back off your call first."

"Well, you're a hell of a guy, Jack," Bentley says. "But I'm not backing off shit. Now go back to cheating widows and orphans."

"You need to reopen—"

"You just can't stand being an insurance adjuster, can you?" Bentley says. "You still wanna be a cop. Well, you're not, Jack. They threw you out, remember?"

I remember, Jack thinks.

"Yeah," he says. "I remember you going belly-up on the stand."

Bentley grabs him by the shirt. Jack grabs back. The two deputies move in to separate them, so they have a real little scrum going when Letty comes around the corner.

"Jack, for Christ's sake—"

"Hey, Jack," Bentley says, "maybe you can *beat* a confession out of him."

"You don't do your job—"

"I told you not to dick around—"

"*Jack*—"

"—with shit you don't know any—"

"—you dumb, lazy—"

"Jack."

Letty takes him by the elbow and walks him up against the wall. "What are you doing?" she asks.

Jack takes a deep breath. "I came to try to get him to back off his report."

She gives him a quizzical look.

"The fire was an arson," he says.

"Oh, you two are together on this, huh?" Bentley says. "What are you, Jack, *doing* her again?"

Jack starts for him but Letty stands in his way.

"Let him go," Bentley says.

Letty says, "Like you want me to."

"And you was told to stay out of this, del Rio," Bentley says.

"She was my sister."

"She was stoned and drunk and she torched herself," Bentley says.

Jack says, "If you'd do your fucking job for once—"

"Get out of here!" Bentley yells. He's straightening out his shirt and patting his hair back into place.

"He's leaving," Letty says. She holds a hand up to the two deputies who are about to escort Jack from the building. She keeps her hand on his elbow as she walks him down the hall. They can both hear Bentley yelling, "You're an asshole, Jack!"

"He might have something there," Letty says.

"Probably."

"Probably," Letty chuckles. Then says, "Arson?"

"I won't be sure until the sample tests, but . . . ," Jack says. Then he asks, "Could Pam have done that, Letty? Could she have been so down she'd take herself out and the house along with her?"

"Pam would never have killed herself."

"How—"

"The kids," Letty says. "She never would have left the kids."

"She was very drunk."

Letty shakes her head. "He killed her, Jack."

"Letty . . ."

"He killed her," she says. Then, "You'd better get out of here."

He gets into his car and drives off. When she gets back into the office Bentley asks her, "So how's the old boyfriend?"

"Shut up, you dumb lazy fuck," Letty says.

46

Dinesh Adjati looks like Bambi.

Not the older Bambi, Jack thinks—the one who kicks the rival buck's ass at the end of the movie—but the *younger* Bambi, Thumper's little buddy.

Dinesh has these big, brown Bambi eyes and long eyelashes and he's slender and has brown skin. However, he also has a Ph.D. in chemical engineering, so to the extent that he resembles Bambi, he's *Doctor Bambi.*

Dinesh works for an outfit called Disaster Inc.

Disaster Inc. is the company you call when something goes very wrong.

You want to know why a train wreck happened, a bridge collapsed, a bus plunged into a river or a fire happened, you call Disaster Inc. Any catastrophe, they'll tell you why it happened.

Disaster Inc. gives its clients a Disaster of the Month calendar every year but Jack's never known anyone sick enough to actually have it on his wall. The calendar features slick Technicolor glossies of that month's featured disaster along with a daily chronicle of past human tragedies like "Hindenburg Explodes," "Chicago School Fire" and a mock-up of "Vesuvius Erupts," which Goddamn Billy amended to read "Vesuvius Erupts and Disaster Inc. Not There to Bill for It."

Disaster Inc. has done some very serious billing in the '90s because the decade has been chock-full of disasters. In California alone you had the '93 fires—Malibu, Laguna, Sherman Oaks—and the good citizens of those towns wanted to know what caused the fires to spread so quickly and burn down so many homes.

Then the Mother of All Disasters hit—the Northridge earthquake. It took thirty seconds of January 17, 1994, to drain a third of Cal Fire and Life's reserves and make the owners of Disaster Inc. rich men.

Dinesh got one whomper of a bonus, because he's the fire guy at Disaster and he billed a lot of hours figuring out the cause of fires that broke out in the aftermath of the quake. A lot of people didn't have earthquake insurance but they did have fire insurance, so a lot of buildings went up in spontaneous combustion that day.

Jack himself knew a lot of insurance claims guys who had figured out how to get total earthquake coverage for a buck sixty-five: you set a gallon of gas on top of your furnace and when the shaking starts—Abracadabra, KABOOM—earthquake coverage.

But most people hadn't figured that out and so were running around pouring accelerants all over their rubble and that's why Dinesh Adjati is twenty-eight years old and has a Porsche, a house in Laguna and a condo in Big Bear.

Jack loves Dinesh, though.

He loves Dinesh because Dr. Bambi works his ass off, gets it right and makes a wonderful witness. He just turns those fawn eyes on the jury and explains the most complicated chemical analyses to them in plain-old American English and they eat him with a spoon.

Anyway, Jack drives straight from the Vale house to Disaster's lab in Newport Beach overlooking the greenway.

He gets a Most Favored Client pass right into Dinesh's lab, where Dr. Bambi is wearing a flameproof smock and a masked helmet and appears to be torturing a pickup truck with a blowtorch.

Dinesh turns it off, flips up the mask and shakes Jack's hand.

"A libel suit against a TV show," he explains. "I'm working for the plaintiff."

Jack tells him that he has a trunk full of samples in the car.

"Can you run the samples for me?" he asks. "Double pronto?"

"Somebody wanted something to burn?"

"Some*one* to burn."

Dinesh makes a face. "No shit?"

"No shit."

"Nasty."

"I need it quick, Dinesh."

"Today?"

"Cool," Jack says. "And I might need you to testify down the road."

"Well," Dinesh says, "I have good news and bad news."

"Tell."

"The good news is that I can get it to you today," Dinesh says. "I'll have to put a crew of techs on it and bill you accordingly, but you'll get it today and you'll get it right."

"What's the bad news?"

"The bad news," Dinesh says, "is that I'm not completely confident that I can testify."

Say *what*?

"What do you mean?"

"I'm not completely confident," Dinesh repeats, "that a gas chromatograph—or even a GC with a mass spectrometer—can accurately determine traces of accelerants."

Jack feels the floor sinking under him.

"We've always used the GC–mass spec," he says. "What's wrong with it?"

"We live in a plastic society," Dinesh says. "In more than just the symbolic sense. The modern home is just chock-full of plastic products, every one of which—when they burn—produces thousands of chemicals that can be confused with hydrocarbons, with accelerants. For example, your basic GC–mass spec reveals about two hundred chemicals in kerosene."

"So?"

"So I've been working with something that shows two *thousand*."

"Two *thousand*?" Jack asks.

"Yeah," Dinesh says. "Let's say that's a little more effective at sorting out the chemical sheep from the chemical goats."

Jack asks, "More expensive?"

Dinesh smiles. "The only thing more expensive than good science is bad science. Let me just say that I don't think I could get up in front of a jury anymore and swear under oath to the absolute accuracy of a GC, even with a mass-spec chaser."

"And with your new process, you could."

"It's not new," Dinesh says. "I've been testing it for months. Something called a GC x GC. Or two-dimensional gas chromatograph, if you prefer. Maybe now is the time to trot it out."

"Do it."

"It's going to cost."

"How much?"

"Run you about another ten grand."

Do it anyway, Jack thinks. You don't want to get hit for a few million on a bad faith suit and then say, *Yeah, but I saved ten thou on the testing.*

"Do it," Jack says.

"This is why I've always loved you, Jack."

"Do it the old way," Jack says. "Then do it the new way. Do it till you're satisfied. But do it."

Whatever it is.

47

Letty's at the regular Thursday-afternoon south coast meeting of Alcoholics Anonymous, which because of its time and location is generally known by the sobriquet "Ladies Who (Drank) Lunch."

This is not the kind of meeting Letty's used to. She's used to night meetings in church basements, meetings with broken cookies and greasy coffee and stories about blowing the rent on beer and bourbon benders.

She's not used to a meeting in broad daylight in a "togetherness space" on a pier in a marina, but that's where the ladies go to share their experience, strength and hope and that's where Pam went to do it with them, and that's why Letty's there.

Thinking, *The ladies are gorgeous.* I mean for a bunch of drunks these babes are put together. Whatever boozy fat they put on in their sinful days these girls worked off on the treadmills and exercise bikes and spinners. Skin glowing with health, eyes bright, hair shiny, full and sexy. If AA ever wanted to do an infomercial, they'd shoot it at the regular Thursday-afternoon south coast meeting.

Even women who weren't alcoholics would go out and get hammered so they could come to the meetings and look like these ladies.

What twelve little steps and a few hundred thousand spare dollars can't do, Letty thinks.

Anyway, she's there, and the ladies aren't drinking greasy coffee—they're sipping Frappuccinos (decaf, low-fat milk) out of clear-plastic go-cups. There are a few guys there, not your nine-to-five types, but real estate brokers and insurance salesmen and other men who can take the middle of the afternoon off to share their experience, strength and hope and maybe get lucky, and as fortune and solid planning would have it there's a Holiday Inn within a hot five-minute walk of the meeting. There are so many pickups happening at this meeting that it could be called Ladies Who (Drank) Lunch and the Men Who Lust After Them, Letty thinks.

Quit being such a bitch, she tells herself.

It's not their fault they're rich and you're not.

They're gorgeous and you're not.

Get over it.

And get over Jack Wade. Twelve years is too long a time to be carrying a torch. Your arm gets tired. Twelve years and the son of a bitch never even called. Never would have called. You never would have seen him again if you didn't need his help, and you're such a bitch that you'd use him like that.

But the truth is she has been carrying a torch for twelve years. She's had a few boyfriends but nothing serious because in the back of her head—in the back of her soul—she's holding out for something she lost.

Jack.

Jack lost his soul and took yours with it.

So you're pushing forty and you have no husband and no kids and no life outside busting skells.

And it isn't these ladies' fault.

It's your own.

So get over it, girl.

So she sits and listens to the preamble and to the speaker and it's the same stuff everywhere: if you're a drunk you're a drunk; no matter what the view is, it turns to shit. She makes small talk with a couple of the ladies during the break, and when the meeting resumes and the chairperson asks if anyone wants to speak, Letty waits for a few people to talk about what's going on with them and then she raises her hand.

My name is Letty. Hi, Letty—blah, blah, blah . . .

"I'm here," she says, "to ask if any of you knew my sister Pam. She died three nights ago and they say she'd been drinking. She was about five-eight, black hair, purple eyes. I know she used to hit this meeting— I don't know what other meetings she used to go to but I'm hoping you can help me."

Amidst the *Oh my God*s and *Not Pam*s and a couple of sudden sobs, about five hands shoot up.

Turns out they can help her.

48

Pam was sober that night, Letty says.

She and Jack are sitting at an outside table at Pirets, beside the main entrance to South Coast Plaza.

"She was at a meeting that night," Letty says between sips of her iced tea. She picks up the glass and the paper napkin blows away in the hot, dry Santa Ana wind. "She was sober then. The meeting broke up at 9:30, then she went out for coffee. With eight other women. She was sober *then*."

"That doesn't mean," Jack says, "that she was sober at four the next morning."

Jack's drinking a Coke. The good folks at Pirets had to search long and hard to find a soda that didn't have the word Diet in front of it. They got it done, though.

"She told her AA friends she was scared," Letty says. "Scared that Nicky was going to kill her. They told her to call the cops. They begged her to stay with them; she said it would just postpone things."

Jack says, "So she went home and the fear and anxiety drove her to the bottle."

"After Nicky left, she didn't keep any booze in the house."

"She bought a bottle of vodka—"

"I checked every liquor store on her route home," Letty says. "I talked with everyone who worked that night. Nobody remembers her."

"You're good."

"I'm motivated."

"Forget about it," Jack says.

"Forget about what?" she asks.

She knows just what he's talking about.

"About getting custody of the kids," Jack says.

"If I get him convicted of murder . . ."

Jack shakes his head. "You're a long way from there. Say it *is* an arson—how did Pam die? Ng's got it as an OD. Say you can *make* the next step, say it's murder. You have nothing puts Nicky there. Say you somehow manage to cross *that* bridge—I don't know how, but say you do—say you get Nicky convicted of murdering Pam . . . Mother Russia is still the declared guardian. Mother gets the kids."

"She was in on it."

"She provided an alibi," Jack says.

"So they'll take the kids from her."

"No, they won't," Jack says. "Besides which, the murder conviction isn't going to happen. Even if you could develop enough information to embarrass Bentley into moving off his call, or enough that the Sheriff's would have to reopen. Or enough to get the DA interested."

It's a long shot. A long shot to get a criminal investigation, a longer shot to get them to charge, a regular NBA three-pointer to get a conviction, because the evidence is getting colder every day.

And Letty knows all this, she just doesn't want to *know* it yet.

No, Nicky and Mother Russia keep the kids.

Nicky gets away with murder.

"So what are you going to do?" Letty asks. "Drop it?"

"No," Jack says. "I'm going to do my job. I'm going to investigate the claim. I'm going to see if Nicky Vale had the motive and opportunity to set the fire and kill his wife. If I find sufficient evidence, I'll deny the claim."

"And that's it?"

"That's it."

"The worst that happens to Nicky is he doesn't get *paid* for killing her?"

"I'm sorry."

"But it works for you, huh, Jack? You don't care what happens to the kids. All you care about is that the claim doesn't get paid, right?"

"That's my job," Jack says.

It's not all I care about—it's all I can do.

Letty gets up, says, "Same old Jack."

"Same old Jack."

"Well, same-old Jack," she says. "I'd like to tell you to go to hell, but you're the only chance I have. If you deny the claim, maybe Nicky will sue you for bad faith. Then maybe there'll be a jury verdict that says that Nicky killed Pam. A family court judge would have to take 'judicial notice' of that verdict in a custody hearing."

"That's a *very* long shot."

"So do your job, Jack," she says.

Like he'd do anything else.

She tosses her napkin down on the table.

"And get a life," she says.

Right, Letty, Jack thinks. Tell me to get a life.

As you walk out, take it with you.

49

Dinesh Adjati takes one of Jack's samples, a small piece of charred wood, and scrapes a fragment into a glass flask. He adds 50 milliliters of pentane to the flask, then pours the whole mess through some filter paper into a clean flask.

The result is a clear liquid.

He repeats this procedure for all of Jack's samples, labeling and placing the flasks in a metal rack as he goes through them.

A robotic machine then caps each flask, inserts a syringe needle into each, withdraws a cubic millimeter of liquid and lines up the samples to go through the gas chromatograph.

One of the allegedly dirty samples goes through first.

The sample gets shot into an injection port which is pressurized at about 60 pounds per square inch of helium gas and heated to 275°C, which vaporizes the liquid. The helium chases the sample vapor into the core of the gas chromatograph.

This is a capillary tube, about 60 meters long and one-quarter of a millimeter in diameter. The inside of it is coated with methyl silicone, a thick viscous liquid. (Here's how Dinesh explains methyl silicone to juries. He says, "If you put methyl silicone in a jar, and tip the jar upside down, and come back a day later, perhaps half of the liquid will have flowed to the bottom of the jar. If you come back another day later, probably most of it will be at the bottom. That's how thick this stuff is.")

The capillary tube (a.k.a. the GC column) starts out at room temperature, so the sample condenses into a liquid again, but the column is gradually heated inside an oven that houses it to 200°C. The effect of all this is that the sample will gradually vaporize again and start a migration down the capillary tube.

Different chemicals make this trip at different speeds, separating from each other as a result. Some of the chemicals dissolve inside the silicone and take a long time to migrate down the tube. Other chemicals race through it lickety-split.

But, one after the other, the chemicals will emerge, each time registering a blip on the computer screen. The height of the blip indicates how much of that chemical is present. At the end of the process, you're looking at a forest of blips or peaks of various heights, which together form a recognizable pattern called the gas chromatogram.

The way Dinesh explains this concept to juries is to talk about cookie recipes. "Look," he'll say, "a recipe might call for a tablespoon of cinnamon and a teaspoon of sugar. That's the composition of that particular cookie dough, if you will—it has cinnamon and sugar in certain defined intensities. Gasoline, kerosene, napalm—any of the accelerants you're testing for—are like cookie dough in this respect: they're made of many different substances, each present in different amounts."

All the substances present in any given mixture will produce a unique and predictable gas chromatogram, a characteristic "signature" of a given mixture.

Dinesh watches as the samples start to sign in.

He starts getting a little ripple at around five minutes. At ten a modest peak. The trace drops way down, then gives him a little hill at twelve minutes. At fifteen the peak goes Himalayan. Shoots up like a rocket. Down again at fifteen minutes, ten seconds. Up again at seventeen. Big peak at eighteen, and then it starts to settle. Modest peaks at twenty, which gradually settle down. At about twenty-eight minutes it's flat again.

Dinesh watches this on a graph.

The sample signs in.

It signs in "Kerosene."

For his next magic trick, he'll analyze the sample through a gas chromatograph with a special instrument, a mass spectrometer, attached to the back.

What happens is that the gases flow out of the GC column into a vacuum port, which sucks them into the mass spectrometer. The mass spec is a steel cylinder about four inches in diameter and two feet long. It has a glass port so you can see inside the guts, which basically consist of vacuum devices, steel plates, cylinders, wires, ceramic tubes and turbopumps which are whirring at about 100,000 rpm.

In the center of all this is a glowing filament which bombards the chemical vapors with electrons, breaking them into electrically charged molecule-sized chunks, or ions. In a microsecond these ions are weighed; in a nanosecond they're counted.

The size and number of these ions produce a characteristic "fragment signature."

(Dinesh explains it to juries like this: "Suppose you throw a flowerpot on the sidewalk. It will shatter into random pieces. It will break into different sizes and different numbers of pieces every time. No two fragments will be alike. But a molecule is a different kind of flowerpot—one with predetermined grooves, if you will. Every time you shatter it, it will break into exactly the same size and number of fragments. Each substance has its own unique, predictable fragment signature.")

Now the computer automatically compares the fragment signatures against the NIST (National Institute of Standards) mass spectral library profiles of certain substances and comes up with a match.

Kerosene.

Which almost every analyst in the country would call a definitive match. Not Dinesh. Not with a GC–mass spec, not with all those plasticizers out there gumming up the works.

So Dinesh takes the samples and runs them through a GC x GC.

"Comprehensive two-dimensional gas chromatography" is the technical term. Dinesh doesn't think of it that way. He thinks of it as looking into chemical mixtures through a Hubble telescope.

It starts off simply enough. Dinesh runs the sample through a gas chromatograph. Same process: the samples are vaporized and shot through a capillary filled with methyl silicone, where they separate into about two hundred groups of chemicals.

Instead of stopping there, or running them through a mass spec, Dinesh shoots them through an interface device into a second gas chromatographic column. See, each peak comes out of the first column for about ten seconds. Every three seconds, a little heater inside the oven is mechanically rotated. It has a slot in it which rotates over the column. It locally heats the column, which drives all the chemicals in that area out. As soon as they get beyond that "hot zone," they come to the unheated "cold zone" and get sucked right back into the methyl silicone. This forms a sharp chemical pulse. This pulse is swept along a short length of column—about fifty millimeters—and eventually is launched down the tube by the heated zone into the second GC column.

Once again, they all travel down the tube and separate.

The trick is in the methyl silicone in the second column.

It's been doped.

Doped with chemicals that produce completely different separation criteria from the methyl silicone in the first column.

("There are three chemical separation mechanisms," Dinesh will tell a floundering jury. "Volatility, polarity and shape. Volatility is how much vapor pressure a substance puts out at a certain temperature—its boiling point, put simply. Polarity refers to the electric property of molecules. Shape is simple—it's the shape of the molecule, whether it's, say, shaped like a chain, or perhaps a closed loop.

"Now, the first GC column only separates by volatility. So two chemicals that have the same volatility will come out of the first column together—unseparated—even though they have different polarities and/or different shapes. But when they hit the doped methyl silicone in the second column, they encounter a chemical mechanism that they haven't seen before, and they separate.

"So: polarity is an electrical property of molecules. Electrostatically, the positive attracts the negative and vice versa. The molecules tend to hug each other. They can maintain this mutual affection through the first GC column, but when they hit the second . . . well, love does not conquer methyl silicone doped with chemicals that have electric charges on their surfaces, and they separate. Same with shape. Two very differently shaped molecules that have the same polarity but different shapes can travel down the first column disguised in happy unity as one. But when they hit the second column they will have a different reaction to the stationary phase—to the doped methyl silicone—and they'll separate.

"The performance then of one GC multiplies the other. They don't *add,* they multiply. So if the first can separate one hundred peaks and the second can separate thirty, then in combination they can separate not one hundred and thirty, but three thousand.")

The net result is that the chromatograms look like stalagmites rising up off a floor, instead of shark fins coming up off lines.

It's the difference between a graph and a kaleidoscope. Between a coloring book and a Matisse. Between, as Dinesh likes to think, the "Beer Barrel Polka" and a Charlie Parker solo. The GC x GC delivers a beautiful multicolored pattern, which will always be exactly the same—every time—for a given mixture. Every time you set the kaleidoscope at the setting marked "Kerosene," you'll get the same beautiful, complex pattern.

Like a signature in 3-D.

Like a fingerprint in Technicolor.

Only better.

And that's what Dinesh sees when he finishes running the first sample through the GC x GC. A two-thousand-piece jigsaw puzzle that portrays one image and one image only.

Kerosene.

Six hours later he and his crew have run all the samples.

The kaleidoscope is always the same.

Kerosene.

He calls Jack with the results.

50

Maybe the best view on the south coast is the one from the patio bar at Las Brisas, with its view of Laguna Bay and Laguna town stretched out beneath you like some old Mediterranean city with its white buildings and terra-cotta-tiled roofs. Especially at sunset, with the sky turning from blue to lavender and the red summer sun starting to kiss the ocean horizon.

"Thanks for coming," Nicky says. He tilts his vodka collins in a salute to Jack.

"Thanks for the drink," says Jack, raising his beer bottle.

Nicky says, "Well, I wanted to thank you for intervening in that ugly situation in the church the other day."

"No," Jack says, "you wanted to find out what Letitia del Rio told me."

Nicky smiles. "That, too."

"She told me some disturbing things."

"No doubt she did," Nicky says. "I am sure that she concocted some wild and wonderful tales for you. I imagine at times she even believes them herself. Letty is a sick woman."

"Yeah?"

"Well, they came from the same dysfunctional family, didn't they."

"Letty says that Pam went to rehab."

"Yes." Nicky laughs. "Would you like to see *those* bills?"

"And?"

"She stayed sober for about two weeks afterwards, I think," Nicky says. "*Not* a bargain."

They sit and drink and watch the progress of the sunset, a spectacular Southern Californian light show gone from lavender to purple as the sky turns into a violent red.

"This might be Paradise," Nicky sighs. Then he says, "Think about this, Jack. The next beneficiary on the life insurance policy after me is Letty, in trust for the children, of course. It would be in her interest to make up stories, wouldn't it?"

Jack watches the bottom of the sun melt into the ocean.

"You know what I think?" Jack asks. He takes a long belt of his beer.

"I wouldn't presume to guess, Jack."

Easy, relaxed, maximum cool.

"What I think," Jack says, "I think that you killed your wife and burned the house down around her. That's what I think."

Grinning at Nicky, who turns pale.

Nicky stares at him for a long moment, then forces his face into a condescending smile. Looks Jack square in the eyes.

Says, "Prove it."

Jack says, "I will."

Behind Nicky the sun, the sky and the ocean are on fire.

This beautiful inferno, Jack thinks.

This drop-dead gorgeous hell.

51

Here's the story on Nicky Vale.

Daziatnik Valeshin grows up in Leningrad, his father a minor apparatchik, his mother a teacher at the state gymnasium. She feels that she has fallen in the world—both her parents were professors and she did brilliantly at university. Were it not for one foolish, unguarded night she would doubtless have become a professor as well. But then, she had a child to raise—alone—as Daz's father splits early, a divorce while young Daz is still in the crawling phase.

Mother he sees.

Constantly, oppressively.

She's raising him to be something, most decidedly *not* a minor apparatchik. They go meatless for weeks to afford ballet tickets, the soup is thinned yet again for a Tchaikovsky recording. At a precocious age he reads his Tolstoy, of course, and Pushkin and Turgenev, and at bedtime she sits and reads Flaubert to him—in French. Not that he understands French, but it is Mother's firm belief that he will somehow absorb the meaning through the rhythm and tone.

Mother teaches him to appreciate the finer things—art, music, sculpture, architecture and design. She teaches him manners—at the table, in conversation, with a woman. They sit and practice an evening out at a fine restaurant—sitting at the fold-up table in their cramped kitchen, she takes him through the various courses and scolds him into making conversation as if she were the young lady and he were the suitor.

She's as brutal about his grades as she is his manners. Nothing but a "first" will do. The moment he comes home she sits him down in front of his books, then has him review his work for her.

It must be perfect.

Otherwise, she tells him, you will end up like the rest of the proletariat, like your father. Stupid, unhappy, bored and with no future but to be stupid, unhappy and bored.

When he gets to the age where he's interested in girls, she chooses them for him. Or more often chooses against them for him. This one is too silly, that one too fat, this one too clever, that one a slut.

Daz knows that her standards are high because she herself is so beautiful. Her face is perfectly formed porcelain, her hair a black-satin sculpture, her neck so long and elegant and white, her manners refined, her intelligence sparkling . . . How Father could leave her he cannot understand.

And he obeys her. He is first in most of his classes. He wins the prize in English, in history, in literature, in math. Not only that, he's a sneaky, mean, underhanded, intimidating little bastard, so he catches the attention of the local talent spotters from the old state security bureau.

And the bit about Afghanistan is true, except Daz doesn't go as some slog-ass foot soldier, a reluctant warrior in someone else's war. Daz goes as a KGB officer attached to a military intelligence unit, his job to interrogate the villagers to find where the *mujahedin* are hiding.

For the first few weeks Daz goes about this job in a civilized way, even though that gets him nowhere. However, after he has found out about the third Russian soldier lying naked, skinned alive with his genitals stuffed in his mouth, Daz takes a different approach. His best routine is to have three villagers trussed up like hogs, cut two of their throats and then offer the blood-spattered survivor a cup of tea and a chance for meaningful conversation. If his hospitality is spurned, Daz usually orders an enlisted man to douse the holy warrior with petrol. Then when Daz is done with his tea he lights a cigarette and tosses the match and warms his hands on the blazing fire. Then he has his unit torch the whole village.

Waits a day or so for word of the incident to filter to the next village and then goes *there* to ask questions. Usually gets some answers.

All the time, Mother is frantic, sick with worry that her son will be killed in this stupid, futile war. She writes him every day and he writes back, but the Soviet mail system being what it is, there are brutal, endless days of no mail when she is convinced that he is dead. The next day's mail brings a letter, and with it, a torrent of tears of relief.

Daz finishes his tour.

Spends his leave with Mother in a state dacha on the Black Sea, his reward for a good war. There they go out for an evening to a fine restaurant on the shore. A table on the veranda, and the moon sparkles on the water. They have an eight-course meal and the conversation sparkles like the water.

Back in the dacha that night she tutors him how to be with a woman.

He needs an assignment and the KGB has one for him.

Back in Moscow his handler, a KGB colonel named Karpotsov, takes him on a stroll through Gorky Park. Karpotsov is quite a number, with a broad Slavic face, silver hair greased straight back on his head, an easy way with the vodka and an easier way with women. A real charmer, Karpotsov is, a word painter, and he works his brush on Daz.

Karpotsov knows talent when he sees it and he sees it in young Valeshin. Valeshin is a ruthless, sociopathic, *smart* little wiseass who would probably torch his own mother, if that's what it took, and that's just the kind of sociopath Karpotsov's looking for. So he walks Daz around the park for a while, looking at women and talking about nothing of any great importance, and then Karpotsov buys two ice creams and sits Daz down on a bench.

And says, "How would you like to go to America?"

He sticks out his broad tongue and takes a lick of the ice cream that is almost obscene. Smiles a Mephistophelian smile.

"I think I would like that very much," Daz says.

Having just been offered a chance at heaven.

"The United States," Karpotsov says—he continues the lecture between licks of ice cream—"is waging economic warfare against the Soviet Union. Reagan knows—and we know—that we can't compete. We can't continue to build missiles and submarines at this pace and still maintain the economy required for a workers' paradise. The ugly truth, Daz, is that they can win the cold war simply by outspending us."

He stops and stares off at the park as if at any moment it is going to disappear along with the Soviet way of life.

He collects himself and continues, "We need cash—hard currency—and the Soviet economy is incapable of generating any. It is simply not to be found here."

"Then where?"

"America," Karpotsov says. "Our expatriate Russian criminals in New York and California are sucking dollars out of the American system like milk from a cow. These are gangsters, mind you, and we have to believe that if common criminals can do this, well . . ."

What could a cadre of KGB-trained agents do?

"It's a brilliant idea, really," Karpotsov says. And it should be—he thought of it. "It has a double benefit—it takes from them and gives to us. Every dollar we make is a dollar they lose. Where better to attack a capitalist system than at its capital?"

"So my assignment would be in the realm of economic sabotage."

"That's one way of putting it," Karpotsov says. "Another would be to say that your assignment is to steal. And steal, and steal."

Daz cannot believe his ears. He's frozen his ass off in that Afghanistan moonscape, and winter is coming so he'll be freezing his ass off in a Soviet Union that is clearly headed down the drain and the *best* he can hope for is sharing a one-bedroom with Mother forever, and maybe one week a summer at a dacha on the Black Sea, and part of him knows, *I must get away from her and this is my chance,* and the other part screams, This is my chance to give her the life she deserves, and now they offer him a transfer to America for the expressed purpose of making a fortune.

So what's the catch?

"Of course you'll have to become a Jew," Karpotsov says.

"A Jew?" Daz asks. "Why a Jew?"

"How else can we get you in?" Karpotsov asks. "Christ, the Americans are always screaming at us—'Release some Jews, release some Jews.' Fine, we'll release some Jews, along with them a few of our agents trained in—how did you put it—economic sabotage."

"But to become a Jew . . ."

"It's a sacrifice, I understand," Karpotsov says. "Perhaps too great a sacrifice to ask . . ."

"No, no, no, no," Daz says quickly. For a heart-stopping second he sees his chance slipping away. "No, of course I accept the assignment."

Karpotsov finishes his ice cream and grins.

"Mazel tov," he says.

So Daz goes to "Jew school."

This is a little course the KGB sets up where Jewish prisoners teach the Torah, the Diaspora, the Holocaust and the whole catalog of Russian outrages against the Jews. Daz studies Zionist history, the history of Israel, Jewish culture and tradition. Jewish artists, writers, composers.

For graduation they do a Passover seder.

And Daziatnik's like, Done that. Hand me my airline ticket.

But Karpotsov is like, Not so fast, Jewboy—first there's a little matter of prison.

"Prison?" Daziatnik asks. "You didn't say anything about prison."

"Well, I'm saying it now," Karpotsov tells him on another stroll through the park. "Daz, we need you to infiltrate the mob, the *Organizatsiya. They're* the people who are sucking the money out of the States. Without being a member, you'd frankly be quite useless. And sadly, the qualification for membership is a stay in the system. To establish your *bona fides,* as it were."

Daz is furious, at Karpotsov and at himself, because he has let the man lure him into a trap, step by step.

"Can't you just create a criminal record for me?" Daz asks.

"We will," Karpotsov says. "But that by itself woudn't be safe for you. No, there is knowledge and experience—and connections—that you can only get in prison."

"How much time?" Daz asks.

"Not a *long* stretch," Karpotsov says. "Eighteen months or so for petty theft. I could *order* you, but I don't want to do that."

Daz's mind is reeling. *A year and a half in prison?*

"I don't know, Colonel . . ."

"And who knows?" Karpotsov asks. "Perhaps we could arrange exit papers for your mother?"

Karpotsov is a slick piece of shit. Like every other piece of shit who handles agents, he knows exactly what buttons can be pushed, and when to push them.

Daz says, "How bad could a few months in jail be?"

Uh-huh.

52

Daz is in the system for maybe ten minutes before a huge old *zek* called Old Tillanin jams him into the corner, shoves the sharp point of a shiv against his ribs and by way of foreplay demands his blanket and his next meal.

Daz is in the system for maybe ten minutes and .00025 seconds before he jams a finger strike into Old Tillanin's left eyeball, which hits the filthy concrete floor about one full second before Old Tillanin does.

He's rolling around, howling in pain, trying to reach out and grab his eyeball before someone in the crowded cell steps on it. As if they're going to send a team of crack surgeons to reattach it.

Daz is in the far corner of the cell before the guards can get over to see who performed the eyeballectomy, and most of the other *zeks* only get from hearsay that it's the new guy, Daz.

Two *zeks* actually witness the action, though. One is a barrel-shaped mugger from Moscow named Lev, the other a tall skinny extortionist from Odessa named Dani, and they're pretty impressed that a new *zek* is either brave enough or stupid enough to take on Old Tillanin, who is the King of the Heap in this cell.

The word on Lev is that he has a way with a chain saw that you don't want to see up close. Lev has a reputation for his skill at performing the "chicken chop," which is *Organizatsiya's* favored method of execution and is just what it sounds like: not to put too fine a point on it, they take a chain saw and cut you into parts. And this is Lev's hobby. He likes it.

The story on Dani is that back in Odessa his own brother ratted some guys out to the cops, and the local mob boss—the *pakhan*— wanted to job out the hit but Dani said no sweat, I'll do him myself.

Dani gutshot *his own brother.*

Dani is such a mean fucker he's doing guys in prison. The guards come in in the morning and one or two *zeks* are tapped out, their necks snapped or their intestines lying on the floor and Dani's standing there with his bowl waiting for his breakfast gruel.

Dani is cold.

When Lev and Dani see the new *zek* take out Old Tillanin like that, they mark him as a guy to, well, keep an eye on.

Anyway, one of the guards asks who did it. He's no more expecting an answer than he's expecting fucking Princess Anastasia to descend through the ceiling on a trapeze, and he's dead right about that because even Old Tillanin keeps his mouth shut.

So the guard grabs up Dani, figuring that mean little fuck had to have a hand in any piece of violent nastiness in the cell, and he's hauling him out into the corridor to give him a going-over with the baton when this new *zek*—a petty thief from Leningrad named Valeshin—yells, "I did."

"What?" the guard asks.

"I did it."

Which is just about the stupidest thing the guard ever saw any *zek* do in a population that is already subpar in the intelligence quotient. The guard is so annoyed by this honor-among-thieves bit that he takes a belt and straps this Valeshin moron to the top of the cell door and whales at him with a piece of rubber hose until the dumb-fuck dickhead passes out. The guard gives him a few more shots to the ribs for good measure, unties him and kicks him back into the cell, there being no point in taking him to the infirmary because (a) they don't have any doctors there, and (b) Old Tillanin's comrades are just going to kill him anyway.

Which is true. Daz is lying unconscious in the cell, and what three of Old Tillanin's buddies are waiting for is a little decent cover of darkness so they can hack him to death before he can wake up and do that finger strike number on one of *them.*

Small chance of that. Even if he were conscious, Daz couldn't lift his hands past his bruised ribs, and even if he could it would have the force of a noodle, so Daz is pretty much on the short-stay program. If he doesn't die of the beating—a very real possibility—Old Tillanin's friends are going to kill him. And if they don't get him, prison life will, because he'll be too weak for the foreseeable future to fight for his food, or his blanket—which, in fact, has already been snatched up—or for his own body, for that matter.

He'll freeze, starve and get raped to death, and that's only if he makes it through the night.

When he comes to, he's wrapped in two blankets, his head in Dani's lap. He can feel the tightness of bandages around his wounded ribs, and a few minutes later Dani, tender as a Madonna, coaxes some tea down his throat. Where he got the wrappings, tea and hot water Daz will never know. What he does know is that Dani and Lev spend the next three weeks nursing him back to a condition where he has a chance to survive.

Which also means guarding him around the clock.

Daz doesn't know it at the time, but Old Tillanin's comrades make three attempts on him. Three stabs at it, if you will. The first comes as Dani and Lev drag Daz into their corner of the cell and wrap him up in Dani's blanket.

"If you want him, Jewboy," one of Old Tillanin's crew warns, "you take all of him."

Meaning the obligations that Daz has accrued in wounding Old Tillanin.

"That's fine," Lev says.

He head-butts the guy, smashing his nose, then shoves the guy's face down as he brings his own knee up. Which ends the first attack.

The second comes later in the night when it looks as if Dani and Lev are asleep. Turns out they're not, when Dani swipes his knife across the stomach of the lead attacker, giving him a deep wound that will get infected and turn fatal some six endless weeks down the line because he doesn't have the price of a simple antibiotic that is for cash only at the infirmary.

The third attack comes in that deadly hour before dawn (you can't say sunrise—the sun doesn't rise on this windowless basement hole), and this time it's four of Old Tillanin's gang at once. Lev and Dani shove Daz into the corner and just stand there and fight it out in front of him, using the corner walls to narrow the lane of attack that they have to defend.

The first attacker lunges with a knife, but he isn't quick enough and Dani grabs his arm and snaps it at the elbow, producing a sound like a tree branch breaking in the winter cold. Lev takes the second guy, who's rushing him, and smashes him into the wall, using his own huge right hand to keep banging the guy's head against the wall while with his left he jabs at the third attacker with his shiv. Dani drops down and shoves his knife upward into the fourth guy's crotch, but Lev's about to get done by number three, who's reaching down into his shoe for his own shiv and is about to swing it up into Lev's ribs, when somehow Daz grabs the guy's hand and holds on for dear life.

Or *Lev's* dear life, but anyway, Daz has crawled between Lev's legs and holds the shiv against the guy's ankle, then bites the guy's hand and won't let go with his hands *or* his teeth even though his ribs are screaming and he's bleeding inside.

Finally Lev drops guy number two and raises his own hands like a club above his own head and brings them down on the third guy's neck and Daz suddenly feels the life go out of the man.

Which it has, because his neck is broken when the guards find the body in the morning.

Anyway, the guy is dead and his blanket is now wrapped around Daz, and when Old Tillanin returns from the infirmary things have changed. He finds this out his first night back when his dreams are broken by a sharp pain in the chest which he at first attributes to a heart attack, which is not entirely mistaken, seeing as how there's a sharpened spoon buried in his chest.

Planted there by one of his own guys, because Old Tillanin isn't the King of the Heap anymore.

That would be Daziatnik Valeshin, but he doesn't get to ascend to the throne right away, because when the guards come in and find Old Tillanin prepped for the dirt nap, they reasonably conclude that Valeshin was just finishing the job he had started and haul him away. Old Tillanin, after all, had kicked in cash and goodies to the guards, so they at least have to make a pretense at investigating his death in case one of his henchmen becomes the new top dog.

So they strip Daz—still sick and hurting from his beating—and toss him naked into a cold isolation cell and he spends the next two weeks freezing and starving, sitting in his own shit and piss, but he doesn't talk. He'll freeze and starve to death but he's keeping his mouth shut.

About all that keeps him going is the fantasy.

America.

Specifically, California.

You're KGB you're privy to a few things—television, movies, magazines—so Daz has seen images of California. Seen the beaches and the sunshine and the palm trees. The sailboats, the surfers, the beautiful girls all but naked, lying in the sun as if they wish to be taken right there and then. He's seen the sports cars, the highways, the homes, and it's these images that keep him going.

Two weeks later the guards decide that they've made their gesture and haul him out. Blind as a mole, naked and shivering, he limps back to the cell.

Which is something of an improvement except his guard, a nasty piece of work from outside Gorky, tells him that he's just going to beat him to death anyway, slowly, on a daily basis.

"There is only one way to stop it," Dani tells him. "You must show him that you can endure more pain than he can give out."

Dani tells him of the old days of *Organizatsiya,* back in Czarist days when it was known as *Vorovskoy Mir*—the World of Thieves. In those days, Dani tells him, the convicts were really tough. Knowing they had no recourse to revenge against the guards, their only choice was to intimidate them not through acts of aggression but through acts of endurance.

"They showed the guards that they could inflict more damage on themselves than the guards could inflict on them," Dani says.

It makes a certain sense to Daz. In a country of such long and deep suffering, endurance is the ultimate power.

Dani tells him stories of convicts who ran knives down their own faces, who sewed their own eyelids shut, stitched their own lips together, to intimidate the guards out of beating them. There is even a story about one spectacularly tough convict who nailed his scrotum to a workbench and waited for the guard to arrive.

The guard was impressed.

Dani tells Daz these stories and then he and Lev sit back to watch.

Daz waits for the guard to come on shift. He borrows a nail and a cell-made "hammer" and sits on the end of the bench by the cell door. When the guard comes to give him his beating, Daz stares at him, takes a deep breath and drives the nail through his hand between the index finger and thumb and into the bench.

Sits there sweating, jaws clenched, staring at the guard.

That night Lev and Dani initiate him into the *Vory v Zakone.*

The Brotherhood of Thieves.

53

Not that there's one Brotherhood of Thieves.

In Russia there are about five thousand—maybe three hundred of which are serious players—but the one that Lev and Dani belong to is as good as any, and they all subscribe to the same basic code of conduct—the *Vorovskoy Zakon*.

Vorovskoy Zakon—the Code of Thieves—makes most of the usual demands you'd expect of a criminal code. It has the Russian version of *omerta*—you keep your mouth shut, you never help the authorities, you never ever rat on another thief—and it has a Mafia-like provision that allows a panel of brothers to convene to settle disputes and punish, if need be, the transgressor.

But it also has a couple of unique features. One is a sort of Catholic priest deal because, strictly speaking, the code forbids marriage. You can have girlfriends, boyfriends and pets. You can date barnyard animals if you want, but if it turns out to be a love connection, you can't marry one.

Then there's an almost Jesuit-like commandment that demands a purity of effort, a single-minded devotion to crime, because the *Vorovskoy Zakon* forbids a member from making an honest living.

These are the points that Dani and Lev instruct Daz in as they tend to his wounds and give him two new ones. One is a jailhouse tattoo behind the left knee. Using a pin, some ink and some smuggled grain alcohol, Lev carefully etches two attached crosses with Stars of David hanging from the crosspieces.

The rationale of the Two Crosses gang being that while Christ was the headliner on that Friday in Jerusalem, there were two nameless *zeks* stuck up beside him, both Jewish thieves.

Then they cut his wrist, likewise open up old scars on their own wrists and touch them together as Daz recites, "I will obey the demands of the *Vorovskoy Zakon:* I will help other thieves whenever possible. I will always come to the aid of my brothers, I will never betray my brothers, I will submit myself to the authority of my older brothers, I will submit all disputes to a convocation of my brothers and abide by its decision, I will carry out the punishment of transgressors if my brothers ask me to do so, I will never cooperate with authorities . . ."

Somewhat melodramatic, Daz thinks, but whatever it takes.

"I will forsake my own family," Dani intones, "I will have no family but the Two Crosses . . ."

Daz balks.

Dani repeats, "I will forsake my own family. I will have no family but the Two Crosses . . ."

Forgive me, Mother, Daz says to himself. I will make it up to you someday.

"I will forsake my own family. I will have no family but the Two Crosses . . ."

"If I transgress against *Vorovskoy Zakon,* may I burn in hell."

For the rest of his stretch no one lays a hand on him. Having kicked Old Tillanin off the top the heap, Daz is firmly entrenched in his place, especially with Dani and Lev as his bodyguards. There's not a *zek* in the cell that wants to take this trio on, knowing that (a) you are far less likely to kill than to be killed, and (b) even if you should incredibly luck out somehow and take out all three of them, you'll eventually have to deal with the three hundred Two Crosses gang members who will either find a way to whack you in prison or whack you the second you step out into the sweet, brief sunshine of freedom.

It's just not something that anyone with *any* brains wants to fuck with.

So Daz gets some breathing room.

A little living space.

And living large by Russian prison standards.

Gets himself a little extra gruel, an extra blanket, the odd cigarette, a little homemade vodka brewed from potato skins in a back room distillery. He's even offered the exclusive use of one of the prison fags, who with a little makeup in dim light bears a passing resemblance to something female.

Daz is like, *Thanks but no thanks* on this. Figures that for eighteen months he can keep his sexuality and self-respect inside and intact. Saves himself for one of his fantasy I-wish-they-all-could-be-California-girls. So he takes a pass on the surrogate and soothes his frustrations with the cigs, vodkas and other little perks he gets from being connected and the King of the Heap.

Daz sees *zeks* drop from exhaustion and just lie there. Just left to lie there and die, and he's seen *zeks* drop and the guards beat them half to death and then leave them for the weather to finish off.

Daz sees this and swears it's never going to happen to him. Not to him or to Dani or Lev, because they *are* brothers and if one drops the others will pick him up. And if the guards don't like it, fuck the guards—they'll have to kill us all before they kill one of us.

But Daz isn't thinking about dying.

He's thinking about living, and he keeps Dani and Lev thinking that way too. Daz knows it's not just your body you have to keep alive—you have to keep your head and your soul alive, too. So at night he tells them stories. Stories from the films and magazines he's seen. Stories about eternal sunshine and fast cars and beautiful homes and even more beautiful women.

I will take you to a new life, he whispers to them.

I promise you, my brothers . . .

You will join me in Paradise.

54

The scene with Mother is pure hell.

Daz finishes his stretch and applies for an exit visa, which Karpotsov shoots through like a bullet. There's no stroll in the park this time—the two men don't meet at all. Those days are over—it just wouldn't do for Daz to be seen with a KGB colonel. Could cause the Two Crosses to have him chopped like a chicken. So Daz gets his instructions through dead drops and the orders are clear: Go forth and prosper, go forth and steal. Here's where and how you send the money.

Now go make.

Mother watches Daz pack his few belongings.

She screams and cries, she wails, she holds him pressed against her, she whimpers, "You said you would take me."

"I can't. Not yet."

"Why not?"

He can't tell her. That he is a sworn member of the Two Crosses. That they would kill him for transgressing the code. Or uncover him as a fraud, and either way he is dead and so is the dream of America.

So he just repeats, "I'm sorry. I can't just now."

"You don't love me."

"I do love you."

She lays her neck against his.

"How can you leave me?"

"I will send for you."

"Liar."

"I will."

"Liar. Ingrate."

She throws herself on the couch and sobs. Refuses to look at him as he tries to say goodbye. The last he remembers of her is her white neck stretched out on a small black pillow.

Then Palm trees.

Daz spots them from the plane as it comes down at LAX and thinks, *This is it.*

California.

He steps out of the terminal onto the baked concrete of the sidewalk and into a phone booth. He has the number of Tiv Lerner, a "brigadier" in the U.S.A. (West Coast) franchise of the Two Crosses, and he has references, and twenty-five minutes later a taxi drops him off at Lerner's home in L.A.'s Fairfax district.

Lerner sits Daz down in the tacky living room of his tacky house and over shots of vodka explains that the organization is set up just like in the old country: The *pakhan* rules over four separate subgangs run by brigadiers. The subgangs are broken down into "cells" which operate various scams like loan-sharking, extortion, fraud and just plain theft. Each cell has a number of street operators who do the actual crimes. In addition to the "brigades," the *pakhan* has an élite group of advisers who help him rule, and a separate "security cell" made up of the heaviest hitters to protect him.

"You'll start at the bottom," Lerner says, "and work your way up. The American way."

"Sure," Daz says.

"I'm your brigadier," Lerner tells him. "You'll go to Tratchev's cell."

"What does it do?"

"Theft," Lerner says. "You steal. Half of what you earn goes to Tratchev. Ten percent goes into the *obochek.*"

The Russians are like Mormons in this sense: they tithe. Ten percent of their earnings goes into the *obochek,* the fund that every *pakhan* maintains as a pool for bribes and payouts. Technically it's not his money, it belongs to the gang—it's there for the gang's safety and welfare. It's there to pay off cops, lawyers, judges, politicians—whoever needs to be greased. The *obochek* is an inviolable fund—the holy of holies—because without the *obochek* the gang's financial welfare and physical safety can't be maintained. The gang would be left floating without a life raft in a hostile sea.

So Daz doesn't mind kicking in to the *obochek*, but this 50 percent to Tratchev . . . well, that ain't gonna last for long. Daz knows that a big chunk of that gets booted up to Lerner and then to the *pakhan* and that's where the serious money is. Ronald Reagan notwithstanding, the cash doesn't trickle down, it pours up, and that's where Daz intends to be.

"Who's our *pakhan*?" he asks.

Lerner smiles. "You don't need to know that."

Daz nods, but he's thinking, I *do* know that, you arrogant cock-sucker. Colonel Karpotsov—speaking of arrogant cocksuckers—ran it all down: the *pakhan* out here is Natan Shakalin, one of the original émigrés.

Daz has seen the whole file—Shakalin's photo, criminal record, the whole bit.

Lerner laughs and says, "Maybe when you're a brigadier you'll meet the *pakhan*."

Which is going to be sooner than you know, Daz thinks.

Now that he's on the Main Chance.

Next afternoon he starts as a limo driver in Lerner's fleet, making runs back and forth from the airport. Daz says something like, "Hold on, didn't I take an oath not to do legit work?" To which Lerner answers, "Grow up, kid."

The gig is that Daz picks up businessmen at their homes and chats them up on the way to the airport. Finds out if they're single, or living alone, or if they have a family, what the family's schedule is. Then he tries to book a round-trip ("When are you coming back, mister? I can pick you up. Be there when you step off the plane, guaranteed"). Also guaranteed that now he knows the businessman's address and when the house will be empty and he gives that info to one of Lerner's stooges and, go figure, the businessman's house gets robbed.

And they toss Daz a cut of the take.

Daz does this for a couple of months but knows that his cut from some cheap B&Es is going to neither destabilize the American economy nor make him rich, so he talks Lerner into letting him go on some car boosts. Daz spends his days driving to and from the airport and his nights boosting Mercedes and Beemers. After a couple of years old Lerner lets him buy in and Daziatnik gets his own chop shop. Cuts up the Mercedes and Beemers and ships the parts back to Russia, where the KGB provides the market outreach and the protection.

Daz is starting to make some good jack doing this, but his real genius shines when he figures out that you can sell the same car twice: once to the parts buyers and once to the insurance company. Just prearrange the theft with an owner who is behind on his payments. The owner parks the car at a ball game, an amusement park, a concert, and when he comes out—surprise—it's gone. The car is chopped up within hours. Shipped abroad within days. The owner gets out from under. Daziatnik takes a commission from the insurance settlement and the price of the parts.

He kicks money to Tratchev, who kicks it to Lerner, who kicks it to Shakalin.

Daz brings in the bucks and gets rewarded with his own unit in Lerner's brigade, which pisses Tratchev off. But Daz isn't through.

Because it's a simple step from car theft fraud to car accident fraud.

Daz nicknames the collective insurance industry "the Big Cow," because you just keep milking it and milking it and milking it . . .

So many nipples from which to suck.

Daz becomes the impresario of staged accidents.

Learns that soft tissue injuries mean hard cash from phony medical bills and accident settlements. Learns how easy it is to buy a doctor, a chiropractor, a lawyer, a judge. Suck on the Big Cow for workmen's comp, pain and suffering compensation ("I hope you got insurance, man") and medical bills: tests, physical therapy, consultations, chiropractic visits. The doctors bill the insurance company and then kick a cut back to Daz in cash.

Then Daz takes the next logical step.

He figures out that you can make even *more* money if the treatments, therapy and consultations never even happen. You just have the doctor sign the documents. The doctors bill the insurance company and then kick a bigger cut back to Daz.

Daz in turn kicks to Lerner, who kicks to Shakalin. Daz also kicks back to Karpotsov, so the KGB is finally getting a taste from the dairy. All this kicking means that Daz is basically drawing the salary of a KGB major (having been promoted in absentia), but that's okay with him on the short term.

On the longer term he has different plans. See, now that he has two of his own cells—car theft and insurance fraud—he's bringing in serious money. But no matter how much he sends home it isn't enough. Karpotsov is back in the old country, where the economy is going downhill in a barrel, so Karpotsov is always sending messages, the main thrust of which is *more more more*. It's like Daz has to make more jack so the KGB can afford *paper clips,* so both he and Karpotsov are sick of having Lerner—never mind Shakalin—as a partner.

Karpotsov is really putting the pressure on him, so Daz comes up with a new plan.

Which he doesn't share with Lerner.

Daz is messing around with serious trouble because what he does is he goes outside the Two Crosses gang and contacts the Armenians. The Armenians are the biggest gang in California. They're all over Hollywood and Glendale, shaking down Armenian merchants, loan-sharking Armenian immigrants, forcing legit Armenians into stealing their own merchandise and turning in insurance claims. Daz has his ear to the ground and knows that you have the same Armenian carpets being "stolen" five, six, seven times all over the west, so he has a sense that the Armenians might be receptive to an insurance scam.

So he sets up a meeting where Daz basically says, *Why are we busting our humps with this little shit? A piece here, a piece there? A car, a carpet, a whiplash? If we work together, we can take down the big chunks. We can hit the Main Chance.*

He and Kazzy Azmekian sit outside at a restaurant on Sunset, speaking Russian, and Daz has come there alone. If Azmekian would rather whack him than do business there's nothing Daz can do about it and they both know, so the other thing that Azmekian knows is that the young Jew has big league balls. Kaz is drinking his coffee, looking at this newcomer and debating whether to snatch him and sell him back to Lerner, or kill him, or listen to him.

Azmekian says, "What do you have in mind?"

Arson.

Is what Daz has in mind.

Buy a warehouse, fill it with overstock, burn it, collect the insurance money.

Azmekian's response is a bored *Been there, done that,* and he's seriously rethinking the kidnap option, except he's not sure he wants to start a war with the Jews right now. The problem with this kid's plan is that it's not a big monkeymaker, because you only gain on the inventory. The fire insurance just pays the value of the building, so you only break even on that.

So Azmekian gestures the waiter "Check, please" as Daz starts to explain what's nifty about his take on this old scam.

"We set up investment companies," Daz says. "Put them in other people's names so they can't be traced. My company buys a warehouse cheap. You buy it for more. Another one of my companies buys it from you. So on and so forth until the value of the building is inflated. Then you fill it with overstock, there's a fire, and we split the profits on the overstock *and* the profit on the building."

"More coffee," Azmekian tells the waiter. Then to Daz, "Why come to me? Why not your own people?"

"Too inbred," Daz says. "Too easy to track."

Plus, I don't want to. I want to make the hit and present it as a fait accompli. And we do it outside L.A., Daz says. We break new ground. And we farm the arson out beyond our own organizations. So there are no connections. No traces.

Azmekian's into it.

He and Daz set up their dummy companies and get ready to go.

First building they buy is the Atlas Warehouse.

There are a few bumps in the fast lane: a security guard dies in the fire, and then it turns out that there's a witness, and the fire inspectors call it an arson and the insurance company denies the claim. But the bumps get smoothed out and Kazzy Azmekian gets an unexpected bonus when he settles his bad faith suit, and now that they know where the potential problems are they won't make *those* mistakes again.

And Daz, he takes in a cool $200,000.

Which he doesn't share with Lerner.

Lerner gets word of it—Daz makes sure he gets word of it—and Lerner screams, *Where is my fucking cut?* and Daz pulls the *Vorovskoy Zakon* on him.

"If you have a grievance," he tells Lerner, "call a convocation. Take it to the *pakhan*."

Lerner would whack him right there on the spot, except that this Valeshin piece of shit is a brother, so he needs permission. Lerner goes before the *pakhan* and the other brigadiers.

Whines like a stuck pig to old Natan Shakalin. Valeshin went outside the organization. Valeshin went to the Armenians. Valeshin set up his own operation. Most of all, Valeshin made a bundle and didn't give me any.

Shakalin listens to all this, nods his wrinkled head, then says while Lerner is an honored and valued old member of the organization— *blahsky blahsky blahsky*—this Valeshin boychick is a *producer,* a hotshot moneymaker, so lay off and give the kid his shot.

In fact, he's going to make Valeshin a brigadier.

Lerner about shits. It's instantly obvious now that Valeshin has just bypassed him and laid a pile of money directly on Shakalin and bought his promotion. Which is not the way it's supposed to work. It's supposed to work like an Amway distributorship, and you just don't bypass a stone on the pyramid.

Lerner is so pissed he thinks for a second about taking on old Natan himself, except the ancient fuck is sitting there flanked by his two bodyguards straight from the old country and the new talent has a serious reputation as very nasty people.

Handy with the old chicken chop.

So Lerner bides his time, and they bring Daz in and Lerner gives Daz his blessing and they kiss and hug and all that happy crap and make a vodka toast to their eternal friendship and mutual prosperity.

Well, the friendship is total bullshit, but as for the prosperity . . .

Daz gets his own brigade and the money rolls in.

Like waves on the California shore.

It's not enough.

Daziatnik wants something more.

Wants something different.

He's living in Fairfax, in the middle of thousands of other Russian immigrants, and it might as well be Leningrad with palm trees. He speaks Russian, he works with Russians, he eats with Russians, he sleeps with Russians.

He makes his money and gives most of it to Russians—to Shakalin and Karpotsov—so they're happy, but Daz is wondering when he gets his piece of Paradise.

Daziatnik reads so he knows his history.

The Irish, the Italians, the Jews.

The grandfathers—gangsters. The grandsons—lawyers.

And bankers and politicians and judges.

And businessmen.

It's a three-generation turnaround, but Daziatnik wonders why.

Why not one generation?

Why not?

If a man can go from spy to *zek,* to driving a limo, to stealing cars, to running a chop shop, to insurance fraud, to brigadier in four short years, why can't he make the leap to legitimate businessman in as short a time?

In this land of opportunity.

In this floating cloud of a land where a man can invent and reinvent himself. Can burn the pages of his history behind him and then his past disappears into the blue California sky like so much smoke.

Daz has a plan to do it.

He knows it's out there, that ineffable thing, the open arms and legs of California, and that's what he wants. He wants freedom, and style, he wants away from his grim émigré comrades—the dull, the stupid, the boring, the mind-numbing soul-stunning *sameness* of it.

He wants to become Nicky.

So he looks for the opportunity. Which isn't hard. The opportunity is so blatant, so transparent, so clear it would take an idiot not to see it.

The sweet, heavy, ripe pear virtually dropping from the tree.

Real estate.

Any fool could see that in California in the mid-'80s real estate is the golden stream. Put money in real estate and watch your investment turn around, sometimes literally overnight. Diversify with longer-term investments: apartment buildings and condo complexes. All the more profitable if you could use your mob outreach to cut a corner here or there—cheaper materials, quicker construction. It was rare they had to twist or even bend an arm: everyone was in a hurry in those days. Get them up, get them sold, get your money into the next one.

His real estate investments make money and that gives him the freedom to stretch the code out even more. He leaves the tight ethnic community in L.A. and moves south to the gold coast. Where he can reinvent himself as Nicky Vale.

Daz changes his name. Daziatnik Valeshin is just too heavy a moniker to carry around. To sign on all the real estate papers. Too hard for customers to remember when they have a good deal and are looking for investors to phone.

Call me, Daz says.

In fact, call me Nicky.

That's his next break with the code, but Nicky says he isn't leaving, he's *colonizing*. Taking the business down to the lucrative gold coast. Going where the money is. Where there's virgin ground for development. Where, dig this, people enter a *lottery* to determine who gets a chance to buy a condo in the new complexes.

You couldn't, Nicky recalls, put the things up fast enough.

Nicky keeps buying up land, putting up buildings.

Leveraging it all like hell, but who cares?

The market outgrows the debt.

And Nicky flourishes.

New house, new clothes, new style, new persona.

Nicky Vale: real estate player.

It's Daz's next violation of the code, of the *Vorovskoy Zakon,* which states in no uncertain terms that making money in legitimate enterprise is like, *outsky,* right? Strictly *nyet.* And some of Daz's soldiers do grumble about it. He tells them to shut their mouths, make money and be happy. Lerner sees his shot and gets on the horn to Shakalin to rat Daz out, telling the old boy that Daziatnik has gone American and is pissing all over *Vorovskoy Zakon.*

Shakalin agrees.

The ties are loosening too much.

Like the Soviet Union, Two Crosses could crumble apart.

It is time to make an example of "Nicky Vale."

55

He's strapped to a wooden chair.

The whole ruling body sits in a semicircle in front of him: the brigadiers, several lieutenants, old Natan Shakalin and his bodyguards, one of whom holds a silenced automatic pistol and the other of whom brandishes a chain saw.

Looking at the saw, Nicky can feel his balls tighten.

Lerner gets up and recites a litany of Nicky's transgressions against the code: Nicky's been doing legitimate business, he's been withholding profits from the organization. In short, "Nicky Vale" has broken faith with his brothers.

He's broken the *Vorovskoy Zakon.*

Nicky's still not too worried. He points to the corruption in the real estate business—the subpar materials, the payoffs to inspectors, the tax dodges, the occasional arson scheme. His basic response to that is, Legit, *hell.* As to not paying his share, Nicky offers to make restitution. It is just an accounting problem; as soon as the books are straight, he will pay his due.

"Perhaps," Lerner says, "the reason that you cannot pay the money you owe is that you send so much to your bosses in KGB."

"Excuse me?"

"*Major* Valeshin?"

Oops.

Now Nicky's worried.

He can practically hear the chain saw warming up.

It's not pleasant, this chicken chop. First they cut off your hands, then your arms, then your feet, then your legs, then your privates—and even though you're probably dead by then, they cut off your head just for a sense of aesthetic unity.

"It *is* major now, isn't it," Lerner says. "Congratulations. *Mazel tov.* Our brothers inside KGB informed us of your promotion."

Lerner demands the death penalty.

Fire up the old McCullough.

Shakalin gets to his feet.

He stands in front of Nicky and says, "Years ago, you took an oath to the Two Crosses. The Two Crosses protected you, nurtured you, took you from a miserable *zek* to riches beyond your knowledge. You came here as nothing and now you are a rich man.

"How do you thank us?

"You cheat us. You turn your back on us. You spit on our traditions and laws. You think you are too good for the Two Crosses, now that you are 'Nicky Vale.'

"And then we learn that you are a traitor. An informer."

He spits in Nicky's face.

Without turning around he asks the board for its verdict.

Guilty.

A huge surprise, Nicky thinks, seeing as they already have the chain saw out.

And realizes, Jesus, sweat is pouring down my back like a river. Shakalin asks what punishment should be rendered.

Death, death, death, death, death, death—right down the line.

Death by dismemberment.

"I validate the verdict and the sentence," Shakalin says, staring down at Nicky. "Burn in hell, Daziatnik Valeshin."

He calls back to his bodyguard, "Execute the sentence."

Lev starts up the $95 Home Depot Special of the Week and slices it through Shakalin's neck. His head topples to the floor just as Dani puts three silenced rounds into Tiv Lerner's face. Dani holds the gun on the rest of them as he unstraps Nicky. Lev puts the chain saw to one of the brigadiers' necks as Nicky says, "All in favor of my becoming *pakhan*, please raise your hands."

He's unanimously elected.

We're in America now, Daziatnik kindly explains when they're done pissing their pants. *California,* and things are different here. Different from Russia or Brighton Beach. Look outside and see the sunshine. Feel the warmth. Contemplate Natan Shakalin's head on the floor. Dig it, men, real estate is the Main Chance. Against the code, true, but the heart of the code is in making money, *da?*

Da.

And this KGB accusation is nonsense, but who cares anyway? Fuck the KGB. In case you missed it, the Union of Soviet Socialist Republics is no more. The cold war is over. They're not the enemy anymore because they're out of business.

Which seems to be true. Nicky tested it out. Stopped sending money to Karpotsov. Stopped answering messages. Stopped sending messages. Just completely went off the radar screen. And what happened?

Nothing.

Nothing happened.

The vaunted KGB is impotent.

It's a new world order.

"You are all reborn in me," Nicky tells them over the buzz of the saw as Lev chops Lerner's body into readily disposable pieces. Nicky makes his speech. He's into it. Dude thinks he's Pacino in *The Godfather.* "I will remain *pakhan* for seven years, after which each brigadier will be free to start his own independent organization. I will use that time to completely legitimize my enterprise. I would recommend that you do the same, but that is your business.

"Parts of the old code are good and we will keep them. Other parts have served their purpose in the past but are now obsolete. I will have a family. I will have a wife. I will have children to inherit what I've worked for. How can we have a dynasty without heirs? Do we work to establish an empire that goes to the grave with us? That is foolishness. If anyone disagrees, speak now."

There is no sound but the saw.

"Then we're agreed," Nicky says. "I am restructuring the organization. Tratchev, seeing as how Tiv Lerner is no longer capable of performing his duties, you're promoted to the command of his brigade. You will do auto accident fraud exclusively. Rubinsky, your brigade will be auto theft. Schaller, arson and extortion. And brothers, reach out to other ethnic groups, the Mexicans, the Vietnamese, the white trash. Make *them* your operators. Insulate yourselves. I do not want to read about the 'Russian Mafia' in the papers or see your faces on television.

"I will keep my security cell. I loaned them to the late Natan Shakalin for a while—for purposes that should be apparent—but now I am taking them back. You will report to them, not to me. You will pay 20 percent—not 50—to me and 10 percent to the *obochek*, which I will maintain and control. Make money and invest it in the economy. Your sons will be senators."

Nicky likes this last line. Came up with it when he was rehearsing this speech. Going over it and over it to maintain his nerve as he hoped that his plan would pay off. That his foresight in persuading Karpotsov to give exit visas to Dani and Lev would work the way they planned it. That Dani and Lev would stay faithful to the vows they had made to each other in prison.

You will join me in Paradise.

There is another promise to keep.

He sends for Mother.

In collapsing, cash-poor Russia, her exit is easier to arrange than a table at Wolfgang Puck's.

Their reunion is cold at first.

She's hurt, she's angry, she's bitter at the six years of separation. She barely speaks on the limo drive from LAX to Dana Point. She starts to brighten when they arrive at the gates of Monarch Bay and the guard trips over himself welcoming them in. She starts to positively warm when she sees the house.

"Daziatnik, it is barely furnished," she says.

"I thought you would like to do that, Mother," he says. "And I count on your taste. Anyway, it is yours."

"Mine?"

"Although I have kept a room for myself. If you find that acceptable."

She kisses him on both cheeks and then fleetingly on the mouth.

"It is acceptable to me."

Nicky separates himself from the Two Crosses. Except for his security cell, he never sees his lieutenants. Lets them run their operations, kick in the money to him. He's satisfied to manage the *obochek* and run his real estate investments.

And collect his furniture. He goes to his first auction with some of his new friends, just as a way to kill a cloudy January Saturday. Ends up falling in love. Not with any of the rich, svelte women he sees there, but with a George II dressing table that calls out to him, *I'm yours.*

More than that.

Calls out to him, I'm *you*.

And before he knows it, Nicky has his hand out and he's plunking down fifteen K on a big piece of walnut.

Which he loves.

There is love that passes and love that lasts. There is love that satisfies the body and the heart, and which is passing, and there is love that nourishes the soul, and which is lasting.

The furniture is the only thing that Nicky has ever found that nourishes his soul.

At first it was a class thing.

He bought it because he *could* buy it, because the ability to pay that kind of money symbolized his triumph over the ghetto. Because the purchase of art—as opposed to cars, or horses, for instance—gave him an entrée into the world of the beautiful people. It made him not just one more real estate tycoon, but a man of culture, polish and, yes, *class*.

Nicky is too smart not to acknowledge to himself the truth of all that.

But in time—and not much time at that—it became more than a status symbol.

It became a true love.

Was it, Nicky wonders, the art itself? But that somewhat begs the question, doesn't it? Perhaps it was the purity of effort that a work of art represents, the genuine desire to create something that is truly beautiful. A purity of effort in such contrast to a corrupt world?

Or is it the beauty itself? Could it be that simple, he wonders, that I am irresistibly drawn to possess beauty? Engaging again in cheap psychoanalysis (Ah, I *have* become an American), it is not difficult to imagine that a boy raised in poverty would wish to own beauty if he could.

It has been, let us face it, for the first thirty or so years an ugly life. The dreary flat, the hideousness of Afghanistan, the horror of the jail cells. Dirty ice, dirty snow, mud, blood, shit and filth.

He wakes up from time to time with nightmares from the war—a hateful stereotype that he finds embarrassing—and it helps to turn on the lights and sit for a while with a fine piece of art. To admire its beauty, study its form and design, to let it take him away from the images of bloated corpses, mutilated comrades, or the recurring dream of the *mujahedin* fighter hit by the flamethrower—staggering forward, on fire, literally a whirling dervish twirling in agony under the swirling flames.

It helps Nicky at such times to look at his artworks.

Other nights sleep takes him back to the jail cells, the filth-encrusted, freezing concrete floors. The stench of sweat and shit and piss, the smell of fear. The screaming psychos, the violent sodomites, the quick deaths by homemade blades or garrotes or simple beatings. Skulls cracked against walls, heads crushed onto floors, faces beaten to mush by club-wielding guards. Not an inch of space to call one's own. Not a moment of privacy. Not a single instance of beauty to be seen anywhere at any price.

Hell.

So to stand in one's own house—in the clean, lovely serenity of one's own home—and contemplate beauty in the form of art, whenever and for however long one wishes . . . well, it nourishes a soul in need of nourishment.

And it is passive, Nicky thinks. It is simply beauty there to be enjoyed. Once purchased it makes no other demands, has no other requirements except to be admired and enjoyed.

And it tells him that he's risen above it all. Risen above the cramped walk-up he shared with Mother, above the dirt, cold, blood and fire of Afghanistan. *Far* above the filth and stench and cold of the prison, above the monotonous kitsch of the Two Crosses.

The cabinet tells him that he's arrived. That he's not even a parvenu new-money California real estate shark but a gentleman.

He starts buying books, visiting dealerships, attending more and more auctions, and it's not long before he's a major collector of antique English furniture. He buys, he sells, he trades—he makes a new set of friends.

He gets a new identity.

Nicky Vale—real estate mogul and collector.

The turnaround inside one generation.

He makes the new friends that come with money, and from the friends he absorbs the south coast style. Discovers the shops at South Coast Plaza and becomes a regular at Armani, Brooks Brothers, Giuducce et al. Becomes a standard figure at the good parties in Newport Beach, Corona Del Mar and Laguna. Gets himself a boat and hosts his own parties out on the blue ocean.

Daziatnik becomes Nicky, and everyone loves Nicky.

Why not? He's charming, rich and funny and has the most wonderful taste in art. He's handsome, he's exotic, and inside a year he's on the A list for the best parties on the south coast.

At one of them he meets Pamela.

56

Incendiary origin, opportunity and motive.

Also known as the Tripartite Proof.

Whatever it's called, you need these three elements to prove arson by an insured in court. And if you deny a claim based on arson, you'd better be able to prove it in court.

Same with the murder, Jack thinks. To deny the life insurance claim, I need to prove that it *was* a homicide, and that Nicky had motive and opportunity.

Incendiary origin is just a fancy way of saying that someone intentionally set the fire. What you need to satisfy this one are such things as traces of accelerants, the remnants of an incendiary device, maybe a timer. You also want the indicators of a hot, fast-moving fire: big V-pattern, alligator char, deep char on the floor, crazed glass, a pour pattern.

Most important of all these is traces of accelerants, and now he has them. Dr. Bambi will come into court and testify that he found heavy traces of kerosene in the flooring and the floor joists. He'll show the jury his charts and graphs and the jury will go back into the room believing that someone poured kerosene around that bedroom.

So Jack checks off incendiary origin and pushes it out of his mind. Opportunity—that is, did the insured have a chance to set the fire or cause to have it set? It goes a little deeper than that. The actual standard is *"exclusive* opportunity"—was the insured the only party to have access to the house during the critical time when the fire was set?

Opportunity is a tricky mother. It's why you look to see if doors and windows were locked. It's why you talk to neighbors to see what—and whom—they might have seen. It's why you take recorded statements to pin the insured down to where they were at the time of the fire.

It's elusive.

One reason being that arsonists—unless they're *really* stupid—tend to use timing devices. For one thing, there is a matter of getting out of the place without setting yourself on fire. You pour some gasoline around and strike a match, you stand a good chance of becoming a human torch. What a lot of amateurs don't know is that it's the fumes that ignite, not the liquid. So they pour the gas, step back, toss the match and then run out flaming into the night.

For another thing, a good timing device gives you the *time* to establish an alibi. You were somewhere else at the moment of ignition so you didn't have the exclusive opportunity to set the fire.

A timing device can be very simple or very sophisticated. As simple as a series of twisted sheets tied together to form a giant wick, which gives you the chance to light it and get away by the time it hits the big pool of gas and goes PHWOOM. Or it can be a simple timer wired to strike a spark into a well of accelerant at a certain time, and that gives you even more space.

Jack's personal all-time favorite for a sophisticated timer, though, was on the file where the couple was definitely in Las Vegas the weekend their house burned down. They had receipts and eyewitnesses for a fifty-some-odd-hour period and there were no remnants of timers found in the house.

But the fire was sure as hell of "incendiary origin" because it had all the indicators and someone had gone to a great deal of trouble to make the house fire-ready. Holes had been punched in the walls to improve circulation (fire eats oxygen), windows had been left open (same) and floor samples tested positive for accelerants.

The security system was intact and there were no signs that anyone had come into the house.

So how was the fire set?

Jack puzzled over it, hell, agonized over it, for weeks. He visited the site again and again. Finally, he found a hot spot on the floor in the upstairs family room. Right below the charred remnants of the VCR.

Jack's favorite all-time timing device: a videocassette timed to eject and tip over a burner into a pool of accelerant.

The couple got away with it, of course, but Jack was relieved to have figured it out.

Anyway, all this is to say that generally speaking, opportunity has to do with time, which often has to do with some kind of timing device.

This is true even if the insureds have hired the arson out. Jack's experience is that this is more often the case in commercial fires, because it really takes a pro to burn a warehouse down. But there have been cases where homeowners have hired an arsonist and then gone off on vacation to establish an alibi, but Jack doesn't think that Nicky hired this one out.

You burn up your wife *in your bed*, it's personal.

So Jack asks himself, Did Nicky have the opportunity to go into the house, kill his wife and set the fire? Not if his mother's story is true, but Jack thinks that Mother's story is bullshit. Then Jack considers the question: Given opportunity, did Nicky have the *exclusive* opportunity to set the fire? Well, the doors were locked, the windows were cracked open. There were no signs of forced entry. So who besides the owner had access to the house?

But it's tricky, it's weak, and unless he can catch Nicky in a lie, proving the opportunity issue is going to be tough.

Which brings Jack to the subject of motive.

57

There are three basic motives for arson: insanity, vengeance and money.

And the greatest of these is money.

Take insanity first, though. Here you're talking about your storied pyromaniac, that specific-type freak who is simply and hopelessly enamored of fire. The sad fact is that there is a striking coincidence between childhood sexual abuse and pyromania. There is something about the all-consuming heat that is evocative of sexuality and at the same time cleansing. It both brings up the heat and makes it go away.

This kind of fire, though, doesn't come up much in insurance fraud anyway, because pyromaniacs tend to burn *other* people's stuff and they tend to get caught doing it. So you pay the claim and move on.

Then there's revenge. A little more common but still unusual, because generally people who are really pissed these days just shoot the object of their pissed-offedness. But there are white supremacist nut jobs who like to lob Molotov cocktails at synagogues, and there's the occasional fired (no pun intended) cleaning lady who cleans the floor with charcoal starter and a match, and there's the husband about to lose his house to the ex-wife and who burns it to the ground by way of saying "Live in *this*, bitch.'"

So there's revenge, and there is something about a fire that's cathartic, no question, but it's not a choice that most people make.

So there's insanity and revenge, but they both pale compared to the numero uno motive for arson—may I have the envelope please—

Money.

Money, honey.

To the tune of some $8 billion a year nationally.

Jack knows that there are about eighty-six thousand arson fires a year. That's about one for every hour of the day and the motive for most of them is money.

Or more properly, the lack of it.

Fire makes all things new again.

A fire in nature burns off the old to make way for the new. Same thing in business—it burns off the old investment to make way for the new. It's an ancient cycle, and the fact is that the incidence of arson directly corresponds to the economic cycle. In boom times, arson goes down. In a recession it goes up. In boom times, people buy a lot of stuff on credit because they're making the money to service the debt. Then the recession hits, the money ain't coming in like it was, but the debt is the same.

It's the same thing with homes. Most people buy more house than they can afford. They buy the house when things are fat, thinking they're going to stay fat forever. Then things get lean but the mortgage is still fat. The mortgage doesn't go on any damn diet.

Most people walk away from the house, say goodbye to their equity and try to start over.

Others say, like, *fuck that*, and get proactive.

Let their insurance company pay off the mortgage.

It happened a lot in Orange County, Jack thinks. In the Reagan years everyone was fat. The whole economy was betting on the income. Then reality hit, and what everyone bought on credit during the Reagan years they burned down during the Bush administration. The Orange County treasurers got caught on the slide and the county went bankrupt. So the real estate market collapsed, the building trades went down the chute and the only industry that was booming was the arson business.

Out with the old, in with the new.

Nature's eternal cycle.

Sometimes nature does it on her own.

It's weird to contemplate, but Jack knows the reality is that the eventual Southern California economic recovery was fueled by disasters, first fire then earthquake.

It's 1993 and the economy sucks. The real estate market and building trades are moribund and everything else comes to a standstill with them. Then the fires hit. Laguna, Malibu, Thousand Oaks. Big out-of-control fires that rise up out of the dry ground and the hot dry wind and burn thousands of acres and hundreds of houses. A lot of people are burned out of their homes and the insurance companies pay out hundreds of millions of dollars in benefits.

Which is where the economic recovery comes in, because the fires restore the building trades. The insurance companies provide the cash to rebuild the burned homes. Contractors get hired, they hire workers, they buy materials from the suppliers, the suppliers start hiring people, the people take their salaries and buy stuff . . .

The cycle goes on an upswing.

Then the earthquake hits.

Nature comes to the rescue because it forces the insurance companies to lolly up billions. Billions of dollars of new money gets pumped into the So-Cal economy and it gets things started again.

So sometimes nature touches off the cycle.

More often, though, it's people.

Touching off their own economic renewal with a match.

And Jack wonders if that's what Nicky Vale did.

Strictly speaking, you don't always need motive to prove arson. The textbook example Jack learned in fire school was: Suppose a person sets fire to his building at noon on Main Street in front of a hundred witnesses, five of whom videotape the event. In that case, you don't need to establish motive, because you have ample direct evidence that your man did the fire.

Jack thinks this example is very useful, because in his experience nothing like this has ever ever happened and it's never ever *going* to happen.

The closest Jack has come to that slice of heaven was the case of the husband who is coming home from work and sees a plume of smoke rising from his town house complex. Fire trucks roar past him, sirens wail, the whole nine yards. The husband pulls up to the security gate only to see his wife sitting on the lawn—a bottle of Jack Daniel's in one hand and a gasoline can in the other, and she looks up at him and says, "I always *hated* that damn house."

That is what is known in the claims business as a slam dunk, and Jack has always retained an awed sense of admiration for the husband's honesty, because it was the husband who told Jack the story.

"So I guess I'm fucked on my claim," the husband says after relating the story to Jack. They're standing beside the charred ruins of what had been the man's very nice $375,000 town house.

"I'm afraid so," Jack says.

Jack almost wants to pay the claim, he feels so bad for the guy, who was, after all, honest about what happened. But the law says that if any permanent resident of the house intentionally sets the fire, the home-owner is shit-out-of-luck.

But Jack offers a suggestion.

"You can *try* saying that your wife is mentally ill and therefore her actions can't be intentional," Jack says.

"You think that would work?"

"Hey, it's California."

To his credit, the guy doesn't try it.

He does file for divorce, though.

Anyway, absent that kind of rare event, you need motive.

Today is Motive Day.

As to the murder, well, in a weird way the murder piggybacks the arson. The motive and the opportunity are the same. The homicide version of incendiary origin comes with the coroner's report proving that she died before the fire. Then if the *fire* was intentional . . . well, it's virtually impossible to conclude that the death was accidental.

Prove it.

You bet your ass, Nicky.

58

So the money first.

Cherchez la buck.

As simple as picking up a phone.

Twenty-four hours a day, seven days a week, you got a name and a Social Security number and you can find out whether someone's servicing debt and for how much.

Jack punches in the number, gets put on hold and tries not to listen to the elevator music coming over the phone. Three annoying minutes later he has an answer, though.

Nicky's maxed out on every piece of plastic in his wallet.

He's on the verge of having his card jerked by the next person who says, "Hi, my name is Diane and I'll be your server today." Like, Nicky has Karl Malden telling him, "Don't leave home *with* it."

Nicky Vale's credit rating is in the Realm of Suck.

Call Me Nicky owes $18,000 plus to the credit card companies.

That ain't all.

Nicky has another creditor.

Uncle Sam.

There's a lien on the Bluffside Drive property for $57,000.

Next Jack hits the Internet.

Gets a service called AmeriData, punches in Nicky's Social Security number and date of birth and in a matter of seconds he gets a rundown on everything Nicky owns.

There's the house on Bluffside, of course—mortgaged to Pacific Coast Mortgage and Finance.

Mother Russia's house is also in his name, also mortgaged to Pacific Coast.

He has five cars. Three bought for cash, two with payments in arrears.

No airplanes.

No boats.

But he had a boat, Jack remembers. What happened to the boat and when?

He makes a note to check it out.

Gets off the Net to take a look at Nicky's bank balance.

Nicky is tapped out.

He has a few thou in the account, enough to make your everyday living expenses, not enough to keep current with the bigger bills.

Back to the computer. Tap in a few numbers and hook in to the California Secretary of State's office database. Does the old name-SS#-DOB drill again and then comes out with a list of any corporation in which Nicky is a principal.

Sees what he expects to see.

Nicky is president and CEO of Vale Investments.

Which must be his real estate development operation, Jack thinks.

There's also ValeArt.

The precious furniture.

And that's it.

Jack taps out of the state database, then taps in to the county's.

Types in "Vale, Nicky DBA" and comes out with three partnerships and two limited partnerships: South Coast Management, Cote D'Or Management and Sunset Investment; TransPac Holding and TransNat Holding.

Jack jots down the names and then hits Dun & Bradstreet and Moody's and also does a credit check.

It all comes out the same.

Nicky Vale's businesses are drowning in the Red Sea.

Nicky as a business entity is about to go down for the third time and there is no life raft in sight. He has apartment buildings that are half-empty, buildings that are under construction with no funds to complete them, and creditors howling at the door.

Motive.

Jack's about to head over to Pacific Coast Mortgage and Finance when Carol buzzes him and tells him to get into Billy's office.

59

"Goddamn it, Jack!" Billy yells.

"What?" Jack asks.

Like he doesn't know.

They're standing in Billy's cactus garden outside the office. Billy's sucking on a cigarette like it's an oxygen mask.

"The Vale file, that's what," Billy says. He tosses the butt on the ground and lights another. Has to cup his hand to get it lit because the wind is blowing like crazy. This puts him in an even worse mood. "You have a little chat with the insured last night?"

Well, that didn't take long, Jack thinks.

"I wanted to see his reaction," Jack says.

"And?"

"He's a cool customer."

"Well, let me tell you about his reaction," Billy says. "Vale called his agent—"

"Roger Hazlitt?"

"Yes, and rattled his cage about you. Hazlitt took time from his busy day humping his secretary to call his Agency manager, who called the VP for Agency, who called me and rattled *my* cage."

"Vale's personal property coverage is *way* over guidelines, Billy. So are his endorsements."

"What are you saying?"

"I'm saying his personal property coverage is way over guidelines and so are his endorsements."

"Don't try to wind me up over Agency, Jack."

Like most insurance companies, Cal Fire and Life is organized into three basic divisions: Agency, Underwriting and Claims. In theory, the three divisions are equal—each has a vice president who reports to the president—but in reality, it's Agency that swings the big hammer. Every guy who plunks his butt down in the executive dining room upstairs on Mahogany Row has come out of Agency. Every suit on the board of directors has come out of Agency.

Because it's Agency that brings in the money, Jack thinks.

You're not going to make money from Claims, Jack knows. All Claims does is pay money out. And you're not going to see any money from Underwriting. The best Underwriting can do is try to set the rates so that you charge the right amount of premiums to make a profit.

But Agency, that's the golden goose, man. That's the pipeline. You have this force of agents out there—selling life, selling auto, selling fire. Taking their commissions—10 percent on fire and auto, 15 percent on life.

That's serious money.

And it regenerates itself. The agent sells the policy once, and all he has to do is keep the policy and he gets his commission every year on renewal. So he wants to keep that customer and he doesn't really care what Claims has to pay out. If that customer has a loss, the agent wants Claims to pay it. Just *pay* it, baby. Because the money doesn't come out of the agent's pocket or his commission.

It comes out of Claims.

Claims gets it, of course, from the Big Pool at corporate, but even Mahogany Row doesn't care all that much how much money is going out as long as a lot more money is coming in. So as long as people are buying California Fire and Life, everything's cool.

Just keep the money coming in.

Of course, it's a little hard to sell to someone when some lunch-bucket from Claims has called him an arsonist and murderer. Then the customer threatens to yank all his policies. And he tells all his friends how he's being fucked by his insurance company, and the next thing you know you have guys flooding off the eighteenth hole to jerk their policies away from you and then it's over.

Then you have to go back to sitting in Mom and Pop's kitchen trying to sell them a homeowner's policy that's maybe going to net you a hundred a year.

So before any of that bad shit happens, you reach out for the telephone and you scream for the big hammer to come down on somebody.

In this case, Goddamn Billy Hayes.

Who tells the So-Cal Agency VP, "We don't pay people to kill their wives and burn their own houses down."

So he doesn't, in fact, need Jack winding him up about Agency.

Or about Underwriting.

"Underwriting?" Jack asks.

"Yeah, they called, too," Billy says. "They want to 'monitor' how we handle this claim."

"What the hell does Underwriting have to do with it?" Jack asks. "Since when do we report to Underwriting?"

"That's what I told them," Billy says. "But if you're keeping score, that's Agency, Underwriting, and, oh yeah, the Sheriff's Department winding my crank about the Vale file."

"Sorry."

"You been over to the Sheriff's?"

"I advised Deputy Bentley that he might want to reconsider his evaluation of the Vale fire."

"Goddamn it, are you *trying* to get us sued?" Billy yells. "You deny a claim based on arson when the Sheriff's already called it an accident, and we'll get sued for bad faith. We might be in bad faith if we even continue to *investigate* the cause of a fire after it's been deemed accidental."

"We have positive samples from Disaster," Jack says. "And Nicky Vale is up to his ears in debt."

Then he tells him about the funeral.

And Letty's story.

When he's finished, Billy says, "Hearsay."

"What do you want?" Jack asks, "Pamela Vale to testify?"

"It would help."

Billy says, "*Maybe* you have incendiary origin, and *maybe* you have motive, but you don't have a goddamn thing on opportunity. Vale was draining the lizard and checking on his sleeping kids."

"The mother's lying," Jack says. "Or maybe he hired the job out."

"Prove it," says Billy.

"I need some time," Jack says.

"I don't know if you got the time," Billy says.

"What do you mean?" he asks.

"They want me to take you off this file, Jack."

"Who's 'they'?"

"They, everybody," Billy says. "Agency, Underwriting, the Sheriff's, shit, I dunno. Anyone else you pissed off on this, Jack?"

"No, but the day is young."

"Keep it up, Jack."

"Billy, you're not telling me they want to pay this fucking claim?!" Jack yells.

"Of course they want to pay it!" Billy yells back. "What the fuck do you *think* they want to do?! They got a millionaire businessman with a load of juicy policies a goddamn camel couldn't carry! They got a guy can put heat on the president's office if he wants to, and by the way, that's his next phone call. Agency knows they fucked up, Underwriting knows they fucked up, you think they want to see that in court? You think they want a fight over this? Not when they cure it with the old Green Poultice!"

The Green Poultice. Billy's phrase for throwing money at a problem claim.

"Is the Green Poultice going to bring Pamela Vale back?" Jack asks.

"Goddamn it, Jack," Billy says. "That's not your job. It's the cops' job."

"They won't reopen the investigation."

Billy taps Jack on the forehead. "Hel*loooo*? Good morning? Doesn't that *tell* you something?"

"Tells me they're not doing their job."

"And you are, right?" Billy asks. "Jack Wade is always right. Everyone else is fucked. Only Jack Wade does the right thing. No matter what it costs other people. Grow up. You can't always be the lone cowboy, riding your surfboard into the sunset."

"What am I supposed to say to that, Billy?"

Because it's true.

Jack stands there with the wind blowing into his face, blowing the green-gray mudge from the cars on the 405 into his eyes and nose.

Billy says, "Just take care of the claim. The claim is your business."

"The claim is wrong."

"Prove it!"

"I need *time* to prove it!"

"You ain't *got* the time!"

Two old friends standing in the middle of a mock desert screaming at each other. They realize it. Billy sits down.

Says, "Shit."

"Sorry."

"Billy," Jack asks, "can you take my back on this one?"

Billy blows out a puff of air and says, "Yeah. For a while. For a *while*, Jack, because I'm telling you—I'm getting heat."

"Thanks, Billy."

"And don't you *ever* talk to an insured like that again," Billy says. "And keep adjusting the claim."

Another bad-faith-phobia demand. The California Fair Claims Practices Act demands that an insurance company has to keep adjusting the claim while at the same time it's investigating. The reason is that if the company spends months investigating without adjusting, and *then* decides to pay the claim, the payment to the insured is unfairly delayed.

"Right," Jack says. "I'll start working up an estimate."

Meaning that he'll do a "scope"—determine what was damaged or destroyed—then a "comp"—an item-by-item estimate of what it will take to replace and repair.

Just what he'd do if he thought this was a righteous claim.

"Just do your goddamn job," Billy says.

"If I have enough evidence," Jack says, "I'm going to deny the claim."

"It's your call," Billy says. "Just do it right."

Which is what Billy's counting on.

60

Jack hates golf.

But the old links are where you want to be if you want to find an insurance agent. Depends on the time of day, of course. Between seven and eleven in the morning, you check the golf course. Lunchtime you check the country club. Early afternoon after lunch, you check the links again, late afternoon you don't check anywhere unless you want to be a witness in a divorce case.

Jack's on the course to buy himself some time.

He finds Roger Hazlitt on the seventeenth hole.

In a foursome with two doctors and a real estate developer.

See, you don't get to be a millionaire insurance agent selling individual policies to Mom and Pop. You get to be a millionaire insurance agent by selling policies to condo complexes, gated communities and the occasional wealthy individual homeowner like Nicky Vale.

Which of course is what Jack wants to talk about.

Roger Hazlitt is less enthused.

You sell a boatload of insurance and the house burns and the wife dies, it completely fucks your loss ratio for the entire year. Not that it's Roger's money—it isn't—but if you're in the top forty on loss ratios at the end of the year Cal Fire and Life sends you and your wife to Rome or Hawaii or Paris or someplace and Roger hates missing those trips.

And he's not all that thrilled to see Jack Wade come striding over the green in his cheap blue blazer and khaki slacks and white shirt and tie, because the two doctors and the real estate developer are putting up a massive condo complex in Laguna Niguel and Roger figures that all he has to do is tank eighteen and blow a putt and he has the policy and 10 percent commission on the premiums.

But he puts on a big smile and pumps Jack's hand and says, "Guys, meet Jack Wade, best damned insurance adjuster in this great land of ours and that is no shit."

Jack, he's thinking that it's all shit, but he smiles and shakes hands as that asshole Roger Hazlitt says, "God forbid, guys, that something should happen with your buildings, but if it does, you know you can call Jack personally and it will get handled. Right, Jack?"

Now Jack feels like an asshole but he says, "You bet."

"Didn't you bring your clubs, Jack?"

I work for a living is what Jack wants to say but what he says instead is, "A quick word with you, Roger?"

"Tell you what," Roger says. "Let me hit my tee shot and then while these guys are in the rough looking for their balls we can have a chat, okay?"

"Sounds like a plan."

"There we go."

Roger has a sweet swing, which he should, because he plays maybe seven times a week plus lessons with his pro, so he hits a long ball and then takes Jack aside.

"I'm going to lose five hundred bucks to these jamokes," he says, "then make a couple hundred K on their premiums, so let's keep this quick, Jack. What are you doing out here? Couldn't you have come to my office?"

"You're never in your office."

"Well, isn't this something one of the gals could handle?"

The "gals" being the women who work in Roger's office.

"You're Nicky Vale's agent," Jack says.

"Guilty."

"You sold him a shitload of special endorsements," Jack says. "Art, custom furniture, jewelry . . ."

"So?"

"*Way* over guidelines, Roger."

"Underwriting okayed it," Roger says, starting to get defensive. Starting to sweat now.

"Who at Underwriting?"

"I don't know," Roger says. "Ask Underwriting."

"Come on, Roger," Jack says. "That kind of overage, you must have a sweetheart in Underwriting."

"Fuck you, Jack."

Jack puts his arm around Roger's shoulders.

Says into his ear, "Roger, I don't begrudge you a living. You go get as much money as your greedy little hands can grab. I know you have a wife, three kids and two girlfriends to support. Plus business expenses."

Roger is like *Mister* Community. For the annual Dana Point Festival of the Whales parade, Roger rents the elephant. In the annual Festival of the Tall Ships, one of the tall ships flies a flag that says Hazlitt Insurance Agency on it. These things cost money. So do tennis bracelets and cosmetic surgery.

"So I know," Jack continues, "that you need to be bringing it in."

"That's goddamn right, Jack."

"Cool," Jack says. "And I don't give a rat's ass that you have to give a taste to someone in Underwriting to okay an overage now and then. I don't care, Claims doesn't care. Unless, you know, I need to go digging and rooting through Underwriting, and then maybe even Mahogany Row might wake up and hear about it."

"You're an asshole."

"Or should I go over to the guys there," Jack says, nudging his chin at Roger's golf partners, "and tell them that by all means they should buy their insurance from you now—today—while you still have your license."

"A real fucking asshole."

"Just give me a name," Jack says. "Someone I can talk to. I don't give a damn about the money, Roger."

"Yeah, you do," Roger says. "All you Joe Lunchbuckets from Claims, you're jealous. How much do you clear, Jack? Thirty-five? Forty-five? Maybe fifty? I shake that much off my dick at the urinal, Jack."

"Good for you, Roger."

But it's true, Jack thinks. All us Joe Lunchbuckets from Claims, we are jealous about the money.

"Bill Reynolds," Roger whispers.

"A black guy?"

"Black guys don't need money?" Roger says. "I kicked him a grand."

"How can you make—?"

"I *don't* make on the endorsements. I make on the home, on the life, on the cars . . ."

"See, this is why you're rich, Roger."

Roger says, "I had to write the endorsements or Vale wouldn't give me his business on all the other shit. You know what those commissions stack up to, year after year? Plus Vale owns three apartment buildings, I get the policies on those, plus I get to solicit the tenants on their renter's insurance and their auto. You know how much money that is?"

"I don't want to know," Jack says. "I'd only get jealous."

"It's serious money."

Jack looks down on the green. Roger's partners are standing there looking back at the tee. I guess they found their balls, Jack thinks. He asks, "Are you and Nicky like *buddies* or something?"

"Screw *buddies*," Roger says. "I don't have time for *buddies*. Maybe we have a drink now and then. Lunch . . . Okay, maybe once or twice I go out on his boat with him for some blow and some babes. Don't look at me like that, Jack."

"I think your buddy killed his wife, Rog," Jack says. "For the insurance benefits. And he burned his house. For the insurance benefits. So fuck his boat and his blow and his babes. And Roger, don't you be making any more calls to my boss or your boss or *anybody's* fucking boss to get this claim paid."

"Just keep me out of this, Jack."

Yeah, you make the bucks and *now* you want out of it. When there's the mess and the dead bodies and the hell to pay.

"Then you just *stay* out of it, Rog," Jack says. "You stick your dick in Claims again I'll see that it gets cut off."

So shake that.

61

Jack drops in at Pacific Coast Mortgage and Finance.

Two-room office shares a building with a swimwear store and an erotic novelty shop on Del Prado in Dana Point. Big glossy photographs of ocean scenes dominate the walls. Handsome guys and sleek girls windsurfing, flecks of ocean spray flying off their bodies, glistening in the sun. Big beautiful sloops cutting through eight-foot swells. A gang of surfer dudes and wahinis carrying their boards against the background of a fiery sunset.

Like, life is beautiful.

Life is short.

Borrow money and get yourself a taste of it before you croak.

Guy sitting behind the desk is a young cool dude with Pat Riley slicked-back hair, a pink polo shirt and a blue blazer. It's like one of those finance-can-be-cool deals—you know, let's get the paperwork over with and go surfing, dude. Nameplate on the desk reads GARY MILLER.

Jack introduces himself and shows him the authorization form that Nicky had signed.

Jack asks, "You're carrying the paper on the Vale house?"

Which is just pro forma—the name of the mortgage company is on the declaration page of the policy and the loss report—but Jack wanted to say it to see if Gary's eyes lit up.

They do.

You can see right in those inane baby blues that the boy is carrying a ton of paper on the Vale house and the payments haven't been coming in. Guy is sphincter-gripping on the paper and now he sees a shot that the insurance company might ride into town and save his ass, man.

Like God bless California Fire and Life.

"Something happen?" he asks, trying to keep the hopeful note out of his voice.

"It burned down," Jack says.

"No shit?"

"And Mrs. Vale was killed," Jack adds.

"What a shame," Gary says.

He's not an *evil* guy. He does feel bad about Pamela Vale, who seemed very nice and was one of the most completely righteous babes he had ever seen. On the other hand, it does seem like Nicky Vale is tapped out and California Fire and Life has some deep pockets.

"Yeah," Jack says. "A shame."

"What happened?" Gary asks. He doesn't want to come right out and ask the, sorry, *burning* question he has on his mind: Was it a total loss?

Please let it be a total, he thinks.

A total loss would pay off the whole loan.

Jack says, "The official report is that Mrs. Vale was smoking in bed."

Gary shakes his head. "A nasty habit."

"Very uncool," Jack agrees. "Would you show me the paper, please?"

"Oh, yeah. Sure."

The paper is heavy.

This is not paper you would like to carry across, say, Death Valley.

But Nicky was carrying it. What Nicky had done was he originally bought the house for cash. *Who the hell,* Jack thinks, *has $2 million in cash?* Turns out Nicky really didn't, because six years later he mortgages the house with Pacific for $1.5 million. He's carrying a six-K-a-month payment.

"He's missed, uh, three payments," Gary volunteers.

He just can't help himself. Somewhere inside burns the ember of a hope that Jack is just going to whip out the old checkbook and say, "Oh, well, *here.*"

If the Vale loan goes down the shitter Gary goes down after it.

"Three payments?" Jack asks. "We looking at foreclosure?"

"It's a consideration," Gary says. "I mean, you know, we don't *want* to."

"No."

"But what are you going to do?"

You're going to try to carry the guy, Jack thinks. At least until the real estate market improves. Otherwise you eat the loan and you have a house you maybe can't sell. And even if you can, you're going to take a bath on it.

Jack asks, "Six K is a little light for that kind of balance, isn't it?"

"Read on."

Jack reads on.

Doesn't take long before he sees what he's looking for.

Prima facie motive for arson.

A $600,000 balloon payment.

Due in six weeks.

No wonder Nicky was in a hurry to start the claim.

"Did *you* write this loan, Gary?" Jack asks.

"Seemed like a good idea at the time," Gary says.

"Different times," Jack says.

He has this image of cool Gary on Nicky's boat—blowing coke, getting some *chucha,* chatting a little business with Nicky. What's a mil and a half between friends?

Party *on.*

"So what do you think?" Jack asks. "Is he going to make the balloon? I mean, if you were a betting man."

Gary laughs. "I *am* a betting man."

"That's no shit."

"Hey, maybe I covered," Gary says. Eyes getting a little angry, a little Fuck you, now *you* gotta pay the loan.

"Yeah, well, before you get too skippy," Jack says, "consider this— Nicky owes fifty-seven thou to the IRS and the California Department of Revenue."

The blood drains from Gary's face.

"Liens?" he asks.

"Oops," Jack says.

"You make the drafts out to *us,*" Gary says.

"Well, to you *and* Vale," Jack says.

Because that's what the law says—a draft on a claim gets made out to the homeowner and the mortgagee. Let them work it out. Of course, in this case, they have to deal with each other and the IRS *and* Sacramento. That'll be fun.

"Come *on,*" Gary whines.

Jack shrugs. "It's the law."

"Fucking Nicky."

"You have a relationship?"

"Yeah, we have a relationship," Gary says. "He fucks me."

The party's over.

Jack asks, "You have other bad paper with him, Gary?"

Gary wants to tell him. Jack can see it in his eyes.

Then Gary backs away.

"Nothing you're carrying," he says.

Meaning nothing he *can* tell me about, Jack thinks. He has other paper, but because Cal Fire's not the insurer on the property, he can't disclose it to me.

"I have authorization," Jack says.

"You have authorization on Nicky Vale," Gary says. Staring at Jack like Good morning, duhh, get it yet?

Jack gets it.

Gary's carrying paper on a company that Nicky has an interest in.

"You want to shoot me a couple of copies of this?" Jack asks, handing the loan papers back.

Gary comes back with the copies, asks, "So how long before you write the draft?"

"If we issue a check," Jack says.

"What do you mean?"

A genuine sphincter moment.

"Just that the claims process isn't finished yet," Jack says, smiling. He gathers the papers and gets up.

"Pray for surf," he says.

62

Jack's at Dana Harbor Boat Brokerage.

He goes up the stairs of the wooden building—he knows the building well. Like every stick, because he and his old man built it.

Anyway, he goes into the office of the brokerage and Jeff Wynand's sitting there where he's always sitting—at his desk on the phone—looking out the window at the thousands of boats in the marina, about half of which he's sold over the years.

He sees Jack and smiles and motions for him to sit down. Jack waits while Jeff gives out the details on a thirty-eight-foot racer. Jeff looks like a yacht broker—he's dressed in just about the same casual clothes as Gary Miller, but on Jeff it looks good. Not a statement, just his clothes, and it goes with the sailboats and motor launches in the harbor. Jeff's been wearing the same clothes since Jack was delivering him his newspapers.

When Jeff hangs up, Jack asks, "Can I buy you lunch?"

"Chez Marsha?"

"Sounds good."

Chez Marsha is actually a little snack shack down by Baby Beach on the West Harbor. When Jack was a kid, the shack sat out at the end of the pier that stretched way out into the harbor. Jack used to dip a pole in the fishing contests Marsha held for the local kids. Then they built the dock for the brig *Pilgrim* and built the Orange County Marine Institute and cut the original pier way back, so now Marsha's sits on the walkway near the base of the truncated old pier.

The shack's not on the water so she doesn't do the fishing contests anymore, but she still has hot dogs with steamed buns and chopped onions, so Jack and Jeff grab a bench at one of the steel picnic tables beside Marsha's shack.

Jack goes up to the window.

"Miss Marsha."

"Jack, what's up?" she asks. "Is that Jeff Wynand with you?"

"Yup."

Marsha's had the place for thirty-some-odd years, so she knows everyone worth knowing at the harbor. If she's not too busy, sometimes she sits down with Jack at one of the tables and they discuss the latest idiocies of progress.

They're redesigning the harbor. Tearing down the old to make place for the new. Going to build a two-story concrete "parking structure" and push out the old stores and restaurants to bring in the chains. So the harbor will look like everywhere else.

"Two hot dogs, please," Jack says. "Mustard, relish and onions on one. Mustard and onions on the other. Two bags of plain chips and two medium Cokes, please."

"You got it." She puts the dogs in the steamer and asks, "So how's life?"

"Good. Yours?"

"Busy," she says. "Too busy. I don't want to be this busy. I'd give it up except I don't know what I'd do for a social life. Is this a business lunch?"

"Sort of."

"I won't join you, then," she says. "Seven-fifty, Jack."

"Miss Marsha, do you know you have a big plastic owl on your roof?"

Marsha rolls her eyes. "The county put it there to keep the pigeons off. They take turns sitting on its head."

Jack looks up again and, sure enough, there's a pigeon perched on the owl's head.

Jack goes back to the table and sets Jeff's mustard-relish-and-onions in front of him. Says, "You're a cheap date."

"There's no better lunch on earth."

Jack tends to agree. Sitting there in the sun beside the building that's been there for a while, with the woman inside who's been there a while. Looking at the boats, looking at the water.

You sit long enough at one of these tables you can find out everything that's going on in Dana Point. Business, politics, real estate, as well as important stuff like what fish are running where and what bait they're hitting on.

"So what's up?" Jeff asks.

"Nicky Vale."

"The *Love Boat* captain."

"Is that right?"

Jeff laughs, "Let's just say that Nicky had a lot of second mates on board."

"Did you handle his boat, Jeff?"

"Sold it to him," Jeff says. "Sold it *for* him."

"I didn't know he sold it."

"I can check on it," Jeff says, "but I'm going to say it was about six months ago."

"Why'd he sell it?" Jack asks. "Did he tell you?"

"You know what they say," Jeff says. "The two happiest days of your life are the day you buy your first boat and the day you sell it."

"He was sick of it?"

"Let me put it this way, Jack. Do you own a sixty-foot cabin cruiser?"

"No."

"Why not?"

"For one thing," Jack says, "I don't have that kind of money."

"There you go."

The other thing, Jack thinks, is that if I *had* the money for a boat I wouldn't buy *that* boat. I'd buy a boat you could do some serious fishing with. A boat you could have a shot at making a living with.

A working boat.

"You got the impression he needed the money?" Jack asks.

"I didn't get the *impression*," Jeff says. "He took a bath on it. The boat market is slow, Jack. Even slower six months ago. Nicky sold it for about fifty grand less than it was worth. I advised him to wait, but he was in a hurry, insisted I make the sale."

Jack notes the frown on his face. Jeff's been in business a long time. He's made a ton of money selling boats for what they're *worth*. Not a lot more, not a lot less. It's not the commission, it's the idea.

"Boats are expensive," Jeff says. "It's not just the cost of the boat. Hell, Nicky bought that boat for cash. But it's insurance, it's fuel, it's maintenance, repairs . . . The slip fees alone on a boat that size, in this harbor, you're looking at two and a half a month. And Nicky threw some *parties* on that boat. So you're talking booze, food . . .."

"Coke?"

"You hear rumors."

"You ever hear that he used to slap his wife around?"

Jeff blows a long sigh. "You know how to take the fun out of a nice lunch."

"Sorry."

"Look, kid," Jeff says, "sometimes you'd hear some arguing from the boat. You know how sound bounces off water. She drank, he had a temper. Once or twice maybe the harbor cops were called. Did he beat her? I don't know. I know most people around here were pretty happy when he sold the boat. Except maybe the liquor store guys. Why are you here, Jack?"

"Vale's house burned down."

"And she died in the fire," Jeff says. "Common knowledge."

"I used to love this harbor when I was a kid," Jack says. "I wish they hadn't messed with it."

"Progress, Jack."

"You think?"

"Nah."

"Now they're going to ruin Dana Strands," Jack says. "Fucking 'Great Sunsets.'"

"Well, we stopped it for a while," Jeff says. Hell of a battle, too. Save the Strands mobilized a lot of the local people, got some councilmen on their side, some environmental groups. Raised money for ads, circulated petitions, even forced the Great Sunsets corporation into court over environmental impact issues, and won. "But they'll be back. They'll get better lawyers, a few councilmen . . . You can't fight money, Jack."

They sit and stare at the boats for a while. Then Jeff balls up his paper wrapper, tosses it into the trash can and says, "So it's a good thing I got Nicky's boat sold, huh? Last thing we need is a fire in the marina."

"I'm not saying anything, Jeff."

"And I hear you, Jack," he says. "I have to go sell some boats."

"Thanks for your time."

"Thanks for the lunch."

They start to leave but hang out chatting with Marsha for a while. Talking about progress.

63

Dr. Benton Howard.

Dr. Howard slides into a red-upholstered banquette at Hamburger Hamblet in Westwood. Already sitting there is a skinny guy with a bad haircut and an equally bad blue suit.

"I asked for nonsmoking," Howard says.

Dani shrugs and sips his iced tea.

Howard says, "I'm a doctor, after all."

Just barely, thinks Dani. He takes another drag of his cigarette and blows it toward the doctor's face. Howard coughs dramatically and waves his hand through the air.

"That stinks," Howard says.

And *you* stink, he thinks but doesn't say. He wants to give Dani the name of his dry cleaner but he's afraid to. But, Jesus, the suit needs cleaning badly. It smells—no, stinks—of stale sweat and old cigarette smoke and whatever the hell it is that Dani puts on his greasy hair.

Some sort of Russian bear grease, Howard decides.

He signals the waitress for an iced tea.

"I was expecting a different person," Howard says.

Viktor Tratchev, who, although somewhat rough, at least has a basic appreciation for personal hygiene.

"You'll be meeting with *me* from now on," Dani says.

"Is that all right with Viktor?" Howard asks.

"Sure," Dani says.

Or at least it *will* be, Dani thinks, when Tratchev finds out about it. And if it isn't, fuck him anyway.

"You have money for me?" Dani asks.

"Fifteen thousand," Howard whispers. "In the briefcase."

Dr. Benton Howard is forty-seven years old and has had a medical career you might charitably describe as undistinguished. Second-to-last in his class on Grenada, he did his residency at a county hospital in Louisiana and then went into private practice in "sports medicine." Dr. Howard's practice kept him very busy, mostly in court defending himself against malpractice suits, because unfortunate things tended to happen to Dr. Howard, not to mention his patients. X rays got reversed, for instance, resulting in the removal of cartilage from the wrong knee,

or reconstructive surgery on an ankle that was already perfectly constructed. Then there were a couple of unfortunate incidents involving
disc surgeries (missed it by *that* much), and Dr. Howard is that close to
delicensing and bankruptcy when the Russians seek him out.

Howard's sitting in his office one day dodging subpoena service
when the Russian fellow comes in and suggests that Dr. Benton Howard set himself up in a subspecialty.

Soft tissue injuries.

The wonderful thing about treating soft tissue injuries, Howard discovers, is that he doesn't have to actually see any patients, never mind
treat them, which is, after all, where all his problems came from in the
first place. No, all Dr. Howard has to do is meet Viktor in restaurants,
sip iced tea and sign diagnoses, treatment reports and recommenda-
tions for chiropractic treatment, massage therapy and rehabilitation
therapy.

Not that the patients don't come to his office; they do. They come
straight from a lawyer's office to Howard's office, sit in the lobby and
read magazines until the nurse calls their name, then they go into a
treatment room and read magazines until Howard comes in and tells
them to go home. Or to the chiropractor, masseur or rehabilitation
specialist.

And the money rolls in. And all his problems go away. The malpractice suits are settled or dropped, the bill collectors quit leaning on his
doorbell, his wife fires her lawyer and crawls back into his bed.

All because of soft tissue injuries.

As long as Howard signs reports that verify that Patient X is suffering
from severe pain and moderate to complete disability from a five-mile-
per-hour rear-ender fender-bender, the money train makes regular
stops at Howard's station.

And it's so easy; because someone else has already written the
reports, all Howard has to do is slip into a banquette in a dark restaurant
and sign until his wrist gets sore.

Dr. Benton Howard actually receives honest-to-goodness physical
therapy—that actually *occurs*—for carpal tunnel syndrome from signing so many forms.

Which is what's happening today. Dani pulls out a stack of medical
reports and Benton starts signing. They have a real system going, a factory. These guys can poop out medical reports like a Xerox machine,
they're that slick.

In fact, they're going so fast (Benton is in a hurry to get away from Dani's offensive odor) that he unwittingly signs treatment reports for seven people who are dead, killed when a fuel tanker slammed into a van on a highway on-ramp.

Howard doesn't realize it, of course, neither does Dani, but it's a potentially ugly fuckup.

Even Benton Howard would have a tough time explaining why he prescribed three months of neck massages for a man who is not only deceased, but actually incinerated.

64

Jack heads over to Laguna Beach.

The fifteen-minute trip south along the Pacific Coast Highway is one of Jack's favorite drives. Skirting the edge of the coastal plateau, the PCH is a mild roller coaster that takes you past Dana Strands and Salt Creek Beach and the Ritz-Carlton, past Monarch Bay and then up a hill that eventually drops you again by Aliso Pier—if you walk out onto the concrete structure around dusk you'll see a spectacular sunset—and Aliso Creek Beach. Then it climbs up another hill into South Laguna, where the hotels and restaurants and art shops really kick in, and you can see the roofs of expensive houses tucked away on the streets that lead down to the ocean.

A few more minutes of this and you hit Laguna Beach.

Laguna Beach got its start in life as an artists' colony.

Bunch of painters and sculptors fled L.A. back in the '20s and came down to the then-pristine bay and put up their artists' bungalows and painted seascapes and carved wooden statues of the fishermen who still lived around there.

It was a great choice for an artists' colony, because Laguna Beach is truly beautiful. Shaped around a crescent of coastline which rises to bluffs and cliffs, a narrow plateau where the town sits and then up to the steep, green Laguna hills. The whole thing madly lush with palm trees and bright flowers and an array of aloes, and when you look at it from a height it brings to mind a painter's palette.

So the artists settled there.

And a few tourists would come down and buy a few paintings and sculptures, so the artists set up some open-air markets where they could put up stands and still paint and carve while they waited for the customers to drift in.

It was a natural step from open-air stands to galleries, from galleries to restaurants, from restaurants to hotels, and after about fifty years the town became a tourist destination. It boomed with everything else in the '80s, got overbuilt, got perhaps a little yuppie, but never quite lost touch with its bohemian origins.

When south coast locals think of Laguna Beach they still think of painters and sculptors, coffee shops and bookstores (and, before it got trendy, bookstores with coffee shops), writers and poets, Hare Krishnas and gay men.

Laguna Beach being the primary locus of gay life on the south coast.

Which is why—and it is no less true for being stereotypical—the service in the restaurants is so friendly and so good. And the zoning is vicious. And the town has a style you won't find elsewhere on the south coast.

Laguna has its own certain sensibility, which is why Jack, like most other old-time locals, treasures the town.

So it was particularly heartbreaking when the fire swept through it.

Jack was actually on vacation that day, taking his vacation in October when most of the tourists were gone but the sun was still hot and the weather dry. Too hot and too dry, as it turned out, because the winds blew the fire across the brown brittle grasses on the bare hills above Laguna Canyon.

Jack was out on his board when he saw a thin plume of smoke rise on the hills east of town, and then the wind came up like a giant trying to fan the embers, and the weirdest thing was that he could hear the crackling of the dry grass burning over the crashing of the waves. He saw the orange-yellow flames burst up over the hills, then race down into the canyon, and the fire trucks race up to meet the fire before it could get into the populated canyon below, but Jack could see from his vantage point in the ocean that that wasn't going to happen, because the fire leaped across the canyon, just jumped Laguna Canyon Road, which runs perpendicular to the ocean and leads into town, and then climbed the opposite slope like it was nothing.

Winds whipping around like a madman.

Wind like God's temper tantrum, and Jack saw that the fire was moving up and over the hills parallel to the coast, and right down the canyon toward the heart of town.

And Jack was thinking, *Why Laguna? Of all the crap and schlock and shit they threw up on the coast, why Laguna?!* He paddled in, threw on his clothes and ran to help fight the fire.

By nightfall they were fighting it at the water's edge.

Then it stopped.

The wind changed and blew the flames back over charred ground already denuded of fuel.

Just like that, Jack thought. It had us beat and it let up. Had us down and let us up. Like God changing his mind. Like some kind of warning, of *what?* Jack wondered. A glimpse of the apocalypse? A preview of hell? Something about this California fire and life?

Jack stood there in the water wondering this as he watched the fire recede. He was hunched over, sucking for air, along with strangers and guys he surfed with, women he'd gone to school with, German tourists who just happened to have been there that night, black guys who shilled B ball on the public courts of Main Beach, glorious queen headwaiters and their partners, millionaires whose hillside homes were now smoking rubble, and they all stood there like soldiers who have stood before an overwhelming attack watching the enemy give it up and retreat. And there were no cheers or whoops—they were all just too damn tired— but what Jack remembers about that moment was that there was no talk of loss, or defeat, or what-if-this-happens-again. All the talk was about one thing.

Rebuilding.

What people were saying was basically, *We got out safely with the cat/dog, with our pictures, a few of our things—the rest of it is just stuff. It's just a hassle, that's all, but shit, no, we're not leaving. We'll live in a hotel, in an apartment, in a trailer until we rebuild.*

And Jack remembers thinking, like, Fucking A—nobody who really loves this place would leave. Not for an earthquake, not for a fire, not for anything.

The other thing Jack remembers about that night is Goddamn Billy.

Goddamn Billy leading a veritable convoy of trucks.

Right behind the fire trucks and ambulances and the like comes Billy in the passenger seat of the lead truck. The road is closed to private vehicles, but Billy leans out the window to the cop and shouts, "These ain't no goddamn private vehicles! I got hoses in here! Face masks and gloves! I got pumps and generators! I got blankets and pillows and food. I got teddy bears and shit like that for the kids!"

They let Billy through.

Billy comes roaring into Laguna like General Patton.

What happened is that Billy was monitoring the radio early in the afternoon when the fires broke out, and Billy looked at the wind and the weather and figured this could be serious shit, so Billy mobilized his Major Disaster Plan which he'd been working on for years, because, "You just had to know this was gonna happen *sometime.*"

Every dog in Claims was immediately called in from whatever he or she was doing. Every adjuster, maintenance person, lunchroom worker, supervisor, whatever, who wasn't already fighting the fires. Cal Fire and Life had some trucks of its own, but Billy also emptied every Ryder and U-Haul lot in Costa Mesa, and within a couple of hours, trucks were loaded with supplies and heading toward the fires. Waiting like benign vultures by the sides of the roads until all the fire trucks had arrived, and then Billy gave the order to get in there.

So Jack knows that while a lot of the supplies that went to the shelters and to the people fighting the fire was brought in by the Red Cross and the National Guard that day, a lot of it also came from Cal Fire and Life. And when he was standing on the beach thinking the fire was going to blow them all into the water—or worse—Goddamn Billy was right down there with him, working a pump and grumbling that they better get this goddamn fire out soon so he could light a goddamn cigarette.

You have to love Goddamn Billy, Jack thinks as he pulls into Laguna this particular day. He's remembering that night because he can't help remembering that night anytime he comes to Laguna.

It'll happen again, Jack thinks. Here or somewhere else.

He parks in the public lot behind Fahrenheit 451 bookstore and walks down PCH to Vince Marlowe's gallery.

The Marlowe Gallery.

Which Jack thinks is a lot better than some cutesy name like Ages Past or Bou-Ant-ique or something.

Vince Marlowe sells furniture. Antique, expensive furniture. Vince furnishes items to the million-dollar homes with ocean views. Jack's used him maybe twenty times to evaluate losses in the aftermath of the big fire.

Jack walks into the shop, which smells of wood polish.

Place is just jam-packed with old wooden cabinets, desks, tables, chairs, dressers, mirrors . . .

Vince himself—early sixties, gray hair, a salmon-colored polo over white slacks and sockless penny-loafers—sits behind one of the desks punching numbers into an adding machine.

"Uh-oh," he says when he sees Jack. "Something burned."

Voice as smooth as old scotch.

He gestures Jack into a seat at the desk.

"Do you know Nicky Vale?" Jack asks.

"Know him?" Vince says. "I named my pool after him. 'The Nicky Vale Memorial Swimming Hole.' Oh God, it's *not* memorial, is it?"

"His wife, Pamela."

Vince slumps in his chair. "Pamela?"

"You really hadn't heard?"

Vince is very wired into the south coast elite.

"I've been out of town," Vince says, as if it needs no explanation. Like, Laguna in August? Please.

"She died in the fire," Jack says.

"The children?"

"They weren't there," Jack says. "Only Pamela."

"They were having problems," Vince says. He mimes a glass tilting toward his lips. "How's Nicky doing?"

"He's concerned about his furniture."

Jack hands Vince a copy of Nicky's inventory and asks, "Could I buy some of your time to take a look at this, tell me if the values are in line?"

Vince scans the pages. Says, "I'll run it in detail, but I can tell you right now that they're about right. Hell, Jack, I sold Nicky half of these pieces."

"So they're the real thing?"

"Oh, very real," Vince says. "Nicky knows his stuff. Sometimes I think he spent more time in this shop than I did."

"Not lately, though."

"Things have been a little flat all over," Vince says.

"Did he try to sell you some pieces?"

"Some," Vince says. "Not the better pieces—he was too attached. But yes, he wanted me to buy some of the lesser works."

"Did you?"

"No."

"Consignment?"

Vince shakes his head. "Space is money. It's a *business* for me. People want to sell when the economy is flat, but of course then no one is buying. You either have all sellers or all buyers, depending on the times."

"How are the times now?"

"Picking up, thank you."

"So you could sell them now."

"Probably."

"For these values?" Jack asks, pointing at the inventory.

"I don't want to harm a customer and a friend," Vince says.

"Are you talking about me or Nicky?"

"Both."

"Relax," Jack says. "If these prices are roughly in line with what he should have paid for them at the time of purchase, we'll pay those numbers. I'm not interested in playing hardball here."

"Then assuming I could sell the pieces, the prices would be a little lower," Vince says. "Call it a market correction."

"Did he try to sell the bed?"

"*Noooo,*" Vince says. "I might have bought that piece for myself. The bed is . . ."

"Ashes."

"A real shame."

"So run these for me, Vince?"

"Of course," Vince says. "Give me a day or two or three?"

"Whatever you need to do it right."

"Can I buy you a cappuccino?"

Doesn't anyone drink just coffee anymore? Jack wonders.

"I have to run," he says. "Rain check."

"Keep it in your pocket."

Jack gets up and shakes his hand. Starts to leave and then asks, "Hey, Vince, you remember the night of the fire?"

Vince actually shudders. "Who could forget?"

"Did you think it was going to be the end of the world?"

"I don't know about the *whole* world," Vince says. "I think I thought it was going to be the end of *our* world."

"Yeah."

The end of *our* world.

65

Letty del Rio has a headache.

She has a headache for precisely the reason she knew she was going to have a headache—she's sitting in Uncle Nguyen's den talking to Uncle Nguyen.

"From one policeman to another," Nguyen is saying, "I know how these things are."

He's a handsome old dog, she thinks. Full head of silver hair, bright eyes, a glow to the skin. Maybe thirty pounds overweight, but it looks good on him. Nice clothes, too—a plum Calvin Klein polo over a pair of white slacks.

"Then perhaps you can help me," she says.

"Difficult," he says. "These cases are difficult."

"Very difficult."

She finds it distracting that Nguyen is looking over her shoulder. The Angels are on television. Edmonds is up in the eighth with one out and a man on base.

I'd rather be watching the game, too, she thinks.

"Tranh and Do?" Nguyen asks.

"Tranh and Do."

For like the seventh friggin' time.

"Missing?" he asks.

Her head feels like someone's drawing needles through her ears.

"Missing," Letty says.

"Who reported them missing?" Nguyen asks.

"Tommy Do's mother."

Nguyen watches Edmonds take a called strike, mulls over the call for a while, then says, "Tommy Do's mother."

Letty thinks maybe she has a brain hemorrhage. She turns around, lowers the volume on the television and says, "Uncle Nguyen, can we cut through the shit?"

Nguyen smiles. "Two cops? Two cops should be able to cut through the shit."

"Good," Letty says. "Then stop jerking my chain. And please stop repeating everything I say. I know you run everything around here. I know that nobody as much as pees in Little Saigon unless they ask you first if they can unzip their fly. I know this, so you don't have to prove anything to me. Okay?"

Nguyen nods his head in acknowledgment.

"So I *know* that you have to know *something* about these two boys."

"They are neighborhood boys."

"They were connected with a chop shop—"

"Chop shop?"

"Oh, come on," Letty says. "Look, I arrested five boys this afternoon who pretended they never heard of Tranh and Do when I know damn well that Tranh and Do worked there."

This is not news to Nguyen, who was informed of the raid before Letty even left the chop shop. Nguyen is royally pissed that one of his shops got busted and that he loses that income *and* has to spring for bail for an entire covey of young incompetents.

Letty del Rio knows that by the time she's back in her car gobbling Excedrin that Uncle Nguyen will be twanging people's wires. Letty del Rio is smart enough to know that Nguyen was not going to tell her word one. The purpose of her visit was to light a firecracker under his smug butt and then watch what happens.

Give *him* a headache for a change.

66

Jack pulls into the Monarch Bay Shopping Plaza and looks for a drugstore. There's only one, so it's easy, and a minute later he's at the pharmacist's counter.

"I'm here," Jack says, "to pick up a prescription for Pamela Vale?"

Asks this with a question mark at the end because that's the Southern California way of being polite while making a demand. Sort of an unspoken If it's okay with you.

"Are you a family member?" the pharmacist asks.

She's young and pretty and her shiny red hair looks great against her white lab coat. The tag on her chest says her name is Kelly.

"I'm kind of a personal assistant," Jack says.

"Hold on," Kelly says, and she consults the computer monitor behind the counter. Then she asks, "Which prescription is it?"

"Sleeping pills?"

"Valium," Kelly says. "But that prescription has already been picked up."

"Really?"

"Three days ago," she says. "And that was the last refill."

"Whoops," Jack says.

"Sorry," Kelly says. "Is she going to be pissed?"

"She's not going to be happy."

Kelly gives him an empathetic frown, then asks, "Has she tried melatonin?"

"What's that?"

"Over-the-counter. Puts you right out and it's totally natural."

"Cool."

"You should try it," Kelly says.

"Me?"

"Sure."

Jack shakes his head. "I sleep like a baby."

"That must be so *cute.*"

Then Kelly says, "I don't want to bum you out, but I don't think you're her only personal assistant."

"No?"

Kelly leans across the counter. "The last guy was hunkier than you."

"Uh-oh."

"But not as good-looking."

Which doesn't describe Nicky Vale, Jack thinks. Nicky Vale is a lot better-looking than me.

Kelly adds, "Real big shoulders and he wore this dorky Hawaiian shirt? The kind you get at, like, every store in Catalina? He looked like a florist shop with hair. Had a foreign accent."

"What kind of accent?"

Kelly asks, "Do you watch the Cartoon Network?"

"I think it's on when I work."

"No, it's on twenty-four hours."

"Okay."

"Anyway," Kelly says. "On the Cartoon Network they have this show? Rocky and Bullwinkle?"

"It was on when I was a kid," Jack says.

"Really?"

"Yup."

"So you know the two bad guys?" Kelly asks. "Boris and Natasha? They always wear black and he has this stiff little mustache?"

"Uh-huh."

"That's what the guy talked like. Like, *Oooh, I'm going to get that moose and squirrel.* Like that."

"That's a pretty good imitation."

"Thank you."

Jack says, "Well, I'd better get going."

Kelly shrugs.

Like, whatever.

Like, personal assistants come in here all the time.

67

The Mustang can *move.*

It ain't Nicky's Porsche, of course, but then again you ain't gonna be doing a hundred and forty on the PCH either. Not on the stretch between Monarch Bay and Dana Point, so the classic '66 is doing just fine, thank you.

See, what Jack does is he drives down to Monarch Bay, ignores the guard and does a U-turn at the gate. Comes to a complete stop.

He checks his watch.

Says, "Go."

Stomps on the gas pedal and leaves a satisfying streak of rubber behind him. Pulls out on the PCH, takes a right and heads south toward Dana Point. Hits the red light at Ritz-Carlton Drive (fuck you, Ritz-Carlton, you get your own friggin' traffic signal), then stomps on it again. Makes it clear down to where the PCH South splits and becomes Del Prado, and turns right on Blue Lantern. Takes Blue Lantern to the top of Harbor Drive and takes another right and bingo, he's at the Vale driveway, 37 Bluffside Drive.

Eight minutes, fifteen seconds.

Jack sits back and takes a little breather.

"Go."

The reverse route. Left onto Harbor. Left on Blue Lantern. Wait for the light and then left onto the PCH. A straight shot back to the gate.

Nine minutes flat.

The guard comes out of the kiosk this time.

"May I help you, sir?" is what he *says*. What he means is What the fuck do you think you're doing?

"Maybe," Jack says. "Hi, I'm Jack Wade, California Fire and Life."

"Mike Derochik."

"Mike," Jack asks, "were you on duty last Wednesday night?"

"I came on at midnight," the guard says.

"Did Mr. Vale go out at anytime during the night?"

The guard says, "We don't discuss the comings and goings of our residents."

Jack hands him his card.

"If Mr. Vale came out of here during those hours," Jack says, "it was probably to kill his wife. You probably knew her, too, right? Nice woman with two little kids? Think it over, huh? Give me a call?"

Derochik puts the card in his pocket.

Jack's about to drive off when the guard says, "I didn't see him go out."

"Okay."

It was worth a try.

"But I saw him come in."

Whoa.

"What time?" Jack asks.

"About a quarter to five," the guard says.

Gotcha, Call Me Nicky.

Caught you in a lie.

Incendiary origin.

Motive.

Now opportunity.

Now if I can just buy a little more time.

68

Jack's waiting in the parking lot of Cal Fire and Life.

Waiting for Bill Reynolds, the executive from Underwriting who okayed a million bucks in coverage for the Vales' personal property, to leave for the day.

Jack's waiting in the parking lot because he doesn't want to go to

Bill's office and embarrass the guy or get the gossip going. Jack doesn't want to hurt Bill Reynolds, he just wants the time to finish his investigation.

Reynolds comes out of the building. Tall guy, has to go six-six, and heavy—in fact, overweight. Wearing an underwriter's gray suit and carrying a briefcase. Guys from Underwriting take work home.

Jack steps up.

"Bill? I'm Jack Wade from Claims."

"Bill Reynolds."

Reynolds has a *What the hell is this* look on his face as he peers through his glasses down at Jack.

"Bill, you okayed some personal property coverage for Roger Hazlitt on the Vale risk?"

"I'd have to look in the file."

Jack lays the Vale policy on the hood of Reynolds's blue Lexus.

"Come see me in my office," Reynolds says. "I'm not standing out here in the parking lot . . . It's 103 degrees . . ."

"You don't want to do this in your office."

"There are channels—"

"You don't want me to go through channels," Jack says.

You're taking bribes from agents, "channels" is not the way you want to go.

Reynolds looks down at him, both literally and figuratively.

"What are you, an M-3?" he asks, citing pay rankings.

"M-4."

"M-4," Reynolds says. "I'm an M-6. You don't have the weight to throw around."

Jack nods. "Roger says he slipped you a thousand bucks to okay this coverage."

Which might add to the weight quotient a little bit.

"Get away from my vehicle."

"Is it true?"

"I said get away from my vehicle."

"Look, typically you'd lay some of that risk off, wouldn't you?" Jack asks. "Work with the customer to get one or two other carriers to pick up some of the coverage? Isn't that the way you'd normally do it if the risk was too high but you wanted to keep the customer?"

"Those are *Underwriting* decisions."

"Which is why I'm asking *you.*"

"You don't understand the business."

"Educate me."

Reynolds takes off his glasses. Looks down at Jack for a long time before he says, "I don't have the time to explain to you things that you don't have the education to understand. So leave it alone."

"Can't."

"What's your name again?"

"Jack Wade. Large Claims."

"That's Billy Hayes's unit?"

"You know it is," Jack says. "You had your boss on the phone banging at him first thing this morning."

"Well, Jack Wade from Large Claims," Reynolds says. "I'm going to tell you once: drop this. Understand?"

"I don't have the education," Jack says. "And that's twice you've told me."

"Well, I'm not going to tell you again."

"Good, because I was getting bored."

"You won't be bored tomorrow morning, I can tell you that."

"You gonna make some more calls, Bill?"

"Get away from my vehicle."

"You gonna bring the *heat* down?"

Reynolds squeezes himself into the driver's seat and starts the engine. Jack takes the papers off the hood.

The car window rolls down with a soft electric hum.

"Pay the claim," Reynolds says.

"No."

"Pay the claim."

"Everyone's telling me that."

"Everyone's right."

"Let me tell you about some basic laws of physics," Jack says. "Before heat can go down, it goes up. Heat rises. So don't drop any more heat on Billy Hayes, because I'll send some up your way, from M-4 to M-6."

The window rolls up.

Reynolds disappears behind blue tinted glass.

Smoked glass, Jack thinks.

69

The parking lot's a rough place today.

Jack's walking into the building when he sees Sandra Hansen heading toward him.

"Sandra," Jack says.

"Jack."

Jack knows this conversation can only be trouble, because Sandra Hansen is the So-Cal head of Cal Fire and Life's SIU. SIU stands for Special Investigative Unit, which means it's the fraud unit. Every big insurance carrier has one, a unit that specializes in handling potentially fraudulent claims. Cal Fire's SIU functions as more of an intelligence organization—it doesn't bother with the small shit; its major job is to track fraud *rings,* the specialized rip-off operations that suck millions of bucks a year in phony claims.

As a former cop, Jack would have been a perfect candidate for SIU, except Jack doesn't want to be a cop of any kind anymore, even a pseudo-cop.

Another reason he's not interested is because SIU also functions as the company's internal affairs unit. You got a Claims guy taking kickbacks for recommending a contractor, or an auto adjuster splitting overcharges with a body shop, or, say, an underwriter taking money from an agent to write bad book, that's SIU's turf.

And Jack would rather be a dog than a rat.

"Were you staking me out, Sandra?" Jack asks her.

"As a matter of fact I was," Hansen says. "Jack, you have a file we're interested in."

"Olivia Hathaway?" Jack asks.

Hansen doesn't think it's funny. She gives Jack her professional SIU hard look and says, "The Vale file."

Surprise, surprise, Jack thinks.

"What about it?"

"We want you to back off it."

"Who's we?"

"SIU."

Like I'm supposed to get all watery in the knees, Jack thinks. Fucking SIU thinks it's the CIA and the FBI except it doesn't have to answer to anybody.

Well, fuck that.

"Why?" Jack asks. "Why does SIU want me to back off the file?"

"Does it matter?"

"To me."

Hansen's pissed. Generally speaking, she says lay off a file, the adjuster lays off it.

"You're walking into something," Hansen says. "You don't know where you're walking."

This is true, Jack thinks.

This is really interesting.

"Tell me," Jack says. "Your guys have something here, for God's sake tell me, Sandra. I could use the help."

"You're going to trip over—"

"So shine me a light," Jack says. "Seriously, show me the way."

"—shit that's too big for you to handle."

Jack says, "Maybe I should decide what's too big for me to handle."

Sandra pulls out the big gun. "Don't make me take this file away from you."

Fucking SIU, they can do that. They can walk in and take the handling of a file.

So why hasn't she already done it? Jack thinks. If she wants the Vale file so badly, why *doesn't* she just take it? Nice big juicy arson file. Lotsa glory for SIU . . .

"I'm trying to do this nicely, Jack," Sandra says. "I'm telling you: back off."

"You're saying pay the claim?"

"I'm not saying anything."

"You're working Vale already, aren't you?" Jack says.

"Shut up, Jack."

"You must have a blind file and Vale's name has—"

"Don't say another word."

"—come up in there somewhere and you're afraid I'm going to trip over it and blow your investigation."

"SIU has no such file."

"Come on."

"I never said that," Hansen says. "And this conversation never happened."

Official-pronouncement-type voice.

"And you're going to pay the claim," Sandra says.

"I'm tired of everyone and his fucking dog telling me to pay this claim," Jack says. "Agency, Underwriting, now SIU? What's going on? Who is this Vale guy, the king?"

"Just pay his claim."

"A woman was murdered."

"This is bigger than that."

Jack stands there and stares at her.

"You're crazy," he says.

"If you force us—"

"Totally whacked."

"If you force us to take over this file," Hansen says, "I promise you a world of trouble. The rest of your short career will be nothing but one long shit shower."

She can do it, too, Jack thinks. All she has to do is get one contractor to say he gave me money and I'm out on my ass. She can do it and she would do it because Sandra Hansen is a tough cookie. Standing there in her white business suit with blond hair like a helmet. Attractive, sexy, a killer. Thirty-five or so and already the head of So-Cal SIU. Her career a bullet and I'm standing in the way.

"Think about it, Jack," she says.

"Stay out of my file, Sandra."

Hansen decides to give it one more try.

"Get on the team, Jack."

"What team?"

"You want to be a claims dog the rest of your life?" Sandra asks. "With your background, you could be SIU. Mayhew's retiring at the end of the year. There'll be a slot open . . ."

"You offering me a deal, Sandra?"

"Whatever."

"I don't do deals."

This pisses Hansen off.

"You're either with us," she says, "or you're against us."

Jack takes Sandra by the shoulders. Gets right in her face.

"If you want to pay this claim," he says, "I'm against you."

He lets her go and walks away.

"That's not where you want to be!" she yells after him. "That is *not* where you want to be."

Jack keeps walking as he flips her off over his shoulder.

Leaving Sandra Hansen thinking what a big, brainless, dumb stud Jack Wade is. She's thinking that Jack's surfboard has landed on his head once—make that twice—too often.

And that she's going to have to take him down.

Three years.

She has three years and God only knows how much of her budget sunk into a long-term investigation of Russian organized crime and she's not going to let one stubborn M-4 of an adjuster flush it down the toilet.

Dead woman or no dead woman.

She feels bad about that.

It makes her sick that Vale gets away with murdering his wife, but that's the way it is.

70

Pamela.

Nicky's biggest break from Mother Russia.

A break with the old code, but Nicky's inaugurated the new code and the brothers are marrying now.

But not California girls—Russian women.

Women of the same culture and language, usually with family ties in the mob. These are wives who understand the way things work, who help bind their husbands to the mob and the code, whose families back home in Russia can be used as hostages if hubby suddenly develops a desire to transgress against the mob.

Not American wives, not California girls.

Who don't know the code, who ask questions, who make demands, who can't keep their mouths shut, who get unhappy and when they get unhappy get divorces.

Marry a Russian girl, Dani tells him when he sees Pamela on his arm two, three, four dates in a row.

"I want children," Nicky argues.

"Have Russian children," Dani advises. He whips open a catalog of Russian would-be brides eager to immigrate. "Pick one out. *Any* one and she's yours. There are some real beauties here."

And there are, Nicky agrees. Stunning Russian women, but that's the point. He doesn't want a Russian woman. He wants an American woman. He doesn't want to strengthen the bond, he wants to break it.

And they don't get it.

Mother does.

She sees exactly what's happening.

"It is a slap in the face," she says.

"No, it isn't."

"You are a Russian."

"I'm an American."

Nicky Vale.

The turnaround in one generation, but to make that a reality he needs to regenerate. To have children.

American children.

Besides which, he *has* to have *her.* She's driving him insane. He knows she dresses to provoke him. Shows him the tops of her white breasts, her long thighs. Wears perfumes that make him hard the second she walks into the room. Kisses him with full warm lips and swipes her tongue across his in a way that makes him feel that tongue on his cock, and then she breaks away and smiles at him to let him know that she knows exactly what he's thinking, and *laughs* at him.

Or she'll press against him. Press her breasts into his arm or his back, or worse—no, better; no, worse—press her pussy against the front of his pants and say, "Oh, baby, I wish we could."

"We can," he'll say.

"No," she'll say, frowning. Then a little whimper, her lips in a frustrated pout. "It's against my beliefs."

Then she rolls against him, sighs, pouts and steps away.

Sometimes even touches herself over her dress and looks at him with sad eyes and he *knows* what she's doing. Knows that she is a cock-teaser extraordinaire, knows this, but can't help himself.

Maybe because she represents to him everything that is so close but just out of reach.

America.

California.

A new life.

A turnaround inside one generation.

And he can see her as the mother of his American children. She is beautiful, free, happy in that careless California way that just doesn't carry the long tragic burden that Russians bear. And if his children come from her, in his mind they come somehow cleansed of all that history.

And besides, he has to have her.

"Then have her as a mistress," Mother says. "If you absolutely must have the little tease, then set her up in an apartment, give her money, give her presents, screw yourself silly until you're tired of her, then give her more money and say goodbye, but *don't marry her.*"

If you marry her, Mother says, she will take your heart, your money and your children because this is America and in America the father has no rights. She will ruin you. She's a gold digger.

"Marry this piece of trash," she says, "and she will leave *you* in the rubbish in her place."

Which, of course, cuts it.

Nicky gives Pam a ring that night.

They marry two months later.

On their honeymoon, on the lawn of the private villa on Maui, she sheds her flowered dress for him. Invites him inside her.

Where she is hot sweet honey.

Liquid gold.

Nicky remembers her neck, the smell of vanilla in the nape of her neck as he stood behind her and put his lips and his tongue against the sweet-smelling white skin below her ear, below her black hair. How she moved against him so he ran his hand down the scooped neck of her dress and felt her breast. Felt the flimsy bra give way and then he rolled her nipple between his thumb and finger and she didn't object so he slid the dress down over her breasts then held them in his hands and slid his thumbs back and forth across the nipples and how she brought her hand around—to stop him, he thought at first, but she just held her palm to the back of his head—so he took one hand and ran it down her stomach, and down, and she was wet.

He remembers the sound she made—mmm-*hmmm,* a sound of unashamed pleasure—and he rubbed her with a finger and she sank back into him.

It's funny what you remember, he thinks again, because what he remembers most is the smell of her neck and the flowered dress. What it looked like as he pushed it over her breasts, and down around her hips, and how it looked lying rumpled at her feet as she stepped out of it, and laid down on top of it, and held her arms up to invite him to come into her.

Strange, he thinks, but that moment was America to him, was California to him, that open-armed, open-legged invitation to unabashed pleasure. The sound of California to him is and always will be: mmm-*hmmm.*

And he remembers her wide purple eyes when later she wrapped her legs around him and pushed him deeper in and held him there as she climaxed, and then he did, and then he laid his face into her neck.

And how she said, "Kiss my neck and I can't stop you."

"Why didn't you tell me this much, *much* earlier?"

"Because then I couldn't have stopped you."

Then she scratched his back with the diamond of the engagement ring he'd given her.

Mmm-hmmm.

71

For quite a while they're happy in their California life.

The money rolls in as they ride the top of the real estate boom. She becomes a south coast housewife. Mornings in the gym, lunch with the ladies, afternoons harassing the interior decorators who come to make the house a showpiece. Or getting her hair, her face, her nails done at this salon or that, usually with the same ladies with whom she'd lunched.

Parties in the evening. Lovely friends, beautiful people.

She becomes pregnant quickly, as he sensed she would, her body a lush field of spring wildflowers. Natalie is born with Daddy in the delivery room doing that American thing, coaching his wife's breathing. But little coaching is needed. Pamela was serenely pregnant—cheerful, relaxed, happy. The birth is as easy as births can be.

"I am a Russian peasant woman," she jokes. "The next baby I'll just drop in a wheat field."

"You are hardly a peasant," Nicky says.

She reminds him that she grew up on a farm.

"Knock me up again," she tells him.

He's delighted to.

Michael's birth is also easy.

Pamela, Nicky thinks, is made to be a mother. She is inseparable from the children. He has to cajole her to get a sitter and go out even once a week. He feigns annoyance, but secretly it pleases him.

That his American wife is a homebody. Content to be with her children. To take them on long walks, play with them in the backyard gym that he has constructed. She paints when they take naps. In the little studio he has built for her beside their bedroom. She stands by the easel and looks out the window and paints watercolor seascapes.

Her paintings are not very good, but she's happy.

And it leaves him free to fuck around.

He has a wife, now he starts collecting mistresses. He still finds Pamela attractive, but now that she is a mother she has lost a certain erotic edge. He seeks it elsewhere, finds it everywhere. Pam is all curves and bosom and hips—he goes for sharp edgy women at the tennis club. Takes them to the Laguna Hills Resort or the Ritz for sweaty postmatch sex. Pamela is sweetness and *Goodnight Moon*—he picks up hard cocktail waitresses and gives them coke and fucks them sometimes on top of the car hood parked at Dana Strand Beach. He takes an especially perverse delight in seducing her friends, not that the seduction is generally a difficult matter, thank you—so while Pamela is committing her mild offenses against art in the sunny room while the children sleep, he is in one of her friend's bedrooms, in one of her friends, in point of fact, and *they* seem to delight in asking, Does Pam do *this* for you? Does Pam do *this* for you? And then doing this and this and that and the other thing and then one of Pam's friends decides to have the ultimate thrill and tell her all about it.

He arrives home that evening and all is well until she puts the kids to bed and then she walks up to where he's sitting and slaps him across the face.

"And that would be for?" he asks.

"Leslie," she says. "If you ever do it again, I'll divorce you and take the children."

He grabs her by the wrist, forces her to her knees on the floor and patiently explains that there have been, are, and will be a lot of Leslies—and Leslie *again* if he has a stirring in that direction—and that she will most definitely not divorce him.

"Here is the deal," he says. "You have the house, the children and all the money and luxuries you could want. All this comes with your position as my wife. Enjoy it. Be happy. Listen to me: *There will never be a divorce. You will never take my children.* You will be their mother *and* my wife *and* my lover. And I will have other women as I wish."

"How about me?" she asks angrily. "Do I get to have other men?"

Which is the first time he hits her.

A ringing slap across the face.

Then he tells her to go up to the bedroom, change into something sexy and be in bed when he gets there. He sits and looks at a furniture catalog for a while and then goes up. She's on the bed, as he told her, in a blue corset, as he told her, looking almost defiantly sexual.

Stunningly beautiful, truly. Black hair shining on her white shoulders. Her neck long and inviting. Her breasts pushed up and glowing white in the soft light. Her black pubic hair naked for him.

As if she could take him back with pure sexual power.

Like, Have your other women, you'll never have anything like *this.*

And that beautiful face with those violet eyes shining with anger and fear and defiance . . .

He lifts her up and flips her over. Places her hands on the headboard and then takes her in the way he saw convicts take the scared young *zeks* in prison.

Does Pam do this for you?

Pam does what I tell her.

Pam starts drinking shortly after that.

72

And things fall apart.

They thought the boom would last forever.

In the land of sunshine and blue water where only good things happen to beautiful people.

But the real estate market slows, then comes to a halt, and Nicky is leveraged to his eyeballs. Nothing is selling, nothing is even renting. Nobody is investing and the creditors want their cash.

Which Nicky doesn't have.

He's gambled it all on the come and it isn't coming.

Condo complexes, apartment buildings, raw land.

All sitting as still as a dead summer day.

And the other business, well, every business needs tending, and Nicky's been neglecting the organization. The two units are pretty much operating on their own, sending a share of their profits up to Nicky and skimming a little more off his share every day. Schaller, Rubinsky and Tratchev are conspiring to do just the thing that Nicky had intended to do *for* them before the recession shut down his cash pipeline—leave Nicky's organization and become independent.

And there are grumblings: Nicky's not putting anything back into the business, Nicky's gotten sloppy, Nicky's gotten soft.

Nicky has gone American.

Dani and Lev try to warn him. Dani tells him to take back control while there's still time. Give his security force something to do, keep them sharp, keep the weapon honed. Nicky tells them no.

Things will turn around. The economy will bounce back. To this extent they're right in what they're saying about him—he has gone soft. He doesn't relish a return to the gun and the knife and the chicken chop.

He sends good money after bad.

Scrapes up what money he can to make the loan payments but it's never enough. Month after month the market spirals down.

He has empty condos, empty apartments. Hell, he has two aparment buildings under construction that he doesn't have the money to complete because he's shifted funds to pay the loans on other properties.

He starts doing more and more coke. It makes him feel better. He buys art he can't sell and can't afford to keep, because it makes him feel better and it keeps up appearances. He spends cash on women who six months ago would have balled him for free. He gives them coke, he gives them art. They get him hard and he feels powerful again for a few minutes.

All the while his own wife is drinking like a fish, taking pills and causing scenes at parties. ("How many people here have fucked my husband? A show of hands, please.") They get into fights, he knocks her around. His kids start looking at him like he's some sort of monster. He hits *them* once or twice. ("Don't you *ever* open your mouth to me.") He spends more and more nights away from home.

None of this escapes the attention of Tratchev, Rubinsky and Schaller.

You listen closely at night, you can hear the wolves circling.

Pam goes to rehab and comes back a raving bitch.

Sober, and the first time Nicky lays a mitt on her she goes to the authorities and lays a TRO on him.

Gets his name in the court system.

I have stolen millions of dollars in this country, Nicky thinks. I have robbed and killed and stolen millions and this is the *first time* my name appears in court. And my *wife* does that to me.

My own *wife*.

Not for long.

Pam files for divorce.

"I told you I would kill you," Nicky says. "I mean it."

"I don't care," Pam says. "I can't live this way."

"If you leave, you leave the way you came. With nothing but some cheap dress on your ass."

"I don't think so," Pam says. "I'll take the children and the house and half of everything. I'll even take your precious furniture, Nicky."

It could happen, Nicky thinks. In this godforsaken country where a man has no rights. They'll give the drunken bitch the kids, they'll give her the house, they'll launch a fishing expedition through my finances that could prove not only costly but dangerous.

It would endanger the plan.

A plan of such simple elegance, such balanced design, such perfect symmetry that it only confirms in him his own sense of genius.

Crime as artful construction.

A plan that, if it works, will achieve his goal of the turnaround in one generation.

And Pamela could stop it.

Take his dream and his identity with it.

In a particularly cruel argument one night she snaps, "My son will *not* be a gangster."

No, he will not, Nicky thinks.

In despair, he goes to Mother.

Goes into her room in the small hours of the morning, sits on her bed and says, "Mother, I could lose—we could lose—everything."

"You have to do something, Daziatnik."

"What?"

"You know, Daziatnik," she says. She takes his face into her hands. "You know what you have to do."

Yes, I know, Nicky thinks as he lies back.

I know what I have to do.

Take back control of my organization.

Protect my family.

He's at home, taking a walk on the lawn when it hits him. He's looking down at Dana Strands, he's thinking about Great Sunsets, and the idea comes to him.

The perfect symmetry of it.

The beautiful balance.

Perfectly structured poetry, like the finest furniture.

Everything, all, in a master stroke.

He watches the sun set over Dana Strands.

73

More likely than not.

Is the phrase that's running through Jack's head as he sits in his cubicle.

More likely than not.

"More likely than not" is the phrase that applies to the standard of proof in civil cases. In criminal cases the standard of proof is "beyond a reasonable doubt" and the distinction is important to Jack's consideration of the Vale file.

If I deny the claim, Jack thinks, we will—*far* more likely than not—get sued. At the end of the trial the judge will instruct the jury as to the burden of proof, and he'll tell the jury that the critical question is, "Is it more likely than not that Mr. Vale either set the fire or caused the fire to be set?"

That's the way the law reads.

In reality it's far more complicated.

The civil burden of proof is "more likely than not," so technically, if it's even 51 percent to 49 percent that your guy did it, the jury should come back and find for the insurance company. That's the way it's supposed to work, but Jack knows that's not the way it does work.

How it *does* work is that the jury is perfectly aware that arson is a crime. No matter what the judge instructs them, they are not going to apply the civil standard, "more likely than not," as the burden of proof. They're going to apply the criminal standard—"beyond a reasonable doubt."

So Jack knows that if you're going to deny a claim based on arson you had better be damn sure that you can persuade a jury that your insured set the fire or caused it to be set . . . *beyond a reasonable doubt.*

So Jack asks himself, Is it more likely than not that Vale set the fire or caused it to be set?

Yes, it is more likely than not.

Beyond a reasonable doubt?

Jack takes out a piece of legal paper and a ruler and draws two straight lines down the paper, creating three columns. At the top of the columns he writes: INCENDIARY ORIGIN, MOTIVE, OPPORTUNITY.

Nicky's up to his ears in debt. He's about to lose the house. He has a balloon payment coming up and no apparent resources to pay it. He owes money to the feds and to the state. His companies are in trouble, too. He sells his beloved boat at a loss to try to get some cash. He has a bundle sunk into antique furniture, and, according to Vince Marlowe, he can't sell the furniture he *wants* to sell. But he doesn't even try to sell the pieces he's *attached* to. His wife is about to divorce him and that would split his meager resources at least in half.

Motive, Jack thinks, is a dead solid lock.

So motive is a win, opportunity is a push, incendiary origin is a comer.

Unless Accidentally Bentley hangs in with his cig-in-the-vodka theory.

Jack draws a dotted line down the center of each column, then alternates plus and minus signs so that each category of proof is divided into pros and cons.

When he finishes the chart, it looks like this:

INCENDIARY ORIGIN		MOTIVE		OPPORTUNITY	
+	−	+	−	+	−
accelerant	Bentley	mortgage balloon		doors locked	alibi
pour pattern	cig/vodka			windows locked	
points of origin	fuel load	taxes		distance to house	
		low income		dog outside	
alligator char		divorce	reconcile	seen at 4:45 a.m.	
annealed bed				lied in statement	
hole in roof					
pebbled glass					
red flame	contents?				

Jack thinks about the chart for a few minutes, then draws a horizontal line across the bottom, subtitles the new section MURDER and starts again.

INCENDIARY ORIGIN		MOTIVE		OPPORTUNITY	
+	−	+	−	+	−
all above plus:	cig/vodka	all above plus hatred?		all above	alibi
no smoke in lungs	alcohol + CO				no witness
carboxyhemo-globin	location of body				
pugilistic					

Okay, Jack tells himself. Take the arson first. Start with incendiary origin. What are your three strongest points? ("The Rule of Three," Billy says. "Always try to present your evidence in sets of three. It's the way juries like to hear it. It's always a minister, a priest and a rabbi in the rowboat.")

So what are my three strongest points? Well, the positive char samples make bullshit of Bentley's cigarette-in-the-vodka hypothesis. So that would be number one. Number two? The pour pattern—there's no way to reconcile that with an accidental fire. Number three? Multiple points of origin. Again, inconsistent with an accidental fire.

Now, what are the points against?

The counterargument is that certain contents in the room might have burned "hot," leaving an erroneous implication of multiple points of origin. And Bentley's point about the fuel load is correct as far as it goes. There was a lot of stuff in the bedroom, and it's possible that the heavy fuel load burn could explain away the other indicators of an accelerated fire.

It could provide reasonable doubt, anyway.

But not with the positive samples.

With a positive sample, Jack thinks, everything falls together.

Motive.

Dead-solid lock. The three strongest points? The balloon payment, the lack of income, the missed payments. It's an embarrassment of riches—no reverse pun intended—and there'll be no problem proving that Nicky had a motive to torch the house. The arguments against? There really aren't any.

Opportunity.

Three strongest points? Locked doors and windows with no sign of forced entry, Leo the pooch outside and Derochik's statement having Nicky coming in at 4:45.

And now Nicky has lied. You have him on tape saying he never went out, that the phone call woke him up. And I guess that just fucks you.

Arguments against? No witness to put Nicky on or near the actual fire scene. No snitch to connect him directly to the fire.

Two: Mother Russia's alibi—but Derochik's statement is going to shoot that down.

So, opportunity?

A tougher call, but when you put it together with incendiary origin and motive, it plays.

Move down to the murder, because it's all connected. A jury will never believe the coincidence of a murder with an accidental fire. Conversely, they'll never buy an accidental death with an intentional fire.

We have a combo plate here, Jack thinks.

Strongest points that Pamela Vale was murdered?

One: She was dead in time proximity to an arson.

Two: Her bloodstream showed alcohol and barbiturates, but witnesses will say that she wasn't drinking, and someone else—probably an associate of her husband's—picked up her Valium prescription.

Arguments against?

Primarily, there's the ME's conclusion of death by overdose.

Second is Bentley's call of CO asphyxiation accelerated by acute inebriation. The alcohol reduces the amount of oxygen in the lungs, making CO poisoning rapid and deadly.

It's possible, Jack thinks.

If she was drinking.

And *if* there was no accelerant.

And if, Jack thinks, you hadn't looked into Nicky's eyes and just known that he killed his wife.

And if the arrogant bastard hadn't lied on tape.

Jack goes in to see Goddamn Billy.

74

Viktor Tratchev is one *très* pissed gangster.

"Valeshin wanted to be a real estate developer," Tratchev says to his head enforcer, an obelisk of a human specimen known simply as Bear, "so he's a real estate developer. Fine. What does he think, that he can just stroll in when he feels like it and be the boss again?"

Bear shrugs. Bear may not know the term "rhetorical question" but he knows one when he hears one.

Tratchev's working himself up.

"What does he think?" Tratchev asks. "That I'm going to lie down and just *take* this shit? I'm supposed to lie down on my belly and let him *fuck* me?!"

This is pretty much exactly what he's supposed to do, actually, according to Dani and Lev, who drop by Tratchev's house that afternoon for a glass of tea and some browbeating.

"You've been shorting the *pakhan* on his share," Dani explains.

By about 100 percent, Dani's thinking.

"Bullshit," Tratchev says.

"Not bullshit," Dani insists. "What do you think, you're playing with children here?"

"I—"

Dani holds up a hand to stop him. "Don't add insult to injury. Keep your lies inside your mouth. Listen, Viktor, between you and me, I'll admit that things have gotten pretty loose. So you take advantage. All right, you take advantage. Human nature. Maybe the fault then is on both sides.

"But I'm here to tell you today, Viktor Tratchev, that the free and easy days are over. The *pakhan* is the *pakhan* again. From now on, until trust is restored, we will take the payments and give you your proper share. You will run a tighter operation that doesn't end up on the evening news. And Viktor Tratchev, if you cause any more problems, I will personally cut off your head and piss into your gasping mouth. Thank you for the tea."

They get up and leave and Tratchev is about to throw a rod.

"I'll kill him," he says.

"Dani?" Bear asks.

"Him too," Tratchev said.

Who he has in mind is Nicky.

He starts working the phones.

75

Tom Casey's in with Billy.

"Let me get this straight, Jack," Casey says. "You want to deny a fire claim because a poodle had to take a piss."

"A Yorkie," Jack says. "Because a Yorkie had to take a piss."

Casey turns back from the window and smiles at him with beatific menace.

"Are you fucking with me, Jack?" he asks.

"I wouldn't fuck with you, Tom."

This is definitely true, because not only are Jack Wade and Tom Casey good friends, but Tom Casey is the Meanest Man in California.

This isn't just Jack's opinion; it's an official title Casey won by unanimous vote at a California Defense Bar Association meeting after he gave a now infamous lecture on the fine art of cross-examination.

Casey's lecture was a joke.

Literally. And it went something like this:

"This accountant goes to prison for embezzlement," Casey tells the audience, "and the second he gets to his cell, his cell mate, an *enormous, mean*-looking guy, says, 'Now, here in this prison we like to play House. Which would you rather be, the husband or the wife?'

"The accountant—who is terrified—doesn't want to be either, of course, but when he considers the various options, he decides he'd rather be the husband. So he manages to croak, 'The husband. I'll be the husband.'

"'Okay, Husband,' the cell mate says, 'now get over here and suck your wife's dick.'"

After the subsequent horrified gasp and burst of laughter, Casey tells the crowd, "And that joke tells you everything you need to know about cross-examination, to wit—when you get to the ultimate question, it shouldn't matter whether the witness says yes or no."

After which, Casey is officially named the Meanest Man in California.

"Goddamn it, Jack," Goddamn Billy Hayes says. He's irritable because Casey has insisted that they meet in the air-conditioned office and there's no smoking in there.

"*Whatever* the fuck kind of dog," Casey says.

Jack gazes on Casey's sartorial splendor. Today he's wearing a pearl gray Halbert & Halbert DB with a two-toned white shirt and red silk tie. Casey's famous for his clothes, especially his ties. The joke around the office is that you can actually take a tour of his walk-in closet at home, and that the bus stops for lunch at the shirt section before setting out for the shrine that is the tie rack.

He lifts his hands in his trademark shrug and asks Jack the same question he often asks (rhetorically) of juries, "I mean, am I *missing* something here?"

"You're missing *a lot*," Jack says.

"Enlighten me," Casey says, then he sits down and crosses his legs. His eyes widen in mock innocence. "Please, teach me."

Like, make your case.

Convince me and maybe you can convince a jury.

Don't convince me and I'll advise Goddamn Billy to pay the claim.

Jack knows the drill. He takes out the chart he made and lays it on Billy's desk.

"Bentley's whole overdose theory relies on Pamela Vale smoking in bed and drinking," Jack says. "I have eight witnesses who will swear that she was sober at least as of 10 p.m."

"That gives her half the night—"

"She didn't keep booze in the house."

"She bought—"

"Not anywhere in Dana Point."

"Go ahead," Casey says.

"The same witnesses will testify that Pam was terrified that night," Jack says. "That she told them Nicky was going to kill her."

"Hearsay."

"You can get it in."

Casey smiles. "Maybe."

"You'll get it in."

"Even if I do," Casey says, "so what? Pamela Vale was afraid and alone. Sadly, she fell off the wagon and went back to the one solace she had—the bottle. She drank herself into unconsciousness, the cigarette slipped from her hand, she died of CO asphyxiation or overdose before the flames hit her. A tragic accident."

"But before she passed out," Jack says, "she poured kerosene from the closet, across the floor, over the bed and under the bed?"

He hands Casey Dinesh's report.

"The formal report will be here in a day or so," Jack says. "Dinesh faxed me the charts."

"You sandbagged me, Jack," Casey says.

"Kerosene," Jack says.

"Volume?"

"Two to five gallons."

Casey says, "Bentley's fucked. Motive?"

Jack lays it out for him.

"It's enough for me," Billy says.

"Not so fast, Cisco," Casey says. "You have incendiary origin. You have motive. But opportunity? You have nothing to put your insured on the scene."

"There's nothing that indicates anyone else had access to the scene," Jack says.

"A boyfriend?" Casey asks. "A lover? Vale says they were going to reconcile. She tells the boyfriend, 'Sorry, Charlie, it was beautiful but now it's over.' The boyfriend is—forgive me—inflamed with rage. Decides, 'I'll show you *over*, bitch.' Strangles her and lights her up. Perfect revenge on her *and* the husband."

"So this phantom lover kills her, sets up the fire, gets a key and locks the doors on his way out?" Jack asks. "Why? Besides which, there's no indication anywhere of any phantom boyfriend. And then there's Leo."

"The poodle."

"The Yorkie," Jack says. "Nicky waits until the kids are asleep, until everything is dead on the streets, then he leaves Mother Russia's and drives to the Bluffside Drive house. He lets himself in. The dog doesn't bark because it's Daddy. Of course, Daddy has a can of kerosene with him, but what does a dog know?"

"What time is it now?" Casey asks.

Jack shrugs. "Three. Three-thirty."

"Okay. Go on."

"Nicky goes into the bedroom," Jack says. "Maybe he has a gun, maybe he has a knife—but he forces her to drink. Maybe he rapes her, I don't know. But he smothers her on the bed. Then he takes the kerosene and pours a big pool in the closet, trails it across the room and pours a bigger pool under the bed and over her body."

"Why?" Casey asks. "If she's already dead?"

"Rage," Jack says. "He pours it from her waist down."

"Go ahead."

"But he just can't barbecue the pooch. Just won't torch little Leo. So he puts Leo outside and shuts the door. We're talking about 4:30 now. He goes back inside and lights the match."

"Timing device?" Billy asks.

"I'm guessing he uses a cigarette tucked into a book of matches. That gives him five to ten minutes before the flame touches off the kerosene. It's a nine-minute drive back to Monarch Bay. The guard sees him come back in around 4:45."

"One minute after Meissner sees the fire," Casey says.

"And the same time Mother sees him checking on his kids," Jack says. "Convenient."

"Will the guard testify?" Casey asks.

"When you subpoena him," Jack says.

"Proving that he could do it," Casey says, "isn't the same as proving that he did do it."

"He lied on tape," Jack says. "Short of Pamela Vale coming back to testify—"

"—this is the strongest case we could have," Casey says. "I agree. The issue is: Is it strong enough?"

The three of them stand there and look at Jack's chart. After a few minutes Goddamn Billy says, "Jack?"

"Deny the claim."

"Tom?"

"I think you're taking a big risk."

He cites Bentley's report and the coroner's conclusion.

"If Vale sues," Casey says, "you'll have to bring two public officials to the stand and make them eat their own reports. Juries don't like that."

Jack says, "If we give Ng the rest of this evidence, he'll be happy to modify his report. As for Bentley . . ."

"Fuck him?" Casey says.

Jack shrugs.

"I still don't know," Casey says.

"What about you, Billy?" Jack asks. "Where are you on this?"

Billy is suddenly *Fuck it* on the No Smoking rule. He draws a Camel from the pack, jams it between his lips, lights it, takes a long draw, then exhales.

Saying, "It's your call, Jack."

"Yeah?"

"Yup."

"Then we deny the life claim and the fire claim," Jack says, "void the policies and sue to get the advance back."

"Write the denial letter," Goddamn Billy says. "Inform the insured of our decision."

Oh, yeah, Jack thinks.

I'll inform him.

76

Sandra Hansen knocks on the door of Room 813 at the Ritz-Carlton. Waits while the FBI agent inside checks her out. The door slides open, she steps in, and the door closes quickly behind her.

The agent's name is Young and she's known him for three years. They've been on the same anti-fraud-ring task force with the two others sitting in the room: Danny Banner, an investigator with the California Attorney General's office Anti-ROC (Russian organized crime) Task Force, and Sergeant Richard Jimenez, from LAPD. Banner and Jimenez are sitting on a sofa by the coffee table, setting up a tape recorder and going over notes.

"Guys," Hansen says.

"Sandy."

"Dr. Howard," Hansen says.

Howard looks up from his easy chair. He's very unhappy.

"I'm Sandra Hansen," she says. "From California Fire and Life. You've taken us for a lot of money, Howard."

"On the phone you said no police," Howard says.

"Gee, I guess I committed fraud on you, huh, Doctor?"

"I should just get up and leave."

"Go."

Howard's not going anywhere. Hansen knows Howard's not going anywhere. She sits down in a chair across from him and lays a file on the table. Opens it and says, "Dr. Howard, yesterday you treated a woman named Lourdes Hidalgo for muscle trauma. Here's the treatment report. That's your signature, isn't it?"

"Yes."

"But, Doctor," Hansen says, "the problem with this is that Lourdes Hidalgo died in a car crash the day before you treated her."

"As I said on the phone," Howard says, "I must have mixed her up with someone else. A mistake in paperwork."

"Well, when did you treat Mrs. Hidalgo?" Hansen asks. "And who did you confuse her with?"

"I don't know."

"You don't know because you screwed up," Hansen says. "You never saw Lourdes Hidalgo, you were just signing paperwork. You were signing phony bills for treatment you never performed. Isn't that right, Doctor? Or did you administer ultrasound therapy to a jar of ashes? Even *you'd* notice that, wouldn't you, Doctor Howard? That your patient is a loose collection of charred bones?"

"There is no need for—"

"I think there's need," Hansen says. "They identified Lourdes through her dental work. Now I'm going to press charges against you for insurance fraud against California Fire and Life. Sergeant Jimenez here is about to read you your rights and arrest you."

"A misdemeanor," Howard says.

"Where did you get your medical degree?" Banner asks. "Because you're very stupid, Doctor. This treatment report connects you to eight murders. Eight people were incinerated in that van."

"I had nothing to do—"

"You had everything to do with it," Hansen says. "Your billing factory is the whole motive for drive-downs like that one that went wrong. That connects you. That makes you a conspirator."

"My lawyers will—"

"Execute your will," Jimenez says. "Because you'll be dead. I know the names of three corrections officers in the downtown jail who are on the Russian payroll. They'll put you in a cell and you'll never make it out. You'll never make it to the arraignment."

Banner says, "We can get you capital punishment just by charging you. We don't have to win a trial."

"If I press these charges," Hansen says, "your partners will kill you. They'll be afraid that you'll talk. Maybe if it *were* a misdemeanor they'd hang in with you, but a seven-count homicide charge?"

Howard is not a tough guy. He starts crying. Asks, "What do you want from me?"

"Only everything," Hansen says. "You're going to start meeting with us. You're going to go over all your records and tell us which ones are phonies. You're going to give us names of who you're working with."

"Starting now," Banner says. "Who brings you the forms to sign?"

"It's changed," Howard says. "Two new guys."

"Names," Banner says.

Howard shrugs.

"You don't *know*?" Banner asks.

"Sorry."

Banner looks at Jimenez and says, "What are we doing here? Read him his rights."

"I don't know."

"Come on," Hansen says. "When they'd call you, they'd say, 'This is . . .'"

"Ivan," Howard says.

"You're shitting me," Banner says.

"Ivan and Boris," Howard says. "It was like, you know, a joke."

"No kidding," Hansen says.

Young says, "Describe them."

Howard describes them. When he's done, Banner takes some pictures out of a file and tosses them on the table.

"Those two," Howard says.

"Who'd they work for?"

"I dunno. I thought they worked for themselves."

"Don't be jerking us, Howard," Banner says. "You're not a moron. You know you're hooked up with the Russian Mafia, not Two Guys from Kiev."

"But they don't tell you," Howard says. "These two, they just came in and said 'Now you report to us.'"

"Did you ever hear anyone mention the name Tratchev?" Hansen asks.

"No."

"Rubinsky?"

"No."

"Schaller?"

"No."

Jimenez turns to Hansen. "You want to press charges?"

"Absolutely."

"No," Howard whines.

Hansen leans forward so her face is real close to his. Says, "Here's the deal, you drunken quack. Listen to me very carefully—I don't care if they kill you. I think that you're bottom-feeding scum and you deserve everything you have coming to you. Now I will keep my finger in the shit dike for just as long as you're useful to me. The second you stop, the second you balk, the second you don't do exactly what we tell you, I'll pull my finger out. I'll have you arrested, and just to make sure, I'll call up Mr. Tratchev and tell him that you met with us and gave up two of his boys. I'll send him an edited version of the videotape. By the way, smile for the camera, Dr. Howard."

"You are a terrible person."

"You bet," Hansen says.

"I want to go into protective custody," Howard says to Banner.

"You don't know enough," Banner says. "There's a price tag for protective custody and you don't even have the ante. You have to go up at least another level to get protection."

"I'll relocate," Howard says.

Young says, "Doctor, what do you think I'm doing here? *Federal* agent? Federal Bureau blah-blah-blah? What are you *thinking* about? That you can set up in Arizona and your former playmates are going to come to a screeching halt at the border? They're nationwide, stupid. They're set up in Arizona, Texas, West Virginia, Ohio, New York . . . Look at me when I'm talking to you. These Russian SOBs take $5 million a week out of my country and you help them do it. You can't run far enough to get away from them or me."

"What's he going to do?" Jimenez asks.

"Next time you meet with them," Banner says, "you're going to wear a wire."

Howard shakes his head. "They'll kill me."

"I don't care," Banner says. "You're going to sit with them and demand a meeting with their boss."

"I'm not doing this."

Jimenez says, "You have the right to remain silent. Anything that you say can and will—"

"Okay, okay."

Howard puts his face in his hands and sobs. This goes on for about two minutes until Hansen says, "I can't take this anymore. Get out."

Jimenez says, "We'll let you know when and where our next rendezvous is. You bring records, we'll bring recording equipment."

"It'll be fun," Hansen says.

She takes Howard's arm and helps him out of the chair. Walks him to the door and says, "Thank you for coming."

She sits back down and Young says, "He'll do."

"That doctor's a corpse," Banner says.

"Tough shit," Sandra Hansen says.

In an operation of this magnitude, you have to expect some casualties.

77

Ding-dong.

Nicky comes to the door; he's holding a glass of champagne.

"Grieving?" Jack asks him.

"To each his own."

"I know you're anxious about the resolution of your claim," Jack says. "So as part of California Fire and Life's continuing commitment to excellent service, I thought I'd come personally to inform you."

"Of what, precisely?"

Jack can see Mother Russia standing a few feet behind Nicky.

"You'll be getting a certified letter tomorrow," Jack says. "Informing you that we're denying both the life insurance and the fire claim on the grounds that you've violated the terms of the policies by intentional acts. To wit, we believe there's sufficient evidence to indicate that you were involved in the death of your wife and in the fire at your home."

Jack watches Nicky's eyes go narrow and hard.

"You're making a very serious mistake," Nicky says.

"Yeah, well, I've made them before."

"And you didn't learn?"

"I guess not."

Cool Nicky shrugs and sips his champagne.

Jack looks over his shoulder and asks, "Aren't you going to ask me in for tea?"

The door shuts in his face.

"I guess that's a *nyet*," Jack says.

He feels better than he's felt in twelve years.

Like a long night's finally ending.

78

The sun comes up like it's been waiting all night to burn somebody.

Jack's out on the water, watching the dawn.

When the sun hits his face it's *personal*. Like, good morning, wake up, dream time is over.

Right behind the sun is the wind.

Blowing wild as a Miles Davis break.

Jack knows it's going to be a hot day in Southern California.

79

Doesn't take long.

Three hours later, Paul Gordon's standing in Tom Casey's conference room, pointing down at Jack, shouting and red in the face. Jack thinks that Paul Gordon is maybe going to be the first-ever witnessed event of self-combustion.

Which would be okay.

There's not a claims dog in California who wouldn't like to see Paul Gordon go up in a ball of flame. Paul Gordon ignites, your basic claims guy is going to spring up and write a letter to the Fire Department to get over there right away.

They used to say that Paul Gordon sits at the right hand of God. Then the lawyer hit Fidelity Mutual Insurance for $40 million in punitive damages on a bad faith suit. Now they say that God sits at the right hand of Paul Gordon.

Gordon has the looks for it, too. Tall, silver hair, ice-blue eyes, craggy features. He's standing by the window in Casey's office, he's got Newport Beach Harbor as a dramatic backdrop and he's telling Jack, Tom and Goddamn Billy that he's going to take Cal Fire and Life down for the biggest punitive damages award in the entire history of bad faith litigation.

Man's gonna break his own record.

". . . make the Fidelity Mutual verdict look like a church bingo pot!" is part of what he's screaming.

"What he did . . . what he did . . . ," Gordon's saying, pointing at Jack, "he told my client—*one day after his wife's funeral*—that he thought my client killed his wife and burned the house down around her! Then he came to my client's home to *hand deliver* a denial letter!"

"Did you do that, Jack?" asks Goddamn Billy.

"Yup."

"Why?"

Billy instantly regrets asking this because Jack turns to Nicky, who's sitting there with this little smile on his face, and says, "Because he killed his wife and then burned the house down around her."

"SEE?! SEE?!!!??" Gordon yells. "He's doing it again!"

"Jack, keep your mouth shut, please," Casey says. He's sitting in his chair sipping coffee and acting like they're all just hanging out discussing the Dodgers' chances of winning the division.

Here's a story about Tom Casey.

Casey goes to a settlement conference with Goddamn Billy, and he has draft authority for $100,000 in his pocket. Plaintiff's attorney comes in and asks for five grand. Casey stands up, slams his fist on the table and yells, "What do I look like, *Santa Claus*?!" The plaintiff settles for two thousand.

So even though Casey has Paul Gordon, the biggest, baddest plaintiff's attorney in Southern California in his office yelling about Armageddon, Casey is not exactly pissing his pants. This is because Casey is the biggest, baddest, *defense* attorney in the Southern Bear Flag Republic.

What you got here—if you're a connoisseur of multimillion-dollar bad faith litigation—is you have the heavyweight championship of the world.

Gordon v. Casey.

You could make a mint from the pay-per-view rights just selling to attorneys who'd watch it in the hopes that they'll actually kill each other.

Funny thing is they're in the same office complex.

Both Casey and Gordon have their offices in the "Black Boxes," a marvel of modern architecture, black glass and hubris that sits astride the Newport Beach greenway. They're called the Black Boxes because that's exactly what they look like, except the bottom right corner of each building is cut away, so they look like black boxes that are about to topple over. Which is where the marvel of modern architecture bit comes in.

Casey calls them the "There Isn't Going to Be Any Fucking Earthquake" buildings, because one good temblor and you got to believe that these babies are coming down, precariously balanced as they appear to be. So you got Casey in one, and Gordon in the other, both on the twelfth floors, and they actually face each other. If they have their curtains open they could exchange friendly morning waves, which is just about as likely as O.J. and Fred Goldman sitting down over a fondue.

Anyway, Casey says, "Jack's conduct was inappropriate, no dispute, Paul."

Gordon nods with some satisfaction but he knows a punch is coming in here somewhere.

Casey throws it. "But Paul, do you think that if a jury concludes that your client is an arsonist and a murderer, it's going to give a rat's ass about some dumb thing Jack did?"

"The jury won't conclude anything of the kind, Tom."

"Maybe not," Tom says, shrugging. "But just to add a jalapeño to the chili, I will tell you right now, if you push this to a trial, I will make sure that it's monitored by the federal prosecutor's office to consider potential criminal charges against your client."

Casey turns to smile at Nicky and explains, "Arson can be considered a *federal* crime, at the discretion of the U.S. Attorney."

Nicky shrugs an exact imitation of Casey's patented shrug.

Like, you can stick your U.S. Attorney up your ass.

And waddle.

Nicky says, "You have no evidence."

"Mr. Vale, to use a technical term," Casey says, "I have evidence up the wazoo."

Lays it all out for him.

Incendiary origin.

Motive.

And opportunity.

Especially opportunity, because he has him in a lie on his whereabouts that night.

"The guard has you coming in at 4:45," Casey says.

"So?"

Oh-so-cool Call Me Nicky.

"So you're hosed," Jack says.

Seeing if he can, you know, set Paul Gordon off.

80

He does.

Gordon goes *totally* off.

It takes Casey a good ten minutes to get him to sit down. What

Casey does is he sends an intern racing to the trendy little coffee shop downstairs to fetch a cappuccino *grande* with low-fat milk and a dash of nutmeg.

"Decaf," Casey stresses to the intern.

It's well known among the greater legal community of Southern California that Gordon has a serious cappuccino jones, that in fact he keeps an associate whose entire job consists of making sure that the attorney has two of them on the table before any meeting begins.

So Gordon's sitting in Casey's office huffing and puffing, face all red, little droplets of sweat bubbling on his forehead.

It's beautiful.

And Casey gets a clue as to how he'll take Gordon in the courtroom if it comes to that: whip him into a froth and let the jury see it.

The decaf cap arrives, Gordon takes a long, soothing sip and then says to Nicky, "Go ahead."

Jack's like, Go ahead and *what*? Go ahead and jump out the window?

It isn't what Nicky has in mind.

Nicky just lays his cool look on Jack and says, "As to one of my employees picking up Pamela's prescription, that's ridiculous. As to this alleged statement by the gate guard, I don't know with whom you talked, or whether you talked to anyone. All I can tell you is that I was home with my children and my mother that entire evening and morning, just as I told you on the recorded statement."

Gordon lays a document on the table. "This is the signed and notarized affidavit from Mr. Michael Derochik, the guard who was on duty the night of the fire, in which he affirms that he did not see Mr. Vale leave or enter the gate after 8:30 that evening."

Jack starts getting this feeling that Nicky's not going out the window.

It's Opportunity that just went out the window.

Nicky continues, "As to my finances, I advised Mr. Wade that because I am in an international business, there is great flux in the liquidity of my assets. The tide, as it were, ebbs and flows. If Mr. Wade would bother to check my accounts today, he will see that I have the money to meet both my personal and commercial responsibilities. As for losing my home, my mortgage payments are current, and I have ample funds to meet the upcoming payment on my home."

Motive is on the ledge.

But I still have Incendiary Origin, Jack thinks. Long as this is an arson fire, everything else follows. And I still have IO.

For about five seconds.

"Your samples that showed traces of accelerants?" Gordon asks. "Deputy Bentley took samples and sent them to the state crime lab, and the samples came up negative. Oh, there's traces of a little Class O combustible—which is probably the turpentine you'd expect from pine flooring—but kerosene? Now, I don't know where Mr. Wade got his so-called samples, but it wasn't from the Vale house, I can tell you that."

So there it is. Jack thinks that if he looks out the window to the ground, he'll see the smashed remains of Incendiary Origin, Motive and Opportunity lying on the sidewalk.

"I'm filing suit today," Gordon adds. "Breach of contract, failure to reasonably investigate and bad faith. If you'd like to settle, come with $50 million in your pocket or don't come."

"Fifty goddamn million?!"

Gordon smiles and nods. "Over and above what you owe on the policies."

"That's just goddamn extortion, is all that is."

"Like a church bingo pot," Paul Gordon tells Casey.

"You'll have your witnesses, we'll have ours."

They're standing out by the elevator when Gordon says, "Oh. Just to add a jalapeño to the chili? As to this story about Dr. Ng trying to contact my client and being rebuffed by an attorney—we have a signed statement from Dr. Ng denying that anything of the sort ever happened. So I don't know where Mr. Wade got his information, but you can bet that we'll sure as hell ask him under oath.

"But seeing as how Mr. Wade is a convicted perjurer with a history of planting evidence . . . well, Mr. Wade, you be thinking now about which you'd rather be, the husband or the wife."

Gordon starts to get into the elevator but does a dramatic about-face instead.

"Oh, I almost forgot," he says. "Mr. Wade is sleeping with Ms. del Rio, who stands to gain insurance benefits if they're denied to my client. We have investigator's photographs of them leaving his condominium together rather early in the morning. Which smacks of collusion to me. We *also* know how to make prosecutors aware of testimony in a civil trial.

"Fifty million to settle," Gordon says. "Over and above, of course, the claim itself. The offer is good for forty-eight hours, gentlemen. Give you some time to get the money together."

Gordon steps into the elevator. Has to push the Hold button, though, because Nicky Vale stops and puts his arm around Jack's shoulders.

Whispers into Jack's ear, "You should have learned the last time. "

Which is when Jack realizes he's been set up.

81

Big time.

Is what Jack's thinking as he races back to the Vale house, hoping he's not too late.

The setup. Nicky Vale wasn't happy just to collect on the claim. Nicky wanted the big bucks, the winning ticket to the California Litigation Lottery, so he put out just enough bait to lure you into denying the claim and then *snap.*

The hook.

And reeled you right in.

You are very stupid, Jack Wade.

He is too late.

They bulldozed it.

Jack pulls up to the house, he can see that the west wing is down.

The only thing standing there in its place is Accidentally Bentley.

With a uniformed deputy.

"Thought you might show up, Jack," Bentley says.

"When did this happen?"

"This morning," Bentley says. "I advised Mr. Vale that the burned portion of the house represented a safety hazard and that he needed to take care of it. You wouldn't want a liability claim, would you, Jack?"

So the evidence is gone, Jack thinks. The holes in the flooring, the splash patterns on the joists.

He says, "I have two sets of photos and videotape, you asshole."

"Yeah, you have *samples,* too," Bentley says. "Get out of here, Jack. You're trespassing."

"Where'd you get your samples?"

"From the house," Bentley says. "Before you came."

"How much is Nicky paying you?"

"Get *out,* Jack. Before I arrest you."

"No, what's your cut?" Jack asks. "How much pension do you get off the dead woman?"

"Walk away *now*, Jack."

"You set me up, Brian."

"You set yourself up," Bentley says. "You always do. I tried to tell you, don't dick around with this thing. You just couldn't help yourself, could you?"

"This isn't over."

"Believe me, Jack. It's over."

Jack gets back in the 'Stang and drives over to Monarch Bay.

Pulls up to the gate.

"May I help you, sir?"

"Where's Derochik?"

"Guy who usually works this shift?"

"Yeah," Jack says. "Do you know where he is?"

"No, do you?" the guard asks. "He just calls up, says he isn't working anymore. Puts us all in a jam."

"Do you know where he lives, where I could get hold of him?"

"You find out, you let *me* know."

Jack knows he'll try to find out but he also knows that he's not going to find Mike Derochik. Derochik is probably in another state already.

Jack drives over to the Monarch Bay Shopping Plaza, to the drugstore. He already knows what he's going to find.

Or what he's not going to find.

Which is Kelly.

There's another chemist behind the counter.

"Is Kelly here?" Jack asks.

The woman smiles at him. "Another broken heart. No, Kelly quit. Very suddenly."

"Do you know where she went? Where I could get hold of her?"

"Yes and no," the woman says. "Yes, I know where she went—no, I don't know how you could get hold of her."

Jack's not in the mood for games.

"What's that supposed to mean?"

"Sorry," the woman says. "It's just that I've had my fill of Kellys. If you were smart, so would you. Kelly flew off to Europe last night. Met a 'great guy' who's going to give her the world. So unless you can give her the world, I think you're out of luck, Kelly-wise."

I don't think luck has anything to do with it, Jack thinks.

They knew every move.

Every move I made.

He drives over to Pacific Coast Mortgage and Finance.

He's not even out of the car when Gary comes bopping out.

"Hey, Nicky came through," Gary says. "Paid the balloon early."

"Is that right?"

"Yeah, dude, we were worried for nothing."

Yeah, dude.

Like very fresh.

Surf on.

Jack finds Ng at home.

A nice tract house on a cul-de-sac in Laguna Niguel. The house newly painted a pale blue. Basketball hoop bolted to the garage at the end of the driveway.

The medical examiner comes to the door in a T-shirt and pajama pants.

"I was sleeping, Jack," he says.

"Can I come in?"

"Why not?"

Jack follows him into the house. Ng leads him into a small room that must be the doctor's study. Antique wooden desk. Walls lined with bookshelves more full of books than knickknacks. Ng sits at the desk chair and motions for Jack to sit down in a big leather chair by the window.

"Anyone else home?" Jack asks.

"Wife's at work," Ng says. "Kids are at school. What do you want?"

"You know what I want."

Ng nods. He reaches under the green blotter on the desk. Pulls out a small stack of Polaroid pictures and hands them to Jack.

Two Asian kids walking out of a playground. A boy and a girl. Each in their little soccer uniforms. You don't need an Ident-A-Kid packet to know that they're Ng's children.

Jack hands the pictures back.

"He killed his wife," he says.

"Probably."

"And he's going to get away with it."

"Probably."

And he's going to make $50 million doing it.

Jack stands up and says, "Okay."

Ng nods.

Back in his car Jack knows that road is closed. Knows that the blood and tissue samples are already parked at a hazardous waste disposal somewhere.

It isn't just money, because if money wants to intimidate a coroner, money sues the coroner, or calls his boss or otherwise leans on him. Money doesn't threaten to hurt his kids.

No, that's a gangster thing.

Jack goes back to Cal Fire and Life, does the whole computer and phone run again and it's the same story.

Nicky's accounts are solid.

Credit card payments up to date.

Money in the business accounts.

And I am one dumb claims dog, Jack thinks.

Nicky set me up. Left evidence out there, waited for me to deny the claim and then jerked the evidence.

Set me and California Fire and Life up for a gigantic bad faith suit.

And he knew every move I was going to make.

82

Jack pushes in the door marked NO ADMITTANCE.

He blows right past the sign that says AUTHORIZED PERSONNEL ONLY and one of the SIU guys lays a hand on Jack's shoulder to stop him. Jack brushes him aside and shoves open the door to Sandra Hansen's office.

She's sitting behind her desk.

Jack leans over it.

"You been reading my file, Sandra?"

Most of the SIU guys are ex-cops and this one—a slab of meat named Cooper—asks her, "You want me to take him out of here, Sandra?"

Jack doesn't turn around as he says, "Yeah, why don't you take me out of here?"

"It's all right," Sandra says.

She gestures for Cooper to leave.

And shuts the door behind him.

She says, "I told you that we were going to monitor this file."

"You didn't tell me that you were going to tip Vale off to every move I was going to make."

"You're paranoid, Jack."

Yeah, Jack thinks, I'm paranoid.

Fucking A, I'm paranoid.

He says, "Vale knew every move I made."

"Then you'd better get some new moves."

"He wants $50 million now."

"You should have settled it before."

She goes back to shuffling papers.

"He's mobbed up, isn't he?" Jack asks.

"What makes you say that?"

Jack says, "He intimidated three witnesses and did a magic act with his money. He set me up, and you guys helped him, and I want to know why."

"You had your chance to play," Hansen says. "Too late now."

Jack slams his hand on her desk. "I'm not *playing*!"

"That's my point."

Jack sighs. "Okay, what do you want?"

"I don't want anything *now*," Hansen says. "You can't give me anything *now*. *Before*, I wanted you to back off. You wouldn't. Now they're going to *make* you back off, so you have nothing to trade."

"Give me what you got on him, Sandra," Jack says. "I'm dying."

Hansen shrugs.

Says, "We didn't give Vale any information. And we don't have any information on Vale to give *you*."

"He killed his wife."

"That's what you say."

"And burned the house down."

"That's your version," Hansen says. "Another version is that you've got an *ancient* hard-on for the sister and that she sold you a bill of goods along with the *chucha*. And you *are* going to back off now, Jack. You're going to lie down like a good dog and die."

"You gonna make me, Sandra?"

"That's right." She pulls some papers from her drawer and lays them on the desk. "A sworn statement from a restoration contractor claiming that he paid you to recommend him to policyholders. Here's another from a homeowner admitting that he gave you a kickback to look the other way on an overcharge. The DA will give them both immunity. It's up to you, Jack: I can stick them back in my desk or I can send them up to Mahogany Row."

"Why don't you stick them in your ass and *then* take them up to Mahogany Row?"

"Same old Jack," she says. "You know what they're going to put on your tombstone, Jack? 'He Never Learned.'"

"So how much is Nicky paying you, Sandra?"

"As usual, you're a hundred and eighty degrees wrong."

"I hope it's enough to retire on," Jack says, "because I'll never quit on this."

"Quitting is the last of your worries," Sandra says. "Is there anything else I can help you with, Jack, or can you just haul your dumb ass out of here now?"

Jack hauls his dumb ass out of there. Pauses just long enough to exchange a bad look with Cooper, then heads back to his cubicle.

Now knowing two things for sure.

One, Nicky Vale is mobbed up.

Two, Sandra Hansen's on the take.

One more thing, Jack thinks.

Unless I take a dive on the Vale file—

—I'm finished at California Fire and Life.

83

Which is pretty much what Casey is telling Goddamn Billy.

He's got him on the horn and he's saying, "It might have been nice if someone over these past twelve years had told their old friend Tom about a perjury conviction."

"Jack Wade's a good man."

"Jack Wade is a good man," Casey says. "Which makes it all the more of a shame that he's going to get fucked."

Jack walks into the office and Billy flips the phone to speaker.

So Jack gets to hear Casey say, "If Gordon wins on the Vale case—and he *will* win on the Vale case—then he'll tie that tail to Cal Fire and Life and use it on the next case. And the next and the next. He'll dig up every claim Jack ever denied—every arson, every fraud—and he'll find a judge who'll let him bring them to trial.

"Except now he not only has Jack's testimony to use forever, he also has the example of the Vale trial. He'll tell the next jury that Cal Fire and Life has already been hit for *x* million, and *that* didn't change their ways so you'd better hit them for *x*-plus. And so on and so on—the tail just keeps getting longer—until the company either buys all the cases or goes out of business.

"And it won't be just Paul Gordon, either. Every shark in town will smell the blood and swarm in for the feeding frenzy. Every plaintiff's attorney in California we ever beat in court will be coming in asking for a retrial, claiming that there's at least a chance that Cal Fire lied and cheated in *their* case. I'll file a truckload of motions to stop it, but some judge in the People's Republic of Santa Monica will think it's his ticket to the Supremes, and seeing how the Ninth Circuit is basically made up of politburo members anyway, we'll get hammered on the appeal.

"And Jack will be everyone's favorite witness. He'll get called to recite a litany of his sins in every bad faith trial for the next ten years. They'll run him right out of the state: I bet he'll leave California, he'll get so tired of being subpoenaed. Of course, if they move a case into federal court, he's screwed nationwide. You along with him, because they'll put you on the stand right behind him to confess how you knowingly hired a corrupt cop.

"Fifty million is a cheap price to stop the bleeding. And save Jack's ass."

"I don't want my ass saved," Jack says.

"Well, *I* want your ass saved, Jack," Casey says. "There is no point dying in a battle you can't win."

"We can win it," Jack says.

"You're going to beat Paul Gordon on the stand?" Casey asks. "With no evidence and *your* baggage? Come on."

"Give me some time to get the evidence," Jack says.

"We don't have the time," Casey says. "Mahogany Row's already banging on me to settle. They have rate hearings coming up. They don't want a high-profile bad faith case. Especially one they can't win. They want to settle."

"They can't settle without me, goddamn it."

Company rules. The regional director of Claims—in this case Billy Hayes—has the last word on a claim. This is to save the corporate mucks from being subpoenaed to testify in every bad faith case. The director makes the call, he takes the fall.

Only this director ain't going down easy.

"They'll take you out if they have to," Casey says.

"They're blowing smoke," Billy says.

"Where there's smoke . . ."

"They know about Jack's checkered past?"

"I haven't told them," Casey says. "I was hoping I'd get your agreement to just lay the Green Poultice on this, then nobody has to know."

All wounds, Billy has said, can be healed with the Green Poultice.

"I don't want it to go away," Jack says.

"You don't have the choice, Jack," Casey says.

"*I* do," Goddamn Billy says. "And we ain't paying this cocksucker a dime."

"Let me offer ten," Casey says. "They'll have a hard time walking away from ten."

"Not a goddamn dime."

"Billy, why—"

"Because he did it and we know he did it."

"You think you can persuade a jury of that?" Casey asks.

"Yes," Jack says.

Walking right into it, because Casey answers, "You got yourself a deal. We'll do a focus group tonight—rent-a-judge, jury, the whole nine yards. You testify, Jack, and I'll cross-examine you."

"When did you schedule this, Tom?" Billy asks.

"This morning," Casey says. "The deal I made with Mahogany Row, trying to save your asses. It's winner take all. You win, we don't settle, you can investigate all the way up to the trial. You lose, we start settlement negotiations first thing in the morning. It's the best deal I could get, guys."

A terrific deal, Jack thinks.

Death.

Death by Focus Group.

84

"We're dead."

Translated from Russian, this is basically what Dani is telling Nicky.

They're taking a walk out on the lawn of Mother's house.

As far from the house as they can get, because the scene *in* the house is driving Nicky crazy.

It's the kids, it's the dog, it's Mother. Actually it's an unholy troika of the kids, the dog and Mother because the kids love the dog and Mother doesn't. The kids want the dog in the house and Mother doesn't, the dog wants to jump up on the couch and Mother has a stroke, the dog wants to sleep with the kids and the kids want to sleep with the dog but Mother wants the dog to sleep outside, which is the same as Mother saying she wants the dog dead—which she does. And last night Nicky experienced the sheer absurdity of making Leo sleep in a doghouse outside and then posting an armed guard by the doghouse so the kids would stop crying and so that little Michael wouldn't, as threatened, sleep in the doghouse with his rubber knife to protect Leo from the coyotes.

Next, Nicky thinks, I'll be stringing barbed wire around the living room sofa.

And Mother will not get off little Michael's back. Natalie she ignores completely. Looks right through the girl as if she were a ghost, but Michael she suffocates with attention. Most of it negative. Poor little Michael cannot do anything right. All day it's Michael, use the napkin not your sleeve, Michael, it's time to do your scales, Michael, a little gentleman walks with his head *up*.

A broken record, Nicky thinks. An oldie but goodie, as the American DJs would say.

Driving the boy crazy.

Driving me crazy.

So it's good to get away from that scene.

Take a walk on the lawn even if it is to hear that you are, more likely than not, dead.

"Tratchev is demanding a meeting," Dani says. "For tonight."

"Tonight?"

"They don't want us to have time to get ready," Dani says.

"But they'll be ready."

"Yes."

"Tell him no."

"Then we're at war."

"So we're at war."

Dani shakes his head. "Given our present strength compared to his, we can't win the war."

Nicky can hear the unspoken rebuke in Dani's voice.

And it's deserved.

In my obsession to be a California businessman, I let things deteriorate. To a point where now we are in mortal danger.

Very uncool.

"So we meet," Nicky says.

Dani shakes his head again.

"At this meeting," he says, "they'll kill you."

Tratchev is selling it to the others and it's an easy sale. Nicky Vale is taking my business—he'll take yours next. Unless we stop him, and soon.

"Tratchev will accuse you of looting the *obochek*," Dani says. "A serious violation of *Vorovskoy Zakon*. And this meeting won't be like the last. They'll be ready."

Nicky takes a moment to inhale the scent of bougainvillea. The luminescent color of the fuchsia. The bright blue of the ocean and sky.

Beautiful.

"All I ever wanted was *this*," he says.

"I know," Dani says.

"I'll go to the meeting," Nicky says. "Alone."

"You can't."

"Why should we all die?"

"Pakhan—"

Nicky puts up his hand. Enough.

I will do what has to be done.

I will deal with Tratchev and all the rest.

Dani says, "There's something else."

"Wonderful."

"The sister."

"What about her?" Nicky asks.

"She's been asking about the two Vietnamese."

"What?" Nicky asks. "How do you know this?"

"She's been making a noise in Little Saigon," Dani says. "Putting real heat on."

"How did she make that connection?"

You think you're safe. You think you've used all your skill and cunning to steer through the rapids and the shoals and then this cunt of a sister . . .

"We'll do what we have to do," Nicky says.

"She's a cop."

"I know that."

"An honest cop."

"I know that, too."

"It's too much for a coincidence," Dani says. "Two sisters—"

"Goddamn it, will you do as I say?!"

I know it's a risk. It's *all* a risk. But I didn't kill my beautiful Pamela and make my children motherless just to lose everything anyway.

We will do what we have to do—however regrettable—and we will do it soon. And the day after tomorrow we will have our share of $50 million, more than enough to start again.

From ashes come new shoots of grass.

Life from death.

85

The ritual sacrifice of Jack Wade starts with peanut M&M's.

Jack stands in the "observation room" behind the one-way mirror, gobbling peanut M&M's and watching the "jury" file in. Jack's been in a couple of dozen focus group facilities and it seems like whatever else they have or don't have, they always have bowls of peanut M&M's.

For nervous chomping.

They always serve dinner, too, except Jack's too edgy to enjoy the lasagna bubbling in the heater trays. The meals at these things are usually pretty good, but tonight it's *really* good—in addition to the lasagna there's roast basil chicken, fettuccine Alfredo, a Caesar salad and profiteroles for dessert. Also, real plates, real silverware and linen napkins.

The quality of the meal is a good news/bad news joke.

The good news is that it's a high-quality meal, the bad news is that the reason it's a high-quality meal is because the muckety-mucks from Mahogany Row are there.

Casey ordered the menu.

Casey knows that the mucks tend to take their meals very seriously, so it's prudent to at least feed them well. Especially when the bill's going to be $50 million.

Not counting the tip.

Jack watches them eat.

Half of freaking Mahogany Row bellied up to the trough. Twelve years with the company, and Jack's never seen these guys in the flesh before, just on a few motivational closed-circuit TV presentations. The boys can eat.

So there they are, VP Claims, VP Legal and VP Public Relations. Goddamn Billy runs it down for him.

"Phil Herlihy, VP Claims," Billy says, pointing to a sixtyish guy with a shock of white hair and a paunch. "Came out of Agency, of course. Doesn't know a claim from a blow job. He's an administrator."

Billy gestures at a tall, thin guy in his fifties. "Dane Reinhardt, VP Legal. Couldn't *buy* a verdict in a goddamn courtroom, so now he's telling *us* what to do.

"Jerry Bourne, VP Public Relations," Billy says, pointing to a short fortyish guy with curly red hair and a red nose. "Basically in charge of arranging hookers for the visiting firemen and hiding the bills in his expenses. He's a fucking idiot, but at least he knows it. So's Reinhardt, except he doesn't know it. All he knows is it's a lot safer to settle claims than to take one to trial and lose. Last thing that no-balls so-called lawyer wants to see is another courtroom. Herlihy's the one to watch out for. He swings the big stick in the president's office."

Herlihy looks over at them.

"Billy," he says, "aren't you going to eat?"

"I'm watching my figure."

Herlihy looks at Jack.

"Are you this Jack Wade I've heard so much about today?"

"Guilty."

Herlihy says, "You Claims cowboys from So-Cal . . ."

Like he's so disgusted he can't even finish.

Jack figures it doesn't require a real answer so all he says is, "Yippi-yi-yo-ky-ay" and walks away, which doesn't score him a lot of points with Phil Herlihy, VP Claims, from the start of this thing.

The observation room itself is shaped like a slice of a lecture hall. A bunch of desks bolted onto the floor slanted down toward the observation window. The dining table is off to the left on the five feet of flat floor by the window and the door. On top of the room, a videographer is getting his camera ready to record the whole mess for the boys at corporate who couldn't make the live show. At the bottom, a table runs the width of the window. Seated at the table are two jury consultants with laptop computers and stacks of questionnaires.

What the two jury consultants also have is a monitor that's hooked up to each of twelve ProCon machines on the desk of each "juror."

The ProCon machines are simple little devices that measure how the juror is "feeling"—generally pro or vaguely con—at any given moment. It's basically a joystick attached to a base and the juror is supposed to keep his or her hand on it at all times. The juror's feeling con about something, he pushes the joystick down. A little con, a little down. A lot con, a lot down. Same with the pro feelings. A little pro, the juror pulls a little back on the joystick, a lot pro, she can whip that puppy all the way back.

It's basically a high-tech version of the old Roman thumbs-up/thumbs-down gladiator deal.

What it does is it allows you to instantly measure the jury's ongoing "instinctive" reaction on a scale from Negative 10 to Neutral to Positive 10 to any witness, question or answer. They're carefully instructed that they don't need a reason for their reaction—they should just react. If they're feeling "bad" they should push the stick down. If they're feeling happy, they should push it up.

Jack knows this is only for the gut reaction, that they'll get the rational response from the questionnaires and the actual decision from a "verdict," but he also knows that the the jury will rationalize its gut reaction onto the questionnaire and then onto the verdict.

Doesn't matter what a lawyer or a judge says; any jury will decide a case on its gut reaction.

So the ProCon machine is an important little fucker in this proceeding.

Everyone in the observation room is going to have their eyes on the ProCon monitor.

Not inside the actual "courtroom."

Inside the actual focus group room, on the other side of the window, the "jurors" are seated in a mock jury box, with individual little tables for their ProCon joysticks. There's a witness stand, tables for the plaintiff and defense, and a judge's bench, where the "rent-a-judge" for the focus group will sit.

The two jury consultants—a yuppie guy and a yuppie gal—and the moderator—a slightly older male yuppie—are all from TSI, Trial Science Inc., and this is what they do for a living. They're all a little frantic at the moment because this is a rush job. They've spent the afternoon assembling a demographically correct focus group that would be an accurate sampling of a potential Orange County jury. Age, gender, race, education, profession have gone into the mix, plus they had to figure in the attorney's preference.

"How do you want this one to come out?" the older yuppie had asked Casey.

Because the attorney is the one they have to keep happy, so they need to know if the attorney wants a real focus group or a dog-and-pony. A lot of times, the attorney is trying to use the focus group to persuade a client to settle or to go to trial, and because the TSI people already know the demographics that tend to be pro-defense or pro-plaintiff, they can slant their recruiting the lawyer's way.

They can also slant the questionnaires and the live discussion, and while they can't guarantee an outcome, they can take a lawyer a long way down his or her chosen path.

Hence the question, "How do you want this one to come out?"

"Accurately," Casey answered.

One, because he's not about to set up a Potemkin village for old friends like Billy Hayes and Jack Wade, and two, he already knows how this one's going to come out anyway.

He's going to kick their ass.

Which is what Jack thinks, too, when he sees the rent-a-judge walk in and take the bench. Dude is wearing black robes, just like this is the real thing.

Dude also looks very familiar.

"We're dead," Jack mutters to Goddamn Billy.

Because the rent-a-judge is none other than retired Justice Dennis Mallon.

From the Atlas Warehouse trial.

86

Mallon bangs on a gavel, which gets the expected chuckle from the group, and he asks them to finish filling out their "pre-stimulus questionnaires," and then he tells them that they're going to hear about a lawsuit involving a fire.

"You'll hear a brief statement from the plaintiff, then one from the defense. Then you'll be asked to fill out a questionnaire based on what you've heard. Then you're going to hear testimony from a witness for the defense, who will be examined and then cross-examined. After which you'll fill out, yes, another questionnaire, and then you'll discuss the case just as you would if you were on a real jury. Then I'll ask you to render a verdict for the defense or for the plaintiff, and if for the plaintiff, how much you would award. I encourage you to take notes; just please be aware that your notes will be collected at the end of the evening.

"During all of this, please manipulate your little ProCon joysticks so the people in the observation room know how you're feeling."

Which gets another appreciative chuckle from the jury.

"Can you believe," Jack whispers to Goddamn Billy, "that with all the law, all the science, everything we do on a file, that a multimillion-dollar decision is going to be made by twelve people who show up for fifty bucks each and all the cookies they can eat?"

"I can believe anything," Billy says.

"Sorry you got dragged into this," Jack says.

"You didn't drag me," Billy says. "I walked."

Casey gets up from the plaintiff's table, looks at the jury for a few moments and says, "This is a story about how a gigantic insurance company, let's call it Great Western Insurance, cheated a policyholder. How it lied, cheated, bullied and oppressed a man who had lost his wife and his home."

Jack looks up at the monitor.

Negative 10.

"How," Casey says, "Great Western Insurance took his premium money for years, assuring him that in his time of need they would be there for him—and then when that time came, when tragedy struck, instead of being there for him, accused him of fraud, arson and murder and denied him the millions of dollars in benefits that he is due.

"This is a story about how a big corporation thinks that it's above the law, because even though the authorities declared that the fire was accidental, and the coroner said the death was accidental, and even though the police have not even investigated, let alone charged, let alone convicted my client of arson or murder, Great Western Insurance accused him of burning his house down and murdering his wife, and convicted him of the crimes of arson and murder without even the benefit of a hearing, let alone a public trial."

Negative 10s across the board.

"And this is a story about a man, an individual, my client—we'll call him Mr. White—who came as an immigrant to this country with only an old suitcase and the clothes on his back. Who through hard work and application and diligence lived the American Dream. Became a millionaire and fulfilled his dream, a dream that is now shattered by a sudden accident, and the deliberate, malicious and oppressive actions of a greedy, powerful corporation that would rather slander a good man and destroy his life than pay what it owes.

"My client's only hope to restore what's left of his life is you. His wife is gone, his children bereaved, his house lies in ashes. You cannot bring back his wife, you cannot comfort his small children, but you can restore to him his home and property and punish the large and callous corporation that, perhaps even more than the fire, has destroyed my client's life. You can rebuild a home for him and his children to live in. You can send a message to the boardroom of Great Western Insurance that they must never, ever engage in this kind of despicable behavior again.

"My client rests his fate in your hands.

"I know that you will see the truth for what it is and act on that truth. Thank you."

Positive 9s and 10s.

The jury, Jack sees, is "happy."

Jack hears Herlihy mutter, "I'm glad that son of a bitch is on our side."

"It's the standard Paul Gordon opening," Reinhardt says. "Just fill in the blanks."

"Shit."

Emily Peters, one of Casey's partners, gets up to respond.

"Go, Emily," Jack whispers.

"It's not easy, following that kind of speech," she says. "That was a great speech, a real tearjerker, a real appeal to your emotions. But ladies and gentlemen, a lawsuit should not be decided by emotions, it should be decided by the law and by the facts. And the law says that if a person burns down his own property, the insurance company cannot—by law—*cannot* pay that claim. And when you listen to the two witnesses that I will bring on, ladies and gentlemen, I am confident that you will recognize that, sadly, those are the facts."

Maybe yes, maybe no, Jack sees. The monitor is hovering around a lot of Neutrals, a few 1s and 2s on either side of the line. The jury doesn't "like" Emily as much as they do Tom.

She goes on anyway. "Mr. White, as we're calling him, is rather like the man who murders his parents and then asks for mercy because he's an orphan—"

Not a laugh or a murmur or a chuckle from the jury. Uh-oh, Jack thinks, they're pissed at us already.

Yup, Negative 4s and 5s.

"—because that is the sad fact of this case.

"Now, my esteemed colleague, Mr. Casey, has told you—correctly—that the authorities ruled the fire an accident and the death an accident. That is true. What he didn't tell you is that those findings are not binding upon an insurance company. Great Western doesn't think itself above the law. The law states that an insurance company has the right, indeed the obligation, to independently investigate a claim and render its own decision. And the law further states that the insurance company may deny a claim if it reasonably concludes that it was 'more likely than not' that an insured set fire to his own property.

"That is the law—'more likely than not'—and when you hear our witnesses, and carefully consider the facts that they present, I am confident that you will also conclude that it is far more likely than not that Mr. White is an arsonist and a murderer. And that far from awarding the millions of dollars that he is asking for, you will be asking, 'Why isn't this man in prison? Why isn't he the defendant in this trial?'

"Now, Mr. Casey asked you to send a message.

"So do I.

"Send a message that you are not going to be swayed by cheap dramatics. You are not going to be swayed by emotion. That you are instead going to consider the facts and send the message that, far from being rewarded, Mr. White should be charged, convicted and punished.

"Thank you."

As the jury starts filling out their questionnaires, Jack hears Reinhardt say, "She came out too strong."

"I liked it," Herlihy says.

It was strong, Jack thinks, but that's what she had to do. You come out half-assed in an arson trial, all you do is get your half-ass totally kicked.

Jack sees the TSI consultants typing like mad. Typing and waiting like vultures for the responses to the opening statements to come in. Jack knows that the responses are key: if Casey "wins" the opening, it's going to be damn hard to convince the jury otherwise. The TSI people would say that 80 percent of jurors have their minds made up after the opening statements.

It's also going to be damn hard to convince Mahogany Row not to settle.

The jury finishes writing and one of the consultants rushes in to get their papers.

Peters says, "Calling to the stand Mr. Smith."

Which is me, Jack thinks.

Now Jack's in an interesting position here.

If he goes in there and does a good job and wins, Sandra Hansen drops the hammer on him.

If he goes in there and does a bad job and loses, then he gets to keep his job but Nicky Vale gets away with arson and murder.

Sort of your basic dilemma.

87

He walks in a Negative 7.

He can't see that, of course, but Jack can look into the jury's eyes and know they already don't like him.

It's one thing to look at a "jury"—even a focus group panel—from behind a one-way mirror. It's a whole different deal, Jack thinks, to be eyeball to eyeball with them, them staring at you like you're some sort of zoo animal.

A bad animal.

Anyway, he does his best to do what Peters advised him: Make eye contact, speak a little slow and a little loud and answer the questions directly. Be calm, be cool, be confident.

Right, Jack thinks. Even as he sits down he can feel the sweat starting to bead on his forehead.

And Mallon staring at him.

Like, I've seen you before.

A long time ago, Judge, in a galaxy far, far away . . .

Peters starts him off with his background, his education, his experience level.

Then asks, "And how many fire claims would you say you've handled for Great Western?"

"I would estimate hundreds."

"As many as a thousand?"

"That's possible."

"And of that thousand," she asks, "how many were eventually denied for arson?"

"Very few."

"Can you give me a number?"

"A handful. Nine, ten."

"It's rare, isn't it?"

"Objection. Leading."

"Sustained."

"Could you give us an idea," Peters asks, "of the frequency of arson denials?"

"It's rare."

A low chuckle from the jury.

"Is it difficult to prove arson by an insured?"

"It can be."

"Why?"

"Arson is a crime that consumes its own evidence," Jack says. "It's also a crime in which the perpetrator tends to leave the scene before the event . . . for obvious reasons."

Jack feels himself flush because he used the word "crime" not once but twice—a supposed no-no in civil arson litigation, but then he thinks, Fuck it, I can't play for a tie here.

"Well," Peters says, "how do you prove arson by an insured?"

"As I understand the law," Jack says, "you need three elements: incendiary origin, motive and opportunity."

She takes him through the meaning of the Tripartite Proof, then asks him, "Did you conclude that the White fire was of incendiary origin?"

"Yes, I did."

"What led you to that conclusion?"

"A number of things."

"Could you tell the jury what they were?"

Oh, yeah, Jack thinks. I sure could.

I could also take a dive, because this is the moment to do it. This would be the place to fumble, mumble, get my shit out of order, just generally look like a doofus.

Do the old two-and-a-half triple gainer with a twist and land head-first in a pool with no water.

Crack.

Jack says, "It would be easier to explain using a chart and some photos I brought."

He gets up and walks over to a tripod stand. Flips the cover over to reveal a big blowup of his INCENDIARY ORIGIN/MOTIVE/OPPORTU-NITY chart.

And runs it.

No mumbling, no fumbling.

Shit *totally* together, Jack runs the jury through the Tripartite Proof. Runs down all the evidence—the kerosene-soaked samples, the holes in the floor, the hole in the roof above the bed, the pour pattern. He matches each item with a blown-up photograph and he talks to the jurors as if they're in the house with him when he took the pictures.

Peters lets him go. You got a Thoroughbred, you give it its head, you let it run, and Jack is running like freaking Secretariat.

His ProCon numbers shoot up into the Positive 8 range.

Jack is amped.

He starts in on motive.

Runs the column.

Tells them how he concluded that White's motives were both personal and financial. Walks the jurors through the Whites' marital problems, their public fights, her drinking and rehab, the restraining order, the separation and the upcoming divorce.

Then he takes them through White's finances: the $600,000 balloon payment on the house, the tax debts, the flat real estate investments, the tapped-out bank account, the delinquent credit card bills, the expensive furniture collection, the threat of alimony and child support, the threat of losing half of his meager assets to his wife.

The jury is tripping on Jack. They're pulling back on their joysticks like they're triggering a cocaine drip. There are 9s and 10s lighting up on the old monitor like Jack is some sort of eighty-five-pound adolescent girl on the uneven parallel bars.

"Did all this lead you to reach any conclusions?" Peters asks.

"Yes," Jack says. "That he was about to lose his home, his business and his furniture."

"You seem to think the furniture is important, why is that?"

"It represented a very considerable investment," Jack says. "Also, it was one of the first things Mr. White asked me about the day of the fire."

"The day of the fire?"

"Yes."

"Mr. White called you about his claim the same day his wife was killed?" Peters asks, looking at the jury, an incredulous little tremor in her voice.

"Yes," Jack says, matter-of-factly. Better to let the *jury* get indignant.

"So the fact that he was about to lose all these things," Peters says, still shaking her head a little, "did that mean anything to you?"

"Yes, it meant to me that he had sufficient motive to set the fire."

"And murder his wife?"

Casey launches up. "Objection!"

Jack says, "It's hard to reach the conclusion that the fire was intentional and the death accidental. There is also forensic evidence to indicate that she was dead before the fire broke out."

"Which is probably beyond the scope of this inquiry tonight," Mallon quickly tells the jury. "Suffice to say that a coroner has ruled that Mrs. White died as the result of an overdose of drugs and alcohol."

And thank you very much, Your Honor, Jack thinks.

Mallon gives Jack a dirty glance, because Pam Vale's death was supposed to be out-of-bounds. Jack gives him an innocent look but he's thinking, *Fuck you—Casey brought it up in his opening and he's not playing by the rules, so I'm not playing by the rules. In fact . . .*

"Mr. Casey told the jury we accused his client of murder," Jack says. "We didn't—we're not the police—but I thought the jury should know why we denied the life insurance claim."

"You're out of order, Mr. Smith," Mallon says.

"Sorry."

Jack looks over at Casey, who is working, albeit none too hard, to suppress a smile.

The jury is grooving on this little spat. Winging happy numbers back to the observation room.

Mallon says, "Ms. Peters, if you would continue your direct . . ."

"Gladly," Peters says. "Let's talk about opportunity."

She says this giving Jack a look like, Get back on the leash, claims dog. He does, and she leads him through his testimony on whether White had the opportunity to set the fire.

Jack takes the jurors through the points on the locked doors and windows, the burglar alarm not going off, the time it would have taken White to drive from his mother's house, set the fire and drive back.

Then Peters asks, "Did you talk to White's mother about his whereabouts that night?"

"Yes."

"What did she tell you?"

"That her son was home watching a movie that night, and that she saw him at her house during the time the fire was being set."

"Did you believe her?"

"No."

"Why not?"

"The guard at the gate told me he saw Mr. White come back in at 4:45 a.m.," Jack says.

To a little *ahhhh* from the jury.

"And the combined weight of all the other evidence argued against her alibi," Jack says. "She had a vested interest in protecting both her son and her own home, which Mr. White had mortgaged to raise capital to cover other debts."

"Any other points on opportunity?"

"The dog."

"The *dog*?"

She looks at him with feigned puzzlement. The jurors don't—their puzzlement is genuine.

Jack looks at them and explains the whole thing about the dog. He finishes with, "I came to the conclusion that Mr. White let the dog out before setting the fire."

Peters can't help herself. "He loved his dog more than his wife?"

"Objection."

"Sustained."

"Did you consider whether there was anyone else who had the opportunity to set this fire?" Peters asks.

"No facts came to light to indicate that there was anyone else," Jack answers.

"Did you reach a conclusion as to the issue of opportunity?"

"Yes."

"What was your conclusion?"

"That Mr. White had sufficient opportunity to have either set the fire or known that the fire was going to be set."

"Earlier, you testified about there being three elements necessary to deny a claim based on arson," Peters says. "Do you recall that testimony?"

He does and she knows he does. She wants the jury to recall it before she goes on.

"I do," Jack says.

"Did you reach a conclusion whether those three elements were sufficiently proved so that you could reasonably deny Mr. White's claim?"

"I did."

"And what was your conclusion?"

Jack says, "Based on the totality of the facts we learned, I concluded that there was sufficient evidence to deny the claim."

"Beyond a reasonable doubt?"

"I don't know if I could describe it in those words," Jack says. "Let me just say that I'd have to be damn sure."

"And were you 'damn sure' that Mr. White was involved in this fire?"

Jack looks at the jury.

Says, "*Damn* sure."

"No further questions. Thank you."

Goddamn Billy breaks into applause.

Turns back to the corporate mucks and points to the monitor.

Solid 10s across the board.

Jack Wade had *killed*.

88

Paul Gordon is making his case in front of Judge John Bickford.

Actually, he's not so much making his case as he is *leaving* his case, the case in question being a Halliburton attaché with twenty K in cash inside.

See, they're seated at this banquette at the Rusty Pelican in Newport Beach, and Gordon has the case underneath the table by his leg, and he and Bickford are discussing an element of the law.

"I'll be filing suit against Cal Fire and Life," Gordon's telling him. "You're going to get the case."

"If it comes up in my rotation," Bickford says.

"It will come up in your rotation," Gordon says.

The assigning judge having been on three fishing trips down on the Mexican coast on Gordon's boat. Fishing trips, Dodgers tickets, a "legal seminar" in Italy compliments of Gordon's firm . . . the case will get assigned where it's supposed to get assigned.

Gordon says, "Tom Casey's going to come whining to you about a discovery issue involving a claims adjuster's prior record. He'll ask you to exclude all discovery prior to the adjuster's handling of the file in suit."

"And?"

"And I'd like you to consider denying that motion."

Bickford sips his scotch. He's sixty-five years old, retirement looms and judges do not make the kind of money, say, plaintiff's attorneys do. Mrs. Bickford has skin cancer . . .

Bickford asks, "Are you writing me a brief?"

"It's in the case."

"How many pages?"

"Twenty."

Bickford sets his glass down. "That's not very long."

"Standard," Gordon says.

"But this is a big case for you, Paul," Bickford says. "I would think you'd want to write more. Nail down every point."

"Twenty's always been good enough in the past," Gordon says. Like, Don't jerk me around at *this* stage of the game. I *own* you, you old bastard.

"The past," Bickford says, "is a fleeting dream. An insubstantial thing."

Like twenty large of my money is now insubstantial? Gordon asks himself.

"You know," Gordon says, "you might be right. Maybe another judge *will* catch this case."

Bickford sighs. It's one thing to acknowledge yourself a whore. To acknowledge yourself a *cheap* whore is yet another level of self-abasement. And yet the money is needed.

"Twenty pages should be adequate to make a persuasive argument," Bickford says.

"Thank you for your consideration," Gordon says. He finishes his drink and gets up. He doesn't have the case with him when he walks out.

Judge John Bickford orders another scotch.

Sits for a long time and watches the boats bob against their slips in the harbor.

He remembers when he believed in the law.

89

"You're a good claims investigator, aren't you, Mr. Smith?"

Tom Casey's first question in his cross-examination of Jack.

A question known in the cross-exam business as an "entry question." Which, just like an entry wound, can be small and even painless.

And it's the smart move, Jack thinks, which is just what you'd expect from Casey. It's smart not to attack me right away, because the jury likes me right now, and Casey doesn't want to antagonize them by attacking me too soon. So he'll lay back and set the trap.

"I hope I'm a good claims adjuster," Jack says.

Cross-exam witness rule number one: Try to answer in complete sentences, not just yes or no. Rule number two: Use your own language, not the lawyer's.

Casey taught him this stuff over the years. That the lawyer's real purpose in a cross-exam is for the lawyer to testify, and just get the witness to nod and shake his head like one of those bobble-head dogs in the rear window of a car.

"Cross-exam," Casey has lectured, "is a 'dig me' game. The lawyer wants to strut his stuff in front of the jury. He wants to show how smart he is, how right he is. Dig me."

Now Casey asks, "And part of adjusting claims is investigating the claim, right?"

"Yes," Jack says. "We need to find out what happened, what is damaged or lost and how much it will cost to repair and replace."

"And the reason you need to find out what happened," Casey says, "is so that you can determine if you are even going to honor the claim in the first place, isn't that right?"

"That's one of the reasons."

"So do you consider yourself a good investigator?"

Knowing that Jack is going to answer more or less yes. If he answers no, he's screwed. If he answers yes, he's another step closer to the ambush.

But there's no choice given the question.

"Yes, I think I do a good job."

"And part of doing a good job is performing a thorough investigation, right?"

They both know the game here. Casey's trying to get Jack to set a standard for himself, a bar that he'll have to jump over down the line. Casey wants to set it as high as possible.

So Jack answers, "We need to find the facts that will let us make a reasonable decision."

"You need to carefully examine all the facts around a loss and make a decision based on your analysis, right?"

"We need to examine all the relevant facts," Jack says.

"So finding and examining all the relevant facts is what makes a good claims investigation?"

"Yes."

"So it stands to reason, doesn't it . . . I mean, you'd agree with me that if you *didn't* consider all the relevant facts, you'd have a *bad* claims investigation, wouldn't you?"

Jack says, "I'd want to consider all the relevant facts."

"And did you do a good job on *this* investigation, Mr. Smith?"

There's no playing around with that question, Jack thinks. It's an ultimate question, a barn burner. You say anything but yes, the case is over.

"Yes, I did."

"You considered all the relevant facts before you made the decision to deny my client's claim?"

Jack can feel the bullet going in, but there isn't a damn thing he can do about it.

"I believe so," he says.

"Okay," Casey says. "Did you know at the time you made the decision that the Sheriff's fire inspector had taken debris samples from the house?"

"No."

"So you didn't consider that fact, did you?"

"The inspector told me on the first visit to the house that he had already established a cause and origin. He said nothing about taking samples so I presumed that he hadn't done that."

Casey pauses, feigns considering the response, then asks, "Was that a no? 'No, I didn't consider that'?"

"I wasn't aware at that time that he had taken samples."

"So you couldn't have considered it, could you?"

"No."

"Are debris samples relevant?" Casey asks, knowing that Jack has no choice but to say yes, because his side of the case put on an expert witness to testify about them, and Jack has already said that they were "significant."

"Yes."

"Okay," Casey says. He turns to face the jury as he asks, "Then you couldn't have been aware at the time you made the decision to deny my client's claim that the debris samples taken by the Sheriff's fire inspector tested *negative* for traces of accelerants, isn't that right?"

"I was not shown those results."

"Did you ask for them?"

"No."

"Isn't that something that would have been important for you to know?" Casey asks. "Would that have been 'relevant'?"

Son of a bitch is taking my own word and beating me over the head with it. Why the hell did I say 'relevant'? Then again, what the hell else could I have said?

"I would have preferred that the inspector share them with me, yes," Jack says. "But he didn't. We weren't made aware of them until after the suit was filed."

"So you didn't consider that fact?" Casey asks. "Is that your answer?"

"I didn't consider those tests."

"Or the results."

"Or the results."

Casey takes a marker from his pocket and crosses out the positive debris sample item on the chart.

Looks at the jury, looks back at Jack.

"Now," he says, "we heard you give a lot of testimony on Mr. White's financial woes. Yup, here it is on your chart. The mortgage, the $600,000 balloon payment, the credit card bills . . . At the time you made your decision, were you aware that Mr. White had paid off the entire $600,000 balloon payment?"

"At the time I made the decision, he hadn't."

"So you didn't consider that, did you?"

"No."

"Would that have been relevant for you to know?"

"It's something I would have considered."

Casey crosses out the $600,000 balloon payment item on the chart.

"Did you know that he's current with his credit card bills?"

"No."

Cross off.

"That he's current with the mortgage on his mother's home?"

"No."

Cross off.

And the jury getting unhappy. Jack can see them pushing the joysticks down.

In the observation room, Reinhardt looks over at Goddamn Billy and asks, "What the hell kind of claims investigations are you guys *doing* down here?"

Casey asks, "That he has over $1 million in liquid assets in his various accounts?"

Come on, Jack thinks, fight back.

"Again," he says, "these were all things we learned only after the suit was filed."

"So that's a no, isn't it?"

"These were things—"

"Yes or no?"

"—that we learned—"

Mallon says, "Please just answer yes or no, Mr. Smith."

"No."

Casey crosses the item off.

"How about the tax liens?" Casey asks. "Did you know that he paid those off?"

"No."

"The divorce," Casey says, "which hadn't happened yet. Did you consider the possibility of a reconciliation?"

"No."

"Would it have been relevant to your investigation, if indeed the Whites were trying to reconcile?"

"They weren't trying to reconcile."

"That's not what I *asked* you, Mr. Smith," Casey snaps. He can get tougher with Jack now because he senses the jury is turning. "I asked you whether that information would have been relevant."

"I would have considered it."

"But you didn't ask, did you?"

"I had information indicating that—"

"You didn't *ask*, did you?"

"Just answer the question, Mr. Smith," Mallon says.

"No, I did not ask."

Casey crosses off the alimony and divorce items.

The whole MOTIVE column is crossed out.

"Opportunity," Casey says. "You've testified that in your opinion, Mr. White was the only person who had the exclusive opportunity to set this fire. Did you look for anyone else?"

"There was no information to point to anyone else."

"That's a no?"

"Yes, that's a no."

"Did Mrs. White have a boyfriend?"

"I had no information to suggest that she had."

"So you didn't consider that, did you?"

"No."

"Wouldn't it have been important to you to know that?" Casey asks. "Wouldn't that have been a relevant fact, the possibility that someone else was in the house—in the bedroom with Mrs. White the night of the fire, the night of her death?"

"Because Mr. White never mentioned it, I had—"

Casey sighs. "Once again, Mr. Smith, that is not the question I asked you. The question I asked you was whether such information might have been relevant to your thorough, fair investigation."

"I asked Mrs. White's sister whether it was possible that the deceased was having an affair."

"Her sister," Casey says. "And what did she tell you?"

"She said that Mrs. White had no boyfriend."

"Mrs. White's sister," Casey asks. "Wasn't she the next beneficiary on the life insurance policy?"

"Yes."

"If Mr. White were found responsible for his wife's death, her sister stood to gain $250,000, isn't that right?"

"That would be correct."

"Did you ever ask her where *she* was the night of the fire?"

"Yes, I did."

"And what did she tell you?"

"That she was at home. About forty miles away."

"And did she offer anyone who could corroborate her alibi?"

"No. She was alone."

"But you believed *her*, right?"

Jack says, "I had no reason to disbelieve her."

"Right," Casey says. "By the way, did you ask her these questions when she spent the night at your condo?"

Audible gasp from the jury.

Audible moan in the observation room.

ProCon numbers plunge into the negatives.

VP Claims looks at Goddamn Billy like he wants to kill him.

Peters jumps to her feet.

"Objection! Lacks—"

"I withdraw that question," Casey says. Then he asks, "Isn't it true that the sister spent the night with you?"

"On my couch, yes."

"On your couch," Casey repeats. "Did you ask anyone else—friends, neighbors—whether Mrs. White was having an affair?"

"No."

"You never asked Mr. White and he didn't volunteer, isn't that correct?"

"Yes."

"So you didn't even consider that possibility, did you, Mr. Smith?"

"Yes, I did. I considered it very improbable."

"Right," Casey says, "because Mr. White had all that *motive*."

Casey pauses for a second to let it sink in with the jury. Then he says, "Now, you've told us that the security guard at the gate of the complex where Mr. White was living saw him come in at a quarter to five, correct?"

"Yes."

"He told you that."

"Yes."

"But you also saw a sworn affidavit from the guard—Mr. Derochik—affirming that he did *not* see Mr. White come in at 4:45 or any other time, isn't that right?"

The jurors get busy with the joysticks.

Jack says, "Mr White presented that statement only *after* we had denied the claim."

"Oh," Casey says. "But we only have your word as to what the guard told you, isn't that right?"

"That's right."

"And you disregarded Mr. Derochik's sworn statement, didn't you?"

"I didn't consider it truthful."

"I see."

He crosses out the items under OPPORTUNITY.

Then he goes for the exit question. And just like with a bullet, it's the exit wound that sprays the blood and flesh and bits of vital organs all over the wall.

"So," Casey says, "you didn't find out about the clean samples, you didn't find out about the mortgage being paid off, you didn't find out about the credit cards being up-to-date, you didn't find out about the bank balance being in excess of $1 million, you didn't find out about a reconciliation, you didn't find out about the lover, and you never considered the sister as a potential suspect. Having failed to consider any of these highly relevant facts, do you still think that you did a good job on this investigation?"

And just like the entry question, he doesn't care if Jack answers yes or no. It doesn't matter, because either way Jack looks bad.

"Yes, I do," Jack says.

Except he doesn't look so bad.

Casey knows it. He can tell without seeing the monitor with its spikes. He can see it just by looking at the jury.

They don't know what to think. They haven't made up their minds.

Casey knows he's fought to a stalemate.

Which just won't do.

So he has to play a card he really doesn't want to play.

90

Letty's at home when the phone rings.

She picks it up; it's a teenager's voice.

"I want to talk with you," he says.

Slight Asian accent.

It's Tony Ky, the wiseass from the chop shop.

"What about?" Letty asks.

She's knows what it's about, but she has to play the game.

There's a hesitation, then the kid whispers, "Tranh and Do."

So, Letty thinks, I guess Uncle Nguyen is feeling the heat.

"Come into the station," she says, just to set a bargaining position.

The kid almost laughs. "No, someplace . . ."

"Isolated?" Letty asks, with this edge in her voice that's like *Go to class*.

"Yeah, isolated."

"You have a ride?"

"Yeah, I have a ride."

She tells him about a turnoff on the Ortega. A picnic spot and hiking trail into the Cleveland National Forest. Park your ride under the trees, walk up the trail a ways.

"Be there at seven," she says.

"In the *morning*?"

"Yeah, learn how to get up," she says.

She hangs up, brushes her teeth, brushes her hair, does all the cream-and-lotion jazz and gets into bed with a book and an intent to turn the light out soon.

Hard to get to sleep.

A lot on her mind.

Pam.

Pam's murder.

Natalie and Michael.

And son of a bitch Jack Wade.

Twelve years, Letty thinks. You'd think that you could take what happened twelve years ago and put it away.

But you can't.

91

"Have you ever lied under oath?"

Casey plays the card. Takes a drink of water, and the next words out of his mouth are, "Mr. Smith, have you ever lied under oath?"

It's the old husband joke. It doesn't matter whether Jack answers yes or no. Either way he's screwed.

Casey didn't want to do it. He'd hoped that Jack would have just laid down on direct exam and let his case fade away. Should have gone down for the count but came out swinging instead, so now Casey has to go for the knockout punch and he hates doing it.

Especially when he sees Jack flush.

Jack can feel himself turning red. My goddamn *shame,* he thinks, blazing red under my skin.

The jurors see it. They lean forward to get a better look.

Jack can feel their eyes.

Burning into him.

Peters jumps to her feet.

"Objection, Your Honor! Relevance?"

"Goes to the witness's credibility, Your Honor."

"Prejudicial, Your Honor," Peters says. "More heat than light."

Mallon looks at the lawyers, then down at Jack.

"Overruled," he said. "You may proceed."

Casey asks again, "Mr. Smith, have you ever lied under oath?"

Get it over with, Jack thinks.

Take the hit.

"Yes," he says.

And leaves it at that.

He and Casey look at each other for a minute. Casey giving him this look like *If you had only stayed on the mat, but . . .*

"That was in connection with an arson trial, wasn't it?" Casey asks.

"That's right."

Casey asks, "You lied about how you obtained a confession, didn't you."

"Yes."

"You swore under *oath*," Casey says, "that you hadn't coerced the confession when you had, isn't that right?"

"Yes."

"In fact, you beat a confession out of a suspect, didn't you?"

"Yes."

"Then told the court that you hadn't."

"Yes."

"And that was a lie."

"That was a lie."

"You told other lies, didn't you?" Casey asks. Thinking, Sorry, Jack, but believe it or not, I'm trying to save your ass. And your job. "You told other lies, right?"

"Yes."

"You lied about evidence, isn't that right?"

"Yes."

"You said that you found evidence at the fire scene, correct?"

"Yes."

"But you hadn't found it at the scene, had you?"

"No."

"How did the evidence get to that fire scene?" Casey asks.

Jack says, "I planted it there."

Jurors shake their heads.

Hands pressing down on the joysticks.

Casey starts to kick the ball downhill. Short questions, rapid fire, all while he looks at the jury, his back to the witness.

"You planted it there," Casey says.

"That's correct."

"You went out and got a gasoline can."

"Yes."

"And you forced the suspect to place his fingerprints on the can."

"Yes."

"And you took the can to the scene."

"Yes."

"And photographed it there."

"Yes."

"And then swore that you had found it there during your initial inspection, isn't that right?"

"That's what happened."

Casey says, "You planted phony evidence because you thought the suspect was guilty, you were 'damn sure,' but you needed physical evidence to confirm that the fire was of incendiary origin, isn't that right?"

"Yes."

Keeping up the pace, he turns to face Jack.

"Now, you testified earlier that you took debris samples from my client's home," Casey says, "and that these samples tested positive for accelerants, is that right?"

"Yes."

"The fire inspector, Deputy Bentley, found *clean* samples, isn't that right?" Casey asks.

"That's what he says."

"He was at the scene first?"

"Yes."

"Before you."

Jack says, "He was there when I arrived."

"The alleged 'dirty' samples only showed up after you got there, isn't that right?" Casey asks.

"I took the samples from the house."

"And the holes in the floor," Casey says. "The fire inspector didn't see those, did he?"

"He didn't do a dig-out."

"There's no mention of them in his report, is there?"

"No."

"They only appear after *you* show up, isn't that true?" Casey asks.

"They 'show up' after I did the dig-out," Jack says.

"It would have been pretty easy to punch out those holes yourself, wouldn't it?"

"I didn't do that."

"Pretty easy to pour a little accelerant into the joists and light a match."

"That's ridiculous, counselor."

"Pretty easy to bring your own contaminated samples to the scene and photograph them there."

"That didn't happen."

"You *swear*?"

"Yes."

"Just like you swore before, right?" Casey says.

"Objection!"

"Sustained."

"Same oath, wasn't it, Mr. Smith?"

"Knock it off, Mr. Casey," Mallon says.

Casey nods and takes a drink of water. Makes a little show of getting his righteous indignation under control.

Then he ups the ante. To show the corporate mucks behind the mirror that they can't just dump Jack and walk away from this thing, he ties a tail onto management.

"You were convicted of perjury, isn't that right?" he asks.

"I pled guilty to several counts of perjury."

"And you were thrown out of the Sheriff's Department," Casey says, "for perjuring yourself, beating up a suspect and planting phony evidence, isn't that right, Mr. Smith?"

"That's correct."

"And shortly after that," Casey says, "California Fire and Life hired you, right?"

Casey looks right into the mirror to make sure the boys in the back get the point.

They do. They're looking at a monitor that's Negative 10 all the way.

"Yes," Jack says.

"Did they know about your record?"

"The man who hired me was aware of my record."

"In fact," Casey says, "he sat through the trial in which you perjured yourself, right?"

"I believe so."

"He knew you were a liar," Casey says.

"Yes."

"A brutal cop."

"Yes."

"That you would plant phony evidence to nail an alleged arsonist."

"He was at the trial."

"And he hired you anyway."

"Yes."

"And he hired you specifically to handle large fire losses for California Fire and Life, isn't that right?"

"That was one of his reasons."

"Does this gentleman still work for California Fire and Life?" Casey asks, looking to the jury.

Several of whom are shaking their heads.

"He does."

"In what capacity?"

"He's the head of Claims."

Jury goes nuts. Pushing the hammer down on those joysticks, shaking their heads; one guy says out loud, "Unreal."

"And he's your boss now, right?" Casey asks.

"Yes."

"Did he supervise your investigation of my client's claim?"

"Yes."

"Have you in any way been punished for what you did in this investigation?" Casey asks.

"No."

"Suspended?"

"No."

"Criticized?"

"No."

Casey looks back into the mirror as he asks, "So this is the way California Fire and Life wants you to handle its claim, right? Strike that question. No further questions. Thank you."

"You may step down, Mr. Smith."

Casey says, "I'm sorry, one further question. Mr. Smith, if you had to handle my client's claim all over again, would you do anything differently?"

It's the standard cross-exam wrap-up question. Another trap where you don't care what the guy answers. If he answers that he wouldn't do anything differently, you get to tell the jury that this arrogant bozo would do the same bad things again if he had the chance. If he says that he would do something different, you get to tell the jury that by the witness's own account, he screwed up.

Jack knows it's over. Can see it in the jurors' eyes. They're looking at him like he's a criminal. They're shocked and pissed off and they're going to award poor tragedy-stricken Mr. White at least $25 million.

And he knows what's going on in the back room. The corporate boys are pissing all over themselves, hopping up and down on one foot they're so eager to lay the Green Poultice on this gaping wound and give Nicky Vale $50 million.

So he says, "Yes, I would. Do something different."

"What would you do?"

Jack turns to the jury, to make eye contact.

"I'd kill the son of a bitch."

Then he gets up and walks out.

92

Casey comes into the observation room, grabs himself a plate of lasagna and says, "For my *next* trick . . ."

Like he's made Wade disappear, he's made their case disappear, now he's going to make $50 million of the company's money disappear, and they'd fire the smart-ass wise guy right now, except that he *is* the smartest lawyer in So-Cal and they need him so that the board doesn't make *them* disappear.

The veeps look at him like *Fuck you, Casey,* but Casey doesn't care. Let 'em be pissed. What are they going to do, fire him? They have that collective *We're the big-dick guys from corporate, cowboy, so watch yourself if you want to stay on the ranch* look in their collective eye, so Casey gives them his favorite John Wayne line, from the old *Stagecoach* movie.

"'You may *need* me and this Winchester, Curly,'" he drawls. "'I saw some ranches burning last night.'"

Phil Herlihy turns his wrath on Goddamn Billy, who's sitting there sucking on a cig like there aren't ten WE THANK YOU FOR NOT SMOK-ING signs in the room. (To which Goddamn Billy's standard response is, "Well, now they don't have to thank me.") Anyway, Herlihy turns to Billy and just about screams, "How the hell could you hire that guy?! What the hell were you thinking about?!"

"I was thinking," Billy says, "that he'd be a damn good claims dog. And he has been."

"One of the best," Casey says. "*The* best."

Herlihy pretends he doesn't hear Casey. Any sane person who watched the cross-exam wouldn't want to get in a debate with Casey.

"Fire him," Herlihy says to Billy. "Tomorrow. Tonight if you can get hold of him."

"I ain't firing him," Billy says.

"I just told you to!"

"I heard you."

The Trial Science Inc. geek walks in. The geek is like white, and his hands are shaking. The verdict forms in his hand rattle like ghosts in the attic.

"Yes?" Casey says. He's still smiling. Tomato sauce looks like blood on his lips.

The TSI geek says, "Two hundred million."

"What?!" Herlihy yells.

"They'd award $200 million in compensatory and punitives," the geek says. "Actually we had to push them to give a dollar figure. What they really wanted to do was put the company's management in jail. One of them wanted to hang you."

"Settle it," Herlihy says.

"Concur," says Reinhardt.

"Absolutely," says Bourne.

"Settle this file now," Herlihy says. "What's the demand?"

"Fifty million," Casey says. "If the real jury goes the way this one does, that's a savings of $150 million. Not counting court costs and, of course, my exorbitant fees. And these days, juries are usually hip enough to figure the plaintiff's attorney's cut into their judgment . . ."

"We lose," Goddamn Billy says. "We appeal."

"On what grounds?" Reinhardt snaps.

"Admissibility," Casey says. "You argue that Wade's background is irrelevant and prejudicial."

"Motions *in limine*?"

"Sure," Casey says. "I'd try to keep Jack's background out before the trial, but I doubt I'd win. We could also instruct him to not answer any questions about his background in deposition, but that would start a discovery battle . . ."

"No discovery battles," Reinhardt says.

Discovery battles have a way of getting out of hand. Subpoenas for documents tend to get broader and broader, and if a judge got annoyed and let Gordon go on a fishing expedition . . . Well, that just can't happen.

"This file is over," Herlihy says. He says to Casey, "Start settlement negotiations tomorrow. See if you can work this down. But you have $50 million settlement authority."

"Hold on," Billy says. "That's not your call to make."

"You need executive authority for anything over a million," VP Claims says.

"If I want it," Billy says. "I ain't said I want a dime yet."

"We're going to settle this case."

"That is *my* call to make, goddamn it."

"Then make it," Reinhardt says.

"I ain't ready to make that call," Billy says.

"I'll make it," Reinhardt says. "I have the authority to settle a lawsuit against the company."

"Yeah, you do," Billy says. "But there ain't no lawsuit yet. There's just a threat of a suit. So it's still in Claims, and I'm Claims."

"I can put an end to that," Herlihy says.

"Well, goddamn it, why don't you just do that?"

"Don't think I won't!"

"Go ahead! I don't give a fuck."

"You boys want to take this outside?" Casey asks. "We have some serious issues to resolve in here. Let me propose a compromise. We settle the case and Jack Wade keeps his job."

"Jack Wade is history," Herlihy says.

"Hold on," Casey says. "If this doesn't go to trial, there's no reason to fire Jack."

"Until the next time," Reinhardt says.

"So take him off fires," Casey says. "Give him slip-and-falls, dog bites, broken pipes . . ."

"Or we could just shoot him," Billy says.

"You're not helping me, Billy."

"Well, goddamn it!" Billy explodes. He gets to his feet. "All Jack Wade did was his job! Tell you something else: all he was doing when he set up that fucking Teddy Kuhl and that fucking Kazzy Azmekian was his goddamn job! They were as guilty as sin and everybody goddamn knew it! 'Perjury' my fucking ass! *Truth* was, those cocksuckers *did* set that fire! And so did Nicky Vale!"

"Billy—"

"Shut up, Tom, I'm talking," Billy says. "I been in this business coming on thirty years, and I can tell you this: if it walks like a dog, barks like a dog, wags its tail like a dog and lifts its hind leg to *pee* like a dog, it's a goddamn *dog*! And Jack Wade knows that—and Tom Casey, you know that—even if these fools don't! And you can bang on your goddamn machines and your goddamn laptop computers all goddamn night and this fire is still a goddamn arson, and Nicky Vale set it, and he murdered his wife, and I ain't paying that motherfucker one goddamn cent and I ain't firing Jack Wade and if you boys don't like it you can just goddamn fire me. I don't goddamn care!"

There's your basic hushed silence as he heads for the door.

He turns around in the doorway and looks at them for a minute.

Shakes his head.

"This company used to stand for something," he says. "Now it'll stand for anything."

Shakes his head again and says, "Any goddamn thing."

He turns and leaves.

"Well . . ." Casey says.

"We pay the fifty," Bourne says. "We're going to the Insurance Commission for a rate hike in ninety days anyway—this will add nicely to the debit side when we argue that we need it."

Casey has stopped listening.

It's a done deal.

93

Jack busts the Mustang south.

Blows right past the exit to California Fire and Life, passes the exit to his condo and shoots down to the Ortega Highway, where he turns east.

You take the Ortega east, what you're letting yourself in for is a series of downhill switchbacks that is like *guaranteed* to make your Labrador throw up in the backseat. You're going over the top of the mountains in the Cleveland National Forest, so you're cruising through some barren, rock-strewn hills—the "forest"—and all of a sudden you're pitching downhill toward the town of Lake Elsinore, and it's like falling off the edge of the fucking earth. Which it is, which you'd know if you've ever actually *been* to Lake 'Snore.

This stretch of road is *not* where you want to fuck up. You slip on the kozmic banana peel coming down *these* switchbacks you are suddenly Lost in Space, man. You are Rocky the Flying Squirrel, you are *airborne*. You may have your four-wheel-drive sports utility vehicle—but you can have eighteen-wheel-drive and it won't matter, if all those wheels are in the sky. What you don't have is wings, or a parachute, which is what you're going to need if you screw up the distinction between centrifugal and centripetal force on one of *these* curves.

Like, bikers have done space launches off this mountain and the

Highway Patrol can't even *find* them; they're in their own little bomb craters six hundred feet below.

You lose the edge on these curves, it's just AMF.

Jack's into it.

Jack's working out his rage on the road; he and the Mustang are taking the Ortega like it's a Nebraska farm road, like *What curves? We don't see no stinking curves.* Jack's doing the gas, brake, shift, gas number, cranking on that wheel like he's on the bridge of the starship *Enterprise.*

As for Jack, well, it isn't *exactly* the Death Ride of Jack Wade. It's not like he's necessarily *trying* to kill himself, it's just that he's not trying real hard *not* to.

Because what's the difference? Jack's thinking.

The job's gone.

And I don't have a life outside the job.

Unless you count the daily surfing ritual at Dana Strand.

Which will be gone soon.

Into the Great Sunsets.

His adrenaline's a little jacked when he has to slow down to figure out where Letty's place is.

In the middle of nowhere.

He finally finds it about a hundred yards down a dirt road that runs between two pastures. There's a stand of trees with several buildings hidden in it and when he pulls up the sign says DEL RIO.

He sits in the car wondering why the hell he's there, decides it's for no good reason at all, and he's just about to put the 'Stang in reverse when he sees lights come on in the house.

He turns off the engine and gets out of the car.

She comes out, she's wearing a T-shirt over jeans and she's barefoot. Hair tussled.

Stands in her gravel driveway looking at him.

Like, What are you doing here?

"It's over," he finally says. "I blew it. We lost."

She thinks about it for a few seconds, then says, "You drove out here to tell me that?"

It's a minute at least before he hears himself speak.

"I have nothing in my life."

Feels like he's standing a long way away, hearing himself say that.

She goes to him and takes him by the arm and leads him into her house.

94

Later, when she takes him into her bedroom, she pulls her T-shirt over her head and steps out of the jeans and gets under the sheet. Jack gets undressed and lies down beside her. She reaches out for him and her skin is white and warm, and they kiss and she presses against him and he pulls the sheet down. When he reaches down to touch her she's moist and warm. He strokes her, feeling her get wetter, feeling her flow to his hand and get hotter, and then she says, *Baby,* and when she reaches for him he's hard and with her open hand she strokes him up and down.

They stroke each other, she starts to move against his hand, she presses up and her eyes get wide as if she's surprised. And her skin is hot and she arches her back and reaches her other hand for his and holds it tight as she cranes her neck back and comes.

He keeps stroking, touching her where she's now so wet but she moves his hand away and says, *In me, I want you* in me, and she guides him inside her and Jack is surprised at how good she feels, hot and ripply as she moves up and down against him, and her breasts flatten against his chest and she doesn't close her eyes but she looks at him as he moves slowly in and out of her. Her black hair rippling on the pillow; he reaches out to grab it and clench it in his hand, bury his face and kiss her neck, lick her salty skin there. She clasps the back of his neck and pulls him close to kiss her. Her mouth is hot and her tongue is hot and her thighs feel fiery against his and he starts to move faster and harder because he wants to feel the heat of the core of her. He can feel it when he lunges hard deep into her. She can feel it too, because she jams herself against him and pushes him up deeper into her. He can feel the head of his cock touch this deep hot place inside her that touches some deep place in him, and she's holding his neck and his ass and rocking with him and he's gripping her neck and her ass and can feel her wet against the tips of his fingers there, and then it feels like inside there is this heat flowing, flowing, and she grips him harder saying, *Yes, baby, it's okay,* as he moans and starts to move faster and harder. There's this heat in him, he feels like he's falling, he feels like he's on fire and falling as she rocks him in and around her, there's that *heat* so deep inside her, so lovely, inside her so lovely, her face so lovely, this falling like riding a wave of flame, *Yes, baby, it's okay, come in me, you can come in me,* and then he is, it's like falling off the world, like a wave of flame crashing, rolling him over and over under this unbearable wave of pleasure, not letting him up, he's crying out, she's cooing, *Yes, baby,* he's under this ocean of pleasure, somewhere up above the water he hears his long scream, he feels his soul race out ahead of him, he's drowning, she's saying, *Baby,* and when finally he comes up it's like he washes up on the white beach of her body, white neck and white breasts, her stomach slick, their sweat like smooth wet sand, and her face is flushed red and her eyes are wet. Black hair sweaty wet clings to her neck and he sees those eyes searching for his and then he finally breathes.

Tears come. Drop from his eyes onto her neck, her chest, her breasts, she holds him tightly to her as he sobs, as he weeps twelve empty years.

95

Jack wakes up in Letty's bed.

At first he's like, *Where the hell am I,* but then he smells the Mexican coffee and remembers. Rolls out of the rack and comes into the kitchen and she's standing there by the toaster sipping on the strong coffee.

"I don't do the bacon-and-eggs thing," she says. "But I can offer you toast and coffee."

"Sounds great."

He plops down on a stool by her curved kitchen counter and looks out the window. The land slopes down through big, old black oak trees to some open pasture. Across a fence, horses are out grazing.

"Your horses?" Jack asks.

"The neighbor's," she says. "I ride them sometimes. You ride?"

"Just surfboards," he says.

"To each his own ride," she says, handing him a plate of buttered toast. She sits on the stool next to his. "What are you going to do now?"

"I'm going to go in to the office," he says, "and clean out my desk."

"You think they're really going to fire you?"

Jack says, "If they don't, I'm going to quit anyway."

"You don't have to do that," she says.

"Yeah I do."

They sit and look out the window. It's pretty out there, Jack thinks. The trees and the pasture. Mountains in the background.

After a few minutes she asks, "So what are you going to do?"

"Dunno."

A few minutes later she says, "You could come here."

"You don't have to—"

"The house needs a remodel," she says. "You could be doing that. You know, fixing things—"

"Sleeping in your bed . . ."

"Well, that would be a bonus."

"For me."

"How gallant."

More coffee, more silence, more window gazing. Then she says, "It's a serious offer."

"Serious?"

"Sincere," she says, looking into her coffee cup. "And sudden. But look, how often do you get a second chance? I mean, me as well."

"Yeah," he says. "Same."

Thinking, you romantic bastard. *Same.* Nice going.

"Yeah?" she asks. Looks up at him now.

"Oh yeah."

"So," she says. "It's a serious sincere offer."

"Thanks," he says. "Can I think about it?"

Because he knows she's offering the whole package. Like this instant life—the home, the woman—and he knows she hasn't given up on the *kids* yet. Which is bad, because she should.

"Letty?"

"Jack?"

"You're not going to get the kids," he says. "It's over."

"For you maybe," she says. She gets up and starts to clean off the counter.

"Letty—"

"Look, you took your best shot and you lost," Letty says. "I'm not *blaming* you for anything, okay? I'm not calling up what you did twelve years ago and saying that cost me the kids. All I'm saying is that I owe those kids *my* best shot, even if you think it's a loser. I'm going to find a lawyer who'll take this in front of a judge, and if I lose I'll find another lawyer and another judge, and if I lose . . ."

"Okay."

"Okay," she says. "I gotta go to work. You want to come back here tonight?"

"Yeah."

"Yeah, you heard me? Or, yeah, you want to."

"Yeah, I want to."

They stand there looking at each other.

"So this is probably the moment when we kiss," she says.

"Yeah."

So they do kiss and then hold on to each other for a minute and he says, "What I did twelve years ago? It was the wrong thing to do. I should have just dropped the case."

"Probably."

"I mean that old man was more important than the case."

"I know that's what you meant."

She walks him out to the 'Stang and he takes off.

Back to California Fire and Life.

96

Jack goes out to Billy's office.

Hotter than hell out there in the cactus garden.

"You ain't fired," Billy says. "They can't fire you until they fire me."

"See you on the unemployment line."

"Shit, I'd just *retire*," Billy says. Gives this private little smile. "Fade into the sunset."

"I'm quitting, Billy."

"Nah, don't do that."

"They gonna pay the demand?"

Billy says, "Probably."

"Then I quit."

"Shit, *Jack*—"

Billy snuffs out the cig and struggles to light another one. Has to turn against the wind and cup his hands to do it. Sucks down the first drag and says, "Just let it go."

"Can't."

Phone rings inside Billy's office. He says, "That's probably Herlihy again. I got Claims, Agency, Underwriting and SIU all banging on me about this claim."

"You better go talk to them, then."

"Don't go anywhere."

"I'll sit out here until the vultures take me away."

Jack takes the files off the chair and sits down.

97

Letty sits in the front seat of her car getting a last sip of her coffee.

She'd rather be doing something else than hiking up some trail in Cleveland Forest to meet a Vietnamese punk teenage chop shop artist to get the word about two of his missing homeboys.

Although I guess I asked for it, Letty thinks as she sets her cup on the floor below the driver's seat. I put the heat on him.

Since busting him in the chop shop, she's cranked up the DA, the Orange County Anti-Gang Task Force and the little moke's probation officer. Plus she's popped three more chop shops, a gambling room and a massage parlor to get Uncle Nguyen wound up. So she wasn't all that surprised when she got the call.

She gets out of the car and walks uphill, up the hiking trail, where she can already see Tony Ky standing there doing the Snitch Hop.

The Snitch Hop is this very distinctive two-step—a little double bounce on one foot, then shift the weight and a double bounce on the other—hands in pockets, shoulders scrunched up, head rhythmically turning from side to side. Letty sees this performance of the Snitch Hop, she knows with some satisfaction that the kid is nervous as hell.

Good, Letty thinks. Serves him right. Maybe he'll get so freaked he'll give it up and get a real job. Yeah, right.

Tony *is* nervous. The kid is definitely not used to meeting with cops to give them information, even if it is about two friends who have dropped off the screen. And Tony has had a brutal week. First there's the bust in the chop shop—which Uncle Nguyen was not happy about. But Tony figures he's still going to cruise through it. Then the DA starts cracking on him about two other chop shops, trying to connect him to some sort of *conspiracy,* then the anti-gang guy is in his face mumbling something about RICO, then his probation officer says he don't have to wait for a conviction to violate, just him being in the presence of other felons . . .

Then, like things weren't shitty enough, Uncle Nguyen reaches out *personally* with the word that if he knows anything about the disappearance of imbecile Tranh and idiot Do, he had better get his mouth in gear immediately if not sooner, and when Uncle Nguyen hears that Tranh and Do were last seen doing errands for the Russians, the old bastard like *freaks.* And then tells him to do something totally whacked, which is like call this police bitch and tell her. And Tony is like, *What?* and Uncle Nguyen is like, *Do what I tell you, haven't you caused me enough headaches already, I want this cop off my back,* so the kid makes the call.

Which would be okay—weird but okay—except that the Russian dude shows up again and asks like, *You been talking to the cops?* And Tony is like, *No, man, I don't talk to cops,* and the Russian dude is like, *Well you're going to, you're going to set up a meet,* and Tony is like, *What?*

And the Russian dude is like, *Your head: use it or lose it.*

All of which is to say that, yes, the kid is a little jumpy standing out there on some dirt path in the country waiting for a cop.

98

Billy comes back out and says, "They're going to pay tomorrow morning, with me or without me."

"So which is it?" Jack asks.

"Gotta think about that," Billy says.

"That's fair."

"How 'bout you?"

"I'm gone."

"Jack," Billy says, "you're not going to find another claims job anywhere in the industry."

"I don't want one."

"What are you going to do?"

"I don't know," Jack says. "Maybe remodeling."

Billy frowns. Fights the wind to light another cig and says, "Sleep on this, goddamn it. Take some sick days."

"Fuck it, Billy. These days, they're *all* sick days."

And walks out.

Muy disgusted.

In the lobby the receptionist juts her chin at the waiting bench and says, "Olivia Hathaway for you."

"Not now."

"She's *here*, Jack."

"I don't work here anymore," Jack says. "She's somebody else's headache now."

"Jack?"

She's standing right behind him now.

"Mrs. Hathaway."

"A moment of your time?"

"Not now, Mrs. Hathaway."

"Just one moment," she says.

She's holding a plate of cookies.

"I really don't have the time right now, Mrs. Hathaway."

Two minutes later Jack's sitting across a table from her in Room 117.

Jack starts, "Mrs. Hathaway, I don't have time for this today. I'm in a very bad mood. So, for the last time, I'm not paying for your spoons. Not now, not ever—"

"I didn't come about my spoons."

Say what?

"Then why—"

"I came because a lawyer came to see me," Olivia says. "A Mr. Gordon?"

"Paul Gordon?"

"Do you know him?"

"Sort of."

"Anyway," Olivia says, "he came to ask me to join in a suit against you. A class suit."

"A class action suit?"

"That's right," Olivia says. She takes out her knitting and goes to work. "He said that he had at least twenty other people that you've cheated that are going to join together and sue you for bad faith and punitive damages. He said that we could stand to share millions of dollars."

"Did he tell you who the others were?"

"I don't remember them all," Olivia says. "There was a Mr. Vale, a Mr. Boland, a Mrs. Vecch . . ."

"Veccharrios?"

"Yes," Olivia says. "And a Mr. Azmekian."

"A Mr. Azmekian?" Jack asks.

"Yes."

"*Kazzy* Azmekian?"

"No," she says. "I think it was Kazimir."

Jack sits there while she recites a litany of various claims Jack has turned down for the past seven years. It's like the old lady is reading off his freaking inventory.

And the only way, Jack thinks, that Paul Gordon could go trolling for these clients is that he's had access to all my files.

Jack hears Olivia saying, "So Mr. Gordon wants me to join in this suit against you. He even offered me shares in the Westview," Olivia says.

"In the what?"

"In the Westview Company, my dear. Very confidentially, of course."

What the hell?

"What did you tell him?" Jack asks.

Olivia looks up from her knitting.

"I told him to go fuck himself. Cookie?"

"Yes, ma'am, I'd like a cookie," Jack says.

Her blue eyes look at him very seriously.

"I know a scam when I see one," she says. "Sugar—your favorite."

"A great cookie."

"Now, about my spoons . . ."

99

"So?" Letty asks.

"So what?" Tony says.

Still doing the Snitch Hop.

Kid's dressed up in the official Vietnamese gangsta uniform—black Levi's, black high-tops. Black leather jacket, and it's what, 70 degrees out? Black leather jacket in August . . .

Letty doesn't feel like it. "*You* called *me*."

"Tranh and Do."

"No kidding."

Tony whispers, "They were doing a job for some Russians."

"Okay," Letty says. Like this is telling her something.

"No," Tony says, "they were doing a job for some *Russians*."

Which gets Letty's attention in a hurry.

"How did they get hooked up with the ROC?"

"Maybe we do some cars . . ." Tony says.

"Is that right?"

"Anyway," he says, like he's not here to engage in bigger issues, "Tranh and Do were running an errand for the Russians. These two guys came and said they needed some guys and a truck."

"For what?"

"Boost a truck, pick some stuff up at a house, take it somewhere, lose the truck."

"What *stuff*?" Letty asks. "What house? Take it where?"

Tony says, "They talk with my boys, they call later and leave an address."

"What address?"

"Thirty-seven Bluffside Drive."

Which rocks Letty.

The night Pamela is murdered, two missing Vietnamese gang-bangers are taking "stuff" out of the house.

Tony says, "So they lift a truck. From Paladin Unpainted Furniture. Go over there that night, they don't come back. Now you know everything I know, so lighten up on me."

"What two guys?"

"I don't know," the kid whines. "Two new guys, not the usual guys."

"You got usual guys?"

"We got guys who bring cars," Tony says. "We got guys come for the money. These were not the guys."

"Would you recognize these guys if you saw pictures?"

Tony shakes his head. "No way, lady. No fucking way do I give up these guys. You don't *have* enough weight make me do that."

"Describe them."

"Tall skinny guy. Big fat guy. No style."

"Have you seen them since?"

Tony shakes his head.

Too fast, too hard, Letty thinks.

"*Heard* from them since?"

"No."

"Don't lie to me, you little shit."

"I'm not lying!"

"And don't whine, either," she says. "It annoys me. What did they say to you, 'Keep your stupid fucking mouth shut'?"

"Something like that," Tony mumbles. "Don't tell Uncle Nguyen."

"Do they know I've been bringing the heat on you?"

"They know," the kid says, resentful. "*Every*one knows."

"You're in a tough spot."

"You put me there."

"Yeah, whatever," Letty says. "Come on in. Bring me those guys."

Tony thinks about it for a second. "See how it plays," he says.

"Yeah, see how it plays," Letty says.

The kid already knows how it's going to play. How it's going to play is this gash is about to get whacked, is how it's going to play.

So he says, "Give me a couple of minutes' head start. I don't want to be seen with no cop."

"Out here?" Letty laughs.

There's nothing out here but hills, dry grass and rocks.

"Out anywhere," Tony says. He heads back down the trail.

Letty's mind is racing. She has the Tranh and Do disappearance hooked in with Pamela's death and the fire. She has Nicky Vale connected somehow with ROC. She has a truckload of stuff leaving the Vale house the night of the fire.

She's deep into these thoughts as she walks back.

She has her head down.

She's dead.

Because the hitter is just standing there waiting for her.

She has her head down, she's thinking things through, and the only reason she looks up is that she catches a glint of something metal even though there is nothing metal out there.

She looks up and sees the gun barrel and a glimpse of a face on a body.

She spins to the ground, dropping hard on the dry red dirt. Lands awkwardly and she can feel her shoulder dislocate when she hits. But she has her weapon out and she can see the guy's arm try to follow her down so she aims to the right of the arm and punches out two rounds WHAM WHAM and then two more WHAM WHAM and the first two take him in the chest and the next two in the head, so *that* guy is over.

But then another figure charges toward her.

Letty yells, "Forget him, he's dead!" and she grips her weapon hard, trying to steady it if she needs to fire her last rounds, but then the horizon starts doing goofy flip-flops and she sees the blue sky and thanks *Madre María* she's alive and then it all goes black.

Last thing she hears is this guy bellowing, "Fuck you, bish!"

But he's running away.

Letty lies in the dirt, her shoulder muscle down around her elbow, and it motherfucking *hurts*.

But she figures that pain is a good thing, given the alternative.

100

Jack's watching TV.

He's sitting down in front of two monitors hooked to VCRs and running two tapes side by side.

The Vale home movies of Pamela showing off the furniture, and the tape he made of the Vales' burned and blackened bedroom.

Very weird, watching them simultaneously.

Almost like watching Pamela's ghost—beautiful, sexy, *alive*—walk around the ashes of her bedroom. Watch her point out the chairs, the card table, the desk . . . the bed. Or where they *were*. Where she *was*.

Because he burned them and he burned her.

No, he didn't, Jack thinks.

He sure as hell burned *her*.

But he wouldn't burn the furniture.

No more than Olivia Hathaway would dump her spoons.

Nobody burns what they love, Jack thinks.

Not while there's a chance that they can still have it.

Except me.

I burn what I love and then scatter the ashes.

What was it I said to Letty? *Pintale*?

Get out.

What was that bird? A mythical bird that rose from the ashes. The phoenix.

Like Letty and me.

Like Pamela on the tape.

Like Nicky's precious furniture.

Show me, Pam.

Show me how Nicky's precious antique furniture rose from these ashes. Show me what I'm missing, Pamela's ghost.

Pam's trying to tell you something.

The fire is trying to tell you something.

The fire's running smack like, *Listen up, dummy. I'm trying to give it to you but you're too stupid to see it. I left it all there for you. You speak fluent fire, right? You're the Dalmatian. You the man.*

So read me.

He runs the tapes three times before he sees it.

The heat shadows.

Pam's showing off the cabinet, "a rare bombé-based red-lacquered and japanned bureau-cabinet from about 1730 . . . A very rare piece."

Jack freeze-frames both tapes.

There it is.

He compares where Pam is pointing to the same place on the wall of the fire scene tape.

The heat shadow is the wrong shape.

He rewinds and looks at it again.

No question about it. The paler shape—the "heat shadow" on the wall—is smaller and lower than what it should be if the bureau-cabinet had shielded the wall from the heat.

It's the wrong shadow.

The wrong ghost.

It's the shape of the writing desk.

Jack rewinds to Pam describing the writing desk.

Freeze-frames both tapes.

Again compares what Pam is pointing out to the heat shadow on the wall.

The wrong shape.

It's the shape of the cabinet.

You screwed up, Nicky.

And thank you, Pam.

And thank you, fire.

And thank you, Olivia Hathaway.

101

First thing he sees is the parrot.

It looks like it's just moving along the top of the hedge and then Jack realizes that it's sitting on the shoulder of Mr. Meissner's white shirt.

"Eliot!" Jack says.

"Eliot. Eliot. Pretty bird."

Meissner stops and looks over the hedge.

"It's the space man," he says. "Where's your space suit today?"

"Jack Wade, California Fire and Life."

"I remember, Mr. Wade."

"Jack."

"Jack," Meissner says. "What can Eliot do for you?"

"Chess pieces," Jack says. "You said something about chess pieces, moving in and moving out. I thought you meant the kids."

"Them, too," Meissner says.

"But you meant something else."

Meissner nods. "The truck. With the chess piece on it. The knight. Stuff coming in and out half the night."

"What stuff?"

"Furniture," Meissner says.

"Did you see who—"

"Two Asian boys, two big white guys, Nicky."

"Pretty bird."

"Yes, you're a pretty bird, Eliot," Meissner says. The wind ruffles the bird's feathers and it's digging into Meissner's shoulder to stay on. "Is this important?"

"Could be."

"Something to do with Pamela's death?" Meissner asks.

"I think so."

Meissner looks off toward the water. When he looks back he says, "She was a lovely girl. A sweet girl. With problems, but a sweet girl."

"Yeah."

"If you need me to testify . . ."

"No," Jack says quickly. "I won't need you to testify. Has anyone else interviewed you about this?"

"No."

"Have you talked to anyone else about it?"

"The parrot," Meissner says. "But I don't think he's listening, do you?"

Jack shrugs.

"Mr. Meissner," he says. "Don't tell anyone what you've told me. Not police, not lawyers, no one. If anyone asks you what you saw that night, all you say is that you heard the dog and you saw the flames. It's very important."

"But I want to help."

"You've helped."

Because now I know just what happened.

Nicky swapped the furniture. Brought in a truck, moved some cheap shit in and took the good stuff out.

But one of his boys screwed up.

Put the desk where the bureau was supposed to be and vice versa.

So Nicky still has his precious furniture.

Half a million bucks on the hoof.

Two million when you count the claim.

Add that to the rest of the claim, you've got the sum total of the money that Nicky paid back to revive his financial standing.

"Thank you, Mr. Meissner."

"For nothing."

"For everything."

Jack walks back toward the car.

Nicky has the furniture.

So what?

The heat shadow "evidence" on the tapes will just get dismissed as corrupted. Or Nicky will claim that he "forgot" that he moved the furniture around before the fire.

Yeah, but you have an eyewitness who will testify that he saw the furniture coming in and out.

But you can't use him because the second you name him they'll kill him.

So what are you going to do?

He drives to Laguna.

Ten minutes later he hands a brass cabinet handle to Marlowe.

Marlowe looks at it for at least a second and a half before he says, "Fake."

"How do you know?"

"One, I'm not Helen Keller," Marlowe says. "Two, I'm not Forrest

Gump. Three, I've been selling the real thing for approaching *hmm-mmnn* years and I can tell you that this is not the brass from a Georgian cabinet door. Next?"

A claw handle foot.

"May I saw?" Marlowe asks.

"Knock yourself out."

Marlowe takes a wood saw and makes two angled incisions into the wood, cutting a wedge out. He shines his lamp into the wedge and says, "This was made perhaps a month ago, maybe two. What else do you have for me?"

A copper hasp.

"Eighteenth century?"

"Perhaps in a former life."

"So?"

"So I don't know what to tell you," Marlowe says. "Look, I know every piece in Nicky Vale's collection. I verified most of them for him. Others, Christ, I bid against him but he had deeper pockets. I don't know where you got these *tchotchkes,* but the furniture in Nicky's house was the real thing. These are the work of a master copier, I'd say."

"Any names come to mind?"

"George Scollins," Marlowe says. "The best. He has a studio way out in the boonies, up in Laguna Canyon. Does great restorations, fantastic copies."

"Is that legal?"

"Can be," Marlowe says. "There's a difference between a copy and a counterfeit. It all depends on how it's labeled. A lot of people want antique furniture style without the age. So they buy a Scollins. Or they want a piece of furniture that doesn't exist anymore, so they get Scollins to copy it from a picture. Or they want a rare piece without the rare price tag, so they buy a Scollins. If they pass it off as real to their friends, it's tacky but legal. If they try to auction it as original, that's fraud."

Or if they burn it and try to sell it to their insurance company as the real thing . . .

"You have Scollins's address?" Jack asks.

102

Way out in the boonies is no shit, Jack thinks as he drives on a windy dirt road up one of the dozens of side canyons that stretch out like fingers from Laguna Canyon.

Tucked away inside a little grove of trees, the Scollins place is more like the Scollins places, a number of little one- and two-story buildings tacked together on the sloped landscape.

Or they *were*, anyway.

Because when Jack gets closer he knows he's not going to get a chance to talk to George Scollins. Because now what you have are a bunch of little burned-out shells gripping the slope.

Hell of a view, though.

Jack gets out of the car, he feels like he's on the top of the world. He can see all across the dry, brown hills, and the ocean is like a rectangle of pure blue.

From this angle the water looks almost vertical.

Nice place to live.

He goes into the Scollins house.

To go dick around in there.

Place still smells of turpentine and shellac and a host of other carbon-based chemicals that must have made a hell of a fuel load.

The fire would have gone up fast and hot.

Ravenous alligator.

Small cinder block house full of wood.

When the fire broke out, it became an oven.

And a mess. It looks like Scollins lived his work. The metal bed frame sits by the wall, and there are remnants of furniture pieces scattered all over the floor. Heat shadows on the walls.

Jack finds the probable point of origin.

An electrical baseboard heater.

An easy call by the scorching and char around it.

Not to mention the remnants of what look to be cleaning rags.

Accelerant splatter at the base of the heater.

Why would the heat be on in the middle of summer?

Classic Teddy Kuhl.

Jack gets on his phone, calls the Sheriff's Department.

"Fire Investigation, please."

"One moment."

I need a little luck here, he thinks.

He gets it. Guy gets on and it's not Bentley.

"Hi," Jack says. "John Morici, Pacific Mutual Insurance. Hey, you guys had a fire recently in Laguna Canyon, the Scollins residence?"

"Hold on a sec."

Guy gets back on and says, "I'm showing that to be Farmer's Insurance."

"We have the Life," Jack says. He plays a hunch. "I'm behind on my files and my boss is all over my ass. Can you just give me a C&O so I can release a payment?"

"Hold on."

Jack holds on.

"Yeah," the guy says. "It was ruled Accidental. Let me see, pile of rags by the heater."

"So, Accidental Death?"

"You got it."

"Hey, who was the investigator?"

"Uhhh, that would be Deputy Bentley."

Yeah, that would be.

He's just clicked off when the phone chirps again.

"Yeah?" Jack asks.

It's Goddamn Billy.

"Jack—"

"Yeah, I know. I'm fired."

"It's not that," Billy says. "It's Letty del Rio."

There's been a shooting.

103

She's sitting up on the examining table.

She looks exhausted and weak, but she's alive and Jack is so damn grateful for that he could kiss God on the lips.

"What happened?" he asks her.

"I got stupid," she says. "I went to meet a snitch alone and I wasn't paying attention and they set me up."

"Letty . . ."

"I'm all right," she says.

"Your arm?"

"It's fucked up but they fixed it," she says. "I'll be out of here this afternoon."

"Stay here," Jack says. "Take it easy."

She looks at him and there are tears in her eyes.

"One of them's dead," she says.

"You okay with that?"

"I'm not crazy about it," Letty says, "but I'm not eating myself up, either."

"They have an ID?"

"No."

But Jack sees there's this weird little look on her face.

"What?" Jack asks.

She tells him what the Vietnamese kid told her about Tranh and Do and the Vale house.

"They're dead," Jack says.

"How do you know?"

"I don't, but I do," Jack says. "Nicky took the real furniture out. Substituted it with cheap fakes. The guy who made the furniture is dead. The kids who dropped it off and picked up the real furniture are dead, too."

"And Pam."

"And Pam."

"Jack, I can reopen now . . ."

Voice starting to fade, she's a few moments from the Enchanted Forest.

"Okay," Jack says.

"You stay out of this now."

"Okay."

"Promise?" she asks. "Because these are dangerous people . . ."

"Promise."

"S'good." She closes her eyes. Murmurs, "Funny thing, Jack. I'm about out, and I hear the other guy? The driver? In the Caddy? He called me a 'bish.' Is that weird or what? I guess I am, though, huh? A real ball-busting *bish*."

She's out.

Jack squeezes her hand and leaves.

So angry that it feels like every square inch of his skin is on fire.

Flashover.

104

Jack pulls up across the street from a trashed-out bungalow on a cul-de-sac up in Modjeska Canyon. The house was white once; now it's a sort of whitish with brown patches where the paint has worn off.

Place needs a paint job bad, Jack thinks. But he figures it isn't likely to get one, because there's garbage strewn all across the rickety front porch, including four biker types drinking beer with their feet up on the porch railing.

Some freakin' heavy metal noise some assholes might call rock 'n' roll blasts from the stereo inside.

Jack walks up the steps and asks, "Teddy Kuhl here?"

"It's his house," one of the bikers says.

"I know *that*," Jack says. "What I asked is, Is he here?"

"He's inside."

"Tell him someone wants to see him."

"No."

"How come?"

"He's busy."

This gets a big laugh from the other three.

Jack doesn't mind playing straight man. "Doing what?"

"Fucking."

A group guffaw. Very male bonding.

Jack says, "Tell him to take a break. Tell him someone wants to talk to him."

"Fuck you."

"Yeah, okay. Fuck me."

Jack backs off the porch and walks over to the driveway, where a big black Harley hog is parked. Jack checks back out on the street and counts three other Harleys there. So this one would be Teddy's.

Teddy Cool's Bad Hog.

Jack kicks it over.

Then kicks in the headlight and stomps on the hand brake until it snaps off.

Which raises what might be called a commotion among the boys on the porch. It isn't five seconds before Teddy bursts through the door.

The twelve years haven't been kind to him. His hairline's retreated like a French army, he's got a couple less teeth and he has a paunch around the middle that's bouncing around as he tries to zip the fly on his jeans and pull his boots on at the same time.

He's getting his left boot on when he hollers, "Who's the crazy motherfucker fucking with my bike?!"

Jack smiles and says, "That would be me."

Teddy grins and announces, "Hey, it's Deputy Dawg!"

"*Former* Deputy Dawg," Jack says.

"Well, you're in a world of shit, former Deputy Dawg," Teddy says. He gets his boot on, gestures for his boys to stay where they are and saunters down to the driveway. "I owe you, you cocksucking motherfucker."

Jack shakes like a wet dog. "Ooooooh, I'm scared. Can you be the same Teddy Kuhl that rolled over for me once like a little bitch?"

This sets Teddy off.

One of Jack's favorite truisms is that you can always count on stupid to be stupid and this is what he's counting on. Teddy doesn't let him down, either, because the stupid thing Teddy does is he reaches into the back waistband of his jeans for his piece.

While Teddy's left hand is behind his back, Jack comes over the top of it with a looping left hand that smashes down into the side of Teddy's nose. You can hear the cartilage crunch over the blasting music.

So Teddy's hand is swinging the gun up, but he can't see because his eyes are watering as Jack steps to the side and swings Teddy's gun hand up and in so the gun butt smashes into Teddy's nose.

Which lights Teddy up like a pinball machine.

He can't even feel Jack take the gun out of his hand, he's in so much pain, but he does feel it when Jack brings the butt down on his nose and the bone breaks in two places.

So Teddy's on his knees in the driveway, and his homeboys start down to help him but stop cold when Jack points the pistol at them and says, "Yes?"

They all like Teddy okay, but not enough to take a bullet for him, and this crazy motherfucker is just crazy enough to shoot them all. So, like, Teddy's on his own.

And not doing very well at it, because there's blood all over the driveway, and a couple of teeth, and a whole lot more blood and snot coming out of Teddy's nose.

You can always count on stupid, Jack thinks, because nobody but a truly dumb moke like Teddy gets that close to someone he's intending to shoot. You're going to shoot a guy, you shoot him from *out of reach*. That's the whole point of having a gun in the first place. But oh well . . .

He drags Teddy along the driveway, kicking him in the ribs as they go, punctuating each kick with, "Let me give you some life *advice, Teddy*. You do *not*"—kick—"try to *hurt*"—kick—"*people*"—kick—"that I *love*"—kick. "Do"—kick—"you"—kick—"*get*"—kick—"that?"—kick.

He drags Teddy until he has his head just inside the garage. Then he reaches up and punches the door button and the door comes down on Teddy's neck so Jack is pretty much just talking to Teddy's head.

Which is having some difficulty getting air.

Jack's thinking that the last time he lit up Teddy Kuhl he regretted it for twelve years.

Oh well, Jack thinks, this'll give me something to regret for the *next* twelve.

105

"Kind of like old times, huh, Teddy?" Jack says.

"Fuck you."

Jack says, "You went on a job this morning."

"No I didn't."

Jack leans on the garage door. Hard. Teddy's head looks like it might just pop off.

"All right, I did!" Teddy yells. "But that is *not* an official confession. I was coerced."

Jack lets up on the door.

"Who sent you?"

Teddy clamps his mouth shut.

Jack leans into it. Repeats, "Who sent you?"

"Couple of Russian dudes."

"You're *Kazzy's* butt boy. He's Armenian," Jack says. "What does he have to do with the Russians?"

"They own him. They took him over."

"Nicky Vale," Jack says.

"What about him?"

"You know him."

"Never heard of no Nicky Vale."

Jack leans on the door again. *"Nicky Vale?"*

"I've heard the name," Teddy says. "I heard that kicked around. Some sort of boss. Boss of bosses. *Capo de tutti capi* godfather shit. Kazzy said he went away and now he's back."

"Did you set the fire at his house?"

"No."

But Teddy giggles. Much as you can giggle with a two-hundred-pound garage door on your neck.

"What's funny, Teddy Cool?"

Teddy actually laughs. "We been *workin'* you, dumbass mother-fucker. Cal Fire is our *bish.*"

"You've been waltzing through my files," Jack says. "Who you got inside Cal Fire?"

"Dunno."

"Is it Sandra Hansen? SIU?"

"SIU. M-I-C. K-E-Y. M-O-U-S-E, I dunno."

"Tom Casey?"

"Dunno."

Jack leans down on the garage door.

"I don't know!" Teddy croaks. "Splatter my brains all over the garage, Deputy Dawg. Sanitation comes and sprays 'em away tonight with a hose, I don't fucking know. *Some*body, because we been working you, humpin' you. The Armenians, the Russians, they all been humpin' away at you, Jack."

"You set the Scollins fire?" Jack asks.

"That one I might've done," Teddy says. "But you can't use any of this. You'll be in jail before I will."

"Same old Teddy Cool," Jack says. "Toss in a bunch of soaked rags and a match. You never grow, Teddy. You never develop. I mean, here we both are in the same old place. You being a stupid, sloppy asshole and me whaling on your ass."

Jack lets up on the door.

"Who gave the order to kill that old man, Teddy?"

"What old man?"

"Porfirio Guzman, twelve years ago."

"The old beaner?" Teddy asks. Then looks up and smiles. "Kazzy said his boss told him to. So Kazzy told me to. And you can't do a thing about it, Deputy Dawg."

Problem is, Teddy Cool is right.

You can't do shit because you don't have shit.

You have a witness to Nicky moving furniture in and out the night of the fire. The same witness puts Nicky on the scene, contrary to his recorded statement.

But if you use the witness they kill the witness.

Déjà vu.

You have the fake remnants.

Yeah, you have char samples, too. Look what happened with them.

You have the guy who made the fakes and he's dead.

All burned up.

Okay. You have two missing Vietnamese kids driving the stolen truck that picked up the furniture. And you have an attempted hit on the deputy who was investigating the missing kids.

And nothing to hook any of it to Nicky Vale.

Jack looks around the garage, sees a gas can.

Pours the contents around the floor as Teddy screams.

Jack pours the rest of the gas over Teddy's head. Some of it scatters and seeps down through the garage door.

Jack squats down next to him.

"What did Nicky do with the furniture?"

"What furniture?"

"Shit, where did I put my matches?"

"I DON'T KNOW NOTHING ABOUT NO FUCKING FURNI-TURE!"

Teddy isn't lying. Teddy is too scared to be lying.

"Give me *something*, Teddy," Jack says. "Something I can use."

Teddy's thinking it over. Jack can see that Teddy's weighing relative fears. His fear of Nicky Vale against his fear of burning alive. Jack knows he's going to win because the flame is immediate and the other is still abstract and Teddy doesn't have a good grasp of the abstract.

"Westview," Teddy says.

"What?"

"What I got to give you," Teddy says. "I just hear Kazzy talking about something called Westview. Something he's got going on with Nicky Vale."

Jack pushes the button and the garage door opens.

Teddy's boys are standing there with guns pointed. Three shotguns, two pistols and a Glock.

"Good idea," Jack says. "Let's have a blazing gun battle. Barbecue Teddy Cool."

"Put 'em down! Put 'em down! Put 'em down!" Teddy screams.

Jack walks through them to his car. Gets inside, opens the window and says, "He sang like a little girl. What can I say, guys? He's still my bish."

Starts the car and drives away.

Wondering, what the hell is Westview?

106

Nicky looks across the desk at Paul Gordon, who's sniffing the top of his cappuccino to make sure that it's nutmeg and not cinnamon.

That important task done, Gordon looks up at Nicky like, *I'm ready for you now.*

For his part, Nicky will be glad to leave the man's ego behind.

"Ready?" Nicky asks.

"I'm all yours."

"Tomorrow morning," Nicky says, "Tom Casey will call to offer $50 million to settle my claim."

Gordon freaks. In his wildest imagination he never dreamed that Cal Fire would go for the $50 million. He was counting on them turning it down. What the fuck good is Cal Fire if it suddenly gets smart?

"Don't worry," he says. "I'll turn it down. I'll find a pretext."

Nicky shakes his head.

"You'll accept that offer."

Gordon turns white.

"That's not the plan."

"It is now."

"The hell it is," Gordon says. "I've spent years setting up these suits. I've got the cops, I've got the judges. You can't bail on me now."

Nicky shrugs.

Gordon's voice gets shrill. "Nicky, what the fuck are you thinking about?! We can ride Jack Wade for hundreds of millions of dollars! Don't settle for the short money now!"

"Jack Wade has played his role," Nicky says.

Wade's on his way out.

Then Gordon gets it.

"You son of a bitch," he says. "You cut your own deal."

"Accept the offer," Nicky says. "You'll get your fee."

"Fuck you," Gordon says. "We're taking it to trial. We're taking all of them to trial."

"In that case," Nicky says, "you're fired."

Gordon laughs. "You can't fire me, you jumped-up little hood. You need me. Without me, they'll eat you alive. You think you can stand down Cal Fire and Tom Casey without me?!"

Actually, yes, Nicky thinks. I think I can.

In fact, I know it.

He stands up. Says, "You're fired."

Gordon flips out.

Follows Nicky down the hallway yelling, "You think you're the only heavy hitter in town?! You need *me*, I don't need *you*! I'll have Viktor Tratchev in this office in five minutes! Maybe he has the brains, he has the vision! Or Kazzy Azmekian! He has the balls to see this through! He's not going to let you crash this, you jumped-up little greasy Euro-trash hood! You can't fire me!"

A very tawdry scene, Nicky thinks as he gets in the car. And Gordon should not have played the Tratchev card. Or the Azmekian one. Very self-indulgent. Very uncool.

Two cards he should have held close to the chest.

And "jumped-up little greasy Eurotrash hood"? One might be tempted to take that personally.

Oh, well.

He leans back into the seat.

Almost there, he thinks.

A couple of steps to safety.

And the turnaround inside one generation.

Fifty million dollars tomorrow.

Fifty million dollars of squeaky-clean money.

But there's work to be done first.

"Ritz-Carlton," he tells Dani.

Take the first step.

Dani waits out in the car while the *pakhan* has his meeting.

107

Uncle Nguyen's head is throbbing.

He's just had to tell Tommy Do's distraught mother that her idiot son is probably not coming home for dinner.

Ever.

So there's a lot of wailing and sobbing and other irritating noise—this woman has a piercing shriek that goes through Uncle Nguyen's head. She completely drowns out the Angels game and won't settle down until Uncle Nguyen promises her vengeance.

He finally gets rid of her with that promise and goes down into the basement where he has Tony Ky hanging by his wrists, and just to improve his mood he gives Tony a couple of two-handers across the back with a bamboo rod, which elicits a satisfying grunt of pain, and then he says to Tony, "Tell me who these Russians were."

And Tony tells him—tall skinny Russian, tall fat Russian.

He doesn't know their names so Uncle Nguyen takes a Jim Edmonds swing at his back—like good for a three-bagger in any park in America—and asks him who they were working for.

"Tratchev," Tony says.

Uncle Nguyen has a tough time with this.

He's been doing business with Viktor Tratchev for years and it's always been a good and mutually profitable relationship. So he gets Tratchev on the phone and asks, "What is *this* shit all about?"

"What shit?"

"Two of your people hired two of my boys for an errand and the boys haven't come back."

"Which of my people?"

Uncle Nguyen describes them.

Tratchev is very happy to hear this description. The last thing in the world he needs right now is a beef with the Vietnamese. First thing he needs right now is an ally against Nicky Vale, so he says, "You're talking about Dani and Lev."

"You had better send Dani and Lev over for a chat."

"They're not mine."

"Whose are they?"

Tratchev tells him.

Uncle Nguyen asks, "Do you have a problem if I do what I need to do?"

Go figure, Tratchev doesn't have a problem.

108

Jack walks back into the office, they're all looking at him like they're seeing a ghost.

Jack hears the whispers as he walks down the narrow aisle through the cubicles. *Fired . . . perjury . . . kickbacks . . . crooked cop . . .*

"I'm baa-aack!" Jack sings out.

Some of the dogs turn around in their cubicles, bury their faces in their monitors. Except one who picks up her phone, cups her hand around the receiver and starts whispering.

So Hansen has released a Be on the Lookout For and this babe can't wait to drop the dime. But it'll take them some time to work out how to handle it. There'll be calls up and down, calls to Billy, calls to Mahogany Row . . .

So you have time but not a lot of time.

He sits down and starts banging the computer.

Gets into the California Secretary of State's database and types in "Westview."

Which is not the happiest name to be researching if you happen to be located on the West Coast.

The screen brings up a couple of hundred of them.

Westview Travel, Westview Realty, Westview Retirement, Westview Recreational Vehicles, Westview Condominium Association . . .

Westview Ltd.

Jack goes with Westview Ltd.

A limited partnership will only show the general partners, not the shareholders. They're anonymous until you can get your hands on the actual limited partnership agreement, which would have to be subpoenaed.

So it's a good vehicle to play the ownership shell game.

Jack double-clicks on Westview Ltd. and requests an LP1 statement, which lists the general partners.

A James Johnson, a Benjamin Khafti and an Orange Coast Ltd.

Another limited partnership.

Jack requests an LP1 statement for Orange Coast Ltd.

A Howard Krasner, a Grant Lederer, another limited partnership. CrossCo Ltd.

Jack requests an LP1 for CrossCo.

And on and on and on.

Every hit gets him a couple of hypothetical people and another limited partnership.

The ownership shell game.

Find the moving owners under the shell.

Jack keeps playing.

He's twelve layers deep when he hits on Jerisoco Ltd.

Bingo.

General partners: a Michael Allen, Kazimir Azmekian and something called Gold Coast Ltd.

Gold Coast Ltd.

Back to the shell game. He pops it for an LP1 and gets another meaningless name and two more limited partnerships. Those two get him three more.

And so on and so on and so on and then he hits it.

Great Sunsets Ltd.

Jack's head whirls.

Great Sunsets Ltd.—the company that's trying to develop Dana Strands.

And it's hooked into Kazzy Azmekian and Nicky Vale.

Holy God.

Jack sees two security guys and Cooper, the ex-cop from SIU, coming down the aisle.

Jack requests an LP1 for Great Sunsets Ltd.

The computer hums.

Come on, come on, Jack thinks.

They're fifty feet away.

Come *on,* Jack thinks.

Because he can feel the paranoia crawl up his back like a hot wave.

Jack looks around and feels like the walls are closing in on him.

They are.

109

He's just managed to turn the computer off when Cooper lays a hand on his shoulder.

"You've been suspended, Jack," Cooper says, "pending an investigation."

"Fuck you, I quit."

"Better," Cooper says.

Goddamn Billy comes up.

"What the goddamn hell is going on here?"

"Mr. Wade has been suspended."

"Who says Mr. Wade has been suspended?"

"SIU has uncovered some information involving kickbacks   "

"Bull-fucking-shit!"

"You'll have to take that up with Ms. Hansen," Cooper says.

"You bet your goddamn ass I'll take it up with *Mizzz* Goddamn Hansen!" Billy yells. "This ain't over, Jack."

"It's over, Billy."

You don't know how over.

They're walking him out, Jack can see Sandra Hansen watching him from the corner. He waves at her.

Hansen's not happy.

She's thinking what a brainless, dumb stud Jack Wade is. She's thinking that Jack's surfboard has landed on his head once—make that twice—too often.

But he's a good honest claims dog and it's too bad he's so damn stubborn. Out this morning still chasing the Vale file.

But she has three years and God only knows how much of her budget sunk into ROC and she's not going to let one stubborn M-4 of an adjuster flush it down the toilet.

Not now.

Not when the deal goes down tonight.

So Jack Wade has to go.

Phil Herlihy's watching the whole thing up on Mahogany Row on the security camera.

Phil's gripping.

Seriously.

He's been monitoring Wade's computer screen, saw what he was working on.

Jack Wade has to go.

110

Jack feels like his head's going to blow off his shoulders.

Nicky owns the Strands.

With SIU taking his back.

Very sweet.

Face it, you don't stand a chance.

They beat you. Any move you make they'll find a way to jam it.

They have the execs and the cops and the lawyers and the judges.

And face it, you don't know who else Nicky owns.

So fuck it.

Sorry, Pam.

Sorry, Letty.

Nicky Vale will get richer.

On his wife's body.

And his kids' heartbreak.

And fuck that.

He looks for a place to turn around.

Can't, because there's a big black Caddy coming up on his ass.

111

It's a big humping old black Caddy and it's right on his ass.

The 'Stang is a nice car but it doesn't have the weight to stand off the souped-up Caddy this doofus is pushing at him.

The Caddy's on his tail through a tricky S-curve, which breaks open into a short straightaway that bends into a huge outside turn, and Jack taps the brakes because you do not want to go into this curve too fast unless you want to be Orville Wright.

So he slows down but this asshole stays right on him.

Then he moves to pass.

Jack can't freaking believe it, but this asshole pulls right alongside him as the curve turns in.

Comes around and *stays* beside him.

The Caddy's in the wrong lane on a curve and doesn't pull back in.

"What the fuck are you doing?!" Jack yells, because there's a cliff wall on the inside and a two-hundred-foot drop on the outside and this is bad news.

Which is true, because now another car has come up behind him. A muscle car, a Charger, and now it's right up on his ass.

Which is bad, because now Jack has nowhere to go.

He can't even hit the brakes.

Then he sees the truck coming.

In *his* lane, straight at him.

He either crashes head-on into the trailer truck or he goes off the road.

Which is the plan.

Jimmy Dansky, he's sitting in the cab of the truck and sees the cars headed straight for him. The new guy is good, the new guy is doing just what he's supposed to. Trap the Mustang in place.

A game of chicken.

Which Jimmy figures he's going to win, because he knows it's psychologically impossible for a car to hang in. The driver sees a truck coming he'll hit the brakes and swerve—human nature. And when he swerves he loses it on that curve and he's over the edge.

Bye-bye.

He goes, and then the chase car can take the oncoming lane, and everyone gets home safe.

Except the Mustang.

It's in a crater at the bottom of the canyon.

A very tricky stunt, a real ball tightener, but it's going like a bomb.

So he bears down on the Mustang and waits for it to chicken out.

Jack doesn't swerve or hit the brakes. What he does is he steps on the gas. He pushes the 'Stang toward the trailer truck like she's going to take it out.

Kamikaze Mustang.

Ban-fucking-zai.

Jimmy Dansky can't believe it.

They told him this guy was hardcore, they didn't say he was crazy.

Or suicidal.

Turn, cocksucker, turn is what Jimmy Dansky is thinking.

What Jack is thinking is like, *Fuck you, asshole.*

You turn.

And all this is going on in like seconds and there's about to be a spectacular four-car crash on the Ortega and Jack lets one hand off the wheel and grabs Teddy's pistol with the other, shoots out the driver's window, then wings a shot at the Caddy, and that's when the Caddy driver chickens out. He swerves the Caddy inside toward the rock face.

Jack moves left into the now vacant space in the oncoming lane. The Charger tries to get out of the way, but it's too late.

Dansky's truck sheers the top off the Charger, taking the driver's upper body with it as it smashes through the guardrail and launches into the sky above the canyon.

Like, *Uhh, Houston, we've got a problem.*

Jimmy's up there with half a Charger and half a Charger driver jammed in his grill; the front of the truck is pointing toward the sun. For a second he fantasizes that the truck has enough momentum to sail across the canyon and land on the other side, but then the laws of physics rule against Jimmy and the front of the truck takes a downward tilt.

And Jimmy without his parachute.

A few seconds later the truck smashes headfirst into the lower slope like some suicidal ski jumper, then it does two somersaults and comes to a rest.

But by that time Jimmy Dansky's neck has snapped in numerous locations.

Jack's not doing so great either.

He scrapes the wall, bounces off, plunges toward the edge of the cliff, jerks the wheel, heads for the wall again, pulls out and goes into a spin.

He's doing three-sixties—wall, cliff, wall, cliff, wall, cliff—he's spinning toward the edge of the cliff and then skids to a stop.

With the front of the 'Stang hanging over the edge.

Jack's looking down at eternity.

He gets out—gently—his legs are weak and the world is spinning and the Caddy and Charger are long gone.

He checks out the 'Stang.

Major damage.

Front-left quarter panel banged in. Passenger-side door banged. Gashes and scrapes along the whole passenger side.

You're talking Bondo from here to eternity.

It's never going to be over, he thinks. You know too much, Letty knows too much, they won't let you just give up.

And face it, *you* won't let you just give up.

It won't be over until you've finished your job.

Your job is to not pay claims you don't owe. You don't pay people to burn their own houses down, and you don't pay them to kill their wives, and you don't let them rip off your company. You do the job you started to do.

And do it *right* this time.

So quit your whining and find Nicky's fucking furniture.

And how the hell are you going to do that?

It could be anywhere in the freaking world.

Nicky has apartment buildings, Nicky has condos, Nicky has—

Yeah.

Jack pats the back of the 'Stang.

"Goodbye, old paint."

He puts his shoulder to it and pushes it off the edge.

Watches it somersault down the canyon and explode in a ball of flame at the bottom.

He starts walking west with his thumb out.

Into a *great* sunset.

112

Young waits for the sun to go down.

Has his troops assembled in the parking lot of the Ritz and they all have their assignments. He's edgy as a mother duck because if he pulls this off tonight it's the biggest organized crime roundup since the Appalachia raid. He has names, records, aliases, safe houses. He knows where the weapons are, what they are, who they belong to. He makes *half* these busts, he can start a ball rolling across the whole country. Start winding ROC up in Arizona, Texas, Kentucky, West Virginia, New York.

He's just waiting for dark.

Jimenez is likewise stoked. Got him his share of the list, his share of the collars, because for once the Feds are playing team ball. So he has his guys posted all over So-Cal. Got a freakin' battalion ready to hit in L.A., another squad down here in Orange County, some more troops in San Diego. Just waiting for the sun to go down.

Sandra Hansen, she's sitting in the room at the Ritz, guzzling Diet Cokes like they could settle her nerves. She won't get the satisfaction of going on the busts. She can't ever even admit that Cal Fire funded half this investigation. All she can do is sit by the phone and hope that it goes down right, that something doesn't come along to fuck it up.

Because it's a tricky deal.

The bust's tonight.

Fifty million dollars' payment in the morning.

Then her guy starts filling them in, in exchange for complete and total immunity for anything except a capital offense. The whole deal signed off on by Claims, Mahogany Row and an alphabet soup of law enforcement agencies.

So tonight's a big night.

She looks out the window at the beautiful stretch of beach and one of those incredible red California sunsets and all she wishes is that it would be morning.

Nicky's gazing at the sunset, too.

Lev and Dani behind him on the lawn like lengthening shadows.

"It is as if we're in the cell again," Nicky says. "The three of us in a corner against the world. We are fighting for our lives. New lives. Years ago in that hell I promised you new lives. I promised you Paradise. Tomorrow—if we do what we have to do tonight—we will have those new lives.

"We are just a few steps from safety. Tonight will tell the story."

Just a few steps from safety, but all the plans are made.

It will be a bloody night.

It already has been. Jimmy Dansky and Jack Wade dead in a fiery pas de deux.

And the sister.

There can be no mistakes this time, which is why he's ordered Lev to do it. Lev will make no mistakes.

All other problems will disappear.

And I am a shifting cloud in a twilight sky.

113

Letty's in no mood for sunsets. She feels like hammered shit.

Which is about right, she thinks, considering.

A deputy drives her home. Another drives her car for her.

"Want me to stay?" he asks.

"I'm fine."

"The boss said—"

"I know what the boss said." Letty laughs. "I'm fine."

She has an ice pack and a bottle of Vicodin and some hopes that Jack will show up tonight to pamper her a little.

Fetch me a drink, fluff my pillow, make sure I get a good night's sleep.

Because first thing in the morning, I'm taking my broken wing to Mother Russia's house and questioning Nicky about what two missing kids were doing at his crib the night before they disappeared.

Boss told me to lay off Pam's case and work the missing kids.

Follow it where it leads.

Well, guess what?

It leads to Nicky.

And where the hell is Jack?

You'd think he'd be falling all over himself to do the concerned male number.

She calls him at the office.

Gone.

Calls him at home, gets his tape, leaves a message.

She knows where he is.

He's out working the arson case.

Lifer claims dog on the scent.

Job or no job, Jack will never give up.

It's just one of the things she loves about him.

She loves him and she's worried about him and she says a little prayer that he's okay.

Then she takes two Vikes, gets into bed and turns out the light.

114

Natalie turns on the bedside lamp.

"Go to *sleep,*" she says to Michael.

"I can't."

He's crying again.

"Why not?" Natalie asks.

"Ghosts."

"They're not ghosts, they're shadows."

But they are scary, Natalie admits. The branches of the big eucalyptus tree outside the window are blowing in the wind, making ghostlike arms and heads on the bedroom wall.

"I'm scared," Michael says.

"Of what?"

"Fire," Michael says. "Like burned up Mommy."

"This house won't catch on fire."

"How do you know?"

I don't know, Natalie thinks. She's scared, too.

She has bad dreams.

Where there's fire *everywhere.*

And Mommy's asleep and won't wake up.

"There won't be a fire," she says, "because I am the princess and that's my command."

"Who can I be?" Michael asks.

"The princess's little brother."

Michael whines, "Can't I be something else, too?"

"Like a wizard?"

"What's that?"

"Like a magician," Natalie says. "Only better."

"Can I make things disappear?"

"Yes."

"Like ghosts?"

"Yes," Natalie says. "Now go to *sleep.*"

"Leave the light on."

She leaves the light on.

And lies awake and watches the shadows move.

115

Jack sits in the darkness.

All but invisible against the bluff, he's waiting for there to be just enough light for him to see without being seen.

So he sits down and just watches the ocean.

Like he used to do as a kid.

Just sits at Dana Strand and does nothing.

The waves are silver under the full moon.

They fall on the beach with a sound like *shhhhhhh*.

A Pacific lullaby.

Jack waits for the sun to come up.

116

Letty wakes up with a start.

A sound outside.

Footsteps on the deck.

She picks up her weapon from the side table by the bed and holds it in her good hand as she eases along the wall to the door.

Settle down, girl, she tells herself. Her heart's racing and her hand's trembling.

She gets to the door and looks out through the glass panes.

Can't see a thing.

She lifts the slinged hand up and turns the doorknob. Then kicks the door open and bursts out onto the deck in the shooting position. Swings right—nothing. Swings left—

The raccoon scrambles down the steps.

"Shit," Letty says.

Puffs a long sigh and gets her breath back.

Then she laughs at herself and makes a note to get bungee cords for the garbage cans.

Shuts the door and starts to go back to bed.

But her arm's hurting so she goes into the bathroom, turns on the light and takes a couple more Vikes.

Turns off the light and goes back to bed.

Lev's pressed against the corner of the house.

He watches the light come on and then go off again.

117

Nicky watches Paul Gordon walk out of the Starbucks with a cappuccino in his hand. Arrogantly oblivious to the possibility that the world might injure him.

The driver trails him across the almost empty parking lot toward the bank where Gordon walks up to the automatic teller, rests his cappuccino on the ledge, puts in his card and taps his foot while the machine hums.

Nicky watches from the backseat as Dani lowers the front passenger window and rests the machine pistol on the edge.

Gordon gets his cash, grips his two hundred bucks in one hand and his coffee in the other and turns into the spray of bullets that smash into his chest. The cappuccino splashes all over his bloodstained shirt as he falls to the hot asphalt.

"You're fired," Nicky says.

118

Teddy Kuhl's doing the smart thing.

He's running.

Since motherfucking Deputy Dawg's parting shot that Teddy sang like a bird, Teddy knows it's only a matter of time before one of his tightest buddies rats him out to the Russians.

Teddy knows that he is just cash on the hoof.

So, hurting as he is, he nuts it up, packs a few things, gets on his bike and heads east until this shit cools off. He's thinking maybe Arizona.

He is doing a very smart thing.

Then he does a very stupid thing.

He stops for a beer.

Stupider than that, he stops for a beer at a bikers bar called Cook's Corner, out by Modjeska Canyon. Teddy's thinking he needs a beer, maybe, and this is the last good beer spot for many dry and lonely miles.

The beer tastes so good to him he goes for another.

Gets laughing with some buddies and ends up having five.

Doesn't even notice one of his boys on the phone.

Beer number seven, he decides it's time to hit the road and get out of Dodge, but he needs to take a piss first. Beer bladder pressing down on him like a fifty-pound weight.

So he slides off the stool, pushes the metal door into the men's room and steps up to the stainless-steel trough.

All by his lonesome in there.

George Thorogood song blaring from inside the bar   Teddy's kind of rocking to it as he unzips his fly and lets loose.

"Aaaaaahhhhh."

Hitter steps out from a stall, puts the pistol to the back of Teddy's head and pulls the trigger.

Teddy dies with what's left of his face in the urinal.

Right next to that little white sponge thing.

119

Judge John Bickford gets an anonymous phone call at home, informing him that his years of devoted service to the plaintiff's bar have been duly noted. That an informant has in fact duly noted it to the California Attorney General's office, and that a story will appear in tomorrow's Orange County *Register* linking him to a murdered Paul Gordon and Paul Gordon to the Russian Mafia.

Bickford says goodbye to his wife and drives to a motel in Oceanside where he tranquilizes himself with twelve-year-old scotch and Valium and, in the small hours of the morning, slashes his wrists.

The newspaper story never appears.

Retired Justice Dennis Mallon gets a similar phone call and catches a flight to Mexico with a connection to Grand Cayman. He has a home there.

Dr. Benton Howard steps off a curb into an oncoming car. His injuries are so real that he dies of them.

Word hits the street by morning that Howard was an informant working with the Anti-ROC Task Force.

120

Which is working like a mother.

In what will become known in law enforcement circles as the St. Petersburg Day Massacre, Young's troops roll up Tratchev's brigade like it's the freaking Republican Guard.

Tratchev's guys are caught flat-footed. They're grabbed in bars, they're grabbed in their homes, they're grabbed in bed with their girlfriends.

Viktor Tratchev is having a quiet evening at home watching *Cops* on the Fox network when the door comes crashing in and Special Agent Young comes through with a shotgun in his hands like he's Robert Stack. Tratchev is annoyed because he thought he had guards out there, but the guards now have their hands behind their backs and plastic ties around their wrists, so technically speaking they're not really guards anymore.

"Bad boys, bad boys, what you gonna do?"

Tratchev reaches for his glasses.

Which is a mistake, because one of Young's troops puts two rounds into his chest before Young can scream, *"What the fuck are you doing?!"* but the fact is that the agent knows exactly what the fuck he's doing.

He's getting in position for a big payday from Nicky Vale is what he's doing.

"What you gonna do when they come for you?"

Jimenez's boys are romping in L.A.

Up and down Fairfax, they're crashing in doors, they're jamming cars into curbs, they're blocking off alleys and side streets. They're scooping up car thieves, drive-down artists, extortionists, drug dealers—the whole first and second All-Star Team of Rubinsky's and Schaller's best moneymakers.

They get Rubinsky and Schaller, too.

Rubinsky's in bed with his wife when Jimenez gives him a wake-up call with a pistol barrel to the back of his neck. Schaller's playing poker with some buddies when the game comes to a sudden halt.

The sweep misses Kazzy Azmekian.

He's not at home.

He's twenty nautical miles off Rosarita on his forty-foot Sportscraft for an overnight fishing trip.

Turns out he can't swim, because when his trusted bodyguard launches him over the side, Kazzy just sort of goes glug-glug and then disappears into the darkness.

Anyway, between tragic accidents like this and the task force sweep, Nicky Vale's self-reinvention as a legitimate businessman is pretty much complete.

But not quite.

121

The noise on the deck wakes Letty up.

Rattling of garbage cans.

"Damn raccoons," she says as she gets out of bed.

Stumbles for the door and this time doesn't bother to take her weapon. It's not like she's going to shoot the damn thing.

Lev waits by the corner of the deck.

Make it look like a rape, is what the *pakhan* said. Then tear her up with the knife. Just another psycho-sex murder in the Southland. Film at eleven.

He poises the knife in his left hand.

Hears her footsteps.

Hears her open the door.

Sees her step out.

"*¡Vamos!*" Letty yells as Lev starts forward.

Something stops him.

A tight cord around his neck pulls him back and down the steps.

Letty hears the raccoon run off and closes the door.

Locks it and goes back to bed.

Whatever the sound was, it's gone now.

122

Mother Russia finally gets the children to sleep.

Truth be known, she'll be happy when Daziatnik rebuilds his own house and moves back in, because while she loves having little Michael with her, the girl Natalie favors her mother and is a real little bitch.

Quite hopeless, really, genetics being what they are.

Michael—Michael will be a little prince.

With some work.

But Natalie . . .

Mother Russia goes into the bathroom, brushes her teeth, scrubs her face, then takes a brush to her hair.

A hundred strokes, every morning and every night, and that is what will keep it beautiful and full, the way Daziatnik so admires it.

She finishes brushing it and stands back to admire her look in the mirror.

That's when she sees the man behind her.

It must be one of the new guards.

But the nerve, to come into her bedroom—

"What—" she starts to snap.

Then the man's hand is over her mouth.

A cloth over her nose.

Then blackness.

123

Nicky lights up a joint.

Savors the sweet musky scent, takes a deep hit, lets it swirl around in his lungs and then releases it. Feels all the tension go out with the smoke.

All problems dissolving into the night air.

Tratchev dead.

His troops locked up.

Rubinsky and Schaller swept up with their troops.

The late Dr. Benton Howard's reputation as a police informer firmly established.

Paul Gordon fired.

Kazzy Azmekian is flotsam. Or is it jetsam? Nicky can never remember. Doesn't matter.

He takes another toke, slips out of his clothes and lets himself ease into the Jacuzzi's steaming water.

Fifty million dollars coming his way tomorrow. The turnaround in one generation.

A very good night, and some very good boo.

He feels a small twinge of anxiety. Lev hasn't returned yet, to report that the problem of the sister is no more. Nicky does another hit and lets the problem fly from his mind. What Lev sets out to kill, Lev kills. He'll be back soon.

So Nicky's having a *very* good night. He has the whole thing working for him, Tratchev dead, a big payday coming up on the morrow and life is way cool. He shuts his eyes and stretches out, and then feels something round against his toes.

He's like annoyed, because he has *told* Michael not to kick his soccer ball around the pool and the Jacuzzi.

Nicky goes to pick the ball up and screams.

Falls backward against the side of the Jacuzzi and cowers there.

And just stares at Lev's severed head bobbing up and down in the bubbling water.

Nicky's going fetal when Dani gets there.

Dani plucks Lev's head up by the hair and just howls in pain.

There's a ribbon around Lev's neck.

Something written on it, but even if they weren't so freaked they couldn't read it.

It's written in Vietnamese.

Nicky runs into the house.

To Mother's room.

Her door is ajar and he can see the flickering silver light of the television.

He opens the door without knocking.

"Mother—"

A man sits on the bed watching television. He casually swings his silenced pistol in Nicky's direction.

"Hello, Daz," Karpotsov says. "I'm sorry—it's Nicky now, isn't it?"

"Colonel."

"It's General now," Karpotsov says.

Nicky is like *freaking*, but Nicky stays cool.

"Congratulations," he says.

"Thanks," Karpotsov says. "Is this HBO?"

"Cinemax."

"I like it."

"I'm glad," Nicky says.

"Well," Karpotsov says, "congratulations, Nicky. I understand that you have quite the deal in the works. Well done, your country is proud. You were going to cut us in, weren't you, Nicky? Or did you think I was dead?"

"I had hopes in that direction," Nicky says. "Where is my mother?"

"She'll be staying with us for a while."

"How long is a while?"

"Well, let me put it this way," Karpotsov says. "We want our fucking money."

Dude.

We want our piece.

Of California Fire and Life.

124

The sun comes up enough to make out shapes.

That early-morning hour when everything is in shades of gray.

Jack starts up the ravine that cuts into the bluff. He climbs until he comes to the old fence. Ducks under it, just the way he did when he was a kid, and he's in the old trailer park.

Very weird, *very* strange being here knowing it belongs to Nicky Vale. That Nicky's planning on turning it into a tract of condos and town houses. That he killed his wife by way of raising the capital.

Jack picks his way through the eucalyptus and pine trees. He walks past old trailer pads and then a Dumpster.

He opens the lid of the Dumpster, shines the light in and jumps back.

Two charred, cracked skulls.

Exploded from the inside out by intense heat.

Tommy Do and Vince Tranh.

Jack closes the lid.

Moves on toward the old, decrepit rec hall he used to run around in. When he was eight it was a fort. When he was ten it was a rock 'n' roll hall. When he was fifteen it was make-out heaven.

The old hall is in bad shape. Some boards ripped out, shingles stripped, but the two wide old doors are still intact.

And there's a shiny new padlock on them.

A combination lock.

Jack finds a rock and smashes the hasp.

The door swings open like it's been an exhausting effort to stay shut.

First thing Jack sees is the bed.

He pulls up a dustcover and there it is.

The Robert Adam four-poster canopied bed with the castle on top. Incredibly beautiful with its silk and fabrics and intricately carved coat of arms. The video didn't do it justice.

The freaking room is filled with furniture. All draped in cloth dust-covers, they look like monuments, like ghosts. Jack goes around turning back the covers.

The George III writing desk, the Hepplewhite chair, the Matthias Lock rococo console table.

"It's all here," Jack says to himself.

The mahogany armless chairs, the silent valet, the Kent mirror, the side table, the gilt chairs, the card table—Jack's looking at it but what he sees in his mind is Pamela Vale walking him through. Like she's there in the old rec hall pointing to each piece as Nicky holds the camera.

This is one of our real treasures. A rare bombé-based red-lacquered and japanned bureau-cabinet from about 1730. It has clawed and hairy paw feet. Also, serpentine-shaped corners with attenuated acanthus leaves. A very rare piece.

It's all here.

Nicky's precious furniture. Over half a million dollars' worth.

Times two. Once for the insurance settlement, twice when he sells it again.

It's more than that, though. It's his identity, his ego, his freaking shifting cloud.

What he killed his wife to hold on to.

His wife, the two Vietnamese kids, George Scollins, God only knows who else. For a pile of old wood. *For a bunch of fucking things.* Even though he stood to make $50 million and it would have been safer to burn this stuff, Nicky couldn't stand to do it.

And now it's going to cost him fifty mil.

And his claim.

And everything else, if Jack has his way.

125

Dawn at Mother Russia's.

Very happy place.

Nicky pours himself a cup of coffee and sits trembling on a stool at the kitchen counter.

Two million in cash.

And a big piece of Nicky's deal.

Is what Karpotsov wants to release Mother.

"Or we'll start burning her," Karpotsov said. "We'll send you some of the charred pieces. First a finger, then we'll start getting serious. Then it's a hand, then a foot. When we're fresh out of Mother, we'll grab the kids and start on them. You tried to fuck us, Nicky. You owe us money. Serious money that you stole from your country."

"My country doesn't exist anymore."

"Then from *us*," Karpotsov said.

"KGB doesn't exist anymore, either," Nicky said. "All there is left of my country is a dipso-buffoon and the mob."

"Nicky," Karpotsov said, shaking his head. "Don't you get it? We *are* the mob. The mob is us. *Organizatsiya.* One and the same. We've come to an understanding. And the only reason that I don't chop your mother into little pieces and feed them to you before blowing your brains out is that you're a profitable little motherfucker. A thief's thief, and you're going to start stealing for us again, Nicky. Two million dollars in good faith money. Or we start burning her. That's your old technique, isn't it, Nicky? From Afghanistan? Didn't you like to burn people?"

"I'll get the money for you!"

"You'd better." Karpotsov got off the bed. "Well, I'd like to see the end of the movie but I'm sure you have things to arrange. Like, later, dude."

He got up and left.

Nicky had a *very* restful night.

Closing his eyes, he saw Lev's dome bobbing up and down in the water. Opening his eyes, he saw them taking a torch and—

He spent most of the night pacing the house.

Now, this morning, Nicky loses it. "They came into the house *where my children sleep* and took my *mother!*"

Slams his hand on the kitchen counter.

Temper, temper, he tells himself.

Temper will do you no good.

Think it through.

Karpotsov is a reality that must be dealt with and dealt with quickly.

Or Mother is dead and the children are next.

He calls the number Karpotsov gave him.

"I have an offer to make," Nicky says.

"I hope it's a good one."

"It's a very good one."

A piece of the biggest insurance company on the West Coast.

"A good faith payment," Karpotsov says. "Today."

"You'll get it," Nicky says. "I have money coming in this morning."

So it's all right, he tells himself. It's cool. Tratchev is dead. Azmekian is dead. Gordon is dead. Two Crosses is out, KGB is in, that's all. A simple swap. Money coming in. Money to ransom Mother. Everything will be all right—

The phone rings.

Jack starts reading off the inventory. Finishes off the last item, then says, "Yup, it's all here."

Nicky says, "Where are you?! If you have my furniture, where is it?"

"I thought your furniture was burned up in the fire," Jack says. "Of course, if you'd like to *withdraw* that claim . . ."

"You don't know—"

"If you now say that your furniture's been stolen, I suggest you call the police right away."

"—who you're—"

"Or submit a claim on the theft," Jack says. "It shouldn't be too hard. I think we already have the inventory."

"You don't know who you're dealing with."

"Porfirio Guzman," Jack says.

"What?"

"That name ring a faint bell with you?"

"No."

"That's what I thought," Jack says. "You had him killed twelve years ago. I understand that's a long time to remember a little thing like that."

"What are you going to do?"

"Well, I have a million bucks' worth of stuff which is also enough evidence to connect you to the arson and your wife's murder," Jack says. "What do you think I'm going to do?"

Silence for a second. Then Nicky says, "I'm prepared to be reasonable."

"I'm not."

"One hundred thousand dollars," Nicky says. "Cash."

"That's cheap, Nicky. I'm surprised at you."

"One-fifty."

"Nickel and dime."

"Two hundred thousand," Nicky says.

"No."

"Make your offer."

"Drop your lawsuit," Jack says.

"Would that do it for you?"

"No," Jack says. "Drop your claim."

"If I had the furniture back . . ."

"You can get it back . . ."

"Good."

"After you confess that you burned the house and killed your wife."

Long sigh from Nicky.

"We can still make a deal," he says.

"I already told you," Jack says.

I don't do deals.

Nicky says, "I'll be coming for you."

Jack says, "Bring your lunch."

And hangs up.

Nicky slams his hand on the counter.

He feels someone behind him.

Little Michael is standing there.

"Is Grandma gone?" he asks.

"Yes," Nicky says. "But—"

"Is she all burned up, too?" Michael asks. "Like Mommy?"

Nicky freaks.

126

The sun starts burning off the marine layer.

So the world is coming clear and sharp as Jack steps out of the old rec hall.

He checks the load in Teddy's pistol.

Six shots left.

Should be enough.

When they come, they'll come through the old gate. He'll hear it creak open and then he'll hear their steps. Nicky won't come alone. He'll have his hitters.

Enough to take me out.

But not before I kill him.

Jack slips the pistol in his waistband and waits.

127

Letty del Rio checks the load in her weapon and slips it back into the holster.

This is a tricky operation with one hand.

Trickier still to drive, but she's going to do it.

Show up at Nicky's door like a bad-news Avon lady.

Ding-dong.

She finesses her coffee cup to the floor below her feet and starts the engine. Wondering where the hell Jack is. Why didn't he show up?

Never mind.

Time to go see Nicky.

Ding-dong.

128

The gate creaks open.

Jack hears it scrape against the ground.

One set of footsteps coming up the path.

Let it be Nicky, Jack thinks.

He holds the pistol at his side.

Pulls the hammer back and raises the gun.

Gets a whiff of something in the wind.

The smell of a burning cigarette.

Goddamn.

He tucks the pistol back under his shirt.

Go*ddamn*, Billy.

129

They stand there not looking at each other for a minute or so.

Jack had forgotten how beautiful the view was from up here. The palm trees, the bougainvillea and jacaranda, the wide stretch of white beach that sweeps up to the big rock at Dana Head.

Has to be one of the most beautiful places in the world.

Worth saving.

Worth killing for.

"It ain't too late," Billy says.

"For what?"

"For you to walk away," Billy says. "Forget about what you seen here."

Jack nods.

"It's too late," he says. "How long have you been on their payroll?"

"A long time."

"Since the Atlas Warehouse?"

Billy nods. "Nobody was supposed to die. Just a price buildup and a sale to the insurance company."

"Why, Billy?"

"Money," Billy says. "You bust your ass for this company for dog bones while the agents make the big money and the underwriters take payoffs and the judges take bribes and the lawyers rake it in, and we old dogs are just supposed to roll over for the table scraps? The hell with that."

"You set me up," Jack says. "You gave them my files, you tipped them off to every move. You jerked me like I was on a leash. You knew everything to do, everything to say to keep me pushing. You let me walk deeper and deeper into the trap, Billy, and you didn't say a word."

"I had no choice, Jack," Billy says. "I had no goddamn choice."

"Everyone has a choice."

"So make a good one for yourself," Billy says. "I'm here to offer you a deal, Jack. You can still get on the boat."

"With you and Nicky?"

Billy laughs, "You still don't get it, Jack. It ain't Nicky. It's Mahogany Row. All the VPs and the president. They all got shares."

Jack feels like the world is spinning.

"Shares in what?"

Billy gestures all around them. "In *this*, Jack. Great Sunsets. We own it."

Like the world's falling out from under him.

"California Fire and Life?" he asks. "Owns Great Sunsets? Owns the Strands?"

"Mahogany Row, me and some others," Billy says. "We all have shares."

"Nicky Vale?"

"Partners."

Genius.

Sheer freaking genius, Jack thinks.

"The company's been taking a goddamn pounding," Billy says. "Between the fires and the earthquakes and the fraud and the goddamn lawsuits, the company was about to go belly up. So instead of giving it *all* to the damn lawyers and the other crooks we decided to get a piece of it ourselves. We made some deals—started paying on some of the drive-downs, the phony thefts, the medical buildups, the arsons, and taking our cut on the other end. Pay out the money, get it back in the form of shares in dummy companies."

The perfect way to loot your own company, Jack thinks. Pay bogus claims to yourself. Route the money through policyholders who then invest back into your dummy companies.

Very slick.

And it works both ways. The Russian mob can put dirty money into real estate, suffer a "loss," then get clean money back through the insurance company.

Everybody wins.

Except the legit policyholders who pay the premiums.

And dumb-ass honest claims dogs.

And the occasional victim like Pamela Vale.

It's just a beautiful scam.

So they took it to the next level.

Why dick around with little claims payments when you can hit the California Litigation Lottery? Set your own claims people up for bad faith suits, and then force yourself into settlements? An easy thing to do from Billy's position. A bad decision here, a fucked-up file there. He'd know where all the weaknesses were, or he'd put them there.

Brilliant.

"It had to stop sometime," Billy says. "SIU digging around, and the goddamn task force . . . so we figured one last big payout."

And I was the perfect setup for a huge bad faith settlement, Jack thinks. A whole big dog-and-pony show to justify paying out $50 million.

"So you hauled me out."

"We was saving you up, Jack."

"For twelve years?"

"Give or take."

Billy drops his cigarette butt on the dirt, snuffs it out with his foot, lights another and says, "We dumped a lot of money into Great Sunsets over the years. But you assholes fought us to a standstill. 'Save the Strands.' Just about broke us. When we decided we had to shut down we knew we had to make this one pay off."

"You lured Gordon into whipping up a class action so you could justify a huge payment to head it off," Jack says. "Then pay the money to yourselves."

"There you go," Billy says. "Gordon's dead. Nicky'll get the $50 million this morning."

And fifty million bucks will go into Great Sunsets and that'll be more than enough to bribe the councilmen and the lawyers and the judges. Enough capital to do all that and put up their shitty condos and ruin what small part of the coast they haven't already destroyed.

"How about Casey," Jack asks. "He in on this?"

"Nah."

"Sandra Hansen?"

Billy shakes his head. "Sandra Hansen is a true believer.

"So I need to know," Billy says, "you in or out, Jack? I can offer you shares. You can get a condo here, maybe a town house. Surf all goddamn day."

"What do I have to do?"

"Nothin'," Billy says. "That's the beauty of it. You don't have to do a goddamn thing. Just walk away."

"That's the deal?"

"That's the deal."

Jack looks around him. At the Strand, at the ocean.

"A woman's dead," he says.

"That wasn't supposed to happen," Billy says.

"Nicky lost his temper?"

"I suppose," Billy says. "So what's it gonna be?"

Jack sighs, "Can't do it, Billy."

Billy shakes his head, "God*damn,* Jack."

"Goddamn, Billy."

They stand there looking at each other. Then Jack says, "I'll let you go, Billy. I won't make the call for a couple of hours. You can be in Mexico."

"Well, that's nice of you," Billy says. "But you got it backwards. I'm all that's keeping you alive right now. Shit, Jack, I begged them for the chance to come talk to you before . . ."

"Before what?"

Billy shakes his head and then whistles. A few seconds later Accidentally Bentley comes waddling up with his gun out.

Right behind him, Nicky Vale.

Carrying a gasoline can.

Bentley walks around Jack and takes the pistol from him.

"I told you not to go dicking around, didn't I?" he says.

Jack shrugs as Bentley pushes him inside the building.

Nicky's very wired.

Jabbering something about Afghanistan.

130

He goes into this riff about Afghanistan and *mujahedin*.

"They didn't want to give it up, either," he says to Jack. "But they did. Have you ever seen a whirling dervish? Wait until you set one on fire, you'll see them whirl."

He stands in front of Jack, right in his face. Stares at him and says, "I'm a businessman. I tried to treat you like a businessman. I tried to do *business* with you but you wouldn't do it. You had to be rigid, you had to be unreasonable. You've never seen the inside of a Russian prison. You've never lived in cold and filth. You're a native Californian, you've never seen anything but the sunshine, and can't you see that's all I want, too, a little slice of sunshine?

"Jack, I need my things and I need the insurance settlement because I have to have that money. I owe it to some people who are going to kill me and my entire family if they don't get it. I'm telling you this so you'll understand how serious I am.

"Jack, what I've learned—what I think we *both* have learned—is that you can't walk away from your history.

"But I've made mine work for me and your history can work for you, too, Jack. It can make you rich. It's not too late to turn back from what you've done. We can reinvent ourselves again, Jack. Reinvent this moment. We can't change the past but we can design the future. We can make each other rich. Choose the California life, not the fire, Jack. This doesn't have to end in ashes."

"It already has," Jack says.

Nicky shakes his head. "All you have to do is tell me who, if anyone, you have told. Have you, for instance, told Tom Casey? Letty del Rio? Other police? The newspapers? Answer my fucking questions, Jack!"

"Don't be an asshole, Jack."

"Tell him, Wade."

Nicky is cranked up.

Back on the rant. "You won't be dead when the flames hit *you,* Jack. We'll start with your feet—you wouldn't believe the pain—the nerves down there. *Then* you'll want to tell me, *then* you might still have your life but I wouldn't think about getting on too many surfboards, Jack. This is so unnecessary but I'm desperate, Jack, I'm desperate. I am, as you would say, *strung out.* Lev is dead, they cut his head off and threw it into my mother's home *where my children live.* Dani is back there guarding my children because they already took my mother, they're going to kill her, they're going to burn her if this falls through, so I *need* to know, Jack.

"I will do it, Jack. I'll pour the—what do you like to call it—*accelerant* all over you and fling a match. You won't die from smoke inhalation, you won't die from carbon monoxide asphyxiation, you'll die from the flames, from the fire swirling around you—"

"Like Pamela?" Jack asks.

"No, not like *Pamela*," Nicky says. He looks to Bentley and says, "Open the lid. Let him smell the fumes."

Jack smells them. Hard not to in the closed room.

"I loved her, Jack," Nicky says. "I loved being inside her. I used to *drink* from her. She was sweetness and sunshine—my children came from inside her, my children. But she was going to take . . . that bitch was going to take *everything* from me. She was going to drain me, leave me with nothing. She was going to get up in court and say things about me: Nicky is a womanizer, Nicky is a druggie, Nicky is a crook, Nicky is a *gangster.* Nicky sleeps with his mother—which is *not true,* not the way she meant it. She was going to say those things, she told me that. I told her she would never divorce me, she would never take my possessions. My house, my money, my things, my kids, and she said that if she had to she would say all those things before she let my mother get her hands on the kids and fuck *them* up. That's what she said, quote, fuck them up. But no, I didn't burn her alive. I didn't make her dance in flames, writhe on our bed like the bitch used to except this time in flames. I didn't do that, because I loved her. I just made her go to sleep. I made her drink and take pills and when she was asleep in our bed I climbed on top of her. She had the most graceful, whitest neck. I can remember the first time I kissed her neck. I can remember the first time she took me inside her and her black hair against her neck. Can you remember that incredible warmth, the ineffable heat, the first time *inside* a woman? I used to want her so badly it was like *I* was on fire, and the bitch *knew* that, she knew what she was doing. Cockteasing bitch *should* burn, she deserves it, but I don't do that. I'm on top of her with a pillow—that's amusing now that I recall it because she used to have me put a pillow under her ass so I could go deeper inside—I'm on top of her with the pillow over her mouth, she's unconscious but her hips jerk and strain, her back arches up and then she goes quiet in my arms but *I* can't finish. Cockteasing bitch to the last, *I* can't finish, so I get up and then—and *only* then, Jack—do I pour the kerosene around our marital bed. Around and under and over the bitch. I can't stand to pour it on that beautiful face, just the cockteasing part of her. I poured it there all right. She makes *no more children* she can fuck up. *You cannot walk away from your history, Jack.* The fire swirls around you and I have heard the screams echo for *miles.* Now tell me what I need to know. I'm out of time and out of patience and I will set you on fire, Jack, because I need my money and I need my things and they have my *mother* for *God's sake!!"*

He gestures to Bentley.

Bentley raises the gas can.

"I haven't told anyone," Jack says.

Nicky smiles.

"But how can I believe you?" he asks. Turns to Bentley. "Do him."

Bentley looks sick but he raises the can again.

"Goddamn it," Billy says.

Takes out his old .44 and shoots Bentley square in the gut.

The flash ignites the fumes.

Which in turn ignite Bentley.

He's on fire so he drops the can and the gas gurgles onto the floor and he forgets everything he learns in fire school and goes running out the door.

He's a screaming, swirling ball of flame when he crumples onto the dry grass.

Which is how Accidentally Bentley sets the Great South Coast Fire. Accidentally.

131

Jack doesn't know that.

He's still in the building and it's on fire. The gas pours out of the can, spreading accelerant all over the floor and fumes in the air and the fumes ignite like WHAM and a column of flame shoots upward.

Flame and smoke and darkness and Jack loses sight of Nicky Vale.

All Jack can see is Goddamn Billy heading not for the door but farther *into* the rec hall, in toward the old kitchen, and Jack's thinking, *Get out of here* but he's also thinking, *Get Billy out of here, too,* so he goes after him.

Which is like stupid, Jack tells himself. Which is like *dumb* because all the old wood is igniting, then the covers on the furniture ignite, and the fucking furniture ignites. The fire is free burning, there are flames everywhere, the place is filling up with smoke and that son of a bitch Billy was going to set you up anyway so why are you going after him?

Because you're a dog and that's what a dog does. A dog doesn't leave.

Jack drops down and stays low, down where the air is, and makes his way after Billy.

Into the kitchen.

The old kitchen where they used to cook up hamburgers and hot dogs and big pots of chili.

And there's Goddamn Billy standing by the old stainless-steel counter.

Lighting a cigarette.

"Come on!" Jack yells. "We can get out of here!"

Maybe.

The ceiling's on fire, the roof's involved.

"We can get out of here!" Jack repeats.

"No," Billy says.

Puts the stick to his lips and takes a long drag.

"Billy, I can get us out of here!" Jack shouts. "If we go now!"

His eyes are starting to tear up. Tear up and burn and he can feel the smoke scorching his throat. Looks behind him and sees the flames. Looks up and sees little tongues of flame start to lick the kitchen ceiling.

"Can't do it, Jack."

Jack starts to cry. Goddamn it, Billy. It could be seconds to flashover. Seconds till the fairies start flying and flashover happens and everything ignites.

We can't wait any longer, Billy.

"I CAN CARRY YOU!"

Screaming because the noise of the fire is unbelievable. The starving alligator in a feeding frenzy, crunching on the old house.

Billy shakes his head. "I CAN'T FACE IT, JACK!"

"I'LL LIE FOR YOU, BILLY! I'LL SAY YOU HAD NOTHING TO DO WITH IT! COME ON!"

Tiny balls of flame dance in the air.

The fairies flying.

"IT'S NO GOOD, JACK!"

To hell with arguing, Jack thinks. I'll knock the stubborn old fucker out if I have to.

He starts toward Billy.

Billy shakes his head and pulls his old .44 from out of his jacket.

Points it at Jack.

Then says, "God*damn* it."

Puts the barrel to his head and pulls the trigger.

As the fairies fly.

Flashover.

132

Outside the fire spreads quickly.

The wind picks up the flame like it's been waiting for a lover and sweeps it across the dry grass.

Into the trees and onto the roofs.

The whole sky on fire.

The sun setting over the ocean a ball of fire.

The ocean ablaze in reflected flame.

On land the sky a red-and-orange glow from the fire that's spreading, blowing north from Dana headlands up toward the Ritz and Monarch Bay.

The fire sweeps across the headlands, over the grass and brush, then ignites the juicy eucalyptus trees, which crackle and pop and it sounds like a million firecrackers going off. The fire races on and ignites the trees that flank the Ritz, encircles the gates of the resort like a besieging army while another arm of the fire races across the top of Salt Creek Beach, pushing on toward Monarch Bay.

Where it doesn't stop at the gate. Doesn't wait for the guard to buzz it in. The wind pushes the flames through, into the trees, into the expensive landscaping, burning up the trees, building up the heat to ignite the roofs.

Natalie and Michael stand in their room, looking out the window and watching the fire come toward them. They can't see the flames from where they stand; what they see is an orange sky turning blood red as the sun sets. They can smell the smoke, the acrid burning sensation in their eyes and noses, and they're scared.

Mommy is all burned up.

Daddy is gone again.

Even Grandma is nowhere to be seen.

There's nobody there but the men that Daddy has around and they're busy spraying water on the roof and they're paying no attention and the sirens are screaming and people are yelling and voices from unseen loudspeakers are commanding in stern voices to "evacuate" and there's a yell from a dozen voices as a wood-shake roof ignites, and Natalie struggles to remember if she knows what "evacuate" means as Leo hops and twirls and barks. The fire crackles in the tree outside the window like a voice from a bad dream, and what Natalie is thinking is, *This is how Mommy died.*

Out on the street Letty tries to get in but a cop stops her at the gate and tells her no entry to civilian vehicles, and she yells, *I have children in there!* but they won't let her through so she gets out and leaves the car there and heads in on foot.

Toward the house.

She runs toward the house as the trees hiss and pop over her head. People in cars and on foot stream the other way past her. Here and there a house has gone up now, the smoke is thick, it would be dark but for the flames, and then she's at the house.

It's on fire.

Flames dance on the roof.

"Natalie! Michael!"

A fireman stops her from rushing in. She fights him, screaming, "There are two children in there!"

"There's no one in there!"

"There are two children in there!"

She wrests herself free and runs toward the front door.

Inside it's all smoke, heat and darkness.

133

Jack's crawling through hell.

On his stomach on the floor, down where there's a little air, below where the fire's burning on the counters, he crawls. Feels his way on the walls, praying he remembers where the door is. The smoke, the noise, the heat . . .

Then he feels the doorway.

It has to be an exterior door.

It has to be because if it isn't, when he opens it the fire will blast back and blow him away, but there isn't a choice so he pushes it open and then he's outside.

The grass is on fire.

Shit, it seems like all of California is on fire.

Through the smoke he can just make out a figure.

Nicky running down the bluff.

Jack runs after him.

Coughing, struggling for breath, Jack chases him down to the beach, runs after him along the beach. He can feel his heart pounding, hear the surf pounding almost in rhythm. Nicky's starting to slow down and then Jack catches him.

Nicky whirls and throws a finger strike at Jack's eye.

Jack turns his head and the strike catches him off the side of his left eye, opening a gash, and for a second Jack can't see but he lunges for where Nicky's neck should be and throws Nicky down into the surf.

Lands on top of him, holds on to Nicky's throat and pushes him under.

A wave comes in, breaks close to shore and sends a rush of swirling white water into Jack but he holds on. He feels Nicky's hands around his wrists, pulling and jerking. Nicky's legs kick out and up, trying to get away, but Jack has him by the throat and isn't letting up, even as another wave breaks and smashes into him. He holds on, holds Nicky under. Nicky's bucking and thrashing as Jack thinks about the Atlas Warehouse fire and Porfirio Guzman and the two dead teenagers and George Scollins and his own fucked-up life. And he pushes Nicky down harder until he can feel Nicky's back hit the rocks rolling in the trench. The white water recedes and Jack can see Nicky's face, can see his eyes bulge, and Jack hears himself yelling, "You want a deal, Nicky?! Here's your fucking deal!"

Hears himself yell that.

Hears himself.

And lets up.

Drags Nicky out of the water by the back of his neck and drops him on the beach. Nicky coughing and sputtering and gasping for air.

And Jack swears he can hear a damn dog barking.

He looks up the beach where the Monarch Bay community juts out from the coastline.

The trees are on fire.

Chimneys going up.

Jack starts running.

134

Natalie holds Michael tight.

Keeping him warm.

Shielding him from the cold salt spray coming off the waves.

Evacuate, the voice had said. Evacuate, she remembered, meant to get out, so she grabbed Michael and got out of the house even before the fire had spread from the tree to the roof.

Out onto the lawn and then the street, and all the people were headed out toward the highway, the Pacific Coast Highway, but Natalie decided that all the people were wrong, because they seemed to be heading into the fire.

So Natalie stopped and thought about it for a few seconds and decided that the safest place to be in a fire would be by water, by the ocean, and that way even if the fire burned all the way down to the beach, they could always jump into the ocean and swim until the fire went out.

So she took Leo under her arm and Michael by the hand and led them down toward the beach. Down the steps toward Salt Creek Beach where Aunt Letty had taken them Boogie boarding and they had gone for picnics and looking for crabs and snails in the tidal pools.

Because Aunt Letty will be looking for us, Natalie thinks, and she will know to come here.

Jack's running along the beach, the bluffs above him on fire, the peninsula of Monarch Bay smoking, and the smoke is thickening. It's hard to see and he doesn't know how he's going to find Michael and Natalie and he's just hoping that they got *out* of there, and then he hears this dog yipping.

The kids recognize him.

Go to him because he's an *adult* they know here.

"Where's my daddy?" Michael asks.

Black eyes big and full of tears.

Natalie asks, "Where's Aunt Letty?"

"I don't know," Jack says. "Has she been here?"

Natalie does a little pirouette of anxiety.

Of course she's here, Jack thinks. She's here for the same reason I'm here. Oh, God, I hope she didn't go to the house.

"It's going to be all right," Jack says, holding them. "It's going to be all right."

Because people will lie.

Their mom is dead.

Their dad killed her.

And the last person who loved them is maybe looking for them where they aren't—namely, in another burning house.

And waiting in the wings is Mother Russia.

But Jack repeats, "It's going to be all right."

He heads up for the house.

It's on fire.

He goes in. Hard to see, hard to breathe. The house is filling with smoke.

"Letty! Letty!"

He makes his way up the stairs to the kids' room.

She's facedown on the bed.

"Oh, no. Oh, no."

He turns her over.

"Don't be dead. *Please* don't be dead."

She's unconscious but still breathing. He picks her up and carries her down the stairs.

Which are on fire.

Too many flames, too much smoke.

And she might not have the time.

So he plunges through it.

Comes out the other side, comes out the door into the smoky air and lays her down.

"Please don't die. Please don't die."

She starts to cough. Cough and then breathe and then her eyes open. When she can speak she asks about the kids.

He picks her up again and carries her down the point to the beach.

When they get there, Nicky is standing with his kids, his arms wrapped protectively around them.

Jack leans in to him, whispers something into his ear.

Let's do a deal.

135

The next afternoon.

The sun is high and hot over a landscape burned black. Ashes still float in the mild breeze.

Jack sits waiting in the front seat of a used pickup in the parking lot of Dana Strand Beach. Letty sits beside him. She chews on a broken fingernail.

"He'll *be* here," Jack says.

She nods and goes back to chewing her nail.

Five long minutes go by, and then Jack sees the black Mercedes snake around the curve of Selva into the parking lot.

"Here they come," he says.

The Mercedes pulls alongside. Dani gets out, nods, and then Nicky gets out of the car. Jack gets out of the truck. They meet between the two cars.

"We have a deal?" Nicky asks.

"You have your money, don't you?"

"Yes."

"Then we have *part* of a deal."

Nicky nods.

Then he hands Jack the signed papers terminating his parental rights over Natalie and Michael. Tom Casey drew up the papers, so Jack is confident they're airtight. He checks Nicky's signature and says, "Looks okay to me."

Nicky walks back to the Mercedes. The door opens and the kids come out, blinking in the harsh sunlight. Natalie has Leo under her arm. Nicky puts his arms around their shoulders and says, "Daddy's going to be very busy for the next little while so you're going to stay with Aunt Letty for a few months, all right?"

They nod and hug him and there are a few tears.

Letty comes over and Nicky ushers the children over to her.

"Take good care of them," Nicky says.

"Kids, go wait in the car for Aunt Letty, okay?" she says.

When they're gone, she says, "In six months I adopt them."

"As you wish."

Letty looks hard at him.

"What kind of man trades his own children?" she asks.

"That's what Mother asked me," Nicky says. "She is devastated."

He pauses for a second, then adds, "But alive."

He walks over to Jack.

Nicky laughs. "Our deal is concluded then? Jack Wade, who doesn't do deals?"

Nicky gets the $50 million. Jack and Letty agree never to seek or aid any prosecution. Jack agrees to walk away from everything he knows about Nicky, California Fire and Life and all the rest of it. Sandra Hansen gets her snitch.

Olivia Hathaway gets paid for her spoons.

"It was an accidental fire and an accidental death," Jack says.

"I just wanted to hear you say it," Nicky says. "So, it's over."

"It's history," Jack says. "As long as you never go back on any of it."

"You have my word."

He offers his hand.

Jack says, "Go to hell."

"Are you so sure," Nicky asks, "that I'm not already there?"

Jack and Letty stand and watch the car drive away.

She says, "And he gets away with murder."

"And two kids get a life," Jack says. "That's a deal you'd make every time, right?"

"Yup."

Some deals, Jack thinks, you just have to make.

Part of life, knowing when to settle.

Letty asks, "Will you be coming out tonight?"

"No."

"This weekend?"

Jack shakes his head.

Letty asks, "You aren't coming, are you?"

"Part of the deal," Jack says. "They want me gone. Out of the state."

Out of the country, too. Past subpoena power. They want a little insurance for their part of the deal, Nicky and Cal Fire and Life. They get their money, they get my silence, they get back to business as usual.

And I get gone.

And if you really get honest, you know it's for the best, Jack thinks. The kids are hurt and confused enough. They don't need to deal with a new "Daddy" in their lives. They're going to have a tough enough ride. They need Letty's undivided attention and that's what she's going to want to give. They don't need some Mommy-Daddy Insta-Kit laid on them.

Letty says, "That's a hell of a price, Jack."

"Worth it, though."

He nods toward Letty's car.

"Worth it," she says.

She squeezes his hand. "I love you, Jack."

"I love *you*, Letty."

She lets go.

"Come tell them goodbye, anyway."

Jack walks over to Letty's car. The kids are in the front seat, the dog stretched across their laps.

"So you guys are going out to the country, huh?" Jack says. "Going to ride horses?"

A couple of tearful nods. Brave smiles.

"Well," Jack says, "take care of your Aunt Letty for me, okay?"

He gives Letty a peck on the cheek and a quick hug and gets into the truck. Starts it up and kicks it into gear before he has a chance to look back.

Fires up a Dick Dale & His Del-Tones tape.

Drives past the new sign set at the entrance to the Strands.

PAMELA VALE MEMORIAL PARK.

He points the truck south.

136

Dani pulls the car over on the dirt turnout above Dana Strand.

Nicky asks, "What—"

Dani shoots him through the groin. The bullet pierces Nicky's spinal cord. But he's conscious as Dani gets out, takes a can of gas from the trunk and pours it all around the car.

Dani opens the back door.

He's crying as he rolls up Nicky's pant leg, takes a knife and makes an incision above the Two Crosses tattoo behind Nicky's knee. He slices the knife down and rips off the skin.

Nicky can't feel it.

Tears stream down Dani's face as he says, "If ever I transgress against *Vorovskoy Zakon,* may I burn in hell."

He closes the door, steps away and tosses the match.

Then sticks his gun in his mouth and pulls the trigger.

137

Man's sitting in a car and the car's on fire.

He doesn't get out.

Flames lick at his legs and he doesn't get out.

Just down the hill the Pacific pounds on the rocks.

California fire and life.

138

Jack Wade sits on an old Hobie longboard, riding swells that refuse to become waves.

He watches a plume of smoke rise up from the beach.

The smoke means to him that Hernando has fired up the grill and that the coals will be hot enough in a little while and that he'll have to come and help Hernando cook dinner for the tourists.

If there are any at the fishing camp.

Usually there aren't, and then Jack helps Hernando work on the little lodge that he's putting up. Nothing fancy, a little cinder-block-and-rebar job with a beamed roof, but Jack knows how to build it and Hernando is happy for the help.

The rest of the time, Jack surfs or fishes or drives into town to buy supplies for the camp. When the tourists are in, he'll cook them breakfasts of *huevos rancheros* or pancakes or any other damn thing they want, and he makes lunches of fruit and chicken and cold, cold beer. In the evening he grills the fish they've caught, or the fish he's caught, and after he's done cleaning up he grabs a beer and sits and listens to Hernando sing the old *canciones.*

Or if Hernando doesn't feel like singing, Jack just lies in the bed of Hernando's old pickup and listens to the Dodgers game on the radio. The weather reports talk about big rainstorms coming up in the north.

Sometimes Jack sits back and looks at some crayon drawings that come for "Uncle Jack" in Hernando's mail. At first they were of trees and houses on fire. Now they mostly show horses, or kids on horses, and the kids are usually smiling and the lady with them always has black hair.

Jack thinks a lot about Letty.

He thinks a lot about himself and Letty with the kids.

He rarely thinks about California fire and life.

A NOTE ABOUT THE AUTHOR

Don Winslow, a former private investigator, was a consultant to law firms on litigation involving arson and other fraud. As such he spent countless hours reviewing cases with insurance investigators, police and fire officials, scientists, attorneys and jury consultants, and has participated in numerous arson trials and investigations. He now makes his living as a writer.